Selected Stories
of
Sean O'Faolain

Selected Stories
of
Sean O'Faolain

An Atlantic Monthly Press Book

LITTLE, BROWN AND COMPANY   BOSTON/TORONTO

FIRST AMERICAN EDITION

"The Silence of the Valley" and "Lovers of the Lake" originally appeared in *The Finest Stories of Sean O'Faolain;* "I Remember! I Remember!", "The Sugawn Chair," "Two of a Kind," and "Angels and
Ministers of Grace" in *I Remember! I Remember!;* "In the Bosom of
the Country," "The Heat of the Sun," "Before the Day Star," "Passion,"
and "Dividends" in *The Heat of the Sun;* "The Talking Trees," "Feed
My Lambs," and "Of Sanctity and Whiskey" in *The Talking Trees;*
"The Faithless Wife," "The Inside Outside Complex," and "Something,
Everything, Anything, Nothing" in *Foreign Affairs.*

LIBRARY OF CONGRESS CATALOGING IN PUBLICATION DATA
O'Faoláin, Seán, 1900–
    Selected stories of Seán O'Faoláin.

    "An Atlantic Monthly Press book."
PZ3.032Se 1978   [PR6029.F3]   823'.9'12   78–5780
ISBN 0–316–63285–6

ATLANTIC–LITTLE, BROWN BOOKS
ARE PUBLISHED BY
LITTLE, BROWN AND COMPANY
IN ASSOCIATION WITH
THE ATLANTIC MONTHLY PRESS

*Published simultaneously in Canada
by Little, Brown & Company (Canada) Limited*

PRINTED IN THE UNITED STATES OF AMERICA

To Julia

Contents

Selected Stories
of
Sean O'Faolain

The Silence of the Valley

Only in the one or two farmhouses about the lake, or in the fishing hotel at its edge – preoccupations of work and pleasure – does one ever forget the silence of the valley. Even in winter, when the great cataracts slide down the mountain face, the echoes of falling water are fitful: the winds fetch and carry them. In the summer a fisherman will hear the tinkle of the ghost of one of those falls only if he steals among the mirrored reeds under the pent of the cliffs, and withholds the plash of his oars. These tiny muted sounds will awe and delight him by the vacancy out of which they creep, intermittently.

One May evening a relaxed group of early visitors were helping themselves to drink in the hotel bar, throwing the coins into a pint glass. There were five of them, all looking out the door at the lake, the rhododendrons on the hermit's island, the mountain towering beyond it, and the wall of blue air above the mountain line. Behind the counter was an American soldier, blond, blankly handsome, his wide-vision glasses convexing the sky against his face. Leaning against the counter was a priest, jovial, fat, ruddy, his Roman collar off and his trousers stuck into his socks – he had been up the mountain all day rough-shooting. Leaning against the pink-washed wall was a dark young man with pince-nez; he had the smouldering ill-disposed eyes of the incorrigible Celt – 'always eager to take offence', as the fourth of the party had privately cracked. She was a sturdy, red-mopped young woman in blue slacks now sitting on the counter drinking whiskey. She sometimes seemed not at all beautiful, and sometimes her heavy features seemed to have a strong beauty of their own, for she was on a hair trigger between a glowering Beethoven and *The Laughing Cavalier*. Sometimes her mouth was broody; suddenly it would expand into a half-batty gaiety. Her deep-set eyes ran from gloom to irony, to challenge, to wild humour. She had severe eyebrows that floated as gently as a veil in the wind. She was a Scot. The fifth of the group was a sack of a man, a big fat school inspector, also with his collar off. He had cute, ingratiating eyes. He leaned against the opposite pink-washed wall.

In the middle of the tiled floor was a very small man, a tramp with a fluent black beard, long black curls, a billycock hat, a mackintosh to his toes, and a gnarled stick with a hairy paw. The tramp (a whisper from the priest had informed them all that he had once been a waiter on the Holyhead–Euston Express) held a pint of porter in his free hand and was singing to them in a fine tenor voice a ballad called 'Lonely I Wandered from the Scenes of My Childhood'. They heard him in quizzical boredom. He had been singing ballads to them on and off for nearly two hours now.

Outside, the sun was seeping away behind the far end of the valley. From the bar they could see it touching the tips of the tallest rowans on the island. Across the lake the tip of a green cornfield on a hillock blazed and went out. Then vast beams, cutting through lesser defiles, flowed like a yellow searchlight for miles to the open land to the east, picking out great escarpments and odd projections of the mountains. The wavelets were by now blowing in sullenly on the shore, edging it with froth.

The tramp ended. They applauded perfunctorily. He knew they were sated and when the redheaded young woman cried, 'Tommy, give us "The Inchigeela Puck Goat",' he demurred politely.

'I think, miss, ye have enough of me now, and sure I'm as dry as a lime kiln.'

'More porter for the singer,' cried the priest with lazy authority, and the lieutenant willingly poured out another bottle of stout and rattled a coin into the pint glass.

'I suppose,' asked the Celtic-looking young man, in a slightly critical voice, 'you have no songs in Irish?'

'Now,' soothed the school inspector, 'haven't you the Irish the whole bloody year round? Leave us take a holiday from it while we can.'

'I had been under the impression,' yielded the Celt, with a – for him – amicable smile, 'that we came out here to learn the language of our forefathers? Far be it from me to insist pedantically on the point.' And he smiled again like a stage curate.

'Tell me, brother,' asked the American, as he filled up the tramp's glass, 'do you remain on the road the whole year round?'

'Summer and winter, for fifteen years come next September, and no roof over my head but the field of stars. And would you believe it, sur, never wance did I get as much as a shiver of a cold in my head.'

'That is certainly a remarkable record.'

The proprietor of the hotel entered the bar from the kitchen behind it and planked a saucepan full of fowls' guts on the counter. He was accompanied by a small boy, long-lashed, almost pretty, obviously a city child, who kept dodging excitedly about him.

'Have any of ye a match?' he asked. He was a powerful man, with the shoulders of a horse. He wore neither coat nor vest. His cap was on his poll. His face was round and weather-beaten as a mangold. He had a mouthful of false teeth.

'What do you want a match for, Dinny?' asked the priest with a wink at the others.

The American produced a match. Dinny deftly pinched a fold of his trousers between the eye of his suspenders and inserted the match through the fold: there it effectively did the work of a button. The priest twisted him round familiarly. A nail had performed the same service behind. They all laughed, but Dinny was too preoccupied to heed.

'What's this mess for?' The American pointed to the stinking saucepan.

Dinny paid no attention. He stretched up over the top of the shelves and after much fumbling brought down a fishing rod.

'Give it to me, Dinny, give it to me,' shouted the child.

Dinny ignored him also as he fiddled with the line. He glanced out the door, turned to the kitchen and roared:

'Kitty cows coming home tell Patsy James have ye the buckets scalded blosht it boys the day is gone.'

Or he said something like that, for he mouthed all his words in his gullet and his teeth clacked and he spoke too fast. They all turned back to watch the frieze of small black cows passing slowly before the scalloped water, the fawny froth, the wall of mountain.

'The cobbler won't lasht the night,' said Dinny, pulling with his teeth at the tangled pike line. The priest whirled.

'Is he bad? Did you see him? Should I go down?'

'Still unconscious, Father. No use for you. Timeen was up. He was buying the drink.'

'Drink?' asked the Scots girl grinning hopefully.

'For the wake,' explained the Celt.

'Well, do you know what it is, by Harry?' cried the inspector earnestly to them all. 'He's making a great fight for it.'

'He may as well go now and be done with it,' said Dinny. 'Gimme the guts. We're fishing for eels.'

'Gimme the rod, Dinny, gimme the rod,' screamed the child and taking it he dashed off like a lancer shouting for joy. Dinny lumbered after him with the saucepan.

'I reckon these people are pretty heartless?' suggested the soldier.

'We Irish,' explained the Celt, 'are indifferent to the affairs of the body. We are a spiritual people.'

'What enchanting nonsense!' laughed the young woman and threw back her whiskey delightedly.

'It is nonetheless true,' reprimanded the Celt.

'You make me feel so old,' sighed the young woman, 'so old and so wise.'

'Are you a Catholic?' asked the Celt suspiciously.

'Yes, but what on earth has that to do with anything?'

'Well, I reckon I don't know much about the spirit, but you may be right about the body. Did you see those hens' guts?'

The priest intervened diplomatically.

'Did you ever see them fishing for eels? It's great fun. Come and watch them.'

All but the tramp walked idly to the edge of the lake. The waves were beating in among the stones, pushing a little wrack of straw and broken reeds before them. Dinny had stuck a long string of windpipe to the hook and the boy had slung it out about twelve feet from the shore. To lure the eels a few random bits of guts had been thrown into the brown shallows at their feet and there swayed like seaweed. The group peered. Nothing happened. Suddenly Dinny shouted as fast as a machine gun's burst.

'Look at 'em look at 'em look at the divils blosht it look at 'em look at 'em.'

A string of intestines was streaking away out into the lake. Dark serpentine shapes whirled snakily in and out of the brown water. The eels had smelled the rank bait and were converging on it.

'By golly,' cried the American, 'they must smell that bait a mile away.'

The reel whirred, the line flew, the rod bent, they all began to shout, the child trembled with excitement.

'You have him pull him you divil,' roared Dinny and seized the rod and whirled a long white belly in over their dodging heads. The girl gave a cry of disgust as the five men leaped on the eel, now lashing in the dust, and hammered savagely at it with heels, stones, a stick, screaming, laughing, shoving. The eel seemed immortal. Though filthy and bleeding it squirmed galvanically. The child circled dancing around the struggling group, half delighted, half terrified.

'Well, Jo,' said the young woman as she looked disdainfully at the last wriggle of the corpse, 'it seems that boys will be boys. Dinny, do you really eat eels?'

'Christ gurl I wouldn't touch one of 'em for a hundred pounds.'

'Then why catch them?'

'For fun.'

Her face gathered, ceased to be *The Laughing Cavalier* and became *Beethoven in Labour*. She saw that the men had now become absorbed entirely in the sport. The American had thrown out the line again and they were all peering excitedly into the water. The sun left the last tips of the mountains. The lake grew sullen. Its waves still hissed. They did not weary of the game until eight eels lay writhing in the dust.

Just as they were becoming bored they observed a silent country-man at the edge of the ring looking down at the eels. The priest spoke to him saying, 'Well, Timeen, how is he?' He was a lithe, lean, hollow-cheeked young man with his cap pulled over his eyes. He lifted his face and they saw that he was weeping.

'He's gone, Father,' he said in a low voice.

'The Lord have mercy on him,' said the priest and his own eyes filled and the others murmured the prayer after him. 'The poor old cobbler. I must go and see herself.'

He hastened away and presently, tidy and brushed and in his Roman collar, they saw him cycle down the road. The child called after him, 'Will you roast the eels for me tonight?' and over his shoulder the priest called, 'I will, Jo, after supper,' and disappeared wobblingly over the first hill.

'By Harry,' cried the inspector, 'there'll be a powerful gathering of the clans tonight.'

'How's that?' from the American.

'For the wake,' explained the Celt.

'I'd certainly like to see a wake.'

'You'll be very welcome, sur,' said Timeen.

'Did he go easy?' asked the inspector.

Dinny threw the guts into the lake and took Timeen by his arm.

'He went out like a candle,' said Timeen, and let Dinny lead him away gently to some private part of the house.

The group dissolved.

'I do wish,' said the American, 'they wouldn't throw guts into the lake. After all, we swim in it.'

'It's very unsanitary, all right,' the inspector agreed.

'What are we all,' said the Celt philosophically, 'but a perambulating parcel of guts?'

The girl sighed heavily and said, 'The lamp is lighting.'

In the hotel window the round globe of the lamp was like a full moon. A blue haze had gathered over everything. They strolled back to the bar for a last drink, the child staggering after them with the heavy saucepan of dead eels.

The cobbler's cottage was on the brow of a hill about a mile down the road. It was naked, slated, whitewashed, two-storied. It had a sunken haggard in front and a few fuchsias and hollies behind it, blown almost horizontal by the storms. On three sides lay an expanse of moor, now softened by the haze of evening. From his front door the dead cobbler used to look across this barren moor at the jagged mountain range, but he could also see where the valley opened out and faded into the tentative and varying horizons of forty miles away.

When the priest entered the kitchen the wife was alone – the news had not yet travelled. She was a tiny, aged woman who looked as if her whole body from scalp to soles was wrinkled and yellow; her face, her bare arms, her bare chest were as golden as a dried apple; even her eyeballs seemed wrinkled. But her white hair flowed upward all about her like a Fury in magnificent wild snakes from under an old fisherman's tweed hat, and her mobile mouth and her loud – too loud – voice gave out a tremendous vitality. When she was a young girl she must have been as lively as a minnow in a mountain stream. The priest had known her for most of his adult life as a woman whose ribald tongue had made the neighbours delight in her and fear her: he was stirred to tears to find her looking up at him now like a child who has been beaten. She was seated on the long settle underneath the red lamp before the picture of the Sacred Heart.

He sat beside her and took her hand.

'Can I go up and pray for him?'

'Katey Dan is readying him,' she whispered, and the priest became aware of footsteps moving in the room over their heads.

She lumbered up the ladderlike stairs to see if everything was ready. While he waited he looked at the cobbler's tools by the window – the last, and the worn hammer, and the old butter box by the fire where the cobbler used to sit. Everything in the kitchen had the same worn look of time and use, and everything was dusted with the grey dust of turf – the kettle over the peat fire, the varied pothooks on the crane, the bright metal of the tongs, the dresser with its pieces of delft, a scalded churn lid leaning in the window to dry. There was nothing there that was not necessary; unless, perhaps, the red lamp and the oleograph of the Sacred Heart, and even that had the stiff and frozen prescription of an icon. The only unusual thing was two plates on the table under the window, one of snuff and one of shredded tobacco for the visitors who would soon be coming down from every corner of the glens. The only light in the cottage came from the turf fire.

As he sat and looked at the blue smoke curling up against the brown soot of the chimney's maw he became aware, for the first time in his life, of the silence of the moor. He heard the hollow feet above the rafters. A cricket chirruped somewhere behind the fire. Always up to now he had thought of this cottage as a place full of the cobbler's satirical talk, his wife's echoes and contradictions. Somebody had once told the old man that he was not only the valley's storyteller but its 'gossip columnist': the old chap had cocked a suspicious eye, too vain to admit that he did not know the phrase, and skated off into one of his yarns about the days when he had cobbled for the Irish workers laying rails out of Glasgow along the Clyde. The priest smiled at the incident. Then he frowned as he looked at the fire, a quiet disintegration: a turf fire never emits even the slightest whisper. He realised that this cottage would be completely silent from now on. Although it was May he had a sudden poignant sensation of autumn; why, he could not tell.

The old woman called him up. After the dusk of the kitchen this upper room was brilliant. She had lighted five wax candles about her husband's head. Snowy sheets made a canopy about his face. The neighbour woman had just finished the last delicately fluted fold on the lacy counterpane that lay ridged over the stomach and toes. Silently the three knelt and prayed.

When they rose, the old woman said, looking down at the calm countenance on the pillow:

'He's a fine corse and a heavy corse.'

'He was a great man. I loved him.'

'He had a fierce veneration for you, Father.'

They lumbered down the steep stairs. She was as quiet as if the business in hand was something that had happened outside the course of nature. She thanked God for the weather. She asked him were there many staying at the hotel. When he told her, she muttered, 'We must be satisfied,' as if she were talking about the hotel and not about her man. When two more neighbour women came, and stood looking at them from the doorway, he took leave of her, saying that he would return later in the night.

The hollies at the door were rubbing squeakingly against each other. The moon was rising serenely over the pass to the east. He felt the cold wind as he rode back to the lake.

They were at supper when he entered the hotel. He joined them about the round table in the bay window through which he could barely discern the stars above the mountains. The rest of the long room, beyond the globe of the lamp, was in shadow. He mentioned that he had seen the cobbler, that they must go down later to the wake, and then set about his food. He paid small heed to the conversation although he gathered that they were loud in discussion over the delay in serving supper.

'Just the same,' the American was saying, 'I cannot see why it would not be perfectly simple to hang up a card on the wall announcing meal times. Breakfast, eight to ten. Luncheon, one to three. And so on. It's quite simple.'

'Just as they do,' suggested the young Scotswoman, 'in the Regent Palace Hotel?'

'Exactly,' he agreed, and then looked in puzzlement at her because she was giggling happily to herself.

'You must admit,' the inspector assured her, following his usual role of trying to agree with everybody, 'that they have a wonderful opportunity here if they only availed of it. Why don't they cater more for the wealthy clientele? I mean, now, suppose they advertised Special Duck Dinners, think of the crowds that would come motoring out of Cork for them on summer afternoons. It's only about forty miles, a nice run.'

'Gee, how often have I driven forty miles and more for a barbecue supper down the coast? I can see those lobster suppers at Cohasset now, two dollars fifty, and the rows and rows of automobile lines outside on the concrete.'

'What does our Celt say to this perfectly hideous picture?' asked the red mop.

'I can see no objection – provided the language spoken is
Gaelic.'

She broke into peals of laughter.

'We,' the Celt went on, dark with anger, 'envisage an Ireland
both modern and progressive. Christianity,' he went on, proud both
of the rightness and intellectual tolerance of his argument, 'is not
opposed to modernity, or to comfort, or to culture. I should not
mind' – his voice was savage, for she was chuckling like a zany –
'if seaplanes landed on that lake outside. Why should I? All this
admiration for backwardness and inefficiency is merely so much
romantic nonsense. Ireland has had enough of it.'

She groaned comically.

'Fascist type. Definitely schizoid. Slight sadistic tendency. Would
probably be Socialist in Britain, if not' – she wagged her flaming
head warningly and made eyes of mock horror – 'dare I say it,
C.P.?'

'You,' cried the Celt scornfully, 'merely like the primitive so long
as it is not in your own country. Let's go to Nigeria and love the
simple ways of the niggers. Let's holiday in Ireland among the
beautiful peasants. Imperialist!'

'I beg your pardon,' she cried, quite offended. 'I am just as happy
in the Shetlands or the Hebrides as I am here. Britain's pockets of
primitiveness are her salvation. If she ever loses them she's doomed.
I very much fear she's doomed already with all these moth-eaten
churchwardens in Parliament trying to tidy us up!'

And she drew out her cigar case and pulling her coffee towards
her lit a long Panatella. As she puffed she was sullen and unbeautiful
again as if his hate had quenched her loveliness as well as her
humour.

'Well, now, now, after all,' soothed the inspector, 'it's all very
well for you. Your country is a great country with all the most
modern conveniences . . .'

'Heaven help it!'

'. . . whereas we have a long leeway to make up. Now, to take
even a small thing. Those guts in the lake.'

'O God!' she groaned. 'What a fuss you make over one poor
little chicken's guts! Damn it, it's all phosphates. The Chinese use
human phosphates for manure.'

The priest shook in his fat with laughter – it was a joke exactly
to his liking – but the other three took the discussion from her and
she smoked in dudgeon until the priest too was pulling his pipe

and telling her about the dead cobbler, and how every night in winter his cottage used to be full of men coming to hear his views on Hitler and Mussolini and the prophecies of Saint Columcille, which foretold that the last battle of the last world war would be fought at Ballylickey Bridge. The others began to listen as he retold some of the cobbler's more earthy stories that were as innocent and sweaty as any Norse or Celtic yarn of the Golden Age: such as the dilemma of the sow eating the eel which slipped out of her as fast as it went into her until, at last, the sow shouted in a fury, 'I'll settle you, you slippery devil!' and at one and the same moment snapped up the eel and clapped her backside to the wall.

Laughing they rose and wandered, as usual, into the kitchen for the night. They expected to find it empty, thinking that everybody would be going down to the wakehouse; instead it was more crowded than ever; it had become a sort of clearinghouse where the people called on their way to and from the cobbler's cottage, either too shy to go there directly or unwilling to go home after visiting their old friend.

The small boy was eagerly awaiting them with the saucepan of eels. The priest set to. He took off his clerical jacket and put on a green windbreaker, whose brevity put an equator around his enormous paunch, so that when he stooped over the fire he looked like one of those global toys that one cannot knock over. When the resinous fir stumps on the great flat hearth flamed up – the only light in the kitchen – he swelled up, shadows and all, like a necromancer. He put an eel down on the stone floor and with his penknife slit it to its tail and gutted it. The offal glistened oilily. While he was cutting the eel its tail had slowly wound about his wrist, and when he tied its nose to a pothook and dangled it over a leaning flame and its oil began to drip and sizzle in the blaze, the eel again slowly curved as if in agony. The visitors amused themselves by making sarcastic comments on the priest as a cook, but four countrymen who lined the settle in the darkness with their caps on and their hands in their pockets watched him, perfectly immobile, not speaking, apparently not interested.

'Aha, you divil, you,' taunted the priest, 'now will you squirm? If the cobbler's sow was here now she would make short work of you.'

That was the only time any of the countrymen spoke: from the darkness of a far corner an old man said:

'I wondher is the cobbler telling that story to Hitler now?'

'I sincerely hope,' said the Scots girl, 'that they're not in the same place.'

The old man said:

'God is good. I heard a priesht say wan time that even Judas might be saved.'

'Jo,' said the inspector, steering as usual into pleasant channels, 'do you think that eel is alive?'

The small boy was too absorbed to heed, lost in his own delight. Now and again a handsome, dark serving-girl came to the fire to tend the pots or renew the sods, for meals were eaten in this house at all hours: she seemed fascinated by the eel and every time she came she made disgusted noises. The men loved these expressions of disgust and tried in various ways to provoke more of them, offering her a bite or holding up the entangled saucepan to her nose. Once the American chased her laughingly with an eel in his fist and from the dark back kitchen they could hear them scuffling playfully. By this time many more neighbours had come into the kitchen and into the bar and into the second back kitchen and two more serving-girls became busy as drinks and teas and dishes of ham passed to and fro, so that the shadows of the men about the fire, the scurrying girls, the wandering neighbours fluttered continually on the white walls and the babble of voices clucked through the house like ducks clacking at a night pond.

Above this murmuring and clattering they heard the tramp singing in the bar a merry dancing tune, partly in Gaelic and partly in English:

> So, little soldier of my heart,
> Will you marry, marry me now,
> With a heigh and a ho
> And a sound of drum now?

'So the little bastard does know Irish,' cried the Celt much affronted as the song broke into Gaelic:

> *A chailin óg mo chroidhe*
> *Conus a phósfainn-se thú*
> *Agus gan pioc de'n bhróg do chur orm* . . .

'Perhaps he suits his language to his company?' the red-haired girl suggested.

> I went to the cobbler,
> The besht in the town,
> For a fine pair of shoes
> For my soldiereen brown,
>   So-o-o . . .
> Little soldier of my heart,
> Will you marry, marry me now . . .

The girl peered around the jamb of the door into the bar and then scurried back dismayed. The tramp had spotted her and at once came dancing fantastically into the kitchen on her heels. His long mackintosh tails leaped, and their shadows with them. His black beard flowed left and right as his head swayed to the tune and his black locks swung with it. His hands expressively flicked left and right as he capered about the girl. His billycock hat hopped.

> But, O girl of my heart,
> How could I marry you
> And I without a shirt
> Either white or blue?

'Would you ate an eel?' asked the green-jacketed porpoise by the fire holding up the shrivelled carcass to the dancer, who at once gaily doffed his hat (into which the priest dropped the eel) and went on his way back to the bar dancing and singing, followed in delight by the boy :

> *So chuadhas dti an tailliúr,*
> The besht to be found,
> And I bought a silken shirt
> For my *saighdiúrin donn* . . .

'Come, lads,' cried the priest, suddenly serious, 'it's time for us to visit the poor cobbler.'

It was full moonlight. The lake crawled livingly under it. The mountains were like the mouth of hell. It seemed to the priest as if the dark would come down and claw at them. He said so to the Celt, who had become wildly excited at the sight of the dark and the light and the creeping lake and strode down to the beach and threw up his arms crying, 'O Love! O Terror! O Death!' – and he

broke into Balfe's song to the moon from *The Lily of Killarney*:
'The Moon Hath Raised Her Lamp Above'.

'If you don't stop that emotional ass,' growled the girl as she
wheeled out her bicycle, 'he'll start singing the "Barcarole",' and
showed her own emotion by cycling madly away by herself.

'Grim! Grim!' said the American and the inspector agreed with,
'In the winter! Ah! In the winter!'

They were cycling now in single file, switch-backing up and
down over the little hills until the glow of the cobbler's window
eyed them from the dark. Near the cottage dark shapes of men
and boys huddled under the hedges and near the walls and as they
alighted drew aside to let them pass, fingers to caps for the priest.
The causeway to the kitchen door was crowded, unexpectedly
noisy with talk, smelling of turf smoke and pipe smoke and bog
water and sweat and hens.

In her corner by the enormous peat fire, the little old woman
seemed almost to be holding pleasant court, her spirits roused by
the friendliness and excitement of the crowds of neighbours.

The babble fell as the strangers entered. It rose again as they
disappeared up the ladder stairs to pay their respects to the cobbler.
It sank again when they clambered down. Then gradually it rose
and steadied as they settled into the company.

They were handed whiskey or stout or tea by Timeen and the
priest began to chat pleasantly and unconcernedly with the nearest
men to him. To the three Irishmen all this was so familiar that they
made no wonder of it, and they left the American and the girl to
the cobbler's wife, who at once talked to them about America and
Scotland with such a fantastic mixture of ignorance and personal
knowledge – gleaned from years upon years of visitors – that all
their embarrassment vanished in their pleasure at her wise and
foolish talk.

Only twice did her thoughts stray upstairs. A neighbour lifted
a red coal in the tongs to kindle his pipe: she glanced sharply and
drew a sharp breath.

'Light away, Dan Frank,' she encouraged him. 'Lasht week my
ould divil used to be ever reddening his pipe, God rest him, although
I used to be scolding him for burning his poor ould belly with all
the shmoking.'

Once when the babble suddenly fell into a trough of silence
they heard a dog across the moor baying at the moon. She
said:

'Times now I do be thinking that with the cobbler gone from me I'll be afraid to be by meself in the house with all the idle shtallions going the road.'

It was her commonest word for men, shtalls or shtallions, and all the neighbours who heard her must have pictured a lone tramp or a tinker walking the mountain road, and she inside listening through the barred door to the passing feet.

Elsewise she talked of things like hens and of prices and several times seemed to forget the nature of the occasion entirely. Then, in her most ribald vein, she became scabrous in her comments on her visitors, to the delight of everybody except the victims, who could only scuttle red-faced out the door without, in respect for her, as much as the satisfaction of a curse. It was after one of these sallies that the priest decided to close his visit with a laughing command to them all to kneel for the Rosary. With a lot of scuffling they huddled over chairs or sank on one knee, hiding their faces reverently in their caps.

Only the soldier did not join them. He went out and found more men all along the causeway and under the hedges, kneeling like-wise, so that the mumbling litany of prayer mingled with the tireless baying of the dog. All about them the encircling jags of mountains were bright and jet, brilliant craters, quarries of blackness, gleaming rocks, grey undergrowth.

The journey back was even more eerie than the journey out, the moon now behind them, their shadows before, and as they climbed the hills the mountains climbed before them as if to bar their way and when they rushed downward to the leaden bowl that was the lake, and into the closed gully of the coom, it was as if they were cycling not through space but through a maw of time that would never move.

The kitchen was empty. The eels lay in the pot. Two old boots lay on their sides drying before the fading fire. The crickets whistled loudly in the crannies. They took their candles and went in their stockinged feet up the stairs to bed, whispering.

The morning was a blaze of heat. The island was a floating red flower. The rhododendrons around the edges of the island were replicated in the smooth lee water which they barely touched. As the American, the girl, and the Celt set off for their pre-breakfast swim from the island they heard the sounds of spades striking against gravel. They saw the tall thin figure of an aged man, with grey side chops, in a roundy black hat and a swallow-tailed coat, standing against the sky. He held a piece of twig in his hand like a water diviner. He was measuring, taking bearings, solicitously encouraging the gravediggers below him to be accurate in their lines. He greeted the strangers politely, but they could see that they were distracting him and that he was weighed down by the importance of his task.

'For do you see, gentlemen, the cobbler was most particular about where he would be buried. I had a long talk with him about it lasht week and the one thing he laid down was for him to be buried in the one line with all the Cronins from Baurlinn.'

'But,' demurred the American, 'would a foot or two make all that difference?'

'It is an old graveyard,' the old man admonished him solemnly, 'and there are many laid here before him, and there will be many another after him.'

They left him to his task. The water was icy and they could bear only to dive in and clamber out. To get warm again they had to race up and down the brief sward before they dressed, hooting with pleasure in the comfort of the sun, the blue sky, the smells of the island, and the prospect of trout and bacon and eggs for breakfast. As they stepped back on the mainland they met a mountainy lad coming from the depths of the coom, carrying a weighted sack. His grey tweed trousers were as dark with wetness to his hips as if he had jumped into a bog hole. He walked with them to the hotel and explained that he was wet from the dew on the mountain heather and the young plantations. He had just crossed from the next valley, about two hours away. He halted and opened the mouth of the sack to show them, with a grin of satisfaction, the curved silver and blue of a salmon. He said he would be content to sell it to the hotel for five shillings and they agreed heartily with him when he said, 'Sure what is it only a night's sport and a walk over the mountain?' Over breakfast they upbraided one another for their lie-abed laziness on such a glorious day.

The day continued summer hot, burning itself away past high noon. The inspector got his car and drove away to visit some distant school. The American took his rod and rowed out of sight to the head of the lake. The girl walked away alone. The Celt went fishing from the far shore. The priest sat on the garden seat before the hotel and read his office and put a handkerchief over his head

and dozed, and when the postman came took the morning paper
from him. Once a farm cart made a crockerty-crock down the
eastern road and he wondered if it was bringing the coffin. In the
farmyard behind the hotel the milk separator whirred. For most
of the time everything was still – the sparkling lake, the idle shore,
the tiny fields, the sleeping hermit's island, the towering mountains,
the flawless sky. 'It is as still,' thought the priest, 'as the world
before life began.' All the hours that the priest sat there, or walked
slowly up and down reading his breviary, or opened a lazy eye
under his handkerchief, he saw only one sign of life – a woman
came on top of a hillock across the lake, looked about her for man
or animal, and went back to her chores.

Towards two o'clock the redheaded girl returned from her walk
and sat near him. She was too tired or lazy to talk: but she did
ask after a time:

'Do you think they really believe that the cobbler is talking to
Hitler?'

'They know no more about Hitler than they do about Cromwell.
But I'm sure they believe that the cobbler is having nice little
chats with his old pals Jerry Coakley and Shamus Cronin – that's
Dinny's father that he will be lying next to – up there in the graveyard – in a half an hour's time.'

She smiled happily.

'I wish I had their faith.'

'If you were born here you would.'

'I'd also have ten children,' she laughed. 'Will you join me in a
drink?'

He could not because he must await the funeral and the local
curate at the chapel on the island, and, rising, he went off there.
She went alone into the bar and helped herself to a whiskey, and
leaned over the morning paper. She was joined presently by the
Celt, radiant at having caught nothing. To pass the time she started
a discussion about large families and the ethics of birth control.
He said that he believed that everybody 'practised it in secret', a
remark which put her into such good humour that, in gratitude,
she made him happy by assuring him that in ten years' time the
birth rate in England would be the lowest in the world; and for
the innocent joy he showed at this she glowed with so much good
feeling towards him that she told him also how hateful birth control
is to the poor in the East End of London.

'I always knew it,' he cried joyfully. 'Religion has nothing to do with these things. All that counts is the natural law. For as I hope you do realise, there is a law of nature!'

And he filled out two more whiskeys and settled down to the unburdening of his soul.

'You see, I'm not really an orthodox Catholic at all. To me religion is valid only because and in so far as it is based on nature. That is why Ireland has a great message for the world. Everywhere else but here civilisation has taken the wrong turning. Here nature still rules man, and man still obeys nature . . .'

'As in the East End?' she said.

He hurried on, frowning crossly.

'I worship these mountains and these lakes and these simple Gaelic people because they alone still possess . . .'

'But you were angry last night when I defended primitive life. You wanted seaplanes on the lake and tourists from Manchester in Austin Sevens parked in front of . . .'

'I have already explained to you,' he reproved her, 'that to be natural doesn't mean that we must be primitive! That's the romantic illusion. What I mean to say is – that is, in very simple words, of course . . .'

And his dark face buttoned up and he became ill disposed again as he laboured to resolve his own contradictions.

She was about to fly from him when, through the wide-open door, she saw a dark group top the hillock to the east. As the sky stirred between their limbs she saw that they were a silhouette of six men lumbering under a coffin. Its brass plate caught the sun. They were followed by a darker huddle of women. After these came more men, and then a double file of horsemen descended out of the blue sky. On the hermit's island some watcher began to toll a bell.

'I'm going to the island,' she said. He followed her, nattering about Darwin and Lamarck.

The priest stood under the barrel arch of the little Romanesque chapel, distant in his white surplice, impressive, a magician. The two went shyly among the trees and watched the procession dissolving by the lakeside. The priest went out to meet the local curate.

Presently the coffin lumbered forward towards the chapel on the six shoulders and was laid rockingly on four chairs. The crowd seeped in among the trees. The widow sat in the centre of the chapel steps, flanked on each side by three women. She was the only one who spoke and it was plain from the way her attendants covered their faces with their hands that she was being ribald about each new arrival; the men knew it too, for as each one came forward on the sward, to meet the judgement of her dancing, wicked eyes, he skipped hastily into the undergrowth, with a wink or a grin to his neighbours. There was now a prolonged delay. The men looked around at the weather, or across the lake at the crops. Some turned their heads where, far up the lake, the American in his boat was rhythmically casting his invisible line. Then the two priests returned and entered the chapel. Their voices mumbling the *De Profundis* was like the buzzing of bees. The men bowed their heads, as usual holding their caps before their faces. Silence fell again as the procession reformed.

In the graveyard the familiar voices of the men lowering the dead into the earth outraged the silence. Nobody else made a sound until the first shovel of earth struck the brass plate on the lid and then the widow, defeated at last, cried out without restraint. As the earth began to fall more softly her wailing became more quiet. The last act of the burial was when the tall man, the cobbler's friend, smoothened the last dust of earth with his palms as if he were smoothening a blanket over a child. The priest said three Aves. They all responded hollowly.

They dispersed slowly, as if loath to admit that something final had happened to them all. As each one went down the path he could see the fishermen far away, steadily flogging the water. But they did not go home. They hung around the hotel all afternoon, the men in the crowded bar, drinking; the women clucking in the back kitchens. Outside the hotel the heads of the patient horses, growing fewer as the hours went by, drooped lower and lower with the going down of the sun, until only one cart was left and that, at last, ambled slowly away.

It was twilight before the visitors, tired and not in a good temper – they had been given only tea and boiled eggs for lunch – could take possession of the littered bar. They helped themselves to drinks and threw the coins into the pint glass. Drinking they looked out at the amber light touching the mountain line.

'It's queer,' murmured the priest. 'Why is it, all today and yesterday, I keep on thinking it's the autumn?'

' 'Tis a bit like it all right,' the inspector agreed pleasantly.

'Nonsense,' said the red-haired girl. 'It's a beautiful May day.'

'Thanks be to God,' agreed the inspector.

A frieze of small black cows passed, one by one, along the beach. They watched them go. Then Dinny put his head in from the kitchen.

'Supper, gentlemen.'

'I hope we'll have that salmon that came over the mountains,' smiled the Celt.

Nobody stirred.

'In America, you know, we call it the Fall.'

'The Fall?' said the priest.

'The fall of the leaves,' explained the soldier, thinking he did not understand.

The priest looked out over the dark lake – a stranger would hardly have known there was a lake if it had not been for the dun edge of froth – and, jutting out his lower lip, nodded to himself, very slowly, three times.

'Yes, indeed,' the inspector sighed, watching his face sympathetically.

'Aye,' murmured the priest, and looked at him, and nodded again, knowing that this was a man who understood.

Then he whirled, gave the Celt a mighty slap on the back, and cried, 'Come on and we'll polish off that salmon. Quick march!'

They finished their drinks and strolled into the lamplit dining room. As they sat around the table and shook out their napkins the soldier said, 'I reckon tomorrow will be another fine day.'

The red-haired girl leaned to the window and shaded her eyes against the pane. She could see how the moon touched the trees on the island with a ghostly tenderness. One clear star above the mountain wall gleamed. Seeing it her eyebrows floated upward softly for sheer joy.

'Yes,' she said quietly, 'it will be another grand day – tomorrow.'

And her eyebrows sank, very slowly, like a falling curtain.

Lovers of the Lake

'They might wear whites,' she had said, as she stood sipping her tea and looking down at the suburban tennis players in the square. And then, turning her head in that swift movement that always reminded him of a jackdaw: 'By the way, Bobby, will you drive me up to Lough Derg next week?'

He replied amiably from the lazy deeps of her armchair.

'Certainly! What part? Killaloe? But is there a good hotel there?'

'I mean the other Lough Derg. I want to do the pilgrimage.'

For a second he looked at her in surprise and then burst into laughter; then he looked at her peeringly.

'Jenny! Are you serious?'

'Of course.'

'Do you mean that place with the island where they go around on their bare feet on sharp stones, and starve for days, and sit up all night ologroaning and ologoaning?' He got out of the chair, went over to the cigarette box on the bookshelves, and, with his back to her, said coldly, 'Are you going religious on me?'

She walked over to him swiftly, turned him about, smiled her smile that was whiter than the whites of her eyes, and lowered her head appealingly on one side. When this produced no effect she said:

'Bobby! I'm always praising you to my friends as a man who takes things as they come. So few men do. Never looking beyond the day. Doing things on the spur of the moment. It's why I like you so much. Other men are always weighing up, and considering and arguing. I've built you up as a sort of magnificent wild, brainless tomcat. Are you going to let me down now?'

After a while he had looked at his watch and said:

'All right, then. I'll try and fix up a few days free next week. I must drop into the hospital now. But I warn you, Jenny, I've noticed this Holy Joe streak in you before. You'll do it once too often.'

She patted his cheek, kissed him sedately, said, 'You are a good boy,' and saw him out with a loving smile.

They enjoyed that swift morning drive to the Shannon's shore. He suspected nothing when she refused to join him in a drink at Carrick. Leaning on the counter they had joked with the barmaid like any husband and wife off on a motoring holiday. As they rolled smoothly around the northern shore of Lough Gill he had suddenly felt so happy that he had stroked her purple glove and winked at her. The lough was vacant under the midday sun, its vast expanse of stillness broken only by a jumping fish or by its eyelash fringe of reeds. He did not suspect anything when she sent him off to lunch by himself in Sligo, saying that she had to visit an old nun she knew in the convent. So far the journey had been to him no more than one of her caprices; until a yellow signpost marked TO BUNDORAN made them aware that her destination and their parting was near, for she said:

'What are you proposing to do until Wednesday?'

'I hadn't given it a thought.'

'Don't go off and forget all about me, darling. You know you're to pick me up on Wednesday about midday?'

After a silence he grumbled.

'You're making me feel a hell of a bastard, Jenny.'

'Why on earth?'

'All this penitential stuff is because of me, isn't it?'

'Don't be silly. It's just something I thought up all by myself out of my own clever little head.'

He drove on for several miles without speaking. She looked sideways, with amusement, at his ruddy, healthy, hockey-player face glummering under the peak of his checked cap. The brushes at his temples were getting white. Everything about him bespoke the distinguished Dublin surgeon on holiday: his pale-green shirt, his darker-green tie, his double-breasted waistcoat, his driving gloves with the palms made of woven cord. She looked pensively towards the sea. He growled:

'I may as well tell you this much, Jenny, if you were my wife I wouldn't stand for any of this nonsense.'

So their minds had travelled to the same thought? But if she were his wife the question would never have risen. She knew by the sudden rise of speed that he was in one of his tempers, so that when he pulled into the grass verge, switched off, and turned towards her she was not taken by surprise. A sea gull moaned high overhead. She lifted her grey eyes to his, and smiled, waiting for the attack.

'Jenny, would you mind telling me exactly what all this is about? I mean, why are you doing this fal-lal at this particular time?'

'I always wanted to do this pilgrimage. So it naturally follows that I would do it some time, doesn't it?'

'Perhaps. But why, for instance, this month and not last month?'

'The island wasn't open to pilgrims last month.'

'Why didn't you go last year instead of this year?'

'You know we went to Austria last year.'

'Why not the year before last?'

'I don't know. And stop bullying me. It is just a thing that everybody wants to do sometime. It is a special sort of Irish thing, like Lourdes, or Fatima, or Lisieux. Everybody who knows about it feels drawn to it. If you were a practising Catholic you'd understand.'

'I understand quite well,' he snapped. 'I know perfectly well that people go on pilgrimages all over the world. Spain. France. Mexico. I shouldn't be surprised if they go on them in Russia. What I am asking you is what has cropped up to produce this extra-special performance just *now*?'

'And I tell you I don't know. The impulse came over me suddenly last Sunday looking at those boys and girls playing tennis. For no reason. It just came. I said to myself, "All right, go now!" I felt that if I didn't do it on the impulse I'd never do it at all. Are you asking me for a rational explanation? I haven't got one. I'm not clever and intelligent like you, darling.'

'You're as clever as a bag of cats.'

She laughed at him.

'I do love you, Bobby, when you are cross. Like a small boy.'

'Why didn't you ask George to drive you?'

She sat up straight.

'I don't want my husband to know anything whatever about this. Please don't mention a word of it to him.'

He grinned at his small victory, considered the scythe of her jawbone, looked at the shining darkness of her hair, and restarted the car.

'All the same,' he said after a mile, 'there must be some reason. Or call it a cause if you don't like the word reason. And I'd give a lot to know what it is.'

After another mile:

'Of course, I might as well be talking to that old dolmen over there as be asking a woman why she does anything. And if she knew she wouldn't tell you.'

After another mile:

'Mind you, I believe all this is just a symptom of something else. Never forget, my girl, that I'm a doctor. I'm trained to interpret symptoms. If a woman comes to me with a pain ...'

'Oh, yes, if a woman comes to Surgeon Robert James Flannery with a pain he says to her, "Never mind, that's only a pain." By God! If a woman has a pain she has a bloody pain!'

He said quietly:

'Have you a pain?'

'Oh, do shut up! The only pain I have is in my tummy. I'm ravenous.'

'I'm sorry. Didn't they give you a good lunch at the convent?'

'I took no lunch; you have to arrive at the island fasting. That's the rule.'

'Do you mean to say you've had nothing at all to eat since breakfast?'

'I had no breakfast.'

'What will you get to eat when you arrive on the island?'

'Nothing. Or next to nothing. Everybody has to fast on the island the whole time. Sometime before night I might get a cup of black tea, or hot water with pepper and salt in it. I believe it's one of their lighthearted jokes to call it soup.'

Their speed shot up at once to sixty-five. He drove through Bundoran's siesta hour like the chariot of the Apocalypse. Nearing Ballyshannon they slowed down to a pleasant humming fifty.

'Jenny!'

'Yes?'

'Are you tired of me?'

'Is this more of you and your symptoms?'

He stopped the car again.

'Please answer my question.'

She laid her purple-gloved hand on his clenched fist.

'Look, darling! We've known one another for six years. You know that like any good little Catholic girl I go to my duties every Easter and Christmas. Once or twice I've told you so. You've growled and grumbled a bit, but you never made any fuss about it. What are you suddenly worrying about now?'

'Because all that was just routine. Like the French or the Italians.

Good Lord, I'm not bigoted. There's no harm in going to church now and again. I do it myself on state occasions, or if I'm staying in some house where they'd be upset if I didn't. But this sort of lunacy isn't routine!'

She slewed her head swiftly away from his angry eyes. A child in a pink pinafore with shoulder frills was driving two black cows through a gap.

'It was never routine. It's the one thing I have to hang on to in an otherwise meaningless existence. No children. A husband I'm not in love with. And I can't marry you.'

She slewed back to him. He slewed away to look up the long empty road before them. He slewed back; he made as if to speak; he slewed away impatiently again.

'No?' she interpreted. 'It isn't any use, is it? It's my problem, not yours. Or if it is yours you've solved it long ago by saying it's all a lot of damned nonsense.'

'And how have you solved it?' he asked sardonically.

'Have you any cause to complain of how I've solved it? Oh, I'm not defending myself. I'm a fraud, I'm a crook, I admit it. You are more honest than I am. You don't believe in anything. But it's the truth that all I have is you and ...'

'And what?'

'It sounds so blasphemous I can't say it.'

'Say it!'

'All I have is you, and God.'

He took out his cigarette case and took one. She took one. When he lit hers their eyes met. He said, very softly, looking up the empty road:

'Poor Jenny! I wish you'd talked like this to me before. It is after all, as you say, your own affair. But what I can't get over is that this thing you're doing is so utterly extravagant. To go off to an island, in the middle of a lake, in the mountains, with a lot of Crawthumpers of every age and sex, and no sex, and peel off your stockings and your shoes, and go limping about on your bare feet on a lot of sharp stones, and kneel in the mud, psalming and beating your breast like a criminal, and drink nothing for three days but salt water ... it's not like you. It's a side of you I've never known before. The only possible explanation for it must be that something is happening inside in you that I've never seen happen before!'

She spread her hands in despair. He chucked away his cigarette and restarted the car. They drove on in silence. A mist began to speckle the windscreen. They turned off the main road into sunless hills, all brown as hay. The next time he glanced at her she was making up her face; her mouth rolling the lipstick into her lips; her eyes rolling around the mirror. He said:

'You're going to have a nice picnic if the weather breaks.'

She glanced out apprehensively.

'It won't be fun.'

A sudden flog of rain lashed into the windscreen. The sky had turned its bucket upside down. He said:

'Even if it's raining do you still have to keep walking around on those damn stones?'

'Yes.'

'You'll get double pneumonia.'

'Don't worry, darling. It's called Saint Patrick's Purgatory. He will look after me.'

That remark started a squabble that lasted until they drew up beside the lake. Other cars stood about like stranded boats. Other pilgrims stood by the boat slip, waiting for the ferry, their backs hunched to the wind, their clothes ruffled like the fur of cattle. She looked out across the lough at the creeping worms of foam.

He looked about him sullenly at the waiting pilgrims, a green bus, two taxiloads of people waiting for the rain to stop. They were not his kind of people at all, and he said so.

'That,' she smiled, 'is what comes of being a surgeon. You don't meet people, you meet organs. Didn't you once tell me that when you are operating you never look at the patient's face?'

He grunted. Confused and hairy-looking clouds combed themselves on the ridges of the hills. The lake was crumpled and grey, except for those yellow worms of foam blown across it in parallel lines. To the south a cold patch of light made it all look far more dreary. She stared out towards the island and said:

'It's not at all like what I expected.'

'And what the hell did you expect? Capri?'

'I thought of an old island, with old grey ruins, and old holly trees and rhododendrons down to the water, a place where old monks would live.'

They saw tall buildings like modern hotels rising by the island's shore, an octagonal basilica big enough for a city, four or five bare, slated houses, a long shed like a ballroom. There was one tree. Another bus drew up beside them and people peered out through the wiped glass.

'Oh, God!' she groaned. 'I hope this isn't going to be like Lourdes.'

'And what, pray, is wrong with Lourdes when it's at home?'

'Commercialised. I simply can't believe that this island was the most famous pilgrimage of the Middle Ages. On the rim of the known world. It must have been like going off in Jerusalem or coming home brown from the sun with a cockle in your hat from Galilee.'

He put on a vulgar Yukon voice:

'Thar's gold somewhere in them thar hills. It looks to me like a damn good financial proposition for somebody.'

She glared at him. The downpour had slackened. Soon it almost ceased. Gurgles of streams. A sound of pervasive drip. From the back seat she took a small red canvas bag marked T.W.A.

'You will collect me on Wednesday about noon, won't you?'

He looked at her grimly. She looked every one of her forty-one years. The skin of her neck was corrugated. In five years' time she would begin to have jowls.

'Have a good time,' he said, and slammed in the gears, and drove away.

The big lumbering ferryboat was approaching, its prow slapping the corrugated waves. There were three men to each oar. It began to spit rain again. With about a hundred and fifty men and women, of every age and, so far as she could see, of every class, she clambered aboard. They pushed out and slowly they made the crossing, huddling together from the wind and rain. The boat nosed into its cleft and unloaded. She had a sensation of dark water, wet cement, houses, and a great number of people; and that she would have given gold for a cup of hot tea. Beyond the four or five whitewashed houses – she guessed that they had been the only buildings on the island before trains and buses made the pilgrimage popular – and beyond the cement paths, she came on the remains of the natural island: a knoll, some warm grass, the tree, and the roots of the old hermits' cells across whose teeth of stone barefooted pilgrims were already treading on one another's heels. Most of these barefooted people wore mackintoshes. They not only stumbled on one anothers' heels; they kneeled on one another's toes and tails; for the island was crowded – she thought there must be nearly two thousand people on it. They were packed between the two modern hostels and the big church. She saw a priest in sou'wester and gum boots. A nun waiting for the new arrivals at the door of the women's hostel took her name and address, and gave her the number of her cubicle. She went upstairs to it, laid her red bag on the cot beside it, unfastened her garters, took off her shoes, unpeeled her nylons, and without transition became yet another anonymous pilgrim. As she went out among the pilgrims already praying in the rain she felt only a sense of shame as if she were specially singled out under the microscope of the sky. The wet ground was cold.

A fat old woman in black, rich-breasted, grey-haired, took her kindly by the arm and said in a warm, Kerry voice: 'You're shivering, you poor creature! Hould hard now. Sure, when we have the first station done they'll be giving us the ould cup of black tay.'

And laughed at the folly of this longing for the tea. She winced when she stepped on the gritty concrete of the terrace surrounding the basilica, built out on piles over the lake. A young man smiled sympathetically, seeing that she was a delicate subject for the rigours before her: he was dressed like a clerk, with three pens in his breast pocket, and he wore a Total Abstinence badge.

'Saint's Island they call it,' he smiled. 'Some people think it should be called Divil's Island.'

She disliked his kindness – she had never in her life asked for pity from anybody, but she soon found that the island floated on kindness. Everything and everybody about her seemed to say, 'We are all sinners here, wretched creatures barely worthy of mercy.' She felt the abasement of the doomed. She was among people who had surrendered all personal identity, all pride. It was like being in a concentration camp.

The fat old Kerrywoman was explaining to her what the routine was, and as she listened she realised how long her stay would really be. In prospect it had seemed so short: come on Monday afternoon, leave on Wednesday at noon; it had seemed no more than one complete day and two bits of nights. She had not foreseen that immediately after arriving she must remain out of doors until the darkness fell, walking the rounds of the stones, praying, kneeling, for about five hours. And even then she would get no respite, for she must stay awake all night praying in the basilica. It was then that she would begin the second long day, as long and slow as the night; and on the third day she would still be walking those rounds until midday. She would be without food, even when she would have left the island, until the midnight of that third day.

'Yerrah, but sure,' the old woman cackled happily, 'they say the fasting is good for the stomach.'

She began to think of 'they'. They had thought all this up. They had seen how much could be done with simple prayers. For when she began to tot up the number of paternosters and Aves that she must say she had to stop at the two thousandth. And these reiterated prayers must be said while walking on the stones, or kneeling in the mud, or standing upright with her two arms extended. This was the posture she disliked most. Every time she came to do it, her face to the lake, her arms spread, the queue listening to her renouncing her sins, she had to force herself to the posture and the words. The first time she did it, with the mist blowing into her eyes, her arms out like a crucifix, her lips said the words but her heart cursed herself for coming so unprepared, for coming at all. Before she had completed her first circuit − four times around each one of six cells − one ankle and one toe was bleeding. She was then permitted to ask for the cup of black tea. She received it sullenly, as a prisoner might receive his bread and water.

She wished after that first circuit to start again and complete a second − the six cells, and the seven other ordeals at other points of the island − and so be done for the day. But she found that 'they' had invented something else: she must merge with the whole anonymous mass of pilgrims for mass prayer in the church.

A slur of wet feet; patter of rain on leaded windows; smells of bog water and damp clothing; the thousand voices responding to the incantations. At her right a young girl of about seventeen was uttering heartfelt responses. On her left an old man in his sixties gave them out loudly. On all sides, before her, behind her, the same passionate exchange of energy, while all she felt was a crust hardening about her heart, and she thought, in despair, 'I have no more feeling than a stone!' And she thought, looking about her, that tonight this vigil would go on for hour after hour until the dark, leaded windows coloured again in the morning light. She leaned her face in her palms and whispered, 'O God, please let me out of myself!' The waves of voices beat and rumbled in her ears as in an empty shell.

She was carried out on the general sliding whispering of the bare feet into the last gleanings of the daylight to begin her second circuit. In the porch she cowered back from the rain. It was settling into a filthy night. She was thrust forward by the crowd, flowed with its force to the iron cross by the shingle's edge. She took her place in the queue and then with the night wind pasting her hair across her face she raised her arms and once again renounced the

world, the flesh, and the Devil. She did four circles of the church
on the gritty concrete. She circled the first cell's stones. She completed the second circle. Her prayers were becoming numb by now.
She stumbled, muttering them, up and down the third steeply sloped
cell, or bed. She was a drowned cat and one knee was bleeding. At
the fourth cell she saw him.

He was standing about six yards away looking at her. He wore
a white raincoat buttoned tight about his throat. His feet were
bare. His hair was streaked down his forehead as if he had been
swimming. She stumbled towards him and dragged him by the
arm down to the edge of the boat slip.

'What are you doing here?' she cried furiously. 'Why did you
follow me?'

He looked down at her calmly:

'Why shouldn't I be here?'

'Because you don't believe in it! You've just followed me to sneer
at me, to mock at me! Or from sheer vulgar curiosity!'

'No,' he said, without raising his voice. 'I've come to see just what
it is that you believe in. I want to know all about you. I want to
know why you came here. I don't want you to do anything or
have anything that I can't do or can't know. And as for believing –
we all believe in something.'

Dusk was closing in on the island and the lake. She had to peer
into his face to catch his expression.

'But I've known you for years and you've never shown any sign
of believing in anything but microscopes and microbes and symptoms. It's absurd, you couldn't be serious about anything like this.
I'm beginning to hate you!'

'Are you?' he said, so softly that she had to lean near him to
hear him over the slapping of the waves against the boat slip. A
slow rift in the clouds let down a star; by its light she saw his
smile.

'Yes!' she cried, so loudly that he swept out a hand and gripped
her by the arm. Then he took her other arm and said gently:

'I don't think you should have come here, Jenny. You're only
tearing yourself to bits. There are some places where some people
should never go, things some people should never try to do – however good they may be for others. I know why you came here. You
feel you ought to get rid of me, but you haven't the guts to do it,
so you come up here into the mountains to get your druids to work
it by magic. All right! I'm going to ask them to help you.'

He laughed and let her go, giving her a slight impulse away from him.

'Ask. You will *ask*. Do you mean to tell me that you have said as much as one single, solitary prayer on this island,'

'Yes,' he said casually, 'I have.'

She scorned him.

'Are you trying to tell me, Bobby, that you are doing this pilgrimage,'

'I haven't fasted. I didn't know about that. And, anyway, I probably won't. I've got my pockets stuffed with two pounds of the best chocolates I could buy in Bundoran. I don't suppose I'll even stay up all night like the rest of you. The place is so crowded that I don't suppose anybody will notice me if I curl up in some corner of the boathouse. I heard somebody saying that people had to sleep there last night. But you never know – I might – I just might stay awake. If I do, it will remind me of going to midnight Mass with my father when I was a kid. Or going to retreats, when we used all hold up a lighted candle and renounce the Devil.

'It was a queer sensation standing up there by the lake and saying those words all over again. Do you know, I thought I'd completely forgotten them!'

'The next thing you're going to say is that you believe in the Devil! You fraud!'

'Oh, there's no trouble about believing in that old gentleman. There isn't a doctor in the world who doesn't, though he will give him another name. And on a wet night, in a place like this, you could believe in a lot of things. No, my girl, what I find it hard to believe in is the flesh and the world. They are good things. Do you think I'm ever going to believe that your body and my body are evil. And you don't either! And you are certainly never going to renounce the world, because you are tied to it hand and foot!'

'That's not true!'

His voice cut her like a whip:

'Then why do you go on living with your husband?'

She stammered feebly. He cut at her again:

'You do it because he's rich, and you like comfort, and you like being a "somebody".'

With a switch of her head she brushed past him. She did not see him again that night.

The night world turned imperceptibly. In the church, for hour after hour, the voices obstinately beat back the responses. She sank under the hum of the prayer wheel, the lust for sleep, her own despairs. Was he among the crowd, Or asleep in a corner of the boatshed? She saw his flatly domed fingers, a surgeon's hand, so strong, so sensitive. She gasped at the sensual image she had evoked.

The moon touched a black window with colour. After an age it had stolen to another. Heads drooped. Neighbours poked one another awake with a smile. Many of them had risen from the benches in order to keep themselves awake and were circling the aisles in a loose procession of slurring feet responding as they moved. Exhaustion began to work on her mind. Objects began to disconnect, become isolated each within its own outline – now it was the pulpit, now a statue, now a crucifix. Each object took on the vividness of a hallucination. The crucifix detached itself from the wall and leaned towards her, and for a long while she saw nothing but the heavy pendent body, the staring eyes, so that when the old man at her side let his head sink over on her shoulder and then woke up with a start she felt him no more than if they were two fishes touching in the sea. Bit by bit the incantations drew her in; sounds came from her mouth; prayers flowed between her and those troubled eyes that fixed hers. She swam into an ecstasy as rare as one of those perfect dances of her youth when she used to swing in a whirl of music, a swirl of bodies, a circling of lights, floated out of her mortal frame, alone in the arms that embraced her.

Suddenly it all exploded. One of the four respites of the night had halted the prayers. The massed pilgrims relaxed. She looked blearily about her, no longer disjunct. Her guts rumbled. She looked at the old man beside her. She smiled at him and he at her.

'My poor old knees are crucified,' he grinned.

'You should have the skirts,' she grinned back.

They were all going out to stretch in the cool, and now dry air, or to snatch a smoke. The amber windows of the church shivered in a pool of water. A hearty-voiced young woman leaning on the balustrade lit a match for her. The match hissed into the invisible lake lapping below.

'The ould fag,' said the young woman, dragging deep on her cigarette, 'is a great comfort. 'Tis as good as a man.'

'I wonder,' she said, 'what would Saint Patrick think if he saw women smoking on his island?'

'He'd beat the living daylights out of the lot of us.'

She laughed aloud. She must tell him that. . . . She began to
wander through the dark crowds in search of him. He had said
something that wasn't true and she would answer him. She went
through the crowds down to the boat slip. He was standing there,
looking out into the dark as if he had not stirred since she saw him
there before midnight. For a moment she regarded him, frightened
by the force of the love that gushed into her. Then she approached
him.

'Well, Mr Wordly Wiseman? Enjoying your boathouse bed?'

'I'm doing the vigil,' he said smugly.

'You sound almighty pleased with yourself.'

He spoke eagerly now:

'Jenny, we mustn't quarrel. We must understand one another.
And understand this place. I'm just beginning to. An island. In a
remote lake. Among the mountains. Night-time. No sleep. Hunger.
The conditions of the desert. I was right in what I said to you. Can't
you see how the old hermits who used to live here could swim
off into a trance in which nothing existed but themselves and their
visions? I told you a man can renounce what he calls the Devil,
but not the flesh, not the world. They thought, like you, that they
could throw away the flesh and the world, but they were using the
flesh to achieve one of the rarest experiences in the world! Don't
you see it?'

'Experiences! The next thing you'll be talking about is symptoms.'

'Well, surely, you must have observed?' He peered at the luminous
dial of his watch. 'I should say that about four o'clock we will
probably begin to experience a definite sense of dissociation. After
that a positive alienation . . .'

She turned furiously from him. She came back to say:

'I would much prefer, Bobby, if you would have the decency to
go away in the morning. I can find my own way home. I hope
we don't meet again on this island. Or out of it!'

'The magic working?' he laughed.

After that she made a deliberate effort of the mind to mean and
to feel every separate word of the prayers – which is a great foolish-
ness since prayers are not poems to be read or even understood;
they are an instinct; to dance would be as wise. She thought that
if she could not feel what she said how could she mean it, and so she
tried to savour every word, and, from trying to mean each word,
lagged behind the rest, sank into herself, and ceased to pray. After
the second respite she prayed only to keep awake. As the first cold

pallor of morning came into the windows her heart rose again. But the eastern hills are high here and the morning holds off stubbornly. It is the worst hour of the vigil, when the body ebbs, the prayers sink to a drone, and the night seems to have begun all over again.

At the last respite she emerged to see pale tents of blue on the hills. The slow cumulus clouds cast a sheen on the water. There is no sound. No birds sing. At this hour the pilgrims are too awed or too exhausted to speak, so that the island reverts to its ancient silence in spite of the crowds.

By the end of the last bout she was calm like the morning lake. She longed for the cup of black tea. She was unaware of her companions. She did not think of him. She was unaware of herself. She no more thought of God than a slave thinks of his master, and after she had drunk her tea she sat in the morning sun outside the woman's hostel like an old blind woman who has nothing in life to wait for but sleep.

The long day expired as dimly as the vapour rising from the water. The heat became morbid. One is said to be free on this second day to converse, to think, to write, to read, to do anything at all that one pleases except the one thing everybody wants to do – to sleep. She did nothing but watch the clouds, or listen to the gentle muttering of the lake. Before noon she heard some departing pilgrims singing a hymn as the great ferryboats pushed off. She heard their voices without longing; she did not even desire food. When she met him she was without rancour.

'Still here?' she said, and when he nodded: 'Sleepy?'

'Sleepy.'

'Too many chocolates, probably.'

'I didn't eat them. I took them out of my pockets one by one as I leaned over the balustrade and guessed what centre each had – coffee, marshmallow, nut, toffee, cream – and dropped it in with a little splash to the holy fishes.'

She looked up at him gravely.

'Are you really trying to join in this pilgrimage?'

'Botching it. I'm behindhand with my rounds. I have to do five circuits between today and tomorrow. I may never get them done. Still, something is better than nothing.'

'You dear fool!'

If he had not walked away then she would have had to, such a gush of affection came over her at the thought of what he was

doing, and why he was doing it – stupidly, just like a man; sceptically, just like a man; not admitting it to himself, just like a man; for
all sorts of damn-fool rational reasons, just like a man; and not at
all for the only reason that she knew was his real reason : because
she was doing it, which meant that he loved her. She sat back, and
closed her eyes, and the tears of chagrin oozed between her lids
as she felt her womb stir with desire of him.

When they met again it was late afternoon.

'Done four rounds,' he said so cheerfully that he maddened her.

'It's not golf, Bobby, damn you!'

'I should jolly well think not. I may tell you my feet are in
such a condition I won't be able to play golf for a week. Look!'

She did not look. She took his arm and led him to the quietest
corner she could find.

'Bobby, I am going to confess something to you. I've been thinking
about it all day trying to get it clear. I know now why I came here.
I came because I know inside in me that some day our apple will
have to fall off the tree. I'm forty. You are nearly fifty. It will have
to happen. I came here because I thought it right to admit that some
day, if it has to be, I am willing to give you up.'

He began to shake all over with laughter.

'What the hell are you laughing at?' she moaned.

'When women begin to reason! Listen, wasn't there a chap one
time who said, "O God, please make me chaste, but not just yet"?'

'What I am saying is "now", if it has to be, if it can be. If I can
make it be. I suppose,' she said wildly, 'I'm really asking for a
miracle, that my husband would die, or that you'd die, or something
like that would make it all come right!'

He burst into such a peal of laughter that she looked around
her apprehensively. A few people near them also happened to be
laughing over something and looked at them indulgently.

'Do you realise, Bobby, that when I go to confession here I will
have to tell all about us, and I will have to promise to give you up?'

'Yes, darling, and you won't mean a single word of it.'

'But I always mean it!'

He stared at her as if he were pushing curtains aside in her.

'Always? Do you mean you've been saying it for six years?'

'I mean it when I say it. Then I get weak. I can't help it, Bobby.
You know that!' She saw the contempt in his eyes and began to talk
rapidly, twisting her marriage ring madly around her finger. He

kept staring into her eyes like a man staring down the long perspective railway line waiting for the engine to appear. 'So you see
why there wasn't any sense in asking me yesterday why I come now
and not at some other time, because with me there isn't any other
time, it's always *now*, I meet you *now*, and I love you *now*, and I
think it's not right *now*, and then I think, "No, not *now*," and then
I say I'll give you up *now*, and I mean it every time until we meet
again, and it begins all over again, and there's never any end to it
until some day I can say, "Yes, I used to know him once, but not
now," and then it will be a *now* where there won't be any other
now any more because there'll be nothing to live for.'

The tears were leaking down her face. He sighed:

'Dear me! You have got yourself into a mess, haven't you?'

'O God, the promises and the promises! I wish the world would
end tonight and we'd both die together!'

He gave her his big damp handkerchief. She wiped her eyes and
blew her nose and said:

'You don't mean to go to confession, do you?'

He chuckled sourly.

'And promise? I must go and finish a round of pious golf. I'm
afraid, old girl, you just want to get me into the same mess as yourself. No, thank you. You must solve your own problems in your own
way, and I in mine.'

That was the last time she spoke to him that day.

She went back to the balustrade where she had smoked with
the hearty girl in the early hours of the morning. She was there
again. She wore a scarlet beret. She was smoking again. She began
to talk, and the talk flowed from her without stop. She had fine
broad shoulders, a big mobile mouth, and a pair of wild goat's eyes.
After a while it became clear that the woman was beside herself
with terror. She suddenly let it all out in a gush of exhaled smoke.

'Do you know why I'm hanging around here? Because I ought
to go into confession and I'm in dread of it. He'll tear me alive.
He'll murdher me. It's not easy for a girl like me, I can promise you!'

'You must have terrible sins to tell?' she smiled comfortingly.

'He'll slaughter me, I'm telling you.'

'What is it? Boys?'

The two goat's eyes dilated with fear and joy. Her hands shook
like a drunkard's.

'I can't keep away from them. I wish to God I never came
here.'

'But how silly! It's only a human thing. I'm sure half the people here have the same tale to tell. It's an old story, child, the priests are sick of hearing it.'

'Oh, don't be talking! Let me alone! I'm criminal, I tell yeh! And there are things you can't explain to a priest. My God, you can hardly explain 'em to a doctor!'

'You're married?' – looking at her ring.

'Poor Tom! I have him worn out. He took me to a doctor one time to know would anything cure me. The old foolah took me temperature and give me a book like a bus guide about when it's safe and when it isn't safe to make love, the ould eedjut! I was pregnant again before Christmas. Six years married and I have six kids; nobody could stand that gait o' going. And I'm only twenty-four. Am I to have a baby every year of my life? I'd give me right hand this minute for a double whiskey.'

'Look, you poor child! We are all in the same old ferry boat here. What about me?'

'You?'

'It's not men with me, it's worse.'

'Worse? In God's name, what's worse than men?'

The girl looked all over her, followed her arm down to her hand, to her third finger.

'One man.'

The tawny eyes swivelled back to her face and immediately understood.

'Are you very fond of him?' she asked gently, and taking the unspoken answer said, still more pityingly, 'You can't give him up?'

'It's six years now and I haven't been able to give him up.'

The girl's eyes roved sadly over the lake as if she were surveying a lake of human unhappiness. Then she threw her butt into the water and her red beret disappeared into the maw of the church porch.

She saw him twice before the dusk thickened and the day grew cold again with the early sunset. He was sitting directly opposite her before the men's hostel, smoking, staring at the ground between his legs. They sat facing one another. They were separated by their identities, joined by their love. She glimpsed him only once after that, at the hour when the sky and the hills merge, an outline passing across the lake. Soon after she had permission to go to her cubicle. Immediately she lay down she spiralled into the bottom of a deep lake of sleep.

She awoke refreshed and unburthened. She had received the island's gift: it's sense of remoteness from the world, almost a sensation of the world's death. It is the source of the island's kindness. Nobody is just matter, poor to be exploited by rich, weak to be exploited by the strong; in mutual generosity each recognises the other only as a form of soul; it is a brief, harsh Utopia of equality in nakedness. The bare feet are a symbol of that nakedness unknown in the world they have left.

The happiness to which she awoke was dimmed a little by a conversation she had with an Englishman over breakfast – the usual black tea and a piece of oaten bread. He was a city man who had arrived the day before, been up all night while she slept. He had not yet shaved; he was about sixty-two or three; small and tubby, his eyes perpetually wide and unfocusing behind pince-nez glasses.

'That's right,' he said, answering her question. 'I'm from England. Liverpool. I cross by the night boat and get here the next afternoon. Quite convenient, really. I've come here every year for the last twenty-two years, apart from the war years. I come on account of my wife.'

'Is she ill?'

'She died twenty-two years ago. No, it's not what you might think – I'm not praying for her. She was a good woman, but, well, you see, I wasn't very kind to her. I don't mean I quarrelled with her, or drank, or was unfaithful. I never gambled. I've never smoked in my life.' His hands made a faint movement that was meant to express a whole life, all the confusion and trouble of his soul. 'It's just that I wasn't kind. I didn't make her happy.'

'Isn't that,' she said, to comfort him, 'a very private feeling? I mean, it's not in the Ten Commandments that thou shalt make thy wife happy.'

He did not smile. He made the same faint movement with his fingers.

'Oh, I don't know! What's love if it doesn't do that? I mean to say, it is something godly to love another human being, isn't it? I mean, what does "godly" mean if it doesn't mean giving up everything for another? It isn't human to love, you know. It's foolish, it's a folly, a divine folly. It's beyond all reason, all limits. I didn't rise to it,' he concluded sadly.

She looked at him, and thought, 'A little fat man, a clerk in some Liverpool office all his life, married to some mousy little woman, thinking about love as if he were some sort of Greek mystic.'

'It's often,' she said lamely, 'more difficult to love one's husband, or one's wife, as the case may be, than to love one's neighbour.'

'Oh, much!' he agreed without a smile. 'Much! Much more difficult!'

At which she was overcome by the thought that inside ourselves we have no room without a secret door; no solid self that has not a ghost inside it trying to escape. If I leave Bobby I still have George. If I leave George I still have myself, and whatever I find in myself. She patted the little man's hand and left him, fearing that if she let him talk on even his one little piece of sincerity would prove to be a fantasy, and in the room that he had found behind his own room she would open other doors leading to other obsessions. He had told her something true about her own imperfection, and about the nature of love, and she wanted to share it while it was still true. But she could not find him, and there was still one more circuit to do before the ferryboat left. She did meet Goat's Eyes. The girl clutched her with tears magnifying her yellow-and-green irises and gasped joyously:

'I found a lamb of a priest. A saint anointed! He was as gentle! "What's your husband earning?" says he. "Four pounds ten a week, Father," says I. "And six children?" says he. "You poor woman," says he, "you don't need to come here at all. Your Purgatory is at home." He laid all the blame on poor Tom. And, God forgive me, I let him do it. "Bring him here to me," says he, "and I'll cool him for you." God bless the poor innocent priest, I wish I knew as little about marriage as he does. But,' and here she broke into a wail, 'sure he has me ruined altogether now. He's after making me so fond of poor Tommy I think I'll never get home soon enough to go to bed with him.' And in a vast flood of tears of joy, of relief, and of fresh misery: 'I wish I was a bloomin' nun!'

It was not until they were all waiting at the ferryboat that she saw him. She managed to sit beside him in the boat. He touched her hand and winked. She smiled back at him. The bugler blew his bugle. A tardy traveller came racing out of the men's hostel. The boatload cheered him, the bugler helped him on board with a joke about people who can't be persuaded to stop praying, and there was a general chaff about people who have a lot to pray about, and then somebody raised the parting hymn, and the rowers began to push the heavy oars, and singing they were slowly rowed across the summer lake back to the world.

They were driving back out of the hills by the road they had come, both silent. At last she could hold in her question no longer:

'Did you go, Bobby?'

Meaning: had he, after all his years of silence, of rebellion of disbelief, made his peace with God at the price of a compact against her. He replied gently:

'Did I probe your secrets all these years?'

She took the rebuke humbly, and for several miles they drove on in silence. They were close, their shoulders touched, but between them there stood that impenetrable wall of identity that segregates every human being in a private world of self. Feeling it she realised at last that it is only in places like the lake-island that the barriers of self break down. The tubby little clerk from Liverpool had been right. Only when love desires nothing but renunciation, total surrender, does self surpass self. Everybody who ever entered the island left the world of self behind for a few hours, exchanged it for what the little man had called a divine folly. It was possible only for a few hours – unless one had the courage, or the folly, to renounce the world altogether. Then another thought came to her. In the world there might also be escape from the world.

'Do you think, Bobby, that when people are in love they can give up everything for one another?'

'No,' he said flatly. 'Except perhaps in the first raptures?'

'If I had a child I think I could sacrifice anything for it. Even my life.'

'Yes,' he agreed. 'It has been known to happen.'

And she looked at him sadly, knowing that they would never be able to marry, and even if she did that she would never have children. And yet, if they could have married, there was a lake . . .

'Do you know what I'm planning at this moment?' he asked breezily.

She asked without interest what it was.

'Well, I'm simply planning the meal we're going to eat tonight in Galway, at midnight.'

'At midnight? Then we're going on with this pilgrimage? Are we?'

'Don't *you* want to? It was your idea in the beginning.'

'All right. And what are we going to do until midnight? I've never known time to be so long.'

'I'm going to spend the day fishing behind Glencar. That will kill the hungry day. After that, until midnight, we'll take the longest possible road around Connemara. Then would you have any objections to mountain trout cooked in milk, stuffed roast kid with fresh peas and spuds in their jackets, apple pie and whipped cream, with a cool Pouilly Fuissé, a cosy 1929 claret, West of Ireland Pont l'Evêque, finishing up with Gaelic coffee and two Otards? Much more in your line, if I know anything about you, than your silly old black tea and hot salt water.'

'I admit I like the things of the flesh.'

'You live for them!'

He had said it so gently, so affectionately that, half in dismay, half with amusement, she could not help remembering Goat's Eyes, racing home as fast as the bus would carry her to make love to her Tommy. After that they hardly spoke at all, and then only of casual things such as a castle beside the road, the sun on the edging sea, a tinker's caravan, an opening view. It was early afternoon as they entered the deep valley at Glencar and he probed in second gear for an attractive length of stream, found one and started eagerly to put his rod together. He began to walk up against the dazzling bubble of water and within an hour was out of sight. She stretched herself out on a rug on the bank and fell sound asleep.

It was nearly four o'clock before she woke up, stiff and thirsty. She drank from a pool in the stream, and for an hour she sat alone by the pool, looking into its peat-brown depth, as vacantly contented as a tinker's wife to live for the moment, to let time wind and unwind everything. It was five o'clock before she saw him approaching, plodding in his flopping waders, with four trout on a rush stalk. He threw the fish at her feet and himself beside them.

'I nearly ate them raw,' he said.

'Let's cook them and eat them,' she said fiercely.

He looked at her for a moment, then got up and began to gather dry twigs, found Monday's newspaper in the car – it looked like a paper of years ago – and started the fire. She watched while he fed it. When it was big enough in its fall to have made a hot bed of embers he roasted two of the trout across the hook of his gaff, and she smelled the crisping flesh and sighed. At last he laid them browned and crackly, on the grass by her hand. She took one by its crusted tail, smelled it, looked at him, and slung it furiously into the heart of the fire. He gave a sniff-laugh and did the same with his.

'Copy cat!' she said.

'Let's get the hell out of here,' he said, jumping up. 'Carry the kit, will you?'

She rose, collected the gear, and followed him saying:

'I feel like an Arab wife. "Carry the pack. Go here. Go there." '

They climbed out of the glens onto the flat moorland of the Easky peninsula where the evening light was a cold ochre gleaming across green bogland that was streaked with all the weedy colours of a strand at ebb. At Ballina she suggested that they should have tea.

'It will be a pleasant change of diet!' he said.

When they had found a café and she was ordering the tea he said to the waitress:

'And bring lots of hot buttered toast.'

'This,' she said, as she poured out the tea and held up the milk jug questioningly, 'is a new technique of seduction. Milk?'

'Are you having milk?'

'No.'

'No, then.'

'Some nice hot buttered toast?'

'Are you having toast?' he demanded.

'Why the bloody hell should it be up to me to decide?'

'I asked you a polite question,' he said rudely.

'No.'

'No!'

They looked at one another as they sipped the black tea like two people who are falling head over heels into hatred of one another.

'Could you possibly tell me,' he said presently, 'why I bother my head with a fool of a woman like you?'

'I can only suppose, Bobby, that it is because we are in love with one another.'

'I can only suppose so,' he growled. 'Let's go on!'

They took the longest way round he could find on the map, west into County Mayo, across between the lakes at Pontoon, over the level bogland to Castlebar. Here the mountains walled in the bogland plain with cobalt air – in the fading light the land was losing all solidity. Clouds like soapsuds rose and rose over the edges of the mountains until they glowed as if there was a fire of embers behind the blue ranges. In Castlebar he pulled up by the post office and tele-

phoned to the hotel in Salthill for dinner and two rooms. When he
came out he saw a poster in a shop window and said:

'Why don't we go to the pictures? It will kill a couple of hours.'

'By rights,' she said, 'you ought to be driving me home to Dublin.'

'If you wish me to I will.'

'Would you if I asked you?'

'Do you want me too?'

'I suppose it's rather late now, isn't it?'

'Not at all. Fast going we could be there about one o'clock. Shall
we?'

'It wouldn't help. George is away. I'd have to bring you in and
give you something to eat, and . . . Let's go to the blasted movies!'

The film was *Charley's Aunt*. They watched its slapstick gloomily.
When they came out, after nine o'clock, there was still a vestigial
light in the sky. They drove on and on, westward still, prolonging
the light, prolonging the drive, holding off the night's decision.
Before Killary they paused at a black-faced lake, got out, and stood
beside its quarried beauty. Nothing along its stony beach but a few
wind-torn rushes.

'I could eat you,' he said.

She replied that only lovers and cannibals talk like that.

They dawdled past the long fiord of Killary where young people
on holiday sat outside the hotel, their drinks on the trestled tables.
In Clifden the street was empty, people already climbing to bed,
as the lights in the upper windows showed. They branched off on the
long coastal road where the sparse white-washed cottages were
whiter than the foam of waves that barely suggested sea. At
another darker strand they halted, but now they saw no foam at all
and divined the sea only by its invisible whispering, or when a star
touched a wave. Midnight was now only an hour away.

Their headlights sent rocks and rabbits into movement. The
heather streamed past them like kangaroos. It was well past eleven
as they poured along the lonely land by Galway Bay. Neither of
them had spoken for an hour. As they drove into Salthill there was
nobody abroad. Galway was dark. Only the porch light of the hotel
showed that it was alive. When he turned off the engine the only
sound at first was the crinkle of contracting metal as the engine
began to cool. Then to their right they heard the lisping bay. The
panel button lit the dashboard clock.

'A quarter to,' he said, leaning back. She neither spoke nor stirred.

'Jenny!' he said sharply.

She turned her head slowly and by the dashboard light he saw her white smile.

'Yes, darling?'

'Worn out?' he asked, and patted her knee.

She vibrated her whole body so that the seat shook, and stretched her arms about her head, and lowering them let her head fall on his shoulder, and sighed happily, and said:

'What I want is a good long drink of anything on earth except tea.'

These homing twelve o'clockers from Lough Derg are well known in every hotel all over the west of Ireland. Revelry is the reward of penance. The porter welcomed them as if they were heroes returned from the war. As he led them to their rooms he praised them, he sympathised with them, he patted them up and he patted them down, he assured them that the ritual grill was at that moment sizzling over the fire, he proffered them hot baths, and he told them where to discover the bar. 'Ye will discover it . . .' was his phrase. The wording was exact, for the bar's gaiety was muffled by dim lighting, drawn blinds, locked doors. In the overheated room he took off his jacket and unloosed his tie. They had to win a corner of the counter, and his order was two highballs with ice in them. Within two minutes they were at home with the crowd. The island might never have existed if the barmaid, who knew where they had come from, had not laughed: 'I suppose ye'll ate like lions?'

After supper they relished the bar once more, sipping slowly now, so refreshed that they could have started on the road again without distaste or regret. As they sipped they gradually became aware of a soft strumming and drumming near at hand, and were told that there was a dance on in the hotel next door. He raised his eyebrows to her. She laughed and nodded.

They gave it up at three o'clock and walked out into the warm-cool of the early summer morning. Gently tipsy, gently tired they walked to the little promenade. They leaned on the railing and he put his arm about her waist, and she put hers around his, and they gazed at the moon silently raking its path across the sea towards Aran. They had come, she knew, to the decisive moment. He said:

'They have a fine night for it tonight on the island.'

'A better night than we had,' she said tremulously.

After another spell of wave fall and silence he said:

'Do you know what I'm thinking, Jenny? I'm thinking that I

wouldn't mind going back there again next year. Maybe I might do it properly the next time?'

'The next time?' she whispered, and all her body began to dissolve and, closing her eyes, she leaned against him. He, too, closed his eyes, and all his body became as rigid as a steel girder that flutters in a storm. Slowly they opened their love-drunk eyes, and stood looking long over the brightness and blackness of the sea. Then, gently, ever so gently, with a gentleness that terrified her he said:

'Shall we go in, my sweet?'

She did not stir. She did not speak. Slowly turning to him she lifted her eyes to him pleadingly.

'No, Bobby, please, not yet.'

'Not yet?'

'Not tonight!'

He looked down at her, and drew his arms about her. They kissed passionately. She knew what that kiss implied. Their mouths parted. Hand in hand they walked slowly back to the hotel, to their separate rooms.

I Remember! I Remember!

I believe that in every decisive moment of our lives the spur to action comes from that part of the memory where desire lies dozing, awaiting the call to arms. We say to ourselves, 'Now I have decided to do so-and-so,' and straightway we remember that for years and years we have been wanting to do this very thing. There it is, already fully created, clear on the horizon, our longed-for island, its palm tree waving, its white hut gleaming, a brown figure standing on the beach, smiling patiently.

I am remembering Sarah Cotter and her infallible memory. If she were not so childlike, so modest, so meekly and sweetly resigned, she could be a Great Bore, as oppressively looming as the Great Bear. She can remember every least thing she ever heard, down to the last detail, even to the hour of the day when it happened. She is a Domesday Book of total recall for the whole of the little town of Ardagh, where she has lived for some twenty-five years in, you might almost say, the same corner of the same room of the same house, ever since an accident to her spine imprisoned her in a Bath chair at the age of eleven. This accident absolved her from all but the simplest decisions: there was no far-off island for her to dream of. It also meant that all she can now know of the world outside is what she reads, or what she is told by her friends, so that if her friends have told her fibs their consciences should prick them when she trustingly retails something that did not happen, or not quite in that way.

She is a little hunched-up woman with a face like a bit of burnt cork, whose plainness, some might say whose ugliness, you forget immediately you notice her gentle expression, her fluent lips, her warm brown eyes. Remember that, because of her ailment, she is always looking upwards at you when you meet her, so that her eyes have the pleading look of a spaniel, as if she were excusing herself for so much as existing. Her only handsome feature, apart from her doggy eyes, is her hair, long and rich and fair, on which she spends hours every morning, brushing it down into her lap over her shoulder, then brushing and pinning it up in a soft cloud, so overflowing that it makes her agile monkey-face seem about the size of a hazelnut. She lives in almost constant pain. She never complains of it. I have met nobody who does not admire her, nobody who has the least fault to find with her, apart from her invulnerable memory, which all Ardagh both enjoys and fears, and whose existence can kill like the sirocco.

The only grumbles ever heard from her are two, as constant and soft as the leaves of a bamboo grove. The first is that she wishes she could see more of her sister Mary, a tall, slim, pretty, volatile girl, who twelve years ago married an American businessman, Richard Carton, a Continental buyer for one of New York's biggest stores.

'Not,' she always adds, 'that I don't realise how lucky the pair of us are. We mightn't be seeing one another at all only for Richard having that wonderful job.'

Because of this job, a cablegram or a letter has come twice a year from Mary saying that Richard is off to Europe on another buying spree, which means that Mary will shortly stop off at Shannon and drive over to Ardagh for a week of heavenly gossip. Sarah at once announces the news to the whole of Ardagh, with burning cheeks and sparkling eyes. Then she may murmur her other grumble:

'Imagine it! I've seen Richard only once in my life. If he wasn't so busy! If only he could come with Mary for a real long holiday! Then she wouldn't have to go away after one little week. But, of course, she's indispensable to him.'

What she does not know, and what Mary intends that she never shall know, though she fears sometimes that one or two people in Ardagh may know it, or at least suspect it – such as Joe Shortall, who picks her up at Shannon in his taxi, or the postmistress, who has sent off an occasional telegram for her – is that for the past six years Richard and she have been living partly in New York and partly in their small, elegant house in Zürich, near which their three children are at an English boarding school – so that, all unknown to Sarah, her sister passes between Switzerland and New York about six times a year. As for being indispensable to Richard in his work, the only time she ever ventured to advise him was in Rome. He looked at the object, a large, handsome blue fruit dish, turned it over and showed her the mark of its Californian manufacturer. What keeps her from visiting Sarah more often is the tireless whisper of the Recording Angel's Dictaphone playing back every lightest word that has passed between the two of them since they could begin to talk. She once incautiously wailed to Richard about it:

'It's not just that it's disconcerting to be reminded about things you've said, or discarded or forgotten years and years ago. Oh, if it was only like that! She brings out these bits and scraps of things I've forgotten since I was ten, like a dog digging up some old thing you've thrown out on the ash heap and laying it lovingly at your feet – grubby, pointless, silly, worn, stupid things – and she says, "That's you." And I don't recognise them. Or don't want to see them. Old toys, old hats, old buried bones. Sometimes she has to remind me and remind me before I can even know what she's talking about. And, anyway, by this time they're no longer bits of me, they're bits of her. She knows more about me than I know myself. I keep on wondering what else does she know about me that I don't know. What's she going to produce next? Isn't my life my own, goddammit, to keep or to lose or to throw away if I want to? Am I me? Or am I her? I sometimes think I'm possessed by that old Chucklepuss the way some people are possessed by the devil!'

Richard had laughed heartily, and she, remembering too late his first, famous, fatal and final session with Sarah, could have bitten her tongue off. She stuck it out at him. Remembering again, he laughed all the more. Because Richard's memory is just as unnerving as Sarah's; and his interest in Mary's past just as avid, or it used to be during the first years of their marriage. He wanted to know everybody she ever knew before he met her, every single thing she had ever done, every thought she had ever thought, every place she had ever been. So, at that first and last meeting between him and Sarah, she had to sit listening, apprehensive or embarrassed, while those two laid out the days of her youth before them like precious things that a pair of antiquaries might love to display to one another but would never part with. As they went on and on she got more and more furious with them:

'Ye make me feel like baby's first shoe. Or a photograph of a First Communion group. Or me aunt's wedding veil. Ye make me feel ninety. Ye make me feel dead!'

Richard only laughed his jolly, buyer's laugh, hang-jawed like a pelican – worth thousands to him in his job – and roared at her to go away and leave them to it.

'This Sally girl knows tons more than you ever told me.'

But how could she go? She was as fascinated as she was furious.

She was also frightened. For, while Sarah did know, or remember, 'tons more', it was all untrue in the way that a police report is untrue, because it leaves out everything except the facts. As she listened, transfixed as a rabbit is by a dazzling light that hides anything behind it, she remembered a wonderful thing she had once read in Stendhal's diaries – that 'True feeling leaves no memory': meaning that every deep feeling is like a peach, to be eaten straight from the tree of life, not spoiled by pawing and pressing. She swore afterwards that she lost pounds in perspiration while listening to them. The worst sequence was when they started talking about Corney Canty:

'Sally!' she heard Richard saying suddenly. 'Tell me about this young Corney Canty of Mary's. She's told me a lot about that wild boyo. As a matter of fact, why don't we meet him?'

'But, darling,' Mary protested, 'I've told you a dozen times over all that there is . . .'

'Now, Mary! Now! Let Sally tell me. Go on, Sally! Mary's told me about how they used to go riding to hounds together. And all the other adventures they had. That must have been a wonderful day – As I recall, Mary, it was the May of nineteen-thirty-seven? – when the two of you, alone with three hounds, flushed a fox out of Ballycoole woods and ran him to the edge of Gaunt's Quarry. And the brave Corney – He must really be a marvellous horseman, Sally – just slid after him down the gravel face of that quarry without a moment's hesitation. And poor little Mary here – Look at her, she's pale again at the thought of it! – God, how I admire you, darling! – terrified out of her wits though she was, slid down after him. And they cornered the fox in that quarry! I'd really love to meet this fellow. Why don't we ask him in for a drink tonight?'

Sarah's eyes dropped.

'God rest him!' she murmured.

'Not dead? Killed on the hunting field? A fine young man like that killed in the prime of life! Did you know this, Mary?'

'Did you say "young", Richard?' Sarah soothed him. 'Sure when he died of the drink there a few years back he was seventy-two to the month.'

'Seventy-two?' – looking wide-eyed at Mary, who was crying out desperately:

'Sarah, you're thinking of Corney's uncle. Or his father. He wasn't a year over forty, and as limber as twenty-five. Of course,' gushing to Richard, 'he was a great rascal, you couldn't trust a word he said, didn't I tell you the time he deliberately made me fall off that gray mare of his, setting me to a stone wall he knew damn well she couldn't take, so that he could come around and kneel over me on the grass, feeling me here and feeling me there with "Does it hurt here, Ducky?" and "Does it hurt there, ducky?' and me with the wind gone out of me so that I couldn't say a bloody worrrd!'

Richard laughed at the familiar story, one of his favourites that he liked to make her tell at every second party, because it brought out the brogue in her voice. Sarah was not to be silenced.

'He was,' she said primly, even a little severely, 'seventy-two years old to the month when he died. No more. No less. I myself witnessed his cross – he couldn't read or write – on the Old Age Pension form on December the first, nineteen hundred and forty-three. He was wearing that old red-flannel-lined raincoat your daddy gave him in thirty-seven when . . .'

'But,' Richard put in, 'that was the year of the quarry hunt.'

'That's right. "I have this coat," said Corney to me, "for six years, and your poor father had it for six years before that, and . . ." '

Mary could see by Richard's face – he could multiply 113 by 113 in his head – that he had already established for himself that 'young Corney' had been an old lad in his middle sixties when she knew him. Sure enough, when Sarah paused, there was a brief silence, suspenseful and decisive, and then he broke into a series of monster guffaws, beating his palms together with delight, relishing with loving malice his wife's scarlet embarrassment. Through his guffaws he managed to utter :

'Mary, you little divil, I always knew you exaggerated a bit, but this . . .'

Wildly she fought for her hour as she had lived it :

'I didn't exaggerate. That was typical of Corney to exaggerate his age to get the pension. He fooled you up to the eyes, Sarah; when we hunted that fox he was forty, forty-two, at the very most, forty-two at the outside limit, not a minute over it.'

One glance from Richard's bubbling shoulders and wrinkled-up eyes to Sarah's prim mouth told her that the battle was hopeless. There Sarah sat, erect in her chair, too nice to contradict further, too honest to compound a felony, giving her head short little shakes that said as plainly as speech, 'Seventy-two. To the month. No more. No less.'

Neither then nor at any time after could Mary have understood that Richard was just as happy with her as a splendid Teller of

Tales as he had been with her as his Wild Irish Girl. Blinded by love, he drew out the session for hour after hour. He only realised his folly that night, in the hour of tenderness, in bed.

'Dammit,' she said, as they lay side by side, in her parents' old room upstairs, the heavy mirror in the coffinlike wardrobe catching the last of the summer daylight, the faint baaing of sheep coming from the Fair Green, 'I did slide down that old quarry. I wasn't codding about it. And he wasn't an old man. And even if he was I think that makes it a hell of a sight more exciting than the sentimental way you want it. Handsome young Irish huntsman. Brave young Irish girl. It makes me sick the way you always want to romanticise everything about me.'

His hands behind his poll, he began to shake all over again until she started to hammer him with her fists on his chest, and he to embrace and fondle her with a new love, a new admiration – he said the words, just so, explicitly – which, she declared, turning her behind to him huffily, was entirely beyond her modest intelligence. She whirled, and sat up and shouted.

'Are you trying to say that you prefer me as a liar?'

'Husssh! My wild little girleen! Sarah will hear you.'

'I don't give a damn if she does hear me. What does she know about it? She wasn't there. It was she started all this, and you kept at her and at her to make me seem more of a liar.'

'Nonsense, darling. It's just that you have this wonderful Irish gift for fantasy.'

'It's not fantasy. It's true, true, true. Every word of it is true. There may be some detail here or there, some trivial, irrelevant thing, some small thing slipped up, but it's all true. And I am not going to have you and old Sarah Sucklepuss down there stealing my life from me with her bloody old...'

And, to his pitying astonishment, she burst into a long, low wail of weeping, sobbing into the pillow like, he thought, as he laid his palm on her wet cheek, a child whose dog had been rolled over by a bus before her eyes.

'You don't understand, Dicky,' she wailed into his armpit. 'It's torture to hear her digging up my life and turning it all into lies that never happened the way she says they happened.'

'But you must have told her they happened that way?'

'I told her the bones. And all she has of anything now is the bones. I can't remember the bones. All I have is the feeling I had at the time. Or else I can't remember at all.'

'Tell her so. Say you forget.'

'It would be like taking her life away from her. All the poor old Sucklepuss has is my bones.'

She wept herself asleep on his shoulder. It is the measure of his distress at what he had done to her, of his natural shrewdness, and of his sensitiveness hidden behind his cocktail-bar laugh that as he lay there, listening to the dim, distant, ceaseless baa-ing, he decided never again to visit Ardagh.

But this was years ago, and since then Mary's life has stopped being the flowing, straightforward river it once was. Not that life ever is like a river that starts from many tributaries and flows at the end straight to the sea; it is more like the line of life on my palm that starts firmly and frays over the edge in a cataract of little streams of which it is impossible to say where each began. Richard has small interest now in her youth. He is rarely amused by her exaggerations: the wind that blew the legs off her, or the bus that went down Fifth Avenue at a hundred miles per hour. Her lovely, lighthearted, featherheaded ways are now her usual scattiness. She finds it more and more difficult to follow Sarah's letters about the latest doings of Ardagh. And the only way Sarah can form any clear pictures of Mary's life in New York is by those intimate gossips, prolonged into the silence of the night, during Mary's precious half-yearly visits to the little house near the end of the Main Street of Ardagh. Yet, it was just when, for this very reason, one might have expected the visits to become either more frequent or longer that they suddenly became so curt that everybody but Sarah foresaw their end.

It all started out as a ridiculous little incident that occurred during Mary's March visit last year. Over the years she had been trying in vain to free herself from Sarah's memory by catching her out in an error of fact. On this wet, March night she suddenly became aware that Sarah was talking of a German air raid on a part of the Irish coast where some old friends of Richard's, working in the American diplomatic service during the war, had had a summer house. Knowing well that no German bombs had dropped on this part of the coast, she felt no overwhelming sense of relief. She did not crow over her. She stayed as quiet as a cat watching a mouse. The whole glorious value of the error was that Sarah must never become aware of it. The night passed with the error uncorrected. At about two o'clock in the morning Mary woke up as if to the sound of a shot, remembering clearly that a floating sea-mine had exploded on that part of the coast and damaged a summer house. She left Ardagh the next day, only three days after she had arrived, to Sarah's dumb dismay, on the feeble excuse of being worried about Richard's health. ('Oh, Sarah, I live in terror that he'll have to give up the job altogether, he's driven *so* hard!')

Six months later, in September, Mary came again, and left after two days.

They were having afternoon tea on the second day of their visit – it was a Sunday afternoon – in the bay of the front room, looking out on the empty autumn street, with Sarah happily squeezing the last drops out of a long, lightly amusing recollection of the famous night seventeen years before when Mary, still at school, organised a secret Midsummer Eve party to hail the sun rising over the Galtee Mountains. She had rowed her party, five in all, across the river in the dark and lit a pagan midsummer-fire in, of all places, the playing fields adjoining the Mercy Convent. The nuns, rising to sing their Matins, had heard the singing and seen the fire, and raised a terrible row about it, which set the whole town talking for weeks after. Sarah happily followed the history of everybody even distantly connected with the affair down to the hour of that afternoon tea. Her comments were largely a string of *Requiescats*, a ritual habit which always secretly tickled Mary: it was as if the Recording Angel had a secondary job as Lady High Executioner. ('Anna Grey? Died nine years back, Mary. Tommy Morgan? Failing. Failing before his people's eyes. Joe Fenelon took to the bottle, poor boy. Molly Cardew? Ah, God rest her . . .') Without a pause Sarah suddenly leaned forward and said:

'Mary, tell me! How is Nathan Cash these days?'

'Nathan who?' Mary had said, parrying wildly at the unexpected transition. This sort of thing was always happening – Sarah suddenly producing some name or event about which she was supposed to know nothing.

'Cash!' Sarah said loudly, rather like people who raise their voices when talking to foreigners in order to be better understood. 'Your friend Nathan Cash. The man who was a director of the Bell Telephone Company in Newark, New Jersey. He married that Jane Barter whose uncle was a partner in Chuck Full O'Nuts before he divorced her last year after playing around, I think I gathered from you, with some other woman, you-never-said-who. And, after all, he didn't marry her either.'

'Didn't he?' Mary said dully, choked with rage against herself for having as much as mentioned Nathan to Sarah.

'When you came last March you told me he was after marrying Carrie Brindle, a rich Jewish girl from Buffalo. Surely you remember?'

Mary could only give a miserable little laugh.

'You told me about it last March! When you came off the *Liberté*. You told me,' Sarah smiled lovingly and admiringly, 'how he gave yourself orchids for your birthday in January.'

'Why, and so he did!' Mary laughed gaily, her anger with herself mounting and spilling. Last March, coming off that damned six-days boat of loneliness, she had had to talk to somebody about him.

'He is a very handsome man,' Sarah smiled gently. Mary stared at her. 'You showed me his photograph.'

'Did I really?' Mary gurgled, and spread her ringed fingers indifferently. 'Richard and I meet so many people.'

Sarah sighed.

'It must be grand getting orchids. That was the only time in my life I saw orchids.' She laughed at her own ignorance. 'I thought they were passion flowers. I forgot to ask you,' with a happy smile, 'was it Mr Cash gave them to you before you sailed?'

Mary looked swiftly at her, but it was plain that she was not probing. Sarah's questions were always innocent, pointless, without guile. She looked out, frowningly, at the granite brown of the old North Gate, under whose arch the almost-silent Main Street of Ardagh flows into the completely silent countryside. She heard the sort of *cric-croc* of a cart entering slowly under the arch from the farther side. The little cart slowly emerged from under the arch, salmon-pink, bearing its pyramid of black peat, drawn by a tiny, grey donkey. It *cric-crocked* slowly past her vision. She found herself murmuring as softly and slowly, feeling as she did so that this was exactly how she had been wheedled last March into talking about Nathan:

'I bought those orchids last March. I just had to have them.'

'Why, Mary?' – gently.

'I was feeling very down.'

'What happened to you?' – sympathetically.

'I'd had a terrible quarrel with a friend.'

'Who, Mary?' – tenderly.

'A friend. Nobody you know. A woman. A woman called Gold.

Nancy Gold. There was nobody to see me off on the boat. Richard had gone by plane direct to Berne. The cabin looked empty. No flowers. No bottle of champagne. No basket of fruit. When I went down to lunch I stood at the turn of the staircase and saw all those men and women chattering around all those white tables and all the women wearing corsages. I turned back and went up to the florist and I bought me two orchids.'

Neither of them spoke for a while.

'Well, well,' Sarah concluded. 'And so he married the Jewish woman in the heel of the hunt. Is he happy with her, would you say?'

'How should I know? We never meet. I'm not sure that I like him very much really.'

Sarah smiled in loyal admiration.

'He liked you once, though. Enough anyway to give you the orchids.'

'That was just one night going to the opera. I thought at the time it was a little plush of him. Still, a woman likes those little attentions.'

'You always liked nice things. You always liked those little attentions. I can see why you bought them for yourself on the boat.'

'It was just that I was down in the mouth.'

'And then there was Richard on your mind, too.'

'Richard?' Mary stared at her as if she was a witch or a fortune-teller.

'I mean you were worried about him.'

'Was I?'

'He was ill. You left here after three days to be with him. I knew the minute you came in the door, Mary, off that old boat, that you weren't your old self.'

Mary gave her a desperate look. She got up.

'I think I'll go for a stroll. I have a bit of a headache.'

She went out, under the arch, so unmistakably a foreigner in her high-collared mink coat, her furry hat and her spiked heels that the few townsfolk who were in the Sunday street stared at her, but sideways so as not to be seen staring. She saw none of them, nothing, none of the familiar names over the shuttered shops, unchanged for as long as she could remember – Fenelon the grocer, Ryan the draper, Shorthall's Garage, Morgan and Corneille, Furnishers, Upholsterers and Undertakers, Saint Anne's Nursing Home and old Dr

Freeman's brass plate polished into holes at the corners. The street petered out where a bright yellow signpost directed her across the bridge to the dark yellow furze on the rising foothills.

She leaned over the limestone parapet, lit a cigarette, and glared along the barely flowing river with its shallow autumn pools and its dry beaches. She pounded the parapet with her gloved fist and said, aloud: 'It's intolerable!' Her cigarette ash floated down into the river. On one side of the river were the long gardens at the back of the Main Street's houses, coming right down to the riverbank; and farther on, plumb with the river, the backs of old donkey-grey warehouses, decaying now, eyeless, little used since the river silted up and ceased to be navigable. The Franciscan belfry was reflected in an island pool among the gravel at the bend of the river, and in the pool a sweep of yellow from the far hills that rose to the farther mountains over whose rounded backs the sailing clouds had long ago seemed so often to call her to come away, to come away. Today the clouds were one solid, frozen mass, tomblike, so that if they moved they moved massively, and she could not tell if they moved at all.

She had rowed across the river down there, that Midsummer Eve, with Annie Grey, and Tommy Morgan, and Joe Fenelon and Molly Cardew. She had borrowed her daddy's gramophone and twelve of his gayest Italian records, and halfway across, the records, which she had placed on top of the gramophone began to slide one by one into the water with gentle plops. Midsummer heat, and a great sky of stars and the whole of Ardagh sound asleep. While waiting for the sun to rise they swam in one of the pools, and then, at the first ghost of light, not light, a hint of morning, they lit the fire and played a muffled 'O Sole Mio' and a wind blew the woodash into the cups of wine that Joe Fenelon had stolen from his father's shop. She had not thought of that grey dust in the wine for seventeen years. It was, she thought savagely, the sort of thing that Sarah's memories never remembered, along with the gaiety of Corney Canty, and the way redheaded Molly Cardew used to tickle the back of Tommy Morgan's neck so that he would hunch up his shoulders and say, affectionately-irritably, 'Go away, you green frog you!' and poor weak-minded Joe Fenelon's lovely tenor voice singing 'I'll Take Ye Home Again, Kathleen' at every party. The ash in the wine was just another piece of her real life immured, with the bones of everything she had ever done or said, in the vaults of Sarah's infallible memoirs. Would Nathan Cash one day join these dead bones? Had he already gone there, with all she had been through because of him? Would all her life, unless she really went away and left her past behind her?

She blew out a long breath of smoke and threw her cigarette into the river. She would call in to Shorthall's Garage on the way home. The car would come for her at nine in the morning. By the evening she would be floating down over the pinewoods on the little hills about the airstrip at Zürich. Blonde hostesses. Pure-white wash-rooms. ('Just like Newark,' Richard had once laughed.) And her ritual first cup of *café au lait* at the tall counter, while Richard waited with Donna, and Biddy and Patrick. But she did not stir until a soft rain began to fall, a dew, a mist, and she was aware that it was dusk. The streets were empty, the slates shone purple. The turf smoke medicinal in the air. She stopped by the garage, passed on, stopped again, hesitated again, half turned back and then, with a groan, went on to the house. She went upstairs to her room and lay there, with the last pallor of the day and the dark great mirror of the wardrobe, until dinnertime.

For their coffee they sat in the bay window. They gossiped amiably, Mary half listening, her head half turned to the footfalls passing down the street to evening Benediction at the Franciscan priory. Sarah said:

'By the way, Mary, wasn't it very sad about your poor friend, Mrs Henry Beirne!'

Mary turned her head a little farther towards the window, as if she were trying to hear something out there, but really to hide the look of blank fear that she could feel coming into her eyes. She knew no Mrs Henry Beirne. Her frightened efforts to recall the woman produced nothing clearer than the vague cloud that a drop of absinthe forms in a glass of water, a fume like smoke, a waver-ing embryo without a face. The last ghostly footstep faded. She whispered, groping for information:

'Yes. It was very sad. How did you know about it?'

'The Dublin papers had it on account of the other woman being related to the Bishop of Kilkenny. I don't think she could be more than thirty-two. Would you say so?'

'Surely more?' – groping still. Could it be a divorce? Or an acci-dent? Why couldn't Sarah say what happened? Was the woman dead? The wraith in the water began to curl into another as yet undecipherable shape. She said gently: 'Was her age given in the papers?'

'Not at all, but, sure, 'tis easy to work it out. We know she was the Class of Forty-one. Give her twenty or twenty-one at the Commencement, and wasn't it then she first met Henry Beirne? He proposed to her that very evening on the Common. You danced with him at the Ritz that night. You had the gold dress with the cream insets. How many children was it you said they had?'

As the white shape in the water took on a remembered face, Mary barely stopped herself from saying, 'My God, it must be nine years since I saw that bitch Lucy Burbank.' She said, dully:

'Children? Four' – and immediately regretted it, realizing that to say anything precise to Sarah about anything was only laying the ground for more questions next year, or in three or five years' time, when she would have completely forgotton what she had earlier said.

They talked a little more about Lucy Burbank-Beirne, but Mary never did find out what exactly happened to the woman that was so very sad.

'It's time we lit the lamp,' Sarah said.

It was dark. The rain had stopped and restarted. The footsteps had all returned the way they had come. In another hour the only sound in the long, winding street would be the drip of rain. Not a ground-floor window would be lit. There would not even be a Civic Guard out on a wet night like this. She gathered up the coffee cups and took them out to the kitchen on the old silver-plated salver, with the copper showing through, that her father had won at a golf tournament forty years ago. She returned and lifted off the pink globe of the oil lamp, her back to Sarah, and then lifted off the glass chimney, and put a match to the two charred wicks and watched the flame creep across their ridged edges. She replaced the glass chimney. Still with her back to Sarah, she said:

'I have bad news to break to you, Sarah.'

'Oh, Mary, don't frighten me.'

'I've been trying to get myself to tell you since I came.'

'What is it love?'

Carefully she replaced the pink globe, aware of its warm light under her chin.

'Richard has given up his job. I came alone this time. I came only to tell you. I must go away tomorrow morning.'

She slowly raised the first wick, and then the second wick, and felt the room behind her fill with light. She heard a noise like a drip of rain, or melting snow, or oozing blood.

'Oh, Mary, don't go away from me!'

She turned. For the first time, Sarah was pleading with her, her little brown face smaller than ever under the great cloud of hair, her two brown spaniel's eyes brimming with tears.

'I must go!' Mary cried, her two fists trembling by her side. 'I must go!'

'I'll never see you again!'

Mary sank on her knees and looped her arms lovingly about her waist.

'Of course you will, you silly-billy,' she laughed. 'You'll see me lots of times.'

They gazed at one another fondly for a long while. Then Mary rose and went to the dark window and drew the curtains together with a swish. Arranging the folds of the curtains, she said, reassuringly, like a mother to a child:

'You'll see me lots of times. Lots and lots of times.'

Behind her, Sarah said resignedly:

'Will I, Mary?'

The Sugawn Chair

Every autumn I am reminded of an abandoned sugawn chair that languished for years, without a seat, in the attic of my old home. It is associated in my mind with an enormous sack which the carter used to dump with a thud on the kitchen floor around every October. I was a small kid then, and it was as high as myself. This sack had come 'up from the country', a sort of diplomatic messenger from the fields to the city. It smelled of dust and hay and apples, for the top half of it always bulged with potatoes, and, under a layer of hay, the bottom half bulged with apples. Its arrival always gave my mother great joy and a little sorrow, because it came from the farm where she had been born. Immediately she saw it she glowed with pride in having a 'back', as she called it – meaning something behind her more solid and permanent than city streets, though she was also saddened by the memories that choked her with this smell of hay and potatoes from the home farm, and apples from the little orchard near the farmhouse. My father, who had also been born on a farm, also took great pleasure in these country fruits, and as the two of them stood over the sack, in the kitchen, in the middle of the humming city, everything that their youth had meant to them used to make them smile and laugh and use words that they had never used during the rest of the year, and which I thought magical: words like *late sowing, clover crop, inch field, marl bottom, headlands, tubers,* and the names of potatoes, British Queens or Arran Banners, that sounded to me like the names of regiments. For those moments my father and mother became a young, courting couple again. As they stood over that sack, as you might say warming their hands to it, they were intensely happy, close to each other, in love again. To me they were two very old people. Counting back now, I reckon that they were about forty-two or forty-three.

One autumn evening after the sack arrived, my father went up to the attic and brought down the old sugawn chair. I suppose he had had it sent up from his home farm. It was the only thing of its kind in our house, which they had filled – in the usual peasants' idea of what constitutes elegance – with plush chairs, gold-framed pictures of Stags at Bay, and exotic tropical birds, pelmets on the mantelpieces, Delft shepherdesses, Chinese mandarins with nodding heads, brass bedsteads with mighty knobs and mother-of-pearl escutcheons set with bits of mirror, vast mahogany chiffoniers, and so on. But the plush-bottomed chairs, with their turned legs and their stiff backs, were for show, not for comfort, whereas in the old country sugawn chair my da could tilt and squeak and rock to his behind's content.

It had been in the place for years, rockety, bockety, chipped and well-polished, and known simply as 'your father's chair', until the night when, as he was reading the *Evening Echo* with his legs up on the kitchen range, there was a sudden rending noise, and down he went through the seat of it. There he was then, bending over, with the chair stuck on to him, and my mother and myself in the splits of laughter, pulling it from him while he cursed like a trooper. This was the wreck that he now suddenly brought down from the dusty attic.

The next day, he brought in a great sack of straw from the Cornmarket, a half-gallon of porter and two old buddies from the street – an ex-soldier known to the kids around as 'Tear-'em-and-ate-'em' and a little dwarf of a man who guarded the stage door at the Opera House when he was not behind the sacristan at the chapel. I was enchanted when I heard what they were going to do. They were going to make ropes of straw – a miracle I had never heard of – and reseat the chair. Bursting with pride in my da, I ran out and brought in my best pal, and the two of us sat quiet as cats on the kitchen table, watching the three men filling the place with dust, straw, and loud arguments as they began to twist the ropes for the bottom of the chair.

More strange words began to float in the air with the dust: *scallops, flat tops, bulrushes, cipeens, fields in great heart* . . . And when the three sat down for a swig of porter, and looked at the old polished skeletons in the middle of the floor, they began to rub the inside of their thighs and say how there was no life at all like the country life, and my mother poured out more porter for them, and laughed happily when my da began to talk about horses, and harrows, and a day after the plough, and how, for *that* much, he'd throw up this blooming city life altogether and settle down on a bit of a farm for the heel of his days.

This was a game of which he, she and I never got tired, a fairy tale that was so alluring it did not matter a damn that they had not enough money to buy a window box, let alone a farm of land.

'Do you remember that little place,' she would say, 'that was going last year down at Nantenan?'

When she said that, I could see the little reedy fields of Limerick that I knew from holidays with my uncle, and the crumbling stone walls of old demesnes with the moss and saffron lichen on them, and the willow sighing softly by the Deel, and I could smell the wet turf rising in the damp air, and, above all, the tall wildflowers of the mallow, at first cabbage-leaved, then pink and coarse, then gossamery, then breaking into cakes that I used to eat – a rank weed that is the mark of ruin in so many Irish villages, and whose profusion and colour is for me the sublime emblem of Limerick's loneliness, loveliness and decay.

'Ah!' my da would roar. 'You and your blooming ould Limerick! That bog of a place! Oh, but, God blast it why didn't I grab that little farm I was looking at two years ago there below Emo!'

'Oho, ho, ho!' she would scoff. 'The Queen's! The Lousy Queen's! God, I'd live like a tiger and die like a Turk for Limerick. For one patch of good old Limerick. Oh, Limerick, my love, and it isn't alike! Where would you get spuds and apples the like of them in the length and breadth of the Queen's County?'

And she grabbed a fist of hay from the bag and buried her face in it, and the tears began to stream down her face, and me and my pal screaming with laughter at her, and the sacristan lauding Tipperary, and the voices rose as Tear-'em-and-ate-'em brought up the River Barrow and the fields of Carlow, until my da jumped up with:

'Come on, lads, the day is dyin' and acres wide before us!'

For all that, the straw rope was slow in emerging. Their arguments about it got louder and their voices sharper. At first all their worry had been whether the kitchen was long enough for the rope; but so far, only a few, brief worms of straw lay on the red tiles. The sacristan said: 'That bloody straw is too moist.' When he was a boy in Tipp he never seen straw the like o' that. Tear-'em-and-ate-'em said that straw was old straw. When he was a lad in Carlow they never used old straw. Never! Under no possible circumstances! My dad said: 'What's wrong with that straw is it's too bloomin' short!' And they began to kick the bits with their toes, and grimace at the heap on the floor, and pick up bits and fray them apart and throw them aside until the whole floor was like a stable. At last they put on their coats, and gave the straw a final few kicks, and my pal jumped down and said he was going back to his handball and, in my heart, I knew that they were three imposters.

The kitchen was tidy that evening when I came back with the *Evening Echo*. My da was standing by the sack of potatoes. He had a spud in his fist, rubbing off the dust of its clay with his thumb. When he saw me he tossed it back in the sack, took the paper, took one of the plush-bottom chairs and sat on it with a little grimace. I did not say anything, but young as I was, I could see that he was not reading what he was looking at. God knows what he was seeing at that moment.

For years the anatomy of the chair stood in one of the empty attics. It was there for many years after my father died. When my mother died and I had to sell out the few bits of junk that still remained from their lives, the dealer would not bother to take the useless frame, so that when, for the last time, I walked about the echoing house, I found it standing alone in the middle of the bare attic. As I looked at it I smelled apples, and the musk of Limerick's dust, and the turf-tang from its cottages, and the mallows among the limestone ruins, and I saw my mother and my father again as they were that morning – standing over the autumn sack, their arms about one another, laughing foolishly, and madly in love again.

Two of a Kind

Maxer Creedon was not drunk, but he was melancholy-drunk, and he knew it and he was afraid of it.

At first he had loved being there in the jammed streets, with everybody who passed him carrying parcels wrapped in green or gold, tied with big red ribbons and fixed with berried holly sprigs. Whenever he bumped into someone, parcels toppled and they both cried 'Ooops!' or 'Sorree!' and laughed at one another. A star of snow sank nestling into a woman's hair. He smelled pine and balsam. He saw twelve golden angels blaring silently from twelve golden trumpets in Rockefeller Plaza. He pointed out to a cop that when the traffic lights down Park Avenue changed from red to green the row of Christmas trees away down the line changed colour by reflection. The cop was very grateful to him. The haze of light on the tops of the buildings made a halo over Fifth Avenue. It was all just the way he knew it would be, and he slopping down from Halifax in that damned old tanker. Then, suddenly, he swung his right arm in a wild arc of disgust.

'To hell with 'em! To hell with everybody!'

'Ooops! Hoho, there! Sorree!'

He refused to laugh back.

'Poor Creedon!' he said to himself. 'All alone in New York, on Christmas-bloody-well-Eve, with nobody to talk to, and nowhere to go only back to the bloody old ship. New York all lit up. Everybody all lit up. Except poor old Creedon.'

He began to cry for poor old Creedon. Crying, he reeled through the passing feet. The next thing he knew he was sitting up at the counter of an Eighth Avenue drugstore sucking black coffee, with one eye screwed-up to look out at the changing traffic lights, chuckling happily over a yarn his mother used to tell him long ago about a place called Ballyroche. He had been there only once, nine years ago, for her funeral. Beaming into his coffee cup, or looking out at the changing traffic lights, he went through his favourite yarn about Poor Lily:

'Ah, wisha! Poor Lily! I wonder where is she atall atall now. Or she dead or alive. It all happened through an Italian who used to be going from one farm to another selling painted statues. Bandello his name was, a handsome black divil o' hell! I never in all my born days saw a more handsome divil. Well, one wet, wild windy October morning what did she do but creep out of her bed and we all sound asleep and go off with him. Often and often I heard my father say that the last seen of her was standing under the big tree at Ballyroche Cross, sheltering from the rain, at about eight o'clock in the morning. It was Mikey Clancy the postman saw her. "Yerrah, Lily girl," says he, "what are you doing here at this hour of the morning?" "I'm waiting," says she, "for to go into Fareens on the milk cart." And from that day to this not a sight nor a sound of her no more than if the earth had swallowed her. Except for the one letter from a priest in America to say she was happily married in Brooklyn, New York.'

Maxer chuckled again. The yarn always ended up with the count of the years. The last time he heard it the count had reached forty-one. By this year it would have been fifty.

Maxer put down his cup. For the first time in his life it came to him that the yarn was a true story about a real woman. For as long as four traffic-light changes he fumbled with this fact. Then, like a man hearing a fog signal come again and again from an approaching ship, and at last hearing it close at hand, and then seeing an actual if dim shape, wrapped in a cocoon of haze, the great idea revealed itself.

He lumbered down from his stool and went over to the telephones. His lumpish finger began to trace its way down the grey pages among the Brooklyn's *Ban's*. His finger stopped. He read the name aloud. *Bandello, Mrs Lily*. He found a dime, tinkled it home, and dialled the number slowly. On the third ring he heard an old woman's voice. Knowing that she would be very old and might be deaf, he said very loudly and with the extra-meticulous enunciation of all drunks:

'My name is Matthew Creedon. Only my friends all call me Maxer. I come from Limerick, Ireland. My mother came from the townland of Ballyroche. Are you by any chance my Auntie Lily?'

Her reply was a bark:

'What do you want?'

'Nothing at all! Only I thought, if you are the lady in question, that we might have a bit of an ould gosther. I'm a sailor. Docked this morning in the Hudson.'

The voice was still hard and cold:

'Did somebody tell you to call me?'

He began to get cross with her.

'Naw! Just by a fluke I happened to look up your name in the directory. I often heard my mother talking about you. I just felt I'd like to talk to somebody. Being Christmas and all that. And knowing nobody in New York. But if you don't like the idea, it's okay with me. I don't want to butt in on anybody. Good-bye.'

'Wait! You're sure nobody sent you?'

'Inspiration sent me! Father Christmas sent me!' (She could take that any way she bloody-well liked!) 'Look! It seems to me I'm buttin' in. Let's skip it.'

'No. Why don't you come over and see me?'

Suspiciously he said:

'This minute?'

'Right away!'

At the sudden welcome of her voice all his annoyance vanished.

'Sure, Auntie Lily! I'll be right over. But, listen, I sincerely hope you're not thinking I'm buttin' in. Because if you are ...'

'It was very nice of you to call me, Matty, very nice indeed. I'll be glad to see you.'

He hung up, grinning. She was just like his mother – the same old Limerick accent. After fifty years. And the same bossy voice. If she was a day she'd be seventy. She'd be tall, and thin, and handsome, and the real lawdy-daw, doing the grand lady, and under it all she'd be as soft as mountain moss. She'd be tidying the house now like a divil. And giving jaw to ould Bandello. If he was still alive.

He got lost on the subway, so that when he came up it was dark. He paused to have another black coffee. Then he paused to buy a bottle of Jamaica rum as a present for her. And then he had to walk five blocks before he found the house where she lived. The automobiles parked under the lights were all snow-covered. She lived in a brown-stone house with high steps. Six other families also had rooms in it.

The minute he saw her on top of the not brightly lit landing, looking down at him, he saw something he had completely forgotten. She had his mother's height, and slimness, and her wide mouth, but he had forgotten the pale, liquid blue of the eyes and they stopped him dead on the stairs, his hand tight on the banister. At the sight of them he heard the soft wind sighing over the level Limerick plain and his whole body shivered. For miles and miles not a sound but that soughing wind that makes the meadows and the wheat fields flow like water. All over that plain, where a crossroads is an event, where a little, sleepy lake is an excitement. Where their streams are rivers to them. Where their villages are towns. The resting cows look at you out of owls' eyes over the greasy tips of the buttercups. The meadow grass is up to their bellies. Those two pale eyes looking down at him were bits of the pale albino sky stretched tightly over the Shannon plain.

Slowly he climbed up to meet her, but even when they stood side by side she was still able to look down at him, searching his face with her pallid eyes. He knew what she was looking for, and he knew she had found it when she threw her bony arms around his neck and broke into a low, soft wailing just like that Shannon wind.

'Auntie! You're the living image of her!'

On the click of a finger she became bossy and cross with him, hauling him by his two hands into her room:

'You've been drinking! And what delayed you? And I suppose not a scrap of solid food in your stomach since morning?'

He smiled humbly.

'I'm sorry, Auntie. 'Twas just on account of being all alone, you know. And everybody else making whoopee.' He hauled out the peace offering of the rum. 'Let's have a drink!'

She was fussing all over him immediately.

'You gotta eat something first. Drinking like that all day, I'm ashamed of you! Sit down, boy. Take off your jacket. I got coffee, and cookies, and hamburgers, and a pie, I always lay in a stock for Christmas. All of the neighbours visit me. Everybody knows that Lily Bandello keeps an open house for Christmas, nobody is ever going to say Lily Bandello didn't have a welcome for all her friends and relations at Christmastime . . .'

She bustled in and out of the kitchenette, talking back to him without stop.

It was a big, dusky room, himself looking at himself out of a tall mirrored wardrobe piled on top with cardboard boxes. There was a divan in one corner as high as a bed, and he guessed that there was a washbasin behind the old peacock-screen. A single bulb hung in the centre of the ceiling, in a fluted glass bell with pink frilly edges. The pope over the bed was Leo XIII. The snowflakes kept touching the bare windowpanes like kittens' paws trying to get in. When she began on the questions, he wished he had not come.

'How's Bid?' she called out from the kitchen.

'Bid? My mother? Oh, well, of course, I mean to say . . . My mother? Oh, she's grand, Auntie! Never better. For her age, of course, that is. Fine, fine out! Just like yourself. Only for the touch of old rheumatism now and again.'

'Go on, tell me about all of them. How's Uncle Matty? And how's Cis? When were you down in Ballyroche last? But, sure, it's all changed now I suppose, with electric light and everything up to date? And I suppose the old pony and trap is gone years ago? It was only last night I was thinking of Mikey Clancey the postman.' She came in, planking down the plates, an iced Christmas cake, the coffeepot. 'Go on! You're telling me nothing.'

She stood over him, waiting, her pale eyes wide, her mouth stretched. He said:

'My Uncle Matty? Oh well, of course, now he's not as young as he was. But I saw him there last year. He was looking fine. Fine out. I'd be inclined to say he'd be a bit stooped. But in great form. For his age, that is.'

'Sit in. Eat up. Eat up. Don't mind me. He has a big family now, no doubt?'

'A family? Naturally! There's Tom. And there's Kitty, that's my Aunt Kitty, it *is* Kitty, isn't it, yes, my Auntie Kitty. And . . . God, I can't remember the half of them.'

She shoved the hamburgers towards him. She made him pour the coffee and tell her if he liked it. She told him he was a bad reporter.

'Tell me all about the old place!'

He stuffed his mouth to give him time to think.

'They have twenty-one cows. Holsteins. The black and white chaps. And a red barn. And a shelter belt of pines. 'Tis lovely there now to see the wind in the trees, and when the night falls the way the lighthouse starts winking at you, and . . .

'What lighthouse?' She glared at him. She drew back from him. 'Are ye daft? What are you dreaming about? Is it a lighthouse in the middle of the County Limerick?'

'There is a lighthouse! I saw it in the harbour!'

But he suddenly remembered that where he had seen it was in a toyshop on Eighth Avenue, with a farm beyond it and a red barn and small cows, and a train going round and round it all.

'Harbour, Matty? Are ye out of your senses?'

'I saw it with my own two eyes.'

His eyes were like marbles. Suddenly she leaned over like a willow – just the way his mother used to lean over – and laughed and laughed.

'I know what you're talking about now. The lighthouse on the Shannon! Lord save us, how many times did I see it at night from the hill of Ballingarry! But there's no harbour, Matty.'

'There's the harbour at Foynes!'

'Oh, for God's sake!' she cried. 'That's miles and miles and miles away. 'Tis and twenty miles away! And where would you see any train, day or night, from anywhere at all near Ballyroche?'

They argued it hither and over until she suddenly found the coffee was gone cold and rushed away with the pot to the kitchen. Even there she kept up the argument, calling out that certainly, you could see Moneygay Castle, and the turn of the River Deel on a fine day, but no train, and then she went on about the steppingstones over the river, and came back babbling about Normoyle's bull that chased them across the dry river, one hot summer's day . . .

He said:

'Auntie! Why the hell did you never write home?'

'Not even once?' she said, with a crooked smile like a bold child.

'Not a sight nor a sound of you from the day you left Ballyroche, as my mother used to say, no more than if the earth swallowed you. You're a nice one!'

'Eat up!' she commanded him, with a little laugh and a tap on his wrist.

'Did you always live here, Auntie Lily?'

She sat down and put her face between her palms with her elbows on the table and looked at him.

'Here? Well, no . . . That is to say, no! My husband and me had a house of our very own over in East Fifty-eighth. He did very well for himself. He was quite a rich man when he died. A big jeweller. When he was killed in an airplane crash five years ago he left me very well off. But sure I didn't need a house of my own and I had lots of friends in Brooklyn, so I came to live here.'

'Fine! What more do you want, that is for a lone woman! No family?'

'I have my son. But he's married, to a Pole, they'll be over here first thing tomorrow morning to take me off to spend Christmas with them. They have an apartment on Riverside Drive. He is the manager of a big department store. Macy's on Flatbush Avenue. But tell me about Bid's children. You must have lots of brothers and sisters. Where are you going from here? Back to Ireland? To Limerick? To Ballyroche?'

He laughed.

'Where else would I go? Our next trip we hit the port of London. I'll be back like an arrow to Ballyroche. They'll be delighted to hear I met you. They'll be asking me all sorts of questions about you. Tell me more about your son, Auntie. Has he a family?'

'My son? Well, my son's name is Thomas. His wife's name is Catherine. She is very beautiful. She has means of her own. They are very happy. He is very well off. He's in charge of a big store Sears Roebuck on Bedford Avenue. Oh, a fine boy. Fine out! As you say. Fine out. He has three children. There's Cissy, and Matty. And . . .'

Her voice faltered. When she closed her eyes he saw how old she was. She rose and from the bottom drawer of a chest of drawers she pulled out a photograph album. She laid it in front of him and sat back opposite him.

'That is my boy.'

When he said he was like her she said he was very like his father. Maxer said that he often heard that her husband was a most handsome man.

'Have you a picture of him?'

She drew the picture of her son towards her and looked down at it.

'Tell me more about Ballyroche,' she cried.

As he started into a long description of a harvest home he saw her eyes close again, and her breath came more heavily and he felt that she was not hearing a word he said. Then, suddenly, her palm slapped down on the picture of the young man, and he knew that she was not heeding him any more than if he wasn't there. Her fingers closed on the pasteboard. She shied it wildly across the room, where it struck the glass of the window flat on, hesitated and slid to the ground. Maxer saw snowflakes melting as often as they touched the pane. When he looked back at her she was leaning across the table, one white lock down over one eye, her yellow teeth bared.

'You spy!' she spat at him. 'You came from *them*! To spy on me!'

'I came from friendliness.'

'Or was it for a ha'porth of look-about? Well, you can go back to Ballyroche and tell 'em whatever you like. Tell 'em I'm starving if that'll please 'em, the mean, miserable, lousy set that never gave a damn about me from the day I left 'em. For forty years my own sister, your mother, never wrote one line to say . . .'

'You know damn well she'd have done anything for you if she only knew where you were. Her heart was stuck in you. The two of you were inside one another's pockets. My God, she was forever talking and talking about you. Morning, noon and night . . .'

She shouted at him across the table.

'I wrote six letters . . .'

'She never got them.'

'I registered two of them.'

'Nobody ever got a line from you, or about you, only for the one letter from the priest that married you to say you were well and happy.'

'What he wrote was that I was down and out. I saw the letter. I let him send it. That Wop left me flat in this city with my baby. I wrote to everybody – my mother, my father, to Bid after she was your mother and had a home of her own. I had to work every day of my life. I worked today. I'll work tomorrow. If you want to know what I do I clean out offices. I worked to bring up my son, and what did he do? Walked out on me with that Polack of his and that was the last I saw of him, or her, or any human being belonging to me until I saw you. Tell them every word of it. They'll love it!'

Maxer got up and went over slowly to the bed for his jacket. As he buttoned it he looked at her glaring at him across the table. Then he looked away from her at the snowflakes feeling the window-pane and dying there. He said quietly:

'They're all dead. As for Limerick – I haven't been back to Ireland for eight years. When my mum died my father got married again. I ran away to sea when I was sixteen.'

He took his cap. When he was at the door he heard a chair fall and then she was at his side, holding his arm, whispering gently to him:

'Don't go away, Matty.' Her pallid eyes were flooded. 'For God's sake, don't leave me alone with *them* on Christmas Eve!'

Maxer stared at her. Her lips were wavering as if a wind were blowing over them. She had the face of a frightened girl. He threw his cap on the bed and went over and sat down beside it. While he

sat there like a big baboon, with his hands between his knees, looking at the snowflakes, she raced into the kitchen to put on the kettle
for rum punch. It was a long while before she brought in the two
big glasses of punch, with orange sliced in them, and brown sugar
liked drowned sand at the base of them. When she held them out
to him he looked first at them, and then at her, so timid, so pleading,
and he began to laugh and laugh – a laugh that he choked by covering his eyes with his hands.

'Damn ye!' he groaned into his hands. 'I was better off drunk.'

She sat beside him on the bed. He looked up. He took one of the
glasses and touched hers with it.

'Here's to poor Lily!' he smiled.

She fondled his free hand.

'Lovie, tell me this one thing and tell me true. Did she really and
truly talk about me? Or was that all lies too?'

'She'd be crying rain down when she'd be talking about you. She
was always and ever talking about you. She was mad about you.'

She sighed a long sigh.

'For years I couldn't understand it. But when my boy left me for
that Polack I understood it. I guess Bid had a tough time bringing
you all up. And there's no one more hard in all the world than a
mother when she's thinking of her own. I'm glad she talked about
me. It's better than nothing.'

They sat there on the bed talking and talking. She made more
punch, and then more, and in the end they finished the bottle between them, talking about everybody either of them had known
in or within miles of the County Limerick. They fixed to spend
Christmas Day together, and have Christmas dinner downtown,
and maybe go to a picture and then come back and talk some more.

Every time Maxer comes to New York he rings her number. He
can hardly breathe until he hears her voice saying, 'Hello, Matty.'
They go on the town then and have dinner, always at some place
with an Irish name, or a green neon shamrock above the door, and
then they go to a movie or a show, and then come back to her
room to have a drink and a talk about his last voyage, or the picture
post cards he sent her, his latest bits and scraps of news about the
Shannon shore. They always get first-class service in restaurants,
although Maxer never noticed it until the night a waiter said, 'And
what's mom having?' at which she gave him a slow wink out of
her pale Limerick eyes and a slow, lover's smile.

Angels and Ministers of Grace

'You can dress now, Mr Neason,' the doctor said. He went back slowly to his desk and began to write.

Jacky, still holding his shirt in his palms, looked hard at him and he didn't like the look of it at all.

'Well, Doc?' he got out in a kind of choke between the rise and fall of his Adam's apple. 'What's the verdict?'

'The verdict is that your heart is a bit dicky, and your blood pressure is high, but otherwise you're all right.'

'A bit dicky?' said Jacky, suddenly crumpling up the shirt in his fists. Still clutching the shirt he sat down. His heart was fluttering like a slack sail. 'What do you mean, dicky?'

'Well, without going into technical details, the fact is you've been overdoing it and your old ticker has got a bit tired, that's all. If you go to bed and rest up for a couple of months and take things easy from this on you'll probably live to be a hundred. If you don't it could become very serious.'

Jacky forgot his fright.

'Rest? In bed? Sure, flat racing begins next week end!'

'Mr Neason, you are not going to see a racecourse for another two months. If you do you must get another doctor.'

'But, sure, Holy God, I was never in bed for more than four hours any night o' me life! What'll I be doing in bed for two months?'

'You can listen to the radio. And you can read. And well, you can be listening to the radio. And you can read.'

'Read what?'

'Anything not too exciting. Someone once told me that whenever H. G. Wells went on a long journey he used to take a volume of the *Encyclopedia Britannica* with him. I'll come and visit you now and again.'

'Can't I come and see you?' Jacky asked feebly.

'It'll be safer the other way,' said the doctor, and it was then that Jacky knew he was really bad.

'Can I take e'er a drink?' he asked, now sagging on the ropes.

'A little glass of malt, or a bottle of stout, whenever you feel like it will do you no harm in the world. But keep off women. It takes the blood away from the head.'

'I never had much to do with them,' said Jacky sourly, putting his head into his shirt.

He went home, took a stiff whiskey, told his wife the news and got into bed. When she saw him in bed she began to cry, and she went on crying so long that he had to tell her he wasn't dead yet. At that she buttoned her lips to keep from crying more than ever. She managed to ask him was there anything special he wanted.

'Is there such a thing in the house as an encyclopedia?' he asked.

'Such a thing as what?'

'An encyclopedia. The doctor said I must read.'

She looked sadly at him and the tears came again.

'Poor Jacky,' she sobbed, 'I never thought I'd see you reduced to this,' and she went away to look.

It did not take her long – there were not twenty books in the house; bookmakers don't collect that sort of book – so she went around next door to Noreen Mulvey, the schoolmaster's wife. She was soon back with a big black book with red edges called a *Catholic Dictionary*.

'Where the hell did I buy that?' Jacky asked.

'You didn't. I got it from Noreen Mulvey. She said 'tis as good as an encyclopedia.'

Jacky looked gloomily through the funereal volume. He found a green rubber stamp inside the cover. *Saint Jacob's College, Putney Green, Middlesex, London.* There were a lot of queer words in black type, of which the first was *Abbacomites*.

' 'Twill last me out,' he said mumpishly and settled himself to read.

The first article informed him that abbacomites were noble abbots, or count abbots, to whom the courts of the time gave abbacies for pecuniary profit. He was further informed that these abbots included not only the sons of nobles but their daughters, and even their wives.

'Nice blackguarding!' Jacky muttered and settled himself more comfortably to read the next article, which was headed *Abbess*. He read the brief paragraph with interest, especially the part that informed him that in the Brigittine Order and in the Order of Fontevrault, where there were monastaries for both nuns and monks side by side, 'the monks were bound to obey the abbess of the related monastery.'

'My ladies!' he growled sardonically and went on to *Abbots*.

He began to wilt a little here – the article was long and technical – though he rallied at the paragraph describing the bright young abbés, 'fluttering around the Court of Versailles,' who never so much as saw the abbeys from which they drew their incomes. He weakened again at *Abbreviations* and he nearly gave up at *Abjuration of Heresy*, but he was arrested by the *Abrahamites* because it struck him that these fellows were not far wrong when they declared that 'the good God had created men's souls, but the wicked power, or demiurge, had created their bodies.' However, at the end of this article there was a reference to a later entry on Manicheanism, of which Jacky read enough to decide that they were a lot of bloody foolahs and that the writer on Abrahamitism had been right to give them hell.

Abraxas bored him. *Absolution* was full of *a*'s, and *b*'s and *c*'s. As for the *Acaeometi* or Sleepless Monks, it was plain that they were another set of born eedjuts. It was then, as he began to ruffle the pages impatiently, that his eye fell on *Adam*. He read this article not only once but three times. When his wife came in with an eggnog she found him leaning back and staring pensively out of the window.

'Come here to me, Eileen,' he said, taking the eggnog with an absent hand. 'Did it ever occur to you that Adam and Eve made nothing at all of going around in their pelts?'

'Everyone knows that,' she said, tucking in the bed-clothes.

'What I mean is did it ever occur to you that they didn't mind one bit?'

'I suppose the poor things were innocent until the devil tempted them.'

He cocked his head cutely at her.

'I'll go so far with you,' he agreed. 'But did it ever occur to you to ask how did the devil manage it if they were all that innocent?'

'Why wouldn't he?' she scoffed. 'Isn't it the innocent ones that always fall?'

'Fair enough,' he agreed again, and then in the smug voice of a chess player saying 'Checkmate', he said: 'But what you're forgettin' is that this was in the Garden of Eden where sin didn't exist.'

'The devil invented it,' she said hurriedly.

'Heresy!' he pronounced and tapped the book. 'I'm after reading it here under *Abrahamites*.'

'Will you have chops for your supper?' she asked.

He nodded without interest.

'It only stands to reason,' he pointed out. 'You can't tempt a man who is so innocent he doesn't mind seeing a woman going around in her pelt.'

'But what about the apple?' she cried.

'Aha! But what *was* the apple?'

' 'Twas just an apple. Anyway it was something they weren't allowed to have,' she declared with all the vehemence of a woman who knows that he does not understand what she is saying and must therefore say it as emphatically as she can. But Jacky was, by now, beyond arguing along these lines. He said loftily that the Council of Trent left the matter entirely open. She whisked her head in the air, and at the door she turned to remark with proper feminine unfairness, and irrelevance, that it would be better for him to be saying his prayers.

By suppertime he had moved further on. Conquering all the territory that he touched, he learned much that he had not previously even thought it possible to know about the subject of *Adultery*. It was an article with cross references to *Marriage* and *Affinity*. When Eileen came back with the supper tray, bearing two fine chops and a glass of Guinness with a one-inch froth on it, she again found him looking thoughtfully out of the window. As she laid the tray on his unheeding lap he said:

'Did you know that a man can't marry his own mother-in-law?'

'Your mother-in-law,' she informed him coldly, 'is in her grave this seven years. And when she was alive you hadn't as much as a good word to throw her no more than to the cat.'

'I am not,' he told her with a nice and infuriating blend of courtesy and condescension, 'discussing your mother. It is a question of canon law.'

Her breath went up her nose like the whistle of a train.

'Eat your chops while they're hot,' she said, and went out with prim hips.

Milo Mulvey called in about ten o'clock to offer his condolences to the patient. Eileen told him to save his sympathy because her hero (her own term) was full of buck and guff. She led him upstairs and while he sat on a cane-bottomed chair by the bed she leaned over the end of it. Milo adopted the false-jolly manner of all visitors to sick-rooms.

'Well, Jacky my ould tar,' he cried jovially, 'so this is what slow horses and fast women did to you?' – with a wink at Eileen to take the harm out of it.

'Milo!' Jacky addressed him seriously. 'Do you really believe that a thousand angels can stand on the point of a needle?'

Milo looked at him, and then he looked a question at Eileen.

'He's that way all day,' she said. ' 'Tis all on account of that book you gave him.'

'Is that mine?' Milo asked, leaning over to glance at the sombre volume. 'Where did you get it?'

'I borrowed it from Noreen today. Worse luck. The professor here said he wanted to read something.'

'You poor man,' Milo said, 'I'll bring you around half a dozen detective stories.'

'Thanks,' said Jacky, 'but I don't want them. This is the most interesting book I ever read in my life. Barring that book of famous crimes you lent me last year when I had the flu. But do you – and this is a serious question now mind you – do you really and truly believe that a thousand angels can stand on the point of a needle?'

'You're very interested in religion all of a sudden,' Milo said suspiciously.

'For a man,' Eileen agreed dryly, 'who wasn't to church, chapel or meeting for the last five years.'

Jacky leaned out of bed and tapped Milo's knee.

'Milo! Will you tell me how the hell's blazes could even one angel stand on the point of a needle, let alone a thousand of 'em.'

'Answer the professor,' Eileen said wearily to Milo.

'Well,' Milo began, a bit embarrassed and not sure he was not being chaffed by the two of them, 'if you are serious about this the answer is, of course, that angels are pure spirits. I mean they can pass through walls and floors and ceilings. I mean they have neither length, nor breadth, nor depth. I mean they are pure intelligences.'

'What you mean,' Eileen said flatly, 'is that angels have no legs.'

'Well,' Milo conceded unwillingly, 'that is more or less what it comes to.'

'The professor,' she said in a long sigh, 'is now about to ask you how they can stand if they have no legs.'

Milo laughed easily. He turned to Jacky. He was a man who loved explaining things, which was why he was a teacher.

'That's very simple, Jacky. Let me explain it to you. You see when you say "stand" you don't really mean "stand". You mustn't take these things literally. You know very well, for instance, that when you say "going up to heaven" or "going down to hell", you don't mean "up" and "down" the way we mean upstairs and downstairs. It's the same with everything else. I mean you don't think God has whiskers do you? You follow me?'

He found himself faltering. Jacky was looking at him rather coldly, something like the way a boss-gangster might look at one of his gang who is explaining volubly how he happened to be seen coming out of the headquarters of the police precinct the previous night at half past eleven arm in arm with the district prosecutor. Milo turned to Eileen:

'*You* understand me, Eileen, don't you? I mean it's impossible for us to as much as talk of things of this kind without forming misleading pictures of them. But, of course,' with a fluent wave of his hand, 'that doesn't mean that our pictures bear any relation to actuality. I mean we don't think that angels have actual wings and all to that, do we?'

He laughed cajolingly, anticipating her answering smile of approval.

She did not smile. She looked sadly at him. Then she looked at Jacky.

'Go on, professor!'

'All the same, Milo,' Jacky said, 'I believe it is a fact that the angels can commit sin?'

'Well, they certainly did once,' Milo agreed, but his eyes were beginning to get shifty. 'The fallen angels and all that. Milton,' he added absently. '*Paradise Lost.*'

'And what,' Jacky asked with a polite interest, 'do you suppose they did it with? Having no legs and so on?'

'With their minds!' said Milo wildly.

'I see,' said Jacky. 'With their minds.'

There was a long pause. Eileen came to the rescue with 'Would you like a bottle of stout, Milo?' very much like a boxer's second at the end of the tenth round saying to a man whose only wish on God's earth is that he had never come into the ring, 'Would ye care for a small brandy?'

Milo said that he would, yes, thanks, he would, thanks very much, take a, in fact, yes a bottle of stout if she had one handy. As she leaned up and went for the stout she heard Milo acceding to her hero that a lot of these things are difficult to our mortal understanding, and Jacky magnanimously agreeing that he could see that, and:

'Take the Garden of Eden, now, for example!'

When she came back with the tray she found the two heads together, going word for word through a page of the black book. She observed that Milo looked much less jovial than when he sailed into the room a quarter of an hour before.

Milo did not call in again until several nights later. He had not been in the bedroom for ten minutes, chatting about this and that, when the doorbell rang. Eileen went down and came back accompanied by Father Milvey. She showed his Reverence in, and when he and Milo greeted one another with as much astonishment as if they had not met for six months, she looked over at Jacky, caught his eye and gave him a moth-wink out of a porcelain face. (The parish joke about the firm of Mulvey and Milvey had moss on it.) Father Milvey was a tidy little man, always as neat as a cuff straight from the laundry; and he might have been thought of as a tidy, cheerful little man if he had not had a slight squint which gave him a somewhat distant look. He greeted the patient with the usual sickroom cordiality. Eileen went downstairs for the bottle of whiskey, and after she had come back and helped them all round, and helped herself, she took up her usual position leaning over the end of the bed, waiting for his Reverence to mention the Garden of Eden. He did it very simply.

'Yerrah, what's the big book, Jacky? Oh? I hope it's not one of those American things, all written in words of one syllable and as full of pictures as if the Vatican was in Hollywood. Well, the Lord knows 'tis high time you took a bit of interest in something else besides horses.'

Jacky fended him off just as simply. He pushed the book aside with a casual:

'Ach, it passes the time, Father.'

There was a short silence. Then Milo made the approach direct.

'He had a bit of difficulty there the other night, Father, with the Garden of Eden. As a matter of fact it stumped myself.'

'Oho, is that so?' said the little priest with a cheerful laugh. 'Nothing like beginning at the beginning, is there? And what was that now?' he asked Jacky, and Eileen saw his hand moving slowly to his pocket, and protruding therefrom the corner of a pale-green pamphlet. She foresaw the look of surprise, could already hear the words, 'extraordinary coincidence . . .'

'Ah, nothing much,' said Jacky.

'What was it, though?'

'Hell!' said Jacky.

Father Milvey's eyes strayed towards Milo's. The look plainly meant: 'I thought you said angels?' His hand came back to his glass. He smiled at Jacky.

'No better subject for a man in your position, Jacky. Did you ever hear the one about the old lad who was dying, and the priest said, "Now, Michael, you renounce the devil, don't you?" Do you know what the old chap said? "Ah, wisha, Father," says he, in a very troubled sort of voice, "I don't think this is any time for me to be antagonising *anybody*!"' He let the laughter pass, and then he said easily: 'Well, what about hell?'

'Fire!' said Jacky. 'I don't believe a word of it.'

His Reverence's face darkened. Help for the humble was one thing, the proud were another altogether. He adopted a sarcastic tone.

'I think,' he said, 'the old man I was just telling you about was a little more prudent in his approach to the question of hell-fire.'

Jacky took umbrage at his tone.

'There's no such a thing as hell-fire,' he said roundly.

'Oh, well, of course, Mr Neason, if you want to go against the general consensus of theological opinion! What do you choose, in your wisdom, to make, for example, of those words: "Depart from me ye accursed into everlasting fire prepared for the devil and his angels?"'

'Angels?' asked Jackie, lifting his eyebrows.

Milo intervened hastily.

'I think Father, what was troubling Jacky there was the question of angels being pure spirits.'

'What of it?'

Jacky, a man of infinite delicacy, lowered his eyes to his glass.

'I must say I fail to see your difficulty,' his Reverence pursued, and put out his palm when Milo restlessly started to intervene again. 'No, Milo! I *like* to hear these lay theologians talking.'

'Ach, 'tis nothing at all, Father,' Jacky said shyly. 'I'm sure 'tis a very simple thing if I only understood it. Only. Well. Pure spirits, you see? And real fire? I mean, could they, so to speak, feel it?'

'Tshah!' cried Father Milvey. 'Suarez . . .' He halted. It was a long time since he had read his Suarez. 'Origen,' he began. He stopped again. It was even longer since he had read his Origen. He wavered for a moment or two, and then he became a nice little man again. He expanded into a benevolent smile. 'Wisha, tell me, Jacky, why does all this interest you anyway?'

'It just passes the time, Father.'

Father Milvey laughed.

'You know, you remind me of a man – this is a good one, I only heard it the other day . . .'

Eileen leaned up. She knew that the rest of the visit would pass off swimmingly.

It was four days before Milo called in again. Jacky thought he looked a bit dark under the eyes, but he decided not to remark on it. Anyway Milo did not give him time; he threw his hat on the bed, sat on the chair, leaned forward with his two hands on his knees, and stared at Jacky with a fierce intensity. Normally, Milo was a rotund, assured sort of man; his tiny mouth, like a child whistling, pursed complacently; a man as resolutely tidy-minded as the row of three pens in his breast pocket, each with a little coloured dot to indicate the colour of the ink. He did not look like that at all tonight. Jacky looked at his furrowed brow and the deep, forked lines from his nose to his button-mouth, and wondered could he be on a batter.

'Jacky!' he said harshly. 'All this about hell!'

'Yerrah!' Jack waved airily, 'that's only chicken feed. You explained all that to me. 'Tis all figurative.' To change the subject, he leaned over and tapped Milo's taut knee. 'But, come here to me, Milo, did it ever occur to you that the antipopes . . .'

Milo choked. He sat back.

'Look!' he almost sobbed. 'First it was angels. Then it was fallen angels. Then it was hell. Now it's antipopes. Will ye, for God's sake, keep to one thing. I'm bothered to blazes about this question of hell.'

'Don't give it a thought,' Jacky soothed him. 'You mustn't take these things too literally. I mean fire and flame and all that!'

'But Father Milvey says, and he's been reading it up, that you must take it literally. My God, 'tis the cornerstone of Christianity. All the eschatological conceptions of the postexilic writings . . .'

'You're thinking too much about these things,' Jacky said crossly.

'Thinking?' Milo gasped and his round eyes flamed bloodshot. 'I've done nothing for four days and four nights but think about it! My head is addled with thinking!'

'I'll tell you my idea about all that,' Jacky confided. 'I believe there's a hell there all right but there's no one in it.'

'That's what Father Conroy says!'

'Who's he?'

Milo's voice became sullen. He explained unwillingly:

'He's the Jesuit that Father Milvey's consulting about it. But Father Saturninus says . . .'

'I never heard of him. Where'd you dig *him* up?'

'He's the Capuchin who's conducting the mission this week in Saint Gabriel's. The three of them are at it every night inside the presbytery. You know very well that the sermon on hell is the linchpin of every mission. Fire coming out of the noses of the damned, fire out of their ears, fire out of their eyeballs, their hands up for one half-cup of cold water – you know the line! Mind you, not that I approve of it! But it always gets the hard chaws, it gets the fellows that nobody else and nothing else can get. Well, Father Saturninus says all this talk and discussion has put him off his stroke. Think of it! Every night people waiting for the sermon on hell and Saturninus climbing up in the pulpit knowing they're waiting for it, and knowing he won't be able to do it. Of course, he could easily talk about hell as a lonely, miserable, desolate place where everybody was always groaning and moaning for the sight of heaven and having no hope of ever seeing it, but you know as well as I do that a hell without fire, and lots and lots of it, isn't worth a tinker's curse to anybody.'

'Well,' said Jacky impatiently, 'I don't see how I can help you. If you want to believe in fire and brimstone . . .'

Milo grasped his wrist. His voice became a whisper.

'Jacky,' he whispered. 'I don't believe one single bloody word of it.'

'Then what are you worrying about?'

'I'm worrying because I *can't* believe in it! I was happy as long as I *did* believe in it! I *want* to believe in it!'

Jacky threw his hands up in total disgust.

'But don't you see, Jacky, if you don't believe in hell you don't believe in divils, and if you don't believe in divils you don't believe in the Garden of Eden.' His voice sank to a frightened whisper again.

He seized Jacky by the arm. Jacky drew back his chin into his chest, and crushed back into the pillows to get away from the two wild bullet eyes coming closer to him. 'Jacky!' whispered Milo. 'What *was* the apple?'

'A figure of speech!'

Milo dashed his arm away, jumped to his feet, gripped his head in his hands uttered a hollow and unlikely 'Ha! Ha! Ha!' in three descending notes like a stage villain. His voice became quite normal and casual.

'Can *you* eat a figure of speech?' he asked very politely.

'There was no eatin'. That was another figure of speech, like the angels that have no legs.'

'You mean, I presume,' Milo asked, with a gentle and courteous smile, and a delicate shrug of his Rugby-player's shoulders, 'that Adam had no mouth?'

'Adam was a figure of speech,' Jacky said stolidly.

'I'm going mad!' Milo screamed, so loud that Jacky had one leg out of bed to call Eileen before Milo subsided as quickly and utterly as he had soared. He smiled wanly. 'Sorry, old boy,' he said in the stiff-upper-lip voice of an old Bedalian on the Amazon who has rudely trod on the tail of an anaconda. 'A bit on edge these days. Bad show. I only wish I could see the end of it. The worst of it is Father Milvey says it's all my fault keeping such books in the house. And lending them to you. I wish to God I never gave you that book! I wish to God I never laid eyes on it!'

Jacky fished it out of the eiderdown and handed it to him.

'Take it,' he said. 'I'm sick of it. 'Tis all full of "This one says" and "That one says." Have you er'er an ould detective story?'

'But, Jacky! About *hell*?'

'Forget it!' said Jacky. 'Eileen!' he roared. 'Bring up the bottle of whiskey.'

'No thanks,' said Milo, getting up gloomily and putting the obscure volume under his arm. 'Father Milvey is coming around to my place tonight and I'll have to have a jar with him.' He looked down miserably at Jacky. 'You're looking fine!'

'Why wouldn't I, and I living like a lord?'

' 'Tis well for you,' Milo grumbled sourly, and went out slowly.

After a while Eileen came upstairs to him bearing the whiskey bottle, two glasses and a big red book.

'What's that book?' he asked suspiciously.

'Milo gave it to me for you. 'Tis *The Arabian Nights*. He said not to let Father Milvey see it. Some of the pictures in it will raise your blood pressure.'

Jacky grunted. He was watching her pouring out the liquor.

'Come here to me, Eileen,' he said, his eye fixed thoughtfully on the glass. 'Did it ever, by any chance, occur to you that . . .'

'What is it now?' she asked threateningly, witholding the glass from him.

'I was only going to say,' he went on humbly, 'did it ever occur to you that the bottom of a whiskey bottle is much too near the top?'

She gave him one of those coldly affectionate looks of which only wives are capable, added a half-inch to his glass, and handed it over to him.

'You ould savage,' she said fondly, and began to tuck him in for the night. To show her approval of him she left the bottle by his side.

Left to himself he opened the big red book. He savoured it. He began to relish it. He was soon enjoying it. He snuggled into his pillow and, with one hand for the page and one for his glass, he entered the Thousand and One Nights. Thanks be to God, here at least there were lots and lots of legs. Towards midnight he gently let the blind roll up to see what sort of a night it was. His eye fell on the light streaming out from Milo Milvey's sitting room across the grass of his back garden : the theological session in full swing. He raised his eyes to the night sky. It was a fine, sweet open-faced night in May. A star among the many stars beamed at him. There are more things in heaven . . . With renewed relish he returned to the Grand Vizier's daughter. His glass was full.

In the Bosom of the Country

Then, suddenly after all their years of love, ten of them, five a-growing and five a-dying, death came. They were lying side by side in the big, bridal bed under its looped-up canopy of pink silk on whose slope the sunset gently laid the twig-pattern of the elms in her drive. She had tossed aside her fair hair so that it lay in a heavy tangle on her left shoulder, and was pensively watching him brushing up his greying, military moustaches with the knuckle of his fore-finger. She started to scratch his shoulder with her nails, gently at first, then a little more wickedly until he turned to look at her. The sunset revealed the dark roots at the parting of her hair and caught a wrinkle at the corner of her eye. Recognising a familiar mood he smiled nervously at her curl-at-the-corner smile, slightly mocking, shy, minxish, naughty. A prelude to another pretty quarrel? He soon stopped smiling: this time there was substance to her fret.

'Well, my dashing Major? Are you betraying me with one of your great galumphing horsey wenches from the Hunt? Account for yourself. Two months all but a week? And before that how long was it? Keene by name but not so keen by nature? Is this your idea of devotion? Are you getting tired of me?'

'Anna!' he protested.

He wanted to glance at his watch but his left arm still lay under her waist. He glanced at the ruddy sun behind the elm-boles. Half past four? With a sudden blare the telephone rang. 'Botheration!' she snapped, and reached out her long, bare arm for the receiver. He noticed the little purse of skin hanging from her elbow. Poor dear! He really did love her, but, dammit, they weren't either of them as young as they . . . She sat straight up, crying out, 'No! Oh, no!' He heard a few more squawkings from the receiver and her 'I'll be right over!' She hung up and leaped out of bed, scrambling all over the floor for her clothes.

'It's the hospital. Arty's dead. I've lost my poor husband.'

Something there had kept bothering him for days, something out of tune that alerted him, something that did not seem right. It was not the time and the place. Although, dammit, if, instead of the telephone ringing to say that Arty had gone, Arty had opened the door and peeped in he could not have chosen a more awkward moment to impose himself. Nor could it have been guilt – not after all these years. It could not have been anything they said – so little had been said in their haste to dress. It could only be something tiny, like an eye glancing over a bare shoulder or some single word or gesture that was not meant to mean anything but did. Not that he ever got down to thinking it out properly. 'Am I,' he wondered, 'shying off it for fear of finding out?'

A modest man, he knew his worth, She was not the only person who joked about his name. He did it himself. It was inevitable – F. L. Keene. In the army they used to call him Festina Lente and kept him to the rank of Major. A good old dobbin. Sure and steady. But, at least, he tried to be honest, and he had flashes, dammit. Once, long ago, Anna had asked him how many women he had loved, and he truly replied, 'Only you.' 'You seem very adept?' she had said sceptically, at which he had asked her the same question about herself and she had answered, 'Only you! Oh, of course, I thought I loved Arty when I married him. But I was very young. I soon found out.' Considering him she had said, 'We get on well for a pair of ignoramuses.' He had thought about this for a while and then, to his own surprise, came up with, 'Love is like jungle warfare at night, it keys you up, you feel things you can't see.' (Like now, when that indefinable something passed in the air between them.)

For her part, when he said that about love and the jungle, she had laughed merrily, sensitive enough to respond to his doleful humour, not intelligent enough to define it. It was his great attraction, of which he was quite unaware, always to expect the worst – it made him infinitely tender and pitiful towards everybody. 'I am a dull dog,' he used to say to her sometimes and it used to make her throw her arms around him. Her big, stupid, dull, loyal dog would look at her in astonishment and love. She was his opposite, endlessly hoping for the best, and better. Had she been smarter she would have realised that pessimists are usually kind. The gay, bubbling over, have no time for the pitiful. Love lives in sealed bottles of regret.

He went to the funeral, hoping to have a chat with Mabel Tallant, the only person, he hoped, who knew all about the pair of them. There were so many people there that he decided to keep discreetly to the rear of the crowd. He was surprised at the size of the turn-out but supposed that a man cannot be a District Justice without making a pack of friends. Anyway, the Irish have a great gift for death, wakes and funerals. They are really at their best in misfortune. Used to it, I suppose? And sport. Quid pro quo, what? The thing that surprised him most, as he stood watching the mourners file in and out of the church, was that while he knew many of them by sight, and perhaps a dozen by name – the vet, the Guards' Inspector, a couple of doctors, shopkeepers from the town, two or three fellows he had hunted with, and those well enough to nod to – he did not know one of them intimately, apart from Mabel Tallant. With her he just managed to get a word: she said she was taking Anna home with her for a couple of days after the relatives left. 'Give her my love,' he whispered hastily. Mabel had smiled sadly and whispered back, 'Everybody can sleep in peace now.'

He drove away, unaccosted by anybody, wondering what the devil she meant, wondering also why the devil it was that ever since he came to live in Ireland he was always wondering what somebody meant about some damn thing or another. He decided yet once more that they had to talk roundabout because they never had anything to say that was worth saying directly. The yews of his drive were dripping as he drove up to his empty house: nothing would do old Mrs Mac but to go to the funeral. The fire was out. Why had he ever come here? But he had been over all that, too. If his uncle had not left him this place he might never have come back from Kenya; and he might have left after the first year if he had not met Anna Mohan. But now? With Africa gone to hell? Package-safaris all over the place. You might as well think of living in Picca-dilly Circus.

The week after the funeral, as he was hacking home from the hunt, Mabel rode up beside him. She was red as a turnip from the wind, mud-spattered to her stock, a grey hair drooping from under her hat, and on her right jaw a streak of dried blood.

'Hello, Mabel? Fall? No bones broken, I hope? You know, you are looking younger every day. But, then, we all know you are a marvel!'

'My dear Frank,' she laughed in her jolly, mannish way; she always laughed at everything, 'if you're referring to my great age I assure you I'm not giving up for a long time yet. Even if I am fifty I'm not decrepit. And I don't think you can give me many years, can you? I wasn't tossed, I'm more wet than muddy. I stayed behind with the Master to put back a few poles that we knocked at the Stameen. I've got half the stream in my boots this minute.'

They ambled along for a quarter of a mile with no more than a few tired words about the hunt. They had had three good runs. The Master was digging out the last fox. You have to give the farmers some satisfaction. After another silence he said. 'How is Anna?'

'You ask me?'

'I suppose I should call on her soon. I don't want to be indiscreet, you know.'

'You could be a bit too discreet.'

'I was always discreet about Anna. I owed it to her. Nobody but you ever knew about Anna and me.'

'Knew? Knows? Maybe not, but you've lived long enough in these parts to know that there's damn little goes on here that everybody doesn't suspect.' She hooted gaily, 'Sometimes a lot more than they've any reason to suspect. It fills their lives, I suppose.'

'Anna and I used always say that they might suspect but they couldn't be sure, and that was what really counted.'

'Past history?'

She laughed. He frowned. Not because her laugh suggested some unspoken blame of him but that it echoed certain spoken, and un-spoken prophecies about Anna : her unbridled tongue, as of a woman who had been spoiled as a too-pretty girl, her temper, her tears, her enthusiasms, her wanting always to be smarter than she was, her melancholy days that went on and on, her warm days that were too warm to last, like a hot day in summer, her sudden bursts of generosity towards some women and her sudden bursts of jealousy towards other women – always young, pretty women. One by one Mabel had shaken her head over Anna's 'ways', and he had liked her all the more for it because in spite of everything she seemed to love her. Or was it that she, too, felt sorry for her?

It was growing dusk when they got to Bardy Hill. Fumes of fog were lying over the reedy plain. The tired horses slowed to a walk. She tapped his thigh with her crop.

'Frank! You're fooling yourself. I heard a bit of gossip at the meet this morning.'

'What did you hear?'

'Not much. Somebody said, "I wonder is Major Keene going to marry her now." '

He suddenly realised what that 'something' had been. She had said, 'Arty's dead, I've lost my poor husband.' Lost? Or was that the word they said to her on the phone? Dammit, she had lost him ten years ago.

'Mabel! If Arty had died ten years ago, even five, even three, I'd have married her like a shot. We dreamed of it. We lived on the dream of it. Not on the hope, dammit, no! We never said "die". We said, "if anything happened to him". Always talking about how happy we could be together. Just the two of us. Morning, noon and night. Lovers' talk! But, ye know, hope deferred maketh the heart sick. Anna being a Catholic there was no hope of a divorce. And, anyway, she was fond of him. In the end I gave up hope. I'll tell ye something else, Mabel. I was with her the day Arty died. I hadn't been with her for two months before that. And before that I dunno when. That day, I knew it was all over.'

He frowned again when Mabel said nothing. Venus shone, alone, in a green sky above a low spear of clouds. The horses, smelling home, began to trot downhill. They pulled up at Ballymeen Cross – they had each about half a mile to go.

'Do you think she really expects me to marry her?' he asked unhappily.

'I can only give you the woman's point of view. I'd think it damn cheap of you if you didn't make an honest woman of her. It will be pretty lonely for her in that old house at Culadrum. To put it at its lowest a husband is a handy thing to have about a house.' She laughed sourly, 'I should know.'

She jerked the head of her horse, and cantered away. He did the same. Once, and he regretted it, he took out his anger on the animal with his crop. Twice he uttered the word 'Damnation!' A pool of water gleamed coldly on his drive. A blank window held the last of the day. Culadrum would not be much of a home for Anna from now on. He should know.

He ate little, drank too much wine, slept badly, and immediately after breakfast he drove over to Culadrum. He found her in her drawing-room reading *The Irish Times* before the fire, slim-looking in proper black, very becoming, with a tiny white ruff under her chin, and hanging beneath it one of those little pendents called a Lavallière, a small, coloured miniature of Arty as a young man. With her tight-busted dress, and her fair hair done in a coil on the top of her head she had a Victorian look, like a queen in mourning. His heart went out to her. He kissed her and said gallantly, 'Now, my darling, before the whole world you can be all mine!' To his delight she blushed, a thing he had not seen her do for years. They sat in armchairs on either side of the fire.

'Frank! We have waited so long you won't mind waiting another while, will you?'

'As long as you like, Anna.'

'There is a special reason why we must wait a bit. It has to do with local opinion. I want to be married in a Catholic church.'

So, she *had* been thinking about it.

'By all means. I'm not bigoted. In for a penny in for a pound.'

'I want everything to be done regularly. I want to clear up everything. We will live here. In this house our life is before us. All my friends and all Arty's old friends are Catholics. They move in their own circle, just as people do everywhere. I'm not one of the hunting set, as they aren't either, except for one or two maybe. So it is frightfully important that they should all become your friends too. Oh, my darling, it would make all the difference in the world if you were a Catholic!'

He sat back slowly.

'Well, unfortunately, I'm not.'

'Frank! For me? It would make all the difference for me if you became a Catholic. Oh, if you could only become a Catholic, Frank! Won't you? We'd be all together then. And I'd be so happy!'

'But, dammit, Anna, you're not seriously suggesting that they'd look down on you in some way if you married a Protestant?'

'A mixed marriage? They won't have it in this diocese. Anyway we never did it in our family. Even where they do allow it its a hole and corner affair. It's not the same thing at all. Documents. Guarantees. Back-door stuff. Ugh!'

'It's beyond me.'

She laughed her little curl-at-the-corners Anna-laugh.

'You've lived in Ireland, Frank, for ten years, and I honestly don't believe you still understand the Irish.'

'Is there anything to understand?'

'Besides, there is something else we have to face.'

'Something else? What else, for God's sake?'

'We always said they didn't know. But in our hearts we always knew that they did know. They always do know. Bother them! Oh, they mightn't have known *exactly*, but they must have known that there was *something* between us. Of course, there is one way out of it. If you don't marry me now they will say they were wrong.'

'But I don't want a way out of it. I want you!'

'But, Frank, if we do marry, you see, then they will know for certain that they were right all along. They'd never feel happy about us. They'd always be whispering about our past. We'd see it in their eyes. They might never visit us at all! And you couldn't blame them, could you? But if you became a Catholic, Frank, they'd be so happy about it that they'd forget and forgive everything. Besides, it was always the one thing – I mean if there ever was any teeny, little thing at all – that stood between us now and again. Now when we can be married, if we do marry, at last, at long last – Oh, my darling! – I want us to be one in everything before the world!'

'It never seemed to bother you before?'

'Of course it bothered me. I often cried about it when you left me.'

'Why did you never speak to me about it?'

'I was afraid of losing you,' she said sombrely.

He stood up, went to the window and looked glumly out through the frosty leaf-tracery on the glass. Accustomed to his ways she kept looking at his back under her eyebrows, waiting on his digestion. Presently he did a smart right-about turn.

'This,' he declared, 'is a bomb-shell. Dammit, it's an absolute bomb-shell. When we couldn't marry you were so afraid to lose me that you never uttered a word about religion, and now, when we can marry, you give me the choice of being a cad if I don't and a Catholic if I do.'

'Darling, if you can't I shan't blame you. And if you can't I am not going to lose you. No matter what it costs me. Unless you want to ditch me, of course?'

'That I shall never do.'

She joined him at the window, and with one coaxing pussy-cat finger she stroked his moustaches right and left, and kissed his lips.

'Think about it, darling.'

He stared at her, snatched his cap and left abruptly. After driving for an hour he found himself outside Mabel Tallant's house at Bunahown. She was in the stables watching her groom combing her grey hunter. When he told her she laughed so loudly that he saw her gold-tipped molars.

'You're stuck, my boy!'

'But she might just as well ask me to become a Muslim or a Parsee! It isn't fair!'

She laughed gleefully again, then became solemn.

'Frank?'

'Well?'

'Suppose this happened ten years ago when you first fell in love with Anna? Suppose she wasn't married then? Suppose she asked you then to do this for her, would you have done it? Would you have said it wasn't fair?'

He glared at her, shuffled a bit, strode away.

After a week of torture, sitting for hours alone over his fire, or stalking alone about the leafless roads, he drove into town, stiffened himself with a glass of whiskey at The Royal Hotel and asked the waitress where the Catholic presbytery was. She directed him to Pearse Square with an enthusiasm that he found nauseating. The presbytery looked like a home for orphans, tall, Victorian, redbrick, with imitation stone quoins in grey plaster, pointed in black. Every window looked up at the wet February sky over brass-tipped half-screens. He hauled stoutly at the brass bell-handle and stood to attention glaring at the door. He asked the scrubby boy who opened it for the Parish Priest and was shown into a chilly front room. Drawing, Waiting? Committee? Dining? He found himself faced by a lifesize statue of Christ pointedly exhibiting His rosy heart. He turned his back to it. He did not sit down. This was a thing a man met on his two feet.

The door opened, very slowly. The priest who entered was an old man of at least sixty-five or more. He wore a monsignor's russet vest beneath a celluloid Roman collar that brushed the cincture of white hair about his roped neck. His voice was as mild as milk, his manner as courteous as a glass of port. When he told his visitor that he had been a chaplain with the Royal Inniskillings towards the end of the 1914 war, they were both only too happy to sit, smoke and chat about Château Thierry, the Sambre, the Somme, places known to the younger warrior of the two with the reverence proper to ancient history. Then they retired upstairs to the monsignor's sitting-room, the fireside and a whiskey bottle. An old Alsatian bitch lay strewn on the hearthrug between them.

By the time they got down to business the major felt as relaxed in his armchair, prickly with horsehair, as if they had just met in a club. All went well until he uttered the name, Mrs Anna Mohan. The monsignor's eyelids fell.

'Mrs Mohan? Ah, yes! Lives over at Culadrum House. I knew her father and mother very well. I wouldn't say they were exactly zealous Catholics. But they were good people. Hm! Well, well!

Anna Carty, that was. A handsome girl when she was a child. I remember now, they sent her to some convent school in Kent. And after that to some place in Switzerland – Lausanne, I believe – finishing school. Rather a mistake that. Risky.'

'Risky?'

The word could have connotations.

'Oh, I am not criticising them. It is simply that I always feel that if a girl is going to live in Ireland it's wiser to bring her up here. She must have been very young when she married Mohan. Why, we buried him only two, three weeks ago. Hm! I see!'

He looked at the major without expression, but it was plain enough that he did see.

'Well, Major? Tell me this. Would I be wrong in surmising that you are doing this chiefly, if not wholly, to please Mrs Mohan?'

'A fair question, padre. Yes, you've got it. That's about the run of it.'

'I mean, you are not being drawn to the Catholic Church entirely for its own sake, are you?'

'I'll be perfectly straight with you, padre, I don't know anything at all about the Catholic Church. I'll go further. I'm not going to become a Catholic, or anything like it, until I know a lot more about the whole thing.'

'Very wise. In other words, you are not asking me to give you a course of instruction. You are just asking me for some preliminary information.'

'Yes! Yes, that's about the run of it.'

'Is there, then, something that particularly interests you, or shall I say that bothers you, about our Church?'

'Why, dammit, everything about the Catholic Church bothers me. Not that I ever thought about it. But I suppose if you ask me a straight question I might say, well, for example, I might say what's all this about the infallibility of the Pope? It's a tall order, ye know, if somebody comes out every day of the week about something and says "That's it! You've got to take it because I'm infallible!" I mean, supposing the Pope came out tomorrow and said Napoleon was a woman, or that a line isn't the shortest distance between two points, or that the Law of Gravitation is all nonsense, you can't deny it, padre, that that'd be a hell of a tall order. You don't mind my being frank about this, I hope?'

The monsignor patted down the glowing tobacco in his pipe with an asbestos finger and said mildly that no, he did not mind at all.

'Not of course, that what you suggest bears any relation to reality. But I don't mind. I mean, the examples you have chosen are not the very best in the world.' Here he waved his mottled hand. 'Since Mr Einstein, as the old song says, fings ain't wat they used ter be.' He wandered off a bit about Tycho Brahe and the mathematics of planetary attraction until he saw a glaze gathering over his visitor's eyes. 'In fact, His Holiness hardly ever speaks infallibly. The doctrine of Infallibility was pronounced in 1870.' He halted, thinking of such names as Newman and Lord Acton, and went on hastily. 'Since then I don't think the Pope has spoken *ex cathedra* more than . . . Is it twice, or three times? And if I may say so, quite enough, too! Though some people might think even that much was excessive. Things change.' He fell into a private thought. 'Change and expand.'

'Only twice or three times? Is this a fact? Dammit, I never knew this! But,' he pounced, 'when he does we have to believe him, eh?'

'Major Keene, I think all this would seem much simpler to us if we were to think of the whole matter as one of obedience rather than of conviction. You are a soldier. You know about obedience. During the war if your colonel told you to advance on Hill 22 with three men and that old Alsatian there and take Objective 46, which you knew quite well was held by a thousand men, what would you do about it?'

'I'd obey at once.'

'Yes. You would obey. Somebody's got to give the orders.'

Keene stared at him out of his two great, blue eyes like a horse facing a jump.

'By George, you're a hundred per cent right, padre! Somebody's got to be boss. Not like all this damned, modern Whiggery we've got now. When everybody wants to be the boss. All those Trade Unions . . . But, mind you, you've touched on another question there. Only last Sunday my housekeeper, Mrs MacCarthy, told me that, when she was at Mass, right here in town, one of your curates . . . You won't mind my saying this?'

'Fire away, Major. Fire away.'

'She told me . . . Mind you, she's a bit of an old exaggerator, but I wouldn't say she's a liar, just Irish ye know, she told me that one of your curates said from the pulpit that any girl going around this town in tight jeans was walking straight on the road to hell. Now, that's a bit of a tall order, padre! What do you say to that?'

The monsignor sighed wheezily.

'Yes. Well. We do seem to have wandered a bit from papal infallibility. But, since you raise the question . . . You, again as an old soldier, must know what happens to orders by the time they pass down to the lower ranks. It's a case of the sergeants' mess, my dear Major. The sergeants' mess in every sense of the word, and you know what I'm talking about.'

'By George! Don't I? Ye know, padre, it's a downright pleasure to talk to a man like you who knows the ways of the big world. You make me feel quite homesick for it.'

'So? Obedience! And order. And authority. You revere your Queen. The proud symbol of the power of your Empire. We Catholics revere the Pope. The proud symbol of our Empire. The Roman Empire. You and I, each in his own way, respect authority, desire order and uphold power.'

'Splendid! I can see that. In fact I begin to see a lot of daylight. Ye know, if we had a couple of chats I shouldn't be at all surprised if we found we had a good deal of ground in common. Mind you, I'm not going to be rushed into this. I'm sure that when I start thinking about it I'll come up with a lot of things that bother me. Mixed marriages, for instance. There's another tall order. And, let me see, hasn't there been some difficulty about the Virgin? And then, of course, there's contraception – ran into that a lot in India. I need hardly say my interest in the matter is purely academic.'

'So is mine.'

He rose.

'Why don't you come to dinner next week, Major, when as you say you will have thought some more about it, and we can combine business, if I may so call it, with pleasure. I've got quite a sound port.'

'Aha! I know something about port.'

The monsignor warmed.

'Do you now? Tell me, did you ever take port for breakfast?'

The major guffawed.

'Oh dammit no! No! Not for breakfast, padre!'

The monsignor chuckled.

'Then I am afraid you don't know anything at all about port. Wait until you taste mine. But I'm afraid if you are a connoisseur in wine you had better bring your own. Ah! The great wines of France. 1917. Spoiled my palate. I can't afford vintage wine any longer.'

'I've got a dozen of Forty-nine Beaunes-Villages at home. I'll bring a couple of bottles with me. By God, this is a splendid idea! I beg your pardon, monsignor, here I am cursing like a trooper in the presence of your reverence.'

'Pshaw! I'm inured to it. I remember one morning outside Ypres. Just before we went into battle. Two dragoons fighting, one of them an Orangeman and the other a Catholic, shouting like troopers. They had to be heard – the barrage going right over our heads, hell open to Christians, the captain staring at his wristwatch waiting for the second to go over the top. Do you remember – Ah, no, you're too young! – those old wristwatches with little metal grilles over them? I never heard such language in all my life as that Orangeman was giving out of him. In the end the other fellow, he was a Corkman, shoved his bayonet up within an inch of the other fellow's throat and he shouts, "Look, Sammy! I'm in the state of grace now before the battle, but with the help of God I won't be so handicapped before the day is out, and I tell you if I meet you then I'll shove this blank blank..." '

He clasped Keene by the arm for support as he bent over and laughed at the memory of it. Then he straightened and sighed.

'Poor chaps, neither of 'em came back. And I'm sure the good Lord was equally kind to the pair of them. Next Thursday, Major. At nineteen hours. Goodness me, I haven't used that phrase for it must be forty years. We'll be talking of old times together.'

Keene clasped his hand. He left the presbytery, glancing in respectfully at the impassive eyes of the Sacred Heart.

Those Thursday dinners became such a solemn, as well as delightful opening of hearts that within two months the monsignor was straining hard to hold his neophyte from declaring himself a Catholic on the spot. Indeed, one silent April night, during their third month, as he was showing his guest out into the moist emptiness of Pearse Square, he said, 'I shall bless the day, Frank, when you become, if you do become, a Catholic, but I confess I shall have one small regret. The end of our little dinners.'

'Nonsense! Why should they end?'

'They will end.'

By the end of April the major was coming up against the hard stuff: the one sector of the battlefield to whose ground he returned obstinately, uncomfortably, scarred a little, sometimes approaching it as quietly as if he were on a lone night-raid. They might be talking about books – say, *Adam Bede* or *The Three Musketeers* and he might slip in:

'Padre! Can one never, simply never say that there are times when love conquers all? I mean, is that kind of love always, simply always, a sin?'

'I'm afraid, Frank, it is. Always a sin. I'm afraid there just isn't any way around that one. Nor, I fear, could any clergyman of any persuasion say anything else.' He allowed himself a slim smile. 'You remind me of old Professor Mahaffy of Trinity College in Dublin. He was a great wag, you know. One time he confided, or pretended to confide in a fashionable Dublin Jesuit, a close friend of his, that he felt drawn to the Catholic Church. Very naturally his Jesuit friend was only too eager to pluck the plum. Another glass? "Not a drop is sold till it's seven years old." Well, it appeared that there was just one small obstacle. Just one tiny, little problem. "If you can allow me," Mahaffy said, and I am sure he said it with a poker-face, "to believe that Christ was not God I will join your Church tomorrow morning." His Jesuit friend is said to have paused for a long time. And at last he said, very regretfully, as I say to you now about adultery, "I'm afraid there isn't any way around that one." There are some things nobody can get around. Not even the Pope. Let alone me.'

Finally, one night, Frank said, plump out:

'Padre! When, and if, you consider me worthy to be received into the Church shall I have to go to Confession?'

'We will, naturally, have to clear up your past. Not that I think it will bother you very much. There are so few sins, and they repeat themselves endlessly. Even boringly. It is only the circumstances that change.'

'I was coming to exactly that. There is a bit of my past that I would like to clear up right away. I want to tell you that I have been in love with Anna Mohan for some ten years. I mean, we have been lovers in the full sense of the word. And I have never felt guilty about it. My fault, no doubt, but there it is. After all, she was only married to him in theory as you might say. He's gone now and words cannot harm him, everybody knows that he was a roaring alcoholic. Don't those circumstances you speak of alter such cases as mine?'

'He was addicted,' the monsignor agreed sadly. 'As for your case, that he was addicted is sad but it is not relevant to the law. Hard cases make bad laws. Nor is it relevant that you did not feel a sense of guilt. A stern moralist might speak to you of an atrophied con-science. I think it is enough for me to remind you that many men, known to history, men like Hitler or Stalin, committed the greatest crimes without feeling any sense of guilt. I can only repeat to you that adultery is a very grave sin. It is even two sins, for it also sins against the law that thou shalt not steal. She was his wife. I do not wish to overstress the point, but it does arise. Furthermore, chastity is not only of the body. In what is commonly called sex the body and the soul are one. You simply have to accept what I say.'

'She did lose something when he died. I have realised that.'

'I think,' the monsignor added, gravely, 'that this is something that it is your duty to clarify.' He paused and then added, pointedly, 'All round.'

'I accept what you say,' his neophyte sighed. 'It is most troubling.'

The monsignor quietly refilled his glass, wondering a little whether his pupil had some extra reason to be troubled.

He had. By now he was also receiving intermittent instruction from Anna, and on these occasions the tender feelings that she aroused in him were at times more than he could control. On one such occasion, looking up at her pink canopy, he said to her, 'Poor Anna! I can see now why you used sometimes to cry. It was a sin.' She smiled her curl-smile and whispered, 'But, sure, it no longer is.'

'Anna! We must not deceive ourselves. We're not married yet, ye know.'

'We are married in the sight of God,' she said and scratched him a little. 'The Church will bless us.'

'The Church must bless us first.'

'Ah, but sure,' she wheedled, 'it's so much nicer before.'

'It will be much, much nicer when you will lawfully be mine before man and God.'

'Darling!' she cried, and scratched wickedly. 'Don't be a bore! Are you a lawyer or a lover?'

'But the monsignor says . . .'

At this she flew into a rage.

'For Heaven's sake, who are you marrying? Me or the monsignor?'

He forbore to reply. He was troubled, and not for the first time, by the thought, 'Is she in more need of instruction than me?' This, however, was something that, in delicacy, he could not broach to her, or, in loyalty, to the monsignor – unless he might, perhaps, act as a go-between?

'Monsignor! I have one last question. To revert once more to my old problem, I do see, now, that I have indeed been guilty of a grave sin. I no longer contest it. It is undeniable. I cannot understand how I ever doubted it. But, supposing I had lain not with a married woman but with an unmarried woman, may I ask, is it in that case permissible for either party to feel just a little bit less guilty?'

'In such a hypothetical case,' his friend said dryly, 'either party would merely have been breaking one commandment at a time.'

'How stupid of me! How is it that everything becomes so simple when you explain it?'

The occasion to relay the consequences of his question was not long in coming. Under the canopy, he gently pointed out to Anna that they would both have to confess all this sooner or later, as one sin on her part, of two on his. She declared at once and with passion, that she had no intention of doing anything of the sort.

'Do you think,' she cried, drawing blood from him this time, 'that I am going to spoil all our years and years of love by saying now that they were beastly and horrible?' Then seeing in his terrified horse-eyes how deeply she had shocked him, she added, easily, 'One could of course go through the *formality*.'

'Of course!' he agreed, profoundly relieved to find that she really was, after all, a Catholic. She went on :

'Why not? One will say that one has transgressed! That's it. Transgressed. To pass over. To step beyond. Beyond the red line. A little.'

'Indeed,' he agreed happily, 'so we will! I'm so relieved! I'm so glad!'

'But, sure, Frank we'll know in our hearts, of course, that we didn't really do anything very bad at all!'

'But my dear Anna, there is the law! *Thou shalt not commit adultery.*'

At this she sat up, seized him by the hair and shook him like a dog.

'Are you calling me an adulteress?'

He sat up, waved his arms despairingly and wailed at her.

'My darling! I sit in judgement on nobody. But,' he said miserably. 'I *have* been an adulterer.'

She stroked his moustaches and kissed him tenderly.

'Not really, darling. That's just an odd afterthought you are having now. You were as innocent as a child at the time.'

He sank back and rolled his tousled head sadly on the pillow.

'I'm such a simple sort of chap, Anna, and it's all such a simple thing, and I understand it so simply, and I do wish that you didn't make it all so damned complicated.'

She laughed and laughed.

'I make it complicated? It is I who am simple about it – your new friends who are tying everything up in knots with their laws, and rules, and regulations, and definitions, and sub-definitions that nobody can make head or tail of. I was brought up on all that stuff. I know it. You don't. They are at it all the time. So many ounces you may eat during Lent in France, so many in Spain. You can't eat meat on Fridays but it's no harm to eat frogs, and snakes and snails. I suppose you could even eat tripe! How much interest may one businessman draw on his deal. How much may another draw on another. Do you think anybody can really measure things like that? A baby who dies without being baptised must go to some place called Limbo that nobody ever knew what it is or in what corner of creation to put it. All that stuff has nothing to do with religion. How could it? Do you know that Saint Augustine said that all unbaptised children are condemned to suffer in eternal fire? Is *that* religion?'

'Are you sure Saint Augustine said this?'

'I was educated in Lausanne,' she said proudly. 'It's the home of Saint Augustine. All those stinking Calvinists.' She began to sob into the pillow. 'I wish I'd never asked you to become a Catholic. I wouldn't have if I knew you were going to take it as seriously as all this.'

'Don't cry, my daffodil! In a few months it will be over and we will never need to talk of these terrible things again.'

She flew at once into a state of total happiness; she clapped her hands gaily.

'Oh, what fun it will be! In a couple of months you will be my loving husband. We'll be welcomed by everybody with open arms, we'll be known as the greatest lovers in all Ireland, the women will envy me and the men will smile at you and clap you on the back. I can't wait for it.'

'God speed the day when I shall at last be received.'

'And I shall be married!'

For six days and six nights he kept away from the monsignor, thinking of all those millions of babies burning in eternal fire, until his whole soul felt beaten all over by devils armed with sticks, and shovels, and red-hot tongs. On the seventh night he invited the monsignor to dinner. Like a good host he kept from his troubles until the port passed. Then, unsteadily, he said, 'Monsignor, I have another question, a small, tiny little problem. Tell me, where is Limbo?'

The old man paused in the act of raising his glass to his lips and looked at him apprehensively. He had dealt with Transubstantiation, Miracles, the Resurrection, Indulgences, Galileo, the Virgin Birth, the Immaculate Conception, Grace, Predestination, the Will, Mixed Marriages, even Adultery. These great mysteries and problems had presented no lasting difficulty either to him or to his dear friend. But Limbo? He knew from long experience how easily the small things, rather than the big ones, can shatter a man's faith.

'Why did you ask me that question?' he said sadly.

'It just occurred to me,' the major said loyally, and curled a little at his lack of frankness to his friend.

'I see!'

'Is it true, monsignor, as I have read, that Saint Augustine said that all babies who have not been baptised must burn in eternal fire?'

With a whole movement of his arm the monsignor pushed his glass slowly to one side. His night was in ruins.

'I believe so,' he said, and thrust gallantly on. 'Still, there are other and more benignant views. It all arose, I presume, out of the problem of where to place those unbaptised souls who died before Christ, and those others who died after Him without ever hearing of Him. I believe it was the Council of Florence that decreed it.' He faltered. 'It was a rather confused Council. So confused that I gather that its Acts have perished. It laid down, it was in the fifteenth century, that nobody who is unbaptised may enter heaven. Since then many thinkers have, in their mercy, felt a repugnance to the idea. Many theologians have sought out ways of accepting the doctrine while, as you might say, circumventing, or anyway softening, its melancholy implications. Major! Do you really want me to go into this matter of Limbo? It is not a primal question.'

'It bothers me, monsignor.'

'I see. Well, I do know that one Italian theologian, whose name escapes me at the moment, felt that God might instruct the angels to confer baptism on those children – who might otherwise perish without it. Another theologian felt that the sincere wish of the parent that the child might have been baptised could be a fair equivalent. Saint Thomas felt, humanely, that those children suffer no pain of the body, although they must, indeed, always grieve that they can never see God. Just as a bird, or a mouse, might grieve that it can never be a man, or speak to an emperor or king.'

'How sad!'

'Of course, Major,' the monsignor whispered, 'we have to recognise that we have no purely human right to Heaven. Heaven is a gift. God could, without injustice, deny it to us. I suggest it was originally a rabbinical idea.'

The priest looked into the glowing ashes of the fire. The major looked out at the darkness of the night. Through the open window the invisible fields sent in the sweetness of the May-blossom. After a long while the monsignor said, 'There are many mysteries in life that we have to accept in humility without understanding them. Indeed, it is because we do not understand the mystery that we do accept it – and live with it.'

As he drove away the major watched the beams of his car until they touched the last of his yews, and stood there until the smell of his petrol faded in the pure air. He walked up and down his avenue many times. Afterwards he sat before his dying fire until sleep came to him, where he slouched by its ashes.

It was quite early, a bird-singing May morning, gleaming after a light shower of rain, when he faced her fresh and handsome, break-fasting beside her cheerful morning fire. He said firmly, 'Anna, I can never become a Catholic.'

Her cup clattered into its saucer.

'But, Frank, you must! Do you expect me to marry you like a Protestant in a registry office? Or to live with you for the rest of my life with you in what you now think of as a cesspool of sin?'

'I am proposing nothing. I can think of nothing. It is just that I am too old, or too stupid, to be able to follow you both.'

'You just want to be shut of me.' She raised her tear-filled eyes. 'Or is it that it is I who am too old and too stupid? Why can't you be as I am? After all I am a Catholic!'

'I have sometimes wondered, Anna, what you are.'

Her fury burst about him like shrapnel. She dashed down *The Irish Times*.

'How dare you? Of course I am a Catholic. What's wrong with you is that you want everything to be perfect. As clean, and bare and tidy as a barrack square. That's it! All you are is a bloody English major who wants everybody's buttons to be polished and every-body's cap to be as straight as a plate.'

'But it wasn't I who raised the question of Limbo!'

'To hell with Limbo! If there is a hell! Or a Limbo! What's

wrong with you is you're too conceited. You want to cross every I
and dot every T. Why do you want to understand everything? Why
can't you just accept things the way I do?'

'Do you accept Limbo?'

'I never think about Limbo. I never think about stupid things like
that. I think only of God, and the stars, and of Heaven, and of love,
and of you.'

'You put me to a great test, Anna. As the monsignor says I must
also think of the cross and the nails. Just as he says that in love the
soul and the body are one.'

'You're a liar! All this is just a cute device to get out of marrying
me. I see through you. I see through your cheap trickery. I see
through your dirty Saxon guile. If you were the last man on earth
this minute, Frank Keene, I wouldn't marry you now. Please don't
come near me ever again!'

She swept out and crashed the door. He retrieved *The Irish Times*
from the fire, beat out its flames and went away.

He had no one left to talk to. He had pestered the monsignor
beyond endurance. He had never attended the Church of Ireland.
Anyway he doubted if they knew very much about Limbo or the
Council of Naples. Mabel Tallant would only laugh at him. He had
devoted so many years of his life to Anna that he had made no
friends. And now she neither loved him nor respected him, and he
did not... He crushed down the bleak admission.

After three weeks of the blackest misery, he dashed off a letter:

Monseigneur, Mon General, Mon ami,
    If I may be allowed to declare my belief in things that I do not
understand and to accept in humility things that I do not approve
I am ready, at your command, to take Mount Sion, even unaccom-
panied by your Alsatian bitch. Give me your order. I will obey.

> Your obedient servant,
> Francis Lancelot Keene,
> Major,
> LRCPE and LM,
> Late RAMC,
> Dunkirk, Tunisia, Libya, Egypt, Italy,
> Dispatches, medal and clasp, DSO,
> 1940–1945.
> Retired.

The reply came by telegram the next day. At the sight of the single word of command a sudden rage boiled up in him. Who did he think he was? A bloody general? One man? And no dog? Against an army of doubts...

He chose July 9th for it, the feast day of two English saints, John Fisher, bishop, and Thomas More, chancellor, both martyrs.

It was raining as he entered the presbytery. In the monsignor's parlour the old Alsatian half looked up at him and sank back into its doze. The two men walked silently across to the church where the monsignor invested himself in his surplice and stole, and the major knelt by the rails of a side-chapel, feeling nothing whatsoever as he repeated the words of recantation and of belief. They then retired to the presbytery where the major knelt by the monsignor's chair for his first confession. During the previous days he had been girding himself for his complete life-story. The monsignor truncated even that piece of the ceremony, saying, 'I imagine I know it all. Women, and drink, and I suppose swearing like a trooper. Unless there is some special sin of your past life that you want to mention'

Humbly the major said, 'Sloth,' and got a faint satisfaction from the painful admission.

Then sunshine flooded his heart when the monsignor told him that his penance would be to say, that night, three Ave Marias.

'So little? After so long?'

'God loves you,' the monsignor said, and bade him to say his Act of Contrition.

The major's eyes filled with tears as he heard the murmuring words of absolution mingle with his own. The monsignor then raised him to his feet and warmly shook both his hands.

'My dear friend in Christ. Now you are one of us. Do your best. In the bosom of the Church. And,' briskly removing his vestments, 'let's go back now and have a good dollop of malt.'

Over the glass the major said happily, 'I was afraid I was going to feel nothing at all. Wouldn't that have been awful?'

'My dear Frank, we are strange cattle. Often, even when I say Mass, I don't feel that it is doing me a bit of good. But I know it is, so I don't worry. The heart may be the centre of all things but in the end it's not our feelings that matter but our good works. As you and I know well, more men go weak in battle from feeling too much than from feeling too little.' He chuckled. 'I remember one time we had a Colonel Home-Crean in the Inniskillings who was always carrying on about the martial spirit. He meant well. But the troops called him Old Carry On. It wasn't a bad pun, because whenever he finished one of his speeches he always said, "Carry on, Sergeant." '

The major laughed wryly. 'Pass the buck.'

'I say it still. I say it now, Frank, to you.'

He tore back at sixty miles an hour to Culadrum to meet her, singing all the way at the top of his voice 'When the Saints go marching in'. There was a shower, the sun ebbed and flowed, and 'Blow me,' he cheered, 'if they haven't sent me a rainbow!' He hooted his horn along her drive, and there she was running down the steps on to the gravel to embrace him.

' 'Tis done,' he laughed, and she said, 'You look about seventeen!'

'God loves me!' he said.

'Did you fix up about the marriage?'

'Good Lord! I forgot all about it!'

'You immense dope!' she laughed. 'That was the whole point. Go back tonight and fix it. And do remember – the tenth of August. We've got all the tickets, darling! Promise?'

'You're still sure it's not a bit too soon? I mean that people may think that . . .'

She laughed triumphantly.

'I want them to think! I'll blame it all on my impetuous lover. And, now, you must come and see my new dresses and hats, a whole crateful of them came this morning from Dublin.'

She took him by the hand, and galloped him upstairs to her room's litter of hillocked tissue and coloured cardboard boxes.

'Sit there. And don't dare stir.' She tore off her frock; he sat and beamed at her, in her panties and bra, circling, preening, glaring in the long mirror at herself in pale toques, straw-hats in white, in mauve, in liver-pink, and he was so happy at her childish happiness that for a moment he was terrified that she would next want him to go to bed with her. Thank heaven, she was too excited to think about it. Once as she posed a pale-blue pillbox on the back of her poll, saying, 'Or this one?' he wondered whether she had gone, or when she would go to Confession, and decided that he would not press her about it just now. Perhaps never at all.

They were married before a large congregation in the cathedral. He recognised many whom he had seen six months before at the funeral. He felt a bit self-conscious about his age, and hers, and several times, when it was over, he had to stop himself from interpreting their broad smiles and their hearty congratulations. Still, whether confetti-speckled in his grey topper and tails outside the church door, or mingling with the crowd in his new pin-stripe at the champagne reception in the Royal Hotel, he felt he had carried it all off like a soldier and a gentleman, talking now with the Inspector about tinkers, now with a very serious young librarian about the publications of the Irish Manuscripts Commission, now with Mulcahy the chemist, about the 'extraordinary' number of women in the town who took barbiturates for 'the narves', or listening in polite astonishment to a curate whom he had never met before weighing the comparative merits of President Salazar and General Franco. Then they were in his car driving off amid huzzas and laughter, down along the Main Street, out into the country for Dublin, for London and Lausanne. They were both tipsy, She was weeping softly. He filled with pity and love.

'You're not upset, darling?'

'It's just my nerves,' she smiled bravely, took a pill from her bag, and was soon chortling once more.

Everything turned out afterwards just as she had foretold. They set up house together in Culadrum. All her old friends, and her late husband's friends, came often and regularly to visit them. They played bridge with them at least twice a week. In the season he hunted three times a week. He took complete charge of her garden. He developed an interest in local archaeology. She was entirely happy, scratched him no longer and wept no more. He enjoyed all the quiet self-satisfaction of a man who, at some cost to himself, has done the right thing and found everything turning out splendidly. As he marched the roads erect, chest out, with his stick and his dog, he was admired, liked and envied by all.

Winter came. The rains and the barometer fell. She began to make excuses about going to Mass on account of the awful weather and her health. At first he found, to his regret, that he was often going to Mass alone. Then he found that he was always going alone. He began to wonder at this, ask questions about it, become testy about it, and at last they argued crossly over it every Sunday morning. There were long silences because of it. Once a whole week passed without a word spoken. He finally realised that she had no interest at all in religion, and had never had. There he felt a great hole opening in his belly, crawling like fear, recurrent as a fever, painful as betrayal, until he could no longer bear his misery alone.

'But, monsignor,' he wailed, 'why did the woman insist on my becoming a Catholic if she doesn't believe in it herself? Why in God's name did she do this to me?'

His friend did not hesitate – he never had hesitated.

'Superstition. Fear perhaps? She has memories of childhood. Of the dark. The thin red line that may not be crossed.'

'But we crossed it over and over again, for years!'

'That was not for ever.'

'Could we not have had a mixed marriage?'

'It could have been managed. Somehow. Somewhere. She wanted the Real Thing. The laying on of hands. The propitiation. The magic touch. I suspect, Frank, that your wife is a very simple woman. We have millions of them in the Church. Full of what I call ignorant innocence. They don't do much harm to anybody, except themselves. Or if they become vain, or proud, or we press them too hard, then they turn on us like a knife. Don't force her. You have a problem. You took a chance and now you must find some way of living with it, in faith, and courage and trust. Just remember that your wife is a little vain, rather spoiled I imagine, possibly a trifle conceited, too. And, or so I feel, very unsure of herself. Hence her superstition. African missionaries tell me that they are very familiar with it.'

The major stared at him, containing the urge to say, 'Why the hell didn't you tell me all this before?'

'And what is my superstition?' he asked curtly.

'You are different. You worked your passage. Only . . .'

Here he did hesitate.

'Only?'

'Only do not expect miracles. You may, of course, pray for one. I suppose it is what we all pray for really.'

He took to going to early Mass every morning, much to her annoyance because no matter how quietly he stole out of her bed she always woke up, turning over and muttering things like, 'For God's sake isn't Sunday enough for you?' or 'My nerves are shot to bits with you and your blooming piety!' By Christmas he had taken to sleeping alone. By February he was praying for the gift of silence and drinking like a fish. In spite of that he had lost eleven pounds weight by March and was thinking of running away to Malaysia. By April he could no longer keep his food down. And then their war suddenly ended, in an explosion of light. He had gone out one morning into her walled garden to jab, stoically, at the grass and the pearlwort between the cracks of her crazy-pavement. The night had been a blur of wet trees; now a skyload of sun warmed his stooped back. He smelled the cosseted earth, glanced at her ancient espaliers, became aware of a thrush's throat, blackbirds skirling, the chaffinches' in-and-out, the powerful robin, two loving tits that flicked into the gleaming cloud of an old cherry tree propped over his head. As he picked on and on, patiently and humbly, his memory slowly expanded in widening circles out to the covert of Easter Hill, out beyond the furze-yellow slopes of the Stameen river, away out after that great wheeling run of a month ago across the reedy plain, past its fallen dolmen and its ruined abbey, losing the scent, finding it again, five glorious nonstop, hammering miles of it. As he shifted the kneeler he noticed the first tiny bells of her white rhododendron. Christ was risen. Steaming roads stretched like wet rulers across the bog, past a pub, a garage, a grey National School, under a procession of elms against a foam-bath of clouds. At his toe he saw a blue eggshell.

At that moment a window in the house was lifted. Looking up, he saw her, in her pink morning-dress, leaning on the sill with both hands, staring over the countryside. He had a vision and in a flash it burst on him that everything she saw and he remembered came out of one eggshell. She waved to him, casually. He waved back wildly with his weeder. She retired.

'Monsignor! It was something that could only happen in Lourdes! How right you were! Never force things. Change and expand. Move slowly. Live with your problems. There are no laws for hard cases. Trust and courage solves everything. And, as you say, most of those laws are just so many old-fashioned rabbinical ideas. And the decrees of the Councils all lost! Heaven is a gift. The heart is the centre. Carry on. We can only all do our best. God loves us. Not a single cross word for two weeks! Everything absolutely ticketyboo. Monsignor, you should be a cardinal!'

They had met in the street. The old man had heard him impassively. Leaning forward on his umbrella he lifted his head from his toes for one quick glance, almost it occurred to the major in his excitement, as if he were not a cardinal but an African missionary.

'You say nothing?' he asked anxiously.

'I was just thinking, Frank. An odd thing! When we were in the

Connaught Rangers we never said "Ticketyboo". What we used to say was "All kiff!" Hindustani, do you suppose? That's good news.' He shook hands limply, turned to go, turned back, said, 'Carry on, Frank,' and went on his slow way down the street, followed by his friend's wide-eyed stare of puzzlement, annoyance, affection and undiminished admiration. Two days later he attended his funeral. It was a damp day, and it did not do his rheumatism any good.

The next morning was a Sunday. The storm woke him. Through the corner of his blind he saw spilling rain, waving treetops and Noreen the maid, wrapped up in yellow cellophane like a lifeboat captain, wobbling on her bicycle down the avenue to Mass. He felt a twinge in his shoulder. He said, 'Well, I was at Mass yesterday,' lay back and dozed for an hour. He heard the soft boom of the breakfast gong, and Anna's door open and close. As he went downstairs in his dressing-gown he smelled bacon and coffee. She was sitting by the breakfast table in her morning-gown. The fire blazed cosily. 'Good morning, love,' he said and kissed her forehead.

'Are you going out?' she asked and looked at the over-spilling gutters dropping great glass beads of water past the window.

'Arthritis,' he said sheepishly.

'Why, in God's name,' she groaned, 'do we live in this climate?'

'We live where we are fated to live, in the bosom of the country,' and he lifted the chased lid of the breakfast dish.

She frowned. They munched silently. To cheer her he suggested that they might go to Italy in May, to Venice, to Rome, and he began to plan how they could go and what they could see there together. Far away a church bell tolled, on the wet wind, like a bell for the dead. He went on talking very gaily, very rapidly, very loudly. She smiled her curl-smile and said, 'Why not Lausanne?'

'Indeed, indeed! Anywhere! To get away!'

The Heat of the Sun

They never said, 'Let's go down to Rodgers',' although it was old
Rodgers who owned the pub; they said, 'Let's go down to Uncle
Alfie.' A good pub is like that, it is the barman who makes it, not
the boss. They gave their custom to Rodgers, they gave their con-
fidence to Alfie. He knew them all, some of them ever since they
were old enough to drink their first pint in a pub. He knew their
fathers, mothers, brothers, sisters, girls, prospects, wages, hopes,
fears and what they were always calling their ideas and their ideals
and that he called their ould guff. Always their friend, sometimes
their philosopher, he was rarely their guide. Your da gave you
money (sometimes) and you hardly thanked him for it. Alfie loaned
it. Your da gave you advice and you resented it. Alfie could give you
a rap as sharp as lightning, and you accepted it because he gave it as
your equal. Your da never had any news. Alfie knew everything. He
was your postman, passing on bits of paper with messages in pencil :
'Deirdre was asking after you, try 803222, Hughesy.' Or, 'For Jay's
sake leave a half-note for me, Paddywhack.' He might hand you out
a coloured postcard with a foreign stamp, taken from the little
sheaf stuck behind the cash register. The sheeting around the register
was as wall-papered as a Travel Bureau with coloured postcards from
all over the word. Best of all, he was there always : his coat off, his
shirtsleeves rolled up, his bowler hat always on his balding red head,
a monument in a white apron, with a brogue like an echo in an
empty barrel.

You pushed the two glass doors in like a king.

'Hi, Alfie !'

'Jakus, Johnny, is that yourself?' With a slap on the shoulder and
your drink slid in front of you unasked. 'Fwhere were you this time?
Did yoo have a good voyage?'

'Not bad. Same old thing – Black Sea, the Piraeus, Palermo, Naples,
Genoa. Crumby dumps !' Your half pint aloft. 'What's the best port
in all creation, Alfie?'

'As if yoo needed to ask me !'

'Here's to it, and God bless it. *Dublin town, O Dublin town/That's where I long to be,/With the friends so dear to me,/Grafton Street where it's all so gay./And the lights of Scotsman's Bay.* Theme-song of every poor bloody exile of Erin. Up the rebels. Long live the Queen of Sheba. How's Tommy? How's Angela? How's Casey. Joanna, Hughesy, Paddywhack? Does my little black-eyed Deirdre still love me?'

'Paddy was in on Chuesday night. He's working with the Gas Company now.'

'Poor old Paddywhack? Has he the gold wristlet still? And the signet ring? Will the poor bugger never get a decent job?'

'His wife had another child. That's six he has now.'

'Sacred Heart!'

'Hughesy is going strong with Flossie.'

(He noticed that Deirdre was being passed over.)

'Sure that line is four years old. When is the bastard going to make an honest woman of her?'

'Is it a busman? She's aiming higher than that. The trouble with yoo young fellows is ye pick gurls beyond yeer means. Yeer eyes are bigger than yeer balls. Leave them their youth. Wedded, bedded and deaded, the world knows it.'

He was anti-woman. Everybody knew he had a wife somewhere, and three kids, separated five years ago. She was before their time – none of them had ever seen her. Poor old Alfie! In hope and in dreams and in insecurity is life. In home and in safety is . . . He should know, he had it every time he came home. Like tonight:

'Oh, no! Johnny! You're not going out from us on your first night home? We haven't seen you for four months! And your father and me looking forward to a nice bit of a chat. About your future, Johnny. About your plans, Johnny. About your prospects. Sit down there now and be talking to us.'

You sat back. They talked. You mumbled. The end of it was always the same. After another half-hour of twitching you said it again.

'I think I'll drop down to Uncle Alfie for an hour to see the boys. I won't be late, Mum. But leave the key under the mat. Don't wait up for me, I'll creep in like a mouse.'

Hating the way they looked at one another, knowing well that you wouldn't be in before one in the morning – if then – shoes in hand, head cocked for the slightest tweak of a bedspring upstairs, feeling a right bastard or, if with God's help, you were tight enough, feeling nothing but your way. Hell roast 'em! Why couldn't they understand that when you cabled, 'Coming home Thursday stop love stop Johnny,' it meant you wanted to see them okay, and you were bringing presents for them, okay, and it would be nice to have your own old room, okay, but what you were really seeing was the gleam of bottles, and the wet mahogany, and the slow, floating layers of smoke, shoulders pushing, hands shooting, everybody talking at the top of his voice to be heard and old Alfie grinning at ye all like an ape. God Almighty! When a fellow has only seven lousy days shore leave ...

It was dry October, the softest twinge of faintest fog, the streets empty, a halo around every light, a right night for a landfall. Tramping downhill, peaked cap slanted, whistling, he foresaw it all. A dollar to a dime on it – Alfie would resume exactly where they left off four months ago :

'Johnny! It is high time yoo thought of settling down.'

'Gimme a chance, Alfie, I'm only twenty-three. I'll settle down some day. Why don't you say that to Loftus or Casey?'

'Loftus will find it hard. With that short leg. Anyway I mean settle down ashore. That wandering life you're leading! It's no life!'

'I'm not ready, Alfie. I want to meet the right girl. I'm mad about Deirdre, but she's always talking about motor-cars, and houses in Foxrock, and Sunday morning sherry parties. I'm not sure of her. The right girl is damn hard to find. It's a funny thing, Alfie, all the nice women I meet are married women.'

'An ould shtory. And the ladies tell me all the nice men are married men. I think the truth is that no wan is ready until they know by heart the music that tames the wild bashte – know it and are beginning to forget it. I don't think Deirdre is the right sawrt for you at all, Johnny. She's too expensive for you. She's too ambitious. She's like Flossie – playing with Hughesy, trying to learn the chune on the cheap, as you might say. Johnny! If I were you, I'd choose a woman of experience. What'd suit you, now, down to the ground would be a nice, soft, cosy, widow-woman that knows every chune in the piper's bag.'

'Oh, for God's sake, Alfie! With a wooden leg? And a yellow wig? And a blue bank-book? I'm young, Alfie. What I dream about, in the middle watch, looking up at the stars, is a young, beautiful, exquisite, lovely, fond, right-dimensional Irish girl of eighteen. Like my little Deirdre. Pure as the driven snow. Loyal and true. Gentle as the dawn. Deirdre, without the motor-car!'

Alfie would draw up from the counter and make a face as if he was sucking alum.

'Yoo could sing it if yoo had the voice for it. *"She was luvely and fair, as the roase of the Summer, But it was not her beauutye aloane tha-at won me..."* '

He would snatch it from him tonight:

' *"Oh no! 'Twas the truth in her eyes ever dawning, That made me love Mary, the Rose of Tra-a-leee."* A hundred per cent right, Alfie. Lead me to her.'

'I wouldn't give you two pinnies for a gurl of eighteen – she couldn't cook an egg for you. And dimensions are all very fine and dandy, but they don't lasht, boy. They don't lasht! Did I ever tell yoo about the fellow that married the opera singer? She was like an angel out of heaven on the stage. In the bed she was no better to him than an ould shweeping brush. He used to wake her up in the middle of the night and say, "Sing, damn yoor sowl!" '

Aboard ship he had told them that one many times. Always the old deck-hands would nod solemnly and say, 'And e's dead right, chum! Feed me and love me, what more can a man ask for?' Well, if he said it tonight he would be ready for him; drawing himself up, with one hand flat on his top, left, brass button:

'Alfie! In this rotten, cheating, stinking, lousy, modern world my generation is going to *fight* for our ideals!'

Four miles out over the shadow sea the light on the Kish bank winked drowsily. Fog? It was so quiet along the promenade that he could hear the small waves below him sucking into the rocks. Wind soft from the south. The only person he passed was a Civic Guard in a cape. He turned right, then left, passed the Coal Harbour, wheeled right again, left, and there were the lights flowing out on the pavement. He pushed the two glass doors in like a king.

'Hi! ...'

He stopped. The young barman was staring at him with uplifted eyebrows. He looked around. The place was like a morgue. He recognised old Molly Goosegog, her fat legs spread, soaking it up as usual with the one-armed colonel. Three business types, their hats on, hunched over a table, talking low. In the farthest corner two middle-aged women were drinking gins and bitters. Dyed, dried, skewered and skivered, two old boiling hens, cigarettes dangled from their red beaks. He moved slowly to the counter.

'Where's Alfie?' he asked quietly.

'On leave.'

'Alfie never took leave in his life unless he took leave of his senses.'

'Well, he's on leave now. What can I get you, sir?'

Sir! Sullenly he said, 'A large whiskey,' although he had been planning a night of draught porter. Alfie would have said, 'Johnny! There is no such thing on earth as a *large* whiskey.' Or he might have said nothing but come back with a half pint of draught and said, 'That'll be better for you.'

Was it because it was Thursday night? Nobody much ever came on Thursday night: less even than came on Friday night. Everyone stony. Behold my beeves and fatlings are all killed, and nobody cometh to eat them. Seven lousy nights and the first a flop? Go forth into the highways and by-ways. From pub to pub? The whiskey appeared before him. The barman stood waiting. He looked up.

'Four and sixpence, sir.'

With Alfie, you let it run for a week, for two, for three, for as long as you liked. Then you asked, 'What's on the slate, Alfie?' and, if you were flush, you paid a half-note over and above for future credit. Man knoweth not the hour nor the night. He paid out four shillings and a sixpenny bit. The barman rang it up and retired down the counter to lean over his *Herald*.

'How long is Alfie going to be on leave?'

The fellow barely glanced up.

'I don't know, I'm only here this past two weeks.'

'Is the boss in?'

'He's gone down to the chapel. The October Devotions.'

Thinking of his latter end. *Dies irae, dies illae.* Back in Newbridge with the Dominicans. All Souls Night. He glanced at the door. Would there be anyone down at The Blue Peter? Or in Mooney's? Maybe in The Purty Kitchen?

'Any message for me there behind the old cashbox?'

'Name?'

'Kendrick.'

The barman, his back to him, went through the light sheaf. Without turning he said, 'Nothing,' shoved it back and returned to his *Herald*. Out of sight out of mind. Bugger the whole lousy lot of them! And Deirdre along with them! The glass doors swished open and there were Paddywhack and Loftus. He leaped from his stool.

'Hi, scouts!'

'Johnny!'

Handshakes all round. Paddy was as hungry-looking as a displaced Arab. His shirtsleeves too long. The gold wristlet. The signet ring. Loftus, as always, as lean and yellow as a Dane. Hoppity Loftus with his short leg. He never worked. He was a Prod and had an English accent, and he lived off his mother. All he did was to get her breakfast in the morning and have her supper ready for her at night. She worked in the Sweep.

'Name it, boys! I'm standing!'

Paddy looked thirstily at the glass of whiskey.

'Are you on the hard tack?'

'Naw! Just this bloody place gave me the willies. The usual?' He commanded the barman. 'Two halfpints. Make it three and I'll use this as a chaser. God, it's marvellous to see ye! Come on, come on! Give! Give! Gimme all the dirt. Tell me more, tell me all. Are you still with the Gas Company, Paddy?'

'I'm with a house-agent now. Looney and Cassidy. In Dame Street.' He made a fish-face. 'NBG Paid on commission. Just to tide me over a bad patch.' He laughed cheerfully. 'The wife is preggers again.'

'Paddy! I dunno how you do it.'

'I'm told,' said Loftus lightly, 'that it's a very simple matter, really.'

'How's your mother, Loftus?'

A rude question. Loftus shrugged it away. They took their drinks to one of the round tables. Paddy lifted his glass.

'Johnny! You don't know how lucky you are. A steady job, cash in your pocket, a girl in every port.'

'And as brown,' said Loftus lifting his glass, 'and as round as a football.'

'Me round?' he shouted, ripped open the jacket of his uniform and banged his narrow waist. 'Feel that, go on, feel it! Hard as iron, boy! Eight stone ten. You,' he said condescendingly, rebuttoning, 'must be about ten stone eight.' He paused. Then he had to say it: Does Deirdre still love me?'

Loftus's eyes glinted as he proffered the sponge on the spear.

'I saw her two weeks ago in a red Triumph. A medical student from Trinity, I believe. She looked smashing.'

His heart curdled, his throat tightened, he laughed loudly.

'So the little bitch is betraying me, eh?'

He could see her, with her dark hair curled down on one shoulder as if she had a monkey on her head. The red lips. The high bosoms.

'It's just because you're not around much,' Paddy said comfortingly. 'Wait until she hears you're home.'

'How are all those girls of yours?' Loftus smiled. 'In foreign ports.'

Paddy poured sad oil.

'Too bad about poor Alfie?'

'I heard nothing,' he said sourly. 'Nobody writes to me. Where *is* the ould devil?'

'You didn't know! Hospice for the Dying. Cancer. These last three months. It'll be any day now.'

It gagged him. There was a long silence. His first death. The double doors let in Hughesy and Flossie; their oldest and youngest – a blonde mop, black lashes, a good looker, but not a patch on his D. Their welcomes were muted. They sat down stiffly like people who did not mean to stay.

' "Here," ' he chanted mournfully, ' "here, the gang's all here." '

'Not all of us,' Paddy said.

'This is a committee meeting, really,' Hughesy said, taking charge of it at once. 'Well?' he asked Paddywhack and Loftus. 'How much can we raise?'

'We're gathering for Mrs Alfie,' Paddywhack explained. 'She hadn't a sou.'

'I managed to borrow five bob,' Flossie said, taking two half-crowns from inside her glove and laying them on the table.

'That,' said Hughesy, putting down half a crown, 'is all I can manage.'

Paddywhack squirmed and said, 'Six kids and another coming, and Thursday night.'

Loftus showed empty palms. 'Unless I could pop something?'

He felt worse than a wanderer – a stranger.

'Mrs Alfie? How in God's name did ye meet *her*?' he asked Hughesy.

'It was Alfie asked us to keep an eye on her and the kids. I saw him again today,' he told the others.

'How is he?' he asked.

Hughesy looked away.

'Alas, poor Yorick,' Loftus said. 'A skull!'

Flossie began to cry.

'But where's the rest of the gang? Joanna, and Tommy, and Angela and Casey.'

He stopped short of Deirdre. Paddywhack shook his head and made faint gestures.

'I nearly didn't come myself. Can you manage anything, Johnny?'

He took out his pocketbook and planked down a pound note.

'Good man!' said Hughesy, and looked up at the barman standing over them, and down at the pound note. He smiled apologetically at Johnny. 'Any more of that nice stuff?'

'Come on, scouts. I'm standing. If it's to be a wake, for Christ's sake let it be a wake. What's yours, Flossie? Still sticking to the dry sherry? Hughesy? The old pint?' He nodded to the barman, who departed silently. 'Let me in on this. Tell me all about Alfie.'

As the drinks warmed them they talked. A man, by God! A true friend if there ever was one. They don't often come like that nowadays. True from his bald head to the soles of his feet. Tried and true. A son of the soil. A bit of old Ireland. Vanishing down the drain. Not one bit of cod about him. His jokes . . . We shall not look upon his like again. The pound note melted. Paddywhack said, 'Life is a mystery all right. She looks such a nice woman, and she *is* a nice woman, and full of guts, not one word of complaint, and three kids. What in God's name happened to them?' They told him, asking how she lived, that she used to work as a dressmaker. 'Yes, he did!' Loftus answered him. 'After a fashion, he did. He supported her. After a fashion.' Flossie said she would never come to this pub again. They agreed with Hughesy that Dublin wouldn't be the same without him. She said the fact was he had nothing to do with all those . . . They followed her eyes down to Molly Goosegog and the one-armed colonel, and the three business types, and the two boiled hakes with the gins and bitters. Hughesy slapped the table. 'And that's a true bill, Flossie! He was one of us. Old in body but young in heart. You agree, Johnny?' He agreed that Alfie was the only man he ever met who understood them. 'He fought for his ideals.' They talked of understanding, and ideals, and truth, and true love, and how well Alfie understood what it means to be young, and to believe in things, that was it – to believe in things. A second pound was melting, and it was after ten when Flossie said to Hughesy that she must go home soon.

'Mind your few quid, Johnny,' Hughesy said. 'What's left there will be enough. A dozen bottles of stout, say a dozen and a half. Just to cheer her up. We'll drop around for a minute, Flossie. Just to cheer her up.'

'One for the road,' he insisted, and held them. They leaned back.

It was nearly eleven when they left in a bunch, carrying the three brown-paper bags of stout, out into the dry streets, the nebulous night, under the dim stars and the gathering clouds that were lit by the city's glow. Loftus said it was a fine night for a ramble. Hughesy laughed and said, 'Or for courting.' Two by two, hooting merrily backwards and forwards at one another, they wound up among shaggy dim-lit squares with names like Albert Gardens,

Aldershot Place or Portland Square, all marked on green and white tablets in Irish and English, until they came to a basement door and, stepping down to it, rang and waited in a bunch under a stone arch. In the dark they were suddenly silent, listening. A light went on over the door. She opened it.

Alfie's youth. She was soft and welcoming. All the parts of her face seemed to be running into one another, dissolving like ice-cream in the sun, her mouth melting, her blue-blue eyes swimming. A loose tress of her grey-fair hair flowed over a high forehead. Her voice was as timid as butter. She was not a bad-looking woman, and for a moment a little flame of youth flared up in her when they introduced him to her, and she laughed softly and said, 'So this is Johnny! He said you were the baby of the lot.' She held his hand in her two hands, moist and warm as if she had been washing some-time, and he remembered a line from a poem they used to read at school, long forgotten, never understood. *Fear no more the heat of the sun* . . .

'Glad to meet you, Mrs Alfie,' he said and realised for the first time that he did not know Alfie's name.

'We brought a few drinks,' Hughesy explained. 'Just to brighten the night.'

'Come in, boys, come in. Talk low,' she begged. 'Jenny is only just gone to sleep.'

The low room was small and untidy, and smelled of soap. The fire was ashen. She had only two glasses. They sat in a circle and drank out of cups, or from the bottle-necks. Moist cloths hung drooping and wet on a line; the stuffing of the chairs tufted out, he saw a toy horse with three legs, torn green paperbacks, a house-of-cards half collapsed on a tray. Staring at her, he heard nothing of their whisper-ing; both surprised and pleased to hear her laugh so often. He be-came aware that Hughesy and Flossie were fading out, for the last bus. Around midnight Paddywhack said he must give the wife a hand with the kids, and slid away. She put a few bits of sticks in the grate and tried ineffectually to remake the fire. Then Loftus clumped off home to his mother and there were only the two of them in the room, stooping over one flicker in the ashes, whispering, heads together.

Only once again did she mention Alfie; when she said, 'They're a grand bunch. Ye are all good boys. Decent young men. It was what he always said about ye.'

'Did you see him often?'

'Hardly at all. He might drop in after he shut the pub. To see the children. He told me he was always at ye to settle down. Hughesy, and Flossie, and Casey, and Loftus and you. Do you like Loftus?'

'He's cold. And bitter.'

'Is Deirdre your girl?'

'Yes. But I think she's letting me down. Did you meet her? She's a smasher.'

'She is a beautiful girl. I don't want to interfere in your life, Johnny, but I would be inclined to think that I would nearly say that she might have a hard streak in her.'

'Not like you?' he smiled.

'I'm not faulting her. A woman must think of her own good.'

There he was off, full-cock, about youth, ideals, loyalty, truth, honesty, love, things that only the gang understood, everybody else talking to you about your future, and good jobs, and making money. 'Ireland is the last fortress. The Noah's Ark of the world. No place like it.' And he should know, an exile! She agreed, she agreed. She said, 'The people here are warm and natural still in spite of all.' He was with her, all the way with her. 'We are not materialists. Not the best of us.' At that they were both off, whispering, breaking into louder talk, hushing, glancing fearfully at the door of the bedroom.

The last flicker of the fire died away. They drank the last bottle of stout between them, passing it from mouth to mouth. Her voice grew softer, her hand when she held his was padded like a cat's. The night became a fugitive. Faintly a foghorn in the bay moaned through a muffled blanket. He looked out and up through the window and saw a yellow blur of street light, and the mist that clung wetly to a fogged tree. She got up to make tea. He followed her into the messy kitchen to help and talk. They came back and she put a few more futile chips of sticks on the warm ashes. She laughed at the slightest thing – when the toy horse toppled, or when he told her about the dog, kicked, and beaten, and mangy, that he bought in Palermo, and how it swam ashore back to its Moorish slum. Or that night in Odessa in the YMCA when he got into a fight by pretending the C stood for Communist.

When it was two o'clock he said, 'You must send me away.' She said, 'Listen to the dripping outside. Oh, don't go away, Johnny!' He said, 'You must sleep.' She said, 'I don't know what sleep is,' and held him by his wrist, frightened to be left alone. 'Listen to the drip-drop,' she wheedled. 'And look! It's yellow as mustard outside.

Sleep here. Sleep in my bed. We're friends, aren't we? Just lie and sleep. You're a good boy. I know you. Go in there and lie down.' She led him into the bedroom with its unmade bed. He barely made out the child asleep on a camp-bed, one arm hooped around its head. She took her nightgown from a chair and went out.

He hung up his jacket, removed his shoes and lay down, gazing out the door at the yellow blur of the street lamp. It was as cold as the grave in the bed. She came back in her rumpled nightdress, her hair about her shoulders, got in under the clothes beside him and put out the light. The yellow street lamp bleared in through the bedroom door.

'It's bloody cold,' he said.

'We'll soon warm up. You should have taken your clothes off and got under the blankets, sure what does it matter?'

They lay in silence for a while, hearing nothing but their breathing and the faint, far fog-horn. He moved closer and began to whisper into her ear about what it means to be homeless, and she whispered to him about the time she came up to Dublin for the first time from County Cavan, for her honeymoon. She never once went back there. He whispered to her, 'You are a heroine.' She said, 'You're a good lad, Johnny.'

After a while more she said, 'We must sleep,' and he lay on his back, his hands clasped behind his head. After a long while he said, 'Deirdre is a bitch,' and she said, 'She is very young.' After another while he whispered, 'Try to sleep,' and she whispered, 'Yes.' After another long time he said, 'You're not sleeping. You are thinking of him. When will you know?' She said, 'It might be any minute. Then I'll sleep. And sleep. And sleep.'

Sleep stole on him. He woke abruptly, at five o'clock. She was no longer in the bed. He saw her in the front room, a man's overcoat on her shoulders, leaning her elbows on the window-sill staring out. In his stockinged feet he went to her and put his arm around her shoulder.

'You can't sleep?'

She did not stir. Her face had melted completely, her two cheeks were wet. He did not know what to say to her. By the cleansed lamplight outside he saw that the fog had lifted. She whispered. 'It's all over.'

'You can't tell!'

'I know it. I'll go out and ring the hospital at six o'clock. But I know it.' Her face screwed up and more tears oozed from her closed eyes. 'You'd better go, Johnny. Your people may be worrying.'

He dressed, shivering, among the empty bottles of stout on the floor, some of them standing to attention, some of them rolled on their sides. He put on his peaked cap with the white top, patted her hooped back, said, 'God help you,' and went out up the steps to the street level. It was black as night. From the pavement he looked down at the shadow of her face behind the misty glass, lifted a hand and walked away.

When he came to the Coal Harbour he halted on the centre of the railway bridge and leaned his hands on the wet parapet. Six miles across the level bay the string of orange lights flickered along the shoreline, and farther west the city's night-glow underlit its mirror of cloud. The harbour water, dark as oil, held the riding-light of a coal-tub. He drew in deep breaths of the raw air and blinked his sanded eyes. He said quietly, 'I still love you, you bitch.' Then he lifted his head, put his two palms about his mouth like a megaphone, and howled in a long, wild howl across the bay, 'Do you love me?'

The city lay remote under its dull mirror.

He rubbed the stone and remembered, 'Quiet consummation have; and renowned be thy grave' – and marched homewards, arms swinging, chin up, white cap slanted. The water of the main harbour was inscribed by a slow wheel of light. Far out from the Kish bank a flight of light beamed and died at regular intervals. The whole way home the only sound he heard was a faint, faraway humming like a bee, a dawn flight out of Dublin across the sea.

As he stole indoors a voice whispered, upstairs, 'Are you all right, darling?

'Okay, Mum?'

'Daddy's alseep.'

'Okay, Mum.'

'Sleep well, love.'

'Okay, Mum. I'll sleep. And sleep. And sleep.'

Before the Day Star

When you come out into the Place Pigalle from its dark side-streets your first impression is of its brightness, then crowds, then noise, and then you become one more aimless wanderer around the jammed pavements. Tonight there was a sharp sense of liveliness, even gaiety, almost like the end of a feast-day, although the streets were cold and damp and a cobweb of pink mist hung suspended over the roofs. It was Christmas Eve, about ten minutes short of midnight.

In a corner of the overcrowded terrace of *Le Rêve* five young people, three young men and two young women, sat crushed about a small table behind the fogged glass partitions, talking loudly to make themselves heard above the gabble. The youth who was doing most of the talking looked like a light-weight boxer. He wore a black polo-necked sweater; his blue-black hair, harsh as metal, peaked over his forehead like a wound-up watch-spring; his smile was a lighthouse flash. The others interrupted him only to spur him on. Their Scherazade? Their pet liar? Indulged. Bantered. Approved.

In a pause in his flow of talk the fair-mousy, pretty girl at his side tilted her scarlet tarboosh so as to tickle his cheek with its blue, silk tassel, and said, 'Happy now, Andy? This is better than Dublin, isn't it? Or isn't it?'

He gave her his white grin, gripped her frail arm and squeezed it.

'As happy, Jenny, as a lamb with two mothers.'

He turned swiftly to the fat youth at his other side. 'Jaysus, Fatso, I wonder what'd we be all doing this minit if we were back in Dublin?'

Fatso raised a finger for silence, groped inside his mustard-and-cress overcoat and slowly, very slowly, drew a vast, silver half-hunter from the well of his fob-pocket. He clicked it open with the air of an ancient out of an ancient world, considered its convex face, smooth, shiny and milk-white as his own; and pronounced in a slow Abbey Theatre brogue.

'I would be afther thinking, dearly beloved, that at this minit we would all be up in the Lamb Doyle's, or in The Goat, or The Cross Guns, or The Purty Kitchen where George the Fourth had his first glass of Guinness, being thrun out on our ears for the fourth time in succession. Althernatively, Andy, you would be snoring in your little white cot in your little white home in Templeogue.'

'Would I now? Well, then, let me tell you, Mister Laurence-O-bloody-well-Toole, I'd be doing no such a thing. I'd be being hauled off by my ma by the short hairs to Midnight Mass. That is, after the usual couple of preliminary breast-wallopings with the Dominican fathers up in Blackhorse Lane.'

He paused to turn to Biddy.

'Our privileged heathen,' he mocked.

Champagne-blonde, older than Jenny, not pretty, her splendid pigeon's bust straining her white sweater.

'Yes?' she queried, in an English voice so tiny that the first time they met her they had asked her if she had the pip.

'I mean Confession,' he explained, politely flicking two imaginary crumbs, one-two, from her bosoms. 'The annual clear-out. Old Father Berengarius. A mile of hardy sinners queueing up before me. The ould chapel as cold as a vault, and the wind under the slates moaning like a hundred banshees. He's as deaf as a post. Very convenient for your's truly. Doesn't hear a blooming word you say. Did I ever tell ye the night he disgraced me ma?'

He received their quizzical attention.

'There she was, late on Saturday night, inside in the confession box, asking him, if you please, was it a sin for her to believe in spirits and ghosts, and the mile of hardy boys outside all grumbling, and growling and rearing to get in and get out before the pubs closed on them. 'Having commerce with ghosts', was what she called it. 'What are ye saying to me?' says he, and his hand to his ear. 'Is it a sin, Father,' says she at the top of her voice, 'to have commerce with ghosts?' 'Speak up,' says he in a roar that you could hear down at O'Connell Bridge. 'To have commerce with ghosts, Father,' she squawks, and the buckos outside all leaning sideways to hear the pair of them. 'You have been having commerce with goats!' he roars at her. 'At your age?'

Once more they gave him the soft accolade of their laughter. Modestly rejecting the honour he turned aside and as suddenly turned back. Crook-necked he gestured to the dark street behind their corner café.

'Will yez look, boys! The foxy-headed whore is back again.

Trying to click a GI she is this time. They're brazen tonight. Out in the Open. He's twice her height. He'll make pancakes of her.'

They all swayed. The nearest of them to the glass partition was Mackinnon. He peered out under his black Homburg hat, low over the boils on his forehead. She was a small, skinny woman in a sheepskin jacket, a white beret, a white satin bottom as taut as two mushrooms.

'She must be frozen,' said Jenny pityingly.

'Behold the fruits of French logic,' Biddy piped. 'They close the brothels and every woman in Paris gets pneumonia. That foolish man will be streaming at the nose tomorrow morning.'

'I consider it most unseemly,' said Mackinnon. 'On Christmas Eve!'

Andy pointed his index finger at him, pulled the trigger, said, 'Bang, you're dead!' They laughed. They knew their Mac. A tongue of gall. He had never said an original word in his life. He worked at the Irish embassy. He would go far. They called him Mac the Knife.

'Mac!' Andy said, 'I wish you to understand that I am on the side of all rebels, exiles, outcasts and sinners. What Genet called The Saints of the Underworld.'

Biddy calmed his clenched fist with one scarlet-netted palm.

'Easy, Andy! And it was not Genet. Pasolini. And I do trust, dear boy, that you are not going to go all romantic on me tonight. I mean, talking about Dublin. And your mamma. And Midnight Mass. And Confession. And Dominican fathers. And, now, French hoahs.'

He was too fascinated by the comedy in the street to heed her. She enlisted Jenny's help.

'Jenny, is our broth of a boy about to get plawstered on us yet once again?'

'Haven't you observed?' Jenny sniffed. 'Whenever he takes to the bottle in a big way it always means the one thing? Some new crisis with his precious Deirdre.'

'Deirdre?' she whispered. 'But that little Irish fool doesn't mean a thing to him. Deirdre is merely the girl he sleeps with.'

At this Jenny laughed so bitterly that Biddy peered one-eyed at her.

'I trust, my dear, that you are not getting soft on him? I mean, as one old harridan to another, you must be hitting twenty. And,' she whispered out of the side of her mouth, 'he is only a poo-o-oodle!'

Jenny considered him seriously. In Paris less than six months, as Dubliny as the first day they met him, light-headed, light-hearted, feckless, a liar, much too fond of his liquor. Nobody was ever going to travel very far on his roundabout. Certainly not Deirdre. As if he felt her looking at him he grinned at her, and turned back to the street. She said loftily to Biddy, 'I assure you!'

'There is no need to protest, dawrling. We're all gone about Andy. That irresistible Irish charm. He's even gone about himself. It's his disease.'

Under the table Jenny felt his hand creeping slowly over her knee.

'Andy, why didn't you bring Deirdre tonight?'

His hand withdrew. He sighed, 'Poor little Deirdre.' He burst into a sudden passion. 'Jenny! Do you know what I am? I'm a sink!'

'Tell us, Andy,' she said sympathetically, 'why are you a sink?'

'No! You tell me! Examine me! Have no mercy on me! Tell me what's wrong with me.'

Mac the Knife tapped his arm. His speckled forehead became suffused with venom. He assumed a stage-Cockney's wheeze.

'I'll tell you, chum, wot's wrong with you. You're 'omesick for dear, old, dirty Dublin. Your wrists long for the chains. Your back aches for the lash. Cheer up, chum, this time next year you'll be back there for keeps, with no Pigalle, and no cafés, and no night-clubs, and you'll have your eye on a good job, and be wearing more holy medals than a Lourdes veteran, and you'll be running off like a good little boy to Midnight Mass, and Aurora Mass, and Third Mass, and Fourth Mass, and . . .'

Andy leaped up. His chair fell. All over the terrace heads turned lazily towards them. A waiter paused in his stride.

'Do you want a sock in the kisser?' he roared.

The two girls dragged him down.

'Andy!' Jenny chided and stroked his arm as if he was a cross dog. 'Aa-a-ndy!'

He retrieved his chair. He sat down glowering. Then he leaned over, seized Mac's hand and shook it warmly, rapidly, hurtingly.

'Mac! My old pal from schoolboys' happy days! As one uncon-verted and thoroughly corrupted Irish crook to another leave us be honest for one brief moment of our all too long and useless lives. Leave us admit that we've both been emancipated by *La Belle France*. We've killed Mother Ireland. We're free!' His grin fell dead on the table. His visor sank slowly over his toddy. 'We're emancipated. And disbloodywellillusioned.'

'I knew it,' Biddy piped to the striped awning. 'The Celtic Goat of Pure Romance. I saw it coming. I felt it in my bones. And I warn everybody present that I shall not be able to bear much more of it.'

Andy's head shot up.

'Anyway I gave up all that Holy Joe stuff years ago. I was a converted atheist at the age of seven. I was thrown out of school at fourteen for denying the existence of God. I proved it by logarithms.'

'You don't say so?' Mac jeered.

Andy shot him again on a quick draw, turned to Jenny, put his arm about her narrow waist and confided into her ear for all to hear.

'Jenny, my love, I'll tell you why I'm a sink. This morning Deirdre said to me, "Don't go out from me tonight, love! Don't leave me on Christmas Eve," says she. "Okay," says I, "come along with me." "You'll only get tight again, chéri," shays she. "Don't abandon your own loving, little Deirdre," shays she. "Spend it alone with me," shays she. But I did leave her! And I *am* going to get tight! And to hell with her! God Almighty, does she want to turn me into a monk? Imagine a fellow not having a couple of jars with his pals on a Christmas Eve! The trouble with Deirdre is she's not emancipated. There's one for you, Mac, who'll be back in Dublin in six months. In five years she'll have a squawl of kids around her saying the Rosary every night. Still and all I did ditch her. And there's no getting away from it. I'm a lousy sink!'

She stroked his cheek with one long finger.

'I don't think you're a lousy sink, Andy. I think you're a sweet sink. You just can't hold your liquor, any more than you can hold your conscience.'

He tightened his arm about her waist.

'Jenny! You understand me better than anybody else in the entire, global world. You're the grandest girl in all creation!'

'Better than Deirdre?'

He banged the table and shouted.

'I'm worse than a sink. I'm a flamin', flittherin', filthy, finished-off sink!'

'Jesus help me,' Biddy moaned, and began wearily to powder her nose.

Jenny whispered something into the whorls of his ear, he let his head sink on her shoulder, her blue tassel fell over his eye, he put his arm around her again. Mackinnon twirled a palm of antique boredom at Larry Doyle, who beamed pleadingly at him as if begging indulgence for all young lovers. Suddenly Andy flung up his head with a wild jerk.

'Boys and girls! I have a smashing idea! Why don't we all tumble into a taxi and go off to Midnight Mass in the Irish Church?'

'Here it comes,' said Biddy, brightly snapping her compact. 'Back to our vomit. Cassandra the daughter of Priam, that's me. Often heard, rarely heeded, always right. Never let it be said that I am a spoilsport,' she begged them all, gathering up her handbag and a four-foot-long, peacock-blue umbrella. 'Which is this church you mentioned, Charlie? Church of Ireland? Papish? Celtic synagogue? I'm with you all the way even to the Mosque. Or would it do if I led you to some good, old, solid ten-by-twenty Non-conformist tin chapel somewhere?'

Mackinnon rose, took off his black hat, held it to his chest and spoke with Castilian pride.

'Mademoiselle, vous oubliez que je suis Catholique.'

She made a soft noise like a duck getting sick, they all laughed, and while Andy was paying the bill they scrambled out on to the pavement. It was jammed by the crowd outside *Le Jardin d'Eve* looking at lighted photographs of naked women with breasts like udders. Biddy said in annoyance to Jenny. 'I notice they always leave him to pay the bill.'

'The boy is a fool. He loves to play the milord.'

'Tell me, does he always get religion when he starts thinking of Deirdre?'

'You've known him as long as I have. Are you getting soft on him now?'

Biddy shrugged.

'I wouldn't mind having a bash at old Andy.'

'He's not your sort. He is what you said. A poodle. A puppy. He's just a kid. Let him alone.'

The kid rushed out and hooked the pair of them into the crowd. They saw the redheaded whore, her eyes circling slowly about her like a slow waltz, glance at and dismiss Mac and Larry. Andy laughed, 'Business bad tonight.' It occurred miserably to Jenny that her eyeballs would be circling under her green eyelids even in her sleep. Larry called out, 'The Irish Church is miles way, can't we go somewhere else?' The crowd bumped them. The doorman of *Le Jardin d'Eve* barked at them to come and see the most nude women in the whole world. 'Ask him,' Andy suggested, and Larry approached him. While Larry and he were comparing silver half-hunter with gold half-hunter Biddy said he was like Georges Brassens' daddy. Jenny said he was like her own daddy. The barker closed his watch, directed them to the Rue des Martyrs, called after them 'Vite, mes enfants! C'est tard!' Then, behind them his voice soared. 'Les plus nues du monde...'

They turned from the lights, and the crowds, and the rumbling beat of Pigalle's heart into the narrow street whose prolonged silence gleamed distantly with coloured windows. By the time they were filing into the church the congregation were shuffling erect for the Gospel. Biddy halted inside the door. Mac and Larry stayed with her. Andy probed along the aisle and found two empty places in the front row directly facing a small Christmas manger with the Infant, the Virgin, Saint Joseph, the cow, the ass, the shepherds and the coloured kings huddled about a crib under an amber light and a bald electric star. Whoever arranged the *crèche* had perched a stuffed robin redbreast on the edge of the cot. Andy nudged her, nodded at it, and winked conspiratorially.

She was back, one frosty morning, four years ago, at home, awakened by a thud on her bedroom window: it was a robin lying stunned on the window-sill. In her nightgown by the open window she had held it, throbbing between her palms, staring at the one big eye staring up at her, and for that one sleepy moment all life was as simple as a captured bird. She opened her palms, the robin flew off into the frosty air, and the morning star gleamed above the hills and the murmuring beach. *In splendoribus sanctorum.* The priest was intoning the psalm. In the brightness of the saints, she remembered from other midnight masses. *Ex utero anti luciferam ...* From the womb before the day-star, I begot Thee. Did he remember? She touched the hand beside her and they looked at one another. Thereafter, silently from her white shore her bright moment ebbed. It fell as softly as a leaf from a book, a rose petal. Her window empty, her beach dry, she saw, leaning against a pillar beside them, the woman in the sheepskin coat. When the sanctus tinkled everybody else but she knelt. When everyone raised their heads she was still standing there, staring blankly in front of her. Andy was gone. There was no sign of him down the aisle, nor could she see the other three.

Crossly, she made her way back to the doorway, and out to the street. It was so dark that at first she saw nothing: then she made out the four figures on the opposite side of the street clumped like a bunch of gangsters, smoking cigarettes. She crossed over.

'Why did you come out?'

Biddy slowly smoothened her netted fingers and said sullenly, 'It wasn't my show, dawrling.' Larry Doyle looked uncomfortably at Mac the Knife who made a half-moon with his hangdog mouth, performed a high dissociating shrug, and looked at Andy who let out a zany guffaw and then said sulkily, 'We should never have gone!'

'It was you who proposed it!'

'We shouldn't have done it!'

'I thought they were doing it very nicely?'

He appealed to them, boxer-crouched.

'When you don't believe in a thing what is it but tomfoolery?' He stood back, his claws to his chest. 'I don't believe in anything. It's all kid stuff. I felt indecent inside there.' He shot out his left. 'And that bloody redhead in there finished me off. God Almighty, people have to be honest, don't they? They have to come clean, don't they? When I saw that wan in there I felt, Jaysus, what am I but another dirty bloody hypocrite?'

Jenny slapped his face, stepped back in dread, ran a few yards downhill, he after her, turned, a lean hare, ran faster and faster until he caught her, whirling her against a black wall under a street lamp, gasping, her palms spread against him. They panted.

'What's wrong, girleen?'

'What's wrong is that you *are* a hypocrite. First Deirdre. Then that street-walker. Who are you going to blame yourself on next? Me? Biddy? Why don't you go back to Dublin and rot there? It's what you want, isn't it?'

She turned to the wall and burst into tears. He waited while she sobbed. When she was quiet she turned and asked him for his handkerchief, wiped her eyes, said, 'May I blow?' and blew.

'Why should I want to go back to Dublin? I'm happy here, with you, and Biddy, and all the gang.'

'Are you?' she challenged. She gave him back his handkerchief. 'I think, Andy,' she said quietly, 'you'd better go back now to Deirdre. You know she'll be waiting up for you all night.'

He made a noise of disgust.

'She's not the answer.'

'And what is?'

He took her arm and led her back to the group. Sacerdotally, Larry blessed them with a sweeping arm. '*Benedicat vos. Pax vobiscum.*' Mackinnon said, with immense bonhomie. 'A Happy

Christmas to the happy pair!' Biddy said, coldly, 'And what does one do now?' Larry threw his arms around Jenny, and intoned:

> My beloved, drink the cup that cheers
> Today of past regrets and future fears,
> For, ah, tomorrow we may be
> With yesterday's seven thousand years.

Nobody commented. The woman was standing alone on the step of the porch looking across at them. As they looked at her Andy walked over and spoke with her. Then the two walked off slowly, out of sight.

Mac gave a beck of his head to Larry, said to the girls, '*Le Rêve*', and the two of them went off, hunched together, nose to nose, back to Pigalle. Jenny whirled and stared downhill towards the pink glow over Paris. For a while, Biddy considered her rigid back. Then she contemplated her long slim legs. Then she regarded her left thumb, wriggling it double-jointedly. Then she looked up at the sky and said, 'Andy once told me he spent an entire night discussing the works of Guy de Maupassant with a hoah in Marseille. He said they were still at it when the sun rose behind the Château d'If. Odd! Even in Marseille the sun does not rise in the west. I shouldn't worry about him if I were you, Jenny. He will be back in *Le Rêve* in half an hour as chaste as the dawn and without as much as a franc in his pocket. He'll tell us that she has a grandmother in Provence, or a child in hospital, or that she reads Pascal every night. The party's over. The night is bitter cold. And I am sick at heart. We'll get a taxi and I'll drop you at your door.'

'I want to walk,' Jenny said sourly.

Biddy's fledgling's voice took on an edge.

'In this cold? To Saint Germain? Do you want to die for him, like Mimi?'

'What is he up to? Always expiating for something or other? What's the point of it? Why doesn't he grow up? If he does give that woman all his money he'll only leave Deirdre penniless for a month, and borrow from us, and then borrow from his mamma to pay us back.'

'Unlike us he is young and innocent. It is what makes him so appealing. In his bothered way he's different.'

'Or is it just that all Irish men are different? Look at the other two. My God! What are we *doing* with them?'

Biddy hooted.

'Dear child, you obviously have no idea what Englishmen are like. I know! I've put dozens of them through my little white hands. Full to the gullet of guilt, black silences, sudden glooms, damp despairs, floods of tears and then that awful, manny, British laughter and "Let's have another one, old girl". Paris has been absolute bliss after London. Every Frenchman a swine. It's been such a relief. It's his only trouble – he thinks he's a sink and he isn't. It takes centuries to produce a really first-class sink. Still he shows promise. The right woman could do a lot for him. Not Deirdre, a silly little Dublin chit, just as stupid as himself. Let's get a cab. I'll pay for it and drop you right at your door.'

'I still want to walk,' Jenny said stolidly.

'It's savage. My ears are dangling by a thread. A cab, for God's sake!'

'Are you trying to get rid of me?'

Biddy regarded her with admiration, and shrugged.

'Biddy! What do we see in him?'

'Ignorance? Hopelessness? Eagerness? Terror? Charm?'

'But he is such a fraud!'

'And as you said, such a fool!'

'But, you say, innocent?'

'As a rose!' Biddy sighed.

'Let's go back to *Le Rêve* and see if he does come back.'

'He will come back. His type always comes back. One of the lads.'

He came, wildly excited, bustling in, penniless, full to the gullet of lies and boastings – or, if they were not lies, of fantasies, and if they were not boastings, of dreams.

'All our lives,' he pronounced, 'we dream of love, and love eludes us. We have fled, Mac, from the sow that eats its own farrow. And all the time we dream of our childhood and are never free of it. O exiles of Erin, love ye one another. My bloody foot! Two single tickets to Dublin, that's the right ticket. But where shall we find her? Every mis-match Irishman a born matchmaker, and good at it. Saving others who cannot save himself. Sitting in a Dublin pool of drink and dreaming of the Arc de Triomphe. I told her I'd follow any woman to the ends of the earth but not to the end of the world. Nobody would take a fellow up on that! Gimme the Queensberry Rules and be God I'll not complain. I want a loving, lovely, innocent wife!'

'With squads of babies?' Jenny asked and felt his hand start to rove over her knee.

'Squads and squads of them!'

'All chawnting the Rosary?' Biddy piped mockingly, and pressed his other hand.

Their mockery could not halt him. The girls looked at one another with big eyes, shook their heads and made wry mouths of self-astonishment. Mac's eyes kept closing and half opening from sleep and drink. 'What are we waiting for?' he asked dully. Larry Doyle looked at his turnip-watch and sighed, 'It's gone two o'clock.' The terrace was empty. The pink haze fell as glistening rain on the street. Nobody stirred. Even their talker was silent.

After a while he spoke, looking around at them sullenly.

'I'm going to take a plane to Dublin in the morning. Who'll lend me the money?'

Passion

Dearest love. When will we meet again? It is only a few hours since I left you, and I am already full of melancholy thoughts.

Why on earth did I think tonight, after I had left you, of Conny Hourigan, and of that soft, wet night when the lights of Cork down in the valley were weeping through the haze, and everything as still as before dawn; and not a sound but the jolt of an old tram over the worn points, or the drip of the rain on the old tin shed in the backyard?

I think it was because I went to my window and saw the far away lights of Dublin, and at once I was again listening to that silence of twenty years ago drumming in my ears. I was waiting for my aunt to play the next card, and looking across the cosy eye of the fire in the kitchen range at Conny breathing contentedly over his evening paper and stroking his Moses beard.

He suddenly lifts his eyes to look over his spectacles at the tiny window, and he says – 'Them bastards of slugs will be out in their marching orders tonight.' And he is just about to heave himself up and go out to his beloved patch of a garden to kill some of them when we hear a ratatatat at the hall door. With a look over his glasses at my auntie, and a look at the clock, and a 'Who on earth can that be?' he goes shuffling out along the little hall. My aunt suspends her card. We turn our heads when we hear the voices rising sharply and Conny shouting, 'No!' And again, 'I tell you, no!' – and then more loud voices and the slam of the door.

He came back, flushed; gave a hitch to his belly, sat down, growled, 'Bloody cheek!', and tried to resume his reading.

'Who's that, Conny?' said the auntie, still holding up her card.

'Three buckos from Blarney Lane. Asking me to give 'um me six Easter lilies.'

'Oh, law! And why so?'

'Some kid that's dead up in Barrett's Buildings. Name of Delurey. Molly Delurey. Died up in the Fever Hospital. The best I ever heard. God Almighty! Asking me to cut me six Easter lilies for some wan I never heard of in me life before. Did you ever hear the beat of that?'

His sister, of course, wanted to know all about it. Cork may call itself a city, but it is really a big town made up of a lot of little villages, and in each 'village' everybody wants to know everything about everybody else.

'Delurey?' she says 'I don't know any wan now of that name. To be sure, we had a little apple-woman used to come here . . . Ah, but she was a Minny Delaney. And how did they come to know that you have the lilies?'

'You may ask. Your brave milkman. Spotted 'um every morning coming in with the milk. I knew that fellow had his eye on me garden. I always said that fellow's too sweet to be wholesome. "Oh, Mister Hourigan, haven't you the grand geraniums! Oh, isn't the verbena massive, Mister Hourigan!" Making a big man out of himself. "Flowers? I'll get ye the flowers. Go up to Mister Hourigan and tell him I sent you. Ask him for his lilies." The cheek of him! The cool, bloody pig's cheek of him!'

My auntie played her card without looking at it. She forgot to take her trick. I suppose she was seeing the little deal coffin, or the child laid out on the bed in the back bedroom. The rain played its harp strings in the yard. The fire purred.

'What they usually do,' she ventured, 'is to make up a collection to buy the flowers.'

'That's what I said to 'um' – Over his spectacles. 'They wanted to blind me that there's none in the shops. I don't believe wan word of it. An if there isn't,' his voice kept rising and rising, 'why did they come up to *me* for *my* poor little flowers? How fair they wouldn't go down to Bolster has a glasshouse full of 'um? Oh, no! Up to the foola! Me poor little six Easter lilies that I reared, that I looked after as if they were me own children, that I . . . But these buckos have no consideration. "Go up to Mister Hourigan and tell him I sent you." The . . . But what . . . Me poor little lilies. Who ever . . . God Almighty, I . . .'

He choked off into incoherence.

I said, 'Your trick, auntie?'

She gently swept the cards aside with her hand and breathed rather than whispered, 'The poor child'.

Down with his paper, off with his specs.

'That's all very fine, woman, but am I going to give me six Easter lilies because . . . And aren't they me own property? Or aren't they?

Amn't I entitled to do what I like with 'um? Or amn't I? And if I don't want to give 'um to 'um what right have them cafflers to be coming up to me own hall door giving me lip?'

'Conny, I hope you didn't have *words*.'

'And am I going to let a pack of Blarney Lane cafflers tell me up to me puss that there won't be luck nor grace about the house if I don't give me flowers to 'um?'

'Conny! Conny! Conny! You refused the dead.'

He dashed down the paper and tore out of the kitchen. We heard the front door opening. I could imagine the dark and the haze and the smudgy lights down in the valley. He shuffled into the bedroom and struck a match. That was for the candle. I saw how the lilies outside the window would be pale against the smudgy lights of the city.

The wind wailed down from the convent grounds behind the backyard. My auntie was slowly putting the cards back into the old cigar-box. The candle clattered against the basin and ewer and then he came shuffling in along the linoleum of the hall. He blew out the candle, took up his paper firmly, and began to read it. The aunt closed the cigar-box and folded her arms about her and turning to the fire was lost in the little fluttering coming out of the coal.

'The loveliest funeral I ever seen was the time of Lord Mayor MacSwiney. All the bands of the city. And the pipers. And the boys marching. And the Dead marching Saul. And the flag on the coffin. And all the flowers. And people in every window crying down salt tears.' Conversationally she inquired of him: 'Isn't Packey Cassidy buried up there with the Lord Mayor?'

'How do I know where he's buried?'

'Sure aren't they all together up in the one plot?'

'I dunno who you're talking about, let me read me paper, woman.'

'Yerrah is it pretending you don't know Packey Cassidy from the Glen worked with you down in the gas-house? Oh then many the night he brought you home when you had a sup taken. Didn't the two of us stand outside there in the garden and the pipers playing him up the Western Road to the Republican Plot?'

Conny pretended to read. The wind brought us the soft tolling of the nuns' bell. Conny looked over his specs again at the window and gave a poke to the cosy fire.

'That's a nor'-wester. There'll be a flood in the river tomorrow.'

'Ah, God look down on us. 'Tis no harm to say it – once we're dead we're soon forgotten.'

'You'd betther be beatin' your way home, boy, the last tram is gone.'

I hated to leave the warm kitchen. Somehow this talk of processions and bands and floods in the river and the nuns' bell and the squeaks of the last tram had wrapped me into a cosy nest of Time and Memory, and I remembered with pleasure how somebody had said that 'All Cork is out of the wan eggshell', and I understood for the first time what that meant. I wanted desperately that Conny should give the lilies to the dead child, and I felt bitter of him that he wouldn't do it. Timidly I said, 'Wouldn't you give her three of them, Uncle Conny?' He roared at me, 'No, nor wan nor half a wan.' The aunt's face got pale and venomous and miserable and she stabbed at him :

'No nor I don't think you'd give them to meself if it was a thing that I was stretched in the next room !'

After a moment he said, quietly.

'Go home, boy !'

As I left his patch of a garden – it was about as big as a table – I saw the six lilies, calm as sleep, in the pale light of the hall. The child's face would be just as pale. Down in its hollow the little city seemed to have locked every door and window against the storm and the rain. There were few lights.

That was twenty years ago. Why did that wet night flash on me when I walked into my bedroom tonight and saw the land under the full moon?

The sky is bleached, the fields are white, the lights of Dublin are bright as youth. They drained me so that I had to lean on the window-sill and let it all pour over me as if I were a stone under a river. It was like hearing an old, old tune on a brass band; or the sound of church bells on a wet Sunday morning; or the hoot of a ship's siren on Christmas Day. Frightening shadows under everything – under the gooseberry bushes, under the cabbages, under an old ashcan. And nothing between those shadows and that high moon but those lights of the city, low down, and poised over them, one long narrow cloud stretched from east to west like a scythe about to sweep the sky. It is the sort of night that might make a man ache for love, but I was suffused with you, dear heart, and should have been full of joy and content.

That night, so long ago, was very different to this serene moon. All through that stormy night the drums of the rain beat on the roofs of the city. In the morning the river was in flood. Rafts of branches and wrack and reeds torn up by the storm sailed on the muddy water through the city. And Conny's lovely white lilies were battered into the mud. When he saw them he just went back to bed and he stayed there for three days. The aunt didn't say one word to him. But outside his window he could hear everybody who came into the little garden – including the milkman – loud in commiseration. After that I no longer envied him his hobby, as I once used to. I began vaguely to understand that his garden was a sort of torment to him.

Or is it, dearest one, that all passion is an unhappiness? Are we always looking forward to our joy, or thinking back on it, or so drunk with it that we cannot realise it?

The night is nearly finished. The moon is going down. The lights of Dublin are still bright. The shadows are long and pale. You are asleep, with your dear black hair spread on your pillow. I hear a wind creeping up from the north-west.

Dear Love, when will we meet again? Let it be soon, Dear Love, let it be soon!

Dividends

As far as Mel Meldrum was concerned *l'affaire Anna*, as he was to call it, began one wet and windy April morning in 1944 when his chief clerk, Mooney, knocked at the door of his sanctum, handed him my letter, marked *Personal* and *By Hand*, and said that the bearer was an old lady in a black bonnet sitting outside in the main office 'shaking her blooming umbrella all over your new Turkish carpet'. I can see Mel glancing at my signature, smiling at his memories of our college days together twenty years before, rapidly taking the point of the letter and ordering Miss Whelan to be shown in to him at once. He rises courteously, begs her to be seated, watches amusedly while she fumbles in her woven shopping-bag, and produces, proudly I have no doubt, a fat, wrinkled envelope containing the £350 in thirty-five white Bank of England notes. He receives it from her with a small bow. It was why I sent her to him; he was always affable, almost unctuous, with old ladies.

My Aunty Anna Maria was my mother's sister. Until she got this small legacy from another sister, who had recently died in a place called Toogong in New South Wales, she had never before possessed such a lump sum. She had existed for thirty-odd years on a modest salary as cook-housekeeper to a highly successful horse-trainer in County Kildare; and then on the small pension he kindly gave her, supplemented occasionally by miniature subventions from a nephew here and a niece there whenever we had the decency to remember how she used to stuff us with cakes and lemonade during our summer holidays on the edge of the Curragh where we loved to visit her in the staff quarters of the trainer's house. My father died, in Cork, so she came down there when she was about fifty-five, to live with my mother; and when my mother died she had stayed on, alone, in the city, living in a single room in a battered old fabric of a tenement overlooking one of Cork's many abandoned quaysides – silent except for the poor kids from the lanes around playing and screaming in the street, or the gulls swooping over the bits of floating orange-skin, bread-crusts or potato peelings backing slowly up-river on the high tide. When Mel saw her she was turned seventy.

To my shame I had not seen her for twelve years. I had left Cork before she came there, and returned only once, for my mother's funeral. I was now married and living in Dublin.

It had taken me weeks of letter-writing, back and forth, to persuade her to invest her legacy, and I was delighted when she agreed, because I knew that if she did not she would either scatter it in dribs and drabs, or lose it in the street some day, or hide it in some corner of her room and not remember where before the mice had eaten it into confetti.

Mel described in a long, amusing letter how he had accepted the envelope 'with measured ceremony'. He had given her his best advice 'like a pontiff'. He explained to her that the sum was too small for an annuity, and she was too old for growth-shares, so he must advise her to buy an 8% Preference shares in Sunbeam-Wolsey. He refused to charge her his usual stockbroker's fee, and kindest act of all, told her that instead of waiting from one six-month period to the next for her modest dividends (£28 a year) she might, if she so wished, come into the office on the first of every month, and his chief clerk would there pay her the equivalent of her £28 per annum in twelve equal portions. She accepted his offer 'like a queen'. I could henceforth be happy to think of her toddling on the first of every month into Meldrum, Guy and Meldrum, smiling and bobbing under her black, spangled bonnet, and departing, amid the pleased smiles of everybody in the office, with her six shillings and eight pennies, wrapped in two single pound notes, clasped in the heel of her gloved fist.

I sent him my cordial thanks and thought no more about her until exactly one year later when he wrote to me that she ordered him to sell her shares. It appeared that she had become smitten by a sudden longing to possess a blue, brocaded, saddle-back armchair that she had seen one morning in the window of Cash's in Patrick Street. It appeared further that for months past 'a certain Mrs Bastable and a certain Mrs Sealy', two cronies as doddering as herself, also in her tenement on Lavitt's Quay, had been telling her that nobody but 'a born foolah' would leave 'all that lovely money' lying idle in Mister Meldrum's fine office on the South Mall.

It was easy enough to hear these two tempters at work on her:

'Sure, Miss Whalen, you could buy all the armchairs in Cork with that much money! And look at your poor ould room with the paint peeling off the ceiling like snow! And your poor ould curtains in tatthers on yer winda! Why don't you buy an electric fire that would keep you warm all the winter? And two grand, soft Blarney blankets for your bed? And a pink, quilted eiderdown? And, anyway, sure that measley ould two quid that Meldrum gives you wouldn't buy a dead cat! And supposing yeh die, What'll happen it then? Get a hold of your money, girl, and *spend it!*'

Mel counter-argued and counter-pleaded. I pleaded. I got her parish priest to plead with her. I even offered to buy her the brocaded armchair as a present. It was no use. Mel sold her shares, gave her a cheque for £350, wished her well, and we both washed our hands of her.

I next got a long and slightly testy letter from Mel, written on the first day of the following month of May. It began, 'Your good Aunty Anna has this morning turned up again in my office, bright as a new-born smile, bowing and bobbing as usual, calmly asking my chief clerk Mooney for what she calls, if you please, *her* little divvies . . .'

In dismay he had come out to her.

'But, Miss Whelan, you've sold your shares! Don't you remember?'

Aunt Maria smiled cunningly at him.

'Ah, yes!' she agreed. 'But I didn't sell my little divvies!'

'But,' Mel laughed, 'your dividends accrued from the capital sum you invested. Once a client sells his shares he withdraws the capital and there can be no more dividends. Surely you understand that?'

At once Aunty Anna's smile vanished. A dark fright started at the bottom of her chin and climbed slowly up to her eyes.

'Mister Meldrum, you know well that I didn't sell me little divvies. I want me little divvies. You always gave me them. They belong to me. Why can't you give them to me now the way you always gave me them at the first of every month? Why are you keeping them back from me now?'

'Miss Whelan, when a client sells his shares they are gone. And when they are gone the dividends naturally cease forthwith. You instructed me to sell. I did so. I gave you back your money in a lump sum. If you now wish to give me back that lump sum I shall be most happy to buy you more shares and your dividends will begin again. Otherwise we have nothing for you.'

Aunty Anna had burst into floods of tears, and she began to wail, with the whole office staring at the pair of them. 'What do I want with shares? I don't want any more ould shares. I gave you back me shares. Keep 'em! I don't want 'em. All I want is me little divvies. And anyway I haven't the money you gave me, I bought an armchair with it, and an electric fire from the ESB, and a costume from Dowden's, and I gave fifty pounds to the Canon to say Masses for my poor soul when I'm dead, and I loaned ten quid to Mrs Bastable on the ground-floor, and ten quid to Mrs Sealy on the third floor back, and what with this and that and the other all I have left is a few quid, and I don't know where I put 'em, I'd lay down me life I put 'em in the brown teapot on the top shelf but when I went looking for them yesterday I couldn't find them high nor low. Mrs Sealy says I must have made tea with them, but I tell you, Mister Meldrum, I wouldn't trust that one as far as I'd throw her. Mister Meldrum, give me me little divvies. They're all I have to live on bar that mangy old pension. I want me divvies here and now, if you please, or I'll go out there in the street and call a policeman!'

Mel led her gently into his inner sanctum, together with his book-keeper, and the two of them spent an hour explaining to her, in every way they could think of, the difference between shares and dividends. They showed her the receipt for the purchase of the shares, for the dividends they had earned over the year, the nota-tion of the re-sale of the shares, and the red line drawn clearly at the end of her account to show that it was now closed for ever. They might as well have been talking to the carpet. Aunty Anna just could not understand that he who does not speculate cannot accumulate. The upshot of it was that she became so upset, and Mel became so angry with her, and then so upset because he had upset her that, to comfort her, he took £2 6s. 8d. out of his pocket, the equivalent of what she had hitherto lawfully drawn every month, told her that this was the end, the very end, and that she must now reconcile herself, firmly and finally, if she would be so kind, to the plain fact that she was no longer in the market for anything. And so he showed her out, bobbing and smiling and happy, and (he hoped), convinced. He was most forbearing about it all. Three pages he wrote about it to me. All I could do was to write him a properly apologetic and deeply grateful reply, enclosing my cheque for £2 6s. 8d., which, I noted, in some surprise, he duly cashed.

On the morning of the first of the following month of June he was on the telephone. His voice over the wire sounded rather strangled.

'Your good aunt is back here in my office again. She is sitting directly opposite me. She seems to be in very good health. And in good spirits to boot. In fact she is beaming at me. Nevertheless she is once more demanding dividends on shares which she does not possess. Will you kindly tell me at once what you wish me to do with, for, or to her?'

'Oh, Lord, Mel! This is too bad! I'm very sorry! I'm awfully sorry. Look, Mel, couldn't you just explain firmly to the old lady that . . .'

At this his voice rose to a squeak of utter exasperation.

'Miss Whelan has been in my private office for the past three-quarters of a bloody hour with my book-keeper, my assistant book-keeper, my chief clerk . . .'

'Mel! I'll tell you what to do. Just give her the two quid six and eight and I'll send you a cheque for it this minute, and then tell her never, just simply never, to darken your doors again.'

Mel's voice became precise, piercing, priggish and prim in a way that suddenly recalled to me a familiar side of his nature that I had completely forgotten until that moment.

'I have no hope what-so-ever of achieving the entire-ly de-sirable state of affairs that you so blandly de-pict. I am afraid the time has arrived for you to come down to Cork in person and talk to your good aunt. Furthermore, I must tell you that your proposal about a cheque is totally contrary to my principles as a man and as a stockbroker. It is contrary to the whole ethics, and the whole philosophy, the whole morality of stockbroking. It is inconsistent, unrealistic, unprofessional and absurd. As I have explained to Miss Whelan, he who saves may invest, he who invests may accumulate, he who does not save may not . . .

'Mel, for God's sake come off it! How the hell can she save anything at all on that measley old pension of hers? Who do you think she is? Bernard Baruch? Henry Ford? John D. Rockefeller? Gulbenkian?'

'In that case,' he retorted, 'it is as absurd for her to expect as it would be unrealistic for me to pretend that she is entitled to returns on non-existent capital. In the name of justice, equity and realism, above all in the name of realism, I will not and I cannot pretend to pay any client dividends that simply do not exist . . . Excuse me one moment.'

Here I could hear a confused babble of voices as of four or five people engaged in passionate argument, 161 blessed miles away from my study in Dublin.

'Hello!' he roared. 'How soon, for God Almighty's sake, can you come down to Cork and settle this matter with your aunt?'.

I saw that there was no way out of it. It was a Friday. I said that I would take the morning train on Saturday.

'I will meet you at the station.'

'Is this an order?' I asked wryly.

His answer was clipped. He recovered himself sufficiently to add 'Please!' and even to mention that I could get some sort of ragtime lunch on the train. When I said I would be there, he calmed down. He expanded. He even became amiable. When he broke into French I remembered how, in his student days, he used to go to France every summer and Easter with his widowed mother.

'Bon! Nous causerons de beaucoup de choses. Et nous donnerons le coup-de-grace à l'affaire Anna, et à ses actions imaginaires' – and hung up.

Actions? My dictionary told me that the word means *acts, actions, performances, battles, postures, stocks, shares.* As I put back the volume on its shelf I remembered how good he always used to be at social work among the poor of Cork. I also wondered a little how such a man could see nothing wrong with giving charity outside his office in the name of Saint Vincent de Paul but everything wrong with the idea of bestowing largesse inside it in the name of pity. I also realised that I had not met him for some twenty years.

2

It was a perfect June morning. All the way down from Dublin to Cork the country looked so soft and fresh, so green and young, and I lunched so well that my heart gradually warmed both to Aunty Anna and to Mel, the dual cause of this pleasant excursion back to my home-ground. As the fields floated past and the waves of the telegraph wires rolled and sank I started to recall the Mel I used to know. Indeed if anybody at that moment had asked me about him – say, that old priest half dozing on the seat opposite me – I would have launched on a eulogy as long as an elegy.

Stout fellow! Salt of the earth! As fine a chap as you could hope to meet in a day's march. Honest, kind and absolutely reliable. The sort of man who would never, simply never let you down. A worthy inheritor of his father's and his grandfather's business. Handsome, strong, tall, always well dressed – in the old days, we all thought him a bit of a dandy. And so easy! As smooth and easy as that bog-stream outside there. Oh, now and again he could be gruff if you rubbed him the wrong way, and he was sometimes given a bit to playing the big shot. And by that same token he always boasted that he was a first class shot. A real, clean-living, open-air man. What else? Well informed about music. And the opera. Spoke French well – those visits abroad with his mother. A strong civic sense, always proud of his native city. Who was it that told me a few years ago that he is up to his neck nowadays in all sorts of worthy societies in Cork? The Old Folks Association, the Safety First Association, Saint Vincent de Paul, the Archaeological Society, the Society for the Prevention of Cruelty to Animals, the African Mission Brotherhood . . .

I glanced across at my old priest. He was looking at me as if I had been talking aloud to myself. I turned to the fields.

'Well . . . Not exactly sociable, I suppose. Unless a committee meeting in a hotel room can be called a jolly sociable occasion.'

Come to think of it, he always did keep a bit to himself. Not stand-offishly, more of a class thing, being so much richer than the rest of us. Or was he a little shy? And I did hear recently that he has given up shooting and taken to bird-watching – from a weekend cottage he has outside Cork, some place along the valley of the Lee beyond Inniscarra. His private hide-out where he can 'get away from it all'.

The old priest was still looking at me. I turned to watch a racing horse.

'All? I suppose he means the roaring traffic of Cork, which, when I was a student, chiefly meant jarvey-cars, bullocks, dray-horses and bicycles. It is a quiet place. Not really a city at all. And then, of course, we mustn't forget Cork's famous social whirl. Bridge every night, golf every Saturday, and, for the happy few, a spot of sailing in the harbour over the weekend. And tubs of secret drinking in hotel lounges for the happy many, stealing in discreetly by the back door. Or were they the unhappy many? Cork can be a pretty grim place in the winter. As I well know! Lord! don't I know!'

A sunshot shower of rain flecked the windows of the train.

'We may as well face it. Cork is a place where it rains, and rains, and rains, with an implacable and persistent slowness. A frightful place, really, in the winter! Of course, if you have enough piastres you can knock out a good time even in Cork. But you have to have the piastres. And I never did. Mel did. And lots of 'em. Rich? Very. At least by Cork standards. A tight, bloody hole, full to the butt of the lugs with old family businesses that keep a firm grip on their miserly homesteads.'

Was that priest raising his eyebrows at me?'

'Naturally he's a Catholic! A most devoted Catholic. No! A baptised, confirmed and unmarried bachelor. That is odd – because he always had a great eye for the girls. Funny I never thought of it before. In Ireland you don't, somehow. You get so used to the widowed mother in the background, or the uncle who is a bishop, or the two brothers who are priests, or the three sisters who are nuns. The tradition of celibacy. But, by God, he did have that roving eye! Why didn't he marry? And he was quite good-looking. Even if he has slightly prominent teeth, and a rather silly, affected way of shaving that leaves a tuft of hair on each cheekbone.'

I closed my eyes to see him better. I wondered why the hell I was coming down here at all.

'He must be forty-six or forty-seven by now. If his taste in clothes is what it used to be he will be wearing a check sports coat with two splits behind and a check cap slightly yawed over his gamesome eye. The country squire's weekend costume.

'Is there,' I asked the priest, 'a train back out of Cork tonight?'
He smiled crookedly.
'There is. A slow one. You're not staying long with us, I see?'
'I have to get back tonight.'

I felt my face flushing. My wife is not well. My youngest daughter has a fever. I am in a bad shape myself, Mel. In fact I am running a temperature of 102°. My brother is arriving from London on Sunday morning. My best friend is dying. My uncle died yesterday. I simply have to go to his funeral.

'Are you sure, Father, there is a train out of Cork tonight?'
'There is. One of these days they say we are going to have our own airport. With aeroplanes.'

The rain stopped and the sun burst out, but I did not trust it one inch. I recognised familiar fields. Poor-looking fields. The rain. The cold. My poverty-stricken youth in Cork. We passed Blarney. Then we were in the tunnel, and though I knew there is this long tunnel into Cork I had forgotten how long it was, how smelly and how dark.

He was the first person I saw on the platform, in his tweeds and his sporty cap. The wings of his hair were turning white. His teeth were much too white to be his own. He wore spectacles. We greeted one another warmly.

People talk of well-remembered voices. I recognised his slightly hectoring Oxford-cum-Cork accent only when he said, 'Well. So we got Your Highness down to Cork at last?' I laughed, 'Why do Cork people always say "up to Dublin" and "down to Cork"? Here I am, like Orpheus.' He sniffed by way of reply, and we went out of the station yard teasing one another amiably about our advancing years, sat into his white sports Jaguar and shot across the station yard like a bullet.

3

'Well?' I said. 'And how did you finish up yesterday with my dear old Aunty Anna?'

He pretended to be coping with the traffic – at that point a dozen bullocks lurching wild-eyed all over the street before the howls and waving arms of two equally wild-eyed drovers. Then, with a sheepish side glance and a grin that was clearly meant to involve me in his illogicality, he said:

'I gave her the odd two quid again. She will obviously be back in a month. And every month for the rest of her life. Unless we do something drastic about her.'

'I see. Are we going to beard her now?'

'No! I don't work on Saturdays. And I'm not going to break my rule of life for that accursed old hairpin. I'm driving you out to my Sabine farm. We've got the whole weekend. We'll talk about her tonight after dinner. And not one minute before!'

I bridled. After all, I was very fond of my Aunty Anna, even if I had not visited her for the last twelve years, and I objected to being shanghaied like this without as much as a 'If you'd like it', or 'If you can spare the time', or 'By your leave'. Was he at his old game of playing the big shot? The bossy businessman? At close quarters, over a whole weekend, was he going to turn out to be an awful bore? However, he had been very kind to Aunty Anna, and I had got him into this mess, and I was under an obligation to him, so I said, as pleasantly as I could. 'That's very kind of you,

Mel. I can see my aunt tomorrow morning, and I'm sure there must be an afternoon train home.'

'If that's what you want,' he said, rather huffily. Then he said cheerfully, 'If there is a train to Dublin on Sundays I'm sure it takes about ten hours.' Then he said, so smugly that anybody who did not know him could well have taken an immediate dislike to him, 'You're going to like my cottage – it's a real beauty. Nobody in Cork has anything like it!'

I did not talk much during the drive into and out of the city. It reminded me too much of my father and mother, of my lost youth. He blathered on and on about its great future, its economic development, the airport they were sure to have some day, as if he were the Lord Mayor of the damn place. Then we were out of it and in the country again, and presently – it can not have been more than twenty minutes at his mad speed – he said, 'Behold my Sabine farm!'

At first glance, through the trees, it looked like the sort of cottage that would make an estate-agent start pouring out words like 'rustic', 'picturesque', 'antique', 'venerable', 'traditional', 'old-world' and every other kind of pin-headed euphemism for damp, dirty, crumbling, phoney, half ruined, fourth-hand and thoroughly uncomfortable. When we drew up by its little wooden gate, it turned out to be the sort of dream cottage you meet in English detective stories, or on the travel posters of British Railways. It stood under its trim roof of thatch on a sunbathed sideroad, in about two acres of orchard, kitchen garden and lawn, facing a small, old church with a not ungraceful spire in brown-stone, directly above the Lee murmuring far below in a valley scooped aeons ago out of the surrounding hills and covered now with young pine-woods. It was long, low and pink-washed, with diamond panes in its small windows, and its walls were covered by a thick curtain of Albertine roses that would be a mellow blaze within a week or two. The door, painted in William Morris blue, was opened by a brown-eyed young woman whom he introduced as, 'My housekeeper. My invaluable Sheila.' The living-room was long and low-ceilinged, furnished in elegant Adams and Chippendale, carpeted in pale green from wall to wall, with an unnecessary but welcoming wood fire sizzling softly in an old brick fireplace. Later I found that he had put in central heating, electric light and an American-style kitchen. His Sheila brought us Scotch, water and ice-cubes, and we sank into two deep armchairs beside the fire.

'You seem to live pretty well, friend,' I admitted grudgingly.

'I like the simple life,' he breezed. 'But I'm not simple-minded about it, I'm a realist.'

I humphed internally. I recognised the common illusion of most businessmen that writers are all mental defectives, dreamy romancers with about as much commonsense as would fit in one of their small toes. Really, I thought again, all this might well turn out to be a frightful bore.

I became aware that his housekeeper was still standing beside us. Her brown eyes reminded me of two shining chestnuts. If her chin had not been a shadow overshot she would have been a beauty. What struck me most about her was not, however, her face, her trim figure or her straight back, but her air of calm self-possession. He gave her a quick, all-over glance.

'Well, my dear? What are you giving us for dinner tonight?'

'Two roast chickens. Parsley potatoes. New. Your own. And fresh peas from the garden.'

'And for sweet? Apart from yourself?' he asked, with that kind of gawky smile with which elderly men try to curry favour with scowling children, and that celibates overdo for handsome young women.

'Apart from myself,' she replied calmly, 'there will be an apple pie. They are the last apples left in your loft.'

'With cream?'

'Naturally.'

'And the wine?'

She nodded to two bottles standing at a discreet distance from the brickwork of the fireplace. Gevrey Chambertin : 1949.

'Excellent. We will dine at seven-thirty.' He turned away from her. 'Drink up! I saw two kingfishers flashing along the river last week and I want to check whether they are still there. They've just got married,' he added, with a raise-your-eyebrows grin at Sheila, who tossed her head and went off about her business.

'And where did that treasure come from?' I asked, carefully keeping the note of suspicion out of my voice, and noting inwardly that twenty years ago I would have started to pull his leg about her.

'Pure luck. She is a typist in my office. I used to have a dreadful old hairpin, as old and almost as doddery as your mad aunt. Then I suddenly found out that Sheila lives halfway between here and Cork, in a labourer's cottage on the side of the road. When I suggested to her that she might lend a hand and make some extra cash she jumped at it. Every Friday night I drive her home from the office on my way here, collect her on Saturday morning, and Bob's-your-uncle.'

He gathered up his binoculars, notebooks and camera, and we went off after the kingfishers. I enjoyed every minute of it, tramping for about three hours up and down the river bed. He found his kingfishers, a nesting heron, and became madly excited when he picked out through his binoculars, and let me also see, a buff-coloured bird about the size of a thrush but with a long beak, a crest and black and white stripes on its wings, perched on a tall beech tree.

'Can it,' he kept saying in a shouting whisper, 'but it can't be, can it *possibly* be a hoopoe?'

He entered every detail in his field notebook, date, hour, temperature, compass bearings and heaven only knows what else, and he became so boyish about it all that my earlier annoyance with him vanished completely. When, on the way home, I asked him casually how old he was, and he said 'Forty-seven', my earlier suspicions also vanished. He was at least twice her age. By the time we got back to his cottage I felt not only so pleasantly tired but so pleasantly relaxed that I told him I had decided not to return home until the Monday morning.

The wood fire, now that the evening chill had come, was welcoming. I found that there were two baths, and lots of hot water. I wallowed in mine for twenty minutes. When we both emerged his Sheila made us a shaker of martinis, and through them we moved leisurely into a perfect dinner. She had not roasted the chickens, she had broiled them *en papilottes*. She must have spent an hour on the apple pie alone – my wife, who is a first-rate cook, could not have improved on its delicate crust.

'Did you teach her all this cooking, Mel?'

'I confess I have tried to play Professor Higgins to her Pygmalion. But only,' he winked, 'as to her cooking. So far.'

By the time we had finished off the two bottles of Burgundy and retired to our armchairs before the fire we were the old – that is the young – Mel and Sean. She lit two shaded lamps, brought us Italian coffee, a bottle of Hine, two warmed glasses, the cigar-box and our slippers.

'Wonderful woman!' I murmured. 'I hope you never lose her.'

'She is useful,' he agreed shortly, poured the brandy and, like me, stretched out his long legs to the fire.

For a while there was not a sound except the sizzle of the logs and an occasional slight tinkle from the direction of the kitchen. The deep, darkening country closed around us in such utter silence that when I strained my ears to listen I could hear, deep in the valley, the whisper of the river. Did I hear a pheasant coughing? Drowsily I remembered that he had said that we would talk tonight of Aunty Anna. I had no wish to talk about Aunty Anna, and by the sleepy way he was regarding the fire through his brandy glass I hoped he felt the same. Then I heard his voice, and with something sharper than regret I gathered that he had begun to talk about himself.

4

'Sean, I'm very glad you came. For a long time now I've been working out a certain idea, something rather important, and I want to try it out on you, just as a sort of test.'

Just barely holding off the sleep of bliss, I nodded easily.

'Did it ever strike you that every man – which includes every woman – is his own potter? I mean, that sooner or later every man takes up what you might call the clay, or the plasticine, or the mud, call it what you like, of his experience of life, and throws it down on his potter's wheel, and starts the pedal going, and rounds it up into a shape? Into what I call his idea of the shape of his whole life? Are you following me?'

I nodded myself awake.

'Good! Now for the big snag. It is, why do we do this? I can't say we do it to please ourselves, because we can *have* no selves – can we? We can't *see* ourselves, – can we? – or *know* ourselves – can we? – and therefore we cannot *be* ourselves – can we? – until we have made this shape, and looked at it, as one would look in a mirror, and said to ourselves, "That's me! That's my vocation. My ambition. My politics. My faith. My whole life." I mean,' he pounded on, with a force of energy that made me even more tired and sleepy than before, 'I cannot say "That's me" until I have made my shape, because there is no *me* until I have made my shape. Therefore I can get no real pleasure of it all until the job is actually done. That's a pretty disturbing thought, what-what?'

I pulled myself awake. What had I walked into? Two nights of this twaddle? There simply had to be an afternoon train tomorrow!

'And when the job is done, Mel?'

He gave me a powerful slap on the thigh.

'Then I begin to live. When I at last know exactly what I am, I at last know exactly what I want to do, because my shape, my image, now tells me what I do want to do.'

I sighed and stretched.

'And then, Mel, some other fellow comes along and he looks at your portrait of the artist as a young dog, and he says, "No! This may be some crazy dream Mel has of himself, or some crazy dream he has of the world as he would like it to be, but it's not our Mel, and it's not our world." '

'Ha-ha, and I might say the same to him, and to his world?'

'You certainly might. But, of course, I hope you're not so daft as to deny that all the time there must be a real objective world outside there? Made up of stockbrokers and tax-collectors, and physicists, and isoprene, and polymerisation . . .'

'By the way, rubber is going up.'

'. . . and gravitation, electricity, atomic weight, blood pressure, measles, kids getting sick, old people dying and kingfishers mating, and so on and so on. And a real, objective you, me, and Tom, Dick and Harry inside in each one of us, and no fancies and no fooling.' I laughed. 'Mel, you're a joy! I'm glad to inform you that you haven't changed one iota since the days when we used to come out from old Father Abstractibus's philosophy lectures, long ago in University College, Cork, and lie on the grass of the quadrangle, and talk for hours about the Object and the Subject and "What is Reality?", and "What is the stars?", and never got one inch beyond chasing our own tails. And here you are still at it! It's a pointless pursuit, and I'm in no mood for it. Mel! If we have to talk about anything at all on top of that wonderful dinner, and that marvellous Gevrey Chambertin, and this perfect brandy, let's talk about a painfully real subject. Let's talk about my Aunty Anna.'

'That,' he said calmly, 'is what I am talking about. About people who live in imaginations, and fantasies, and illusions about themselves. What, so far as I can see, the whole blessed world is doing all the time. Including your dear Aunty Anna Maria Whelan.' He stretched out his foot and touched my ankle with the toe of his slipper. 'Do you know what your dear Aunty Anna did with that three hundred and fifty quid?'

'You told me. She bought an armchair, and an electric fire, and an eiderdown, and curtains, and Masses for her soul, and she gave loans to ...'

'Rubbish! That's what she said. She bought a fur coat with the three-fifty quid.'

'You're a liar!'

'She is the liar.'

'Then you're joking.'

'It's no joke, my friend. The old divil had the cheek to have it on her back when she came into my office yesterday. When she went out I had a brain-wave. I rang up a friend of mine who works with the Saint Vincent de Paul's in her part of the city and I asked him to drop around and have a look at her place. No armchair, no electric fire, no eiderdown, no new curtains, no nothing. And as for those loans that she invented, as he pointed out to me, the poor don't give anybody loans of ten quid a time. Ten shillings would be more like it. If that! You talk very glibly about the "real, objective world outside there". You don't seem to know so very much about it, after all, do you?'

His air of condescension infuriated me.

'It was probably a cheap, second-hand coat!'

'I checked up on that too. Cork is a small place, and there aren't many shops where you can buy new fur coats for a sum as large as that. I rang up Bob Rohu and I told him the whole yarn. I hit a bull's eye at once. He sold it to her himself. He remembered the transaction very well – as you might expect. A poor old woman like her doesn't come in every day to buy a bang-up fur coat. She paid him two hundred and seventy-five pounds for that fur coat. In notes.' He paused. He concluded with sardonic formality, 'You perceive my trend?'

I was furious, chastened and filled with pity for my Aunty Anna. I saw also that whatever picture Mel had made of himself it would not show him as anybody's fool. I could have choked him. Here was I, who had known Aunty Anna all my life, a man who was supposed to know something about human nature, and here was this fellow who had only met Aunty Anna three or four times in his life, pitilessly exposing her to me as a woman perched out there for thirty years on that big, grassy, empty plain of the Curragh of Kildare, working, since she was twenty, for a wealthy trainer, seeing his rich, horsy clients coming and going in all their finery, and thinking, as she grew older and older, with no man ever asking her to marry him – Why the hell had I never realised that she would think it? – that she would never possess anything even dimly like what they possessed. Until, by pure chance, at the age of seventy-odd, she finds herself drawing dividends like the best of them, trading in the stock-market just like the best of them, being received like a lady by the best stockbroker in Cork – and sees that fur coat in a shop window.

Mel was slowly rolling his brandy around in his brandy glass and watching me slyly.

'Interesting, isn't it?' he said.

'Very,' I said bitterly. After a while of silence I said, 'And this is why she won't get any more of what she thinks are her little divvies? Even if I agreed to pay you for them?'

He answered with anger, almost with passion:

'It is. The woman is fooling herself, and I refuse to encourage her. She is trying to make nonsense of everything I believe in. And I won't let her do it. Would you, as a writer, write something you didn't believe to be true?'

'Don't be silly! I'm pleased and proud any time I think I'm able to tell even one tenth of the truth.'

'Would you, if you were a doctor, tell lies to a patient?'

'Doctors have to do it all the time. To help them to live. To make it easier for them to die.'

'Well, I don't and won't tell lies. Facts are facts in my profession, and I have to live by them.'

'You gamble.'

'I do not.'

'You encourage your clients to gamble.'

'I do not.'

'Then what do you do for a living?'

'I hope.'

We laughed. We calmed down.

'What about charity, Mel?'

'I would have no objection to giving your aunt charity. I like the old thing. She is a nice poor soul. And my friend in the Vincent de Paul assures me that she is a very worthy creature. In fact I'd be quite happy to pay the old hairpin . . .' Here the chill caution of the trained businessman entered his voice, 'I'd be quite happy to go halves with you in paying her the equivalent of her blasted divvies every year. But not as dividends! Strictly as a gift from the pair of us.'

'Mel, that's kind of you! Our whole problem is solved. Let's give her the £28 a year as a present. What are you looking at me like that for?'

'She won't take it.'

'Why won't she take it?'

'Because it's charity. And she doesn't want charity. The poor never want charity. They hate it because it makes them feel their poverty. Any of them that have any pride left in them. And that old lady is stiff with pride. You could take a gift from me, I could take a gift from you, Queen Victoria would have taken all India and hung it on her charm bracelet without as much as a thank you. But not the poor! However, try her. Take the Jaguar to-morrow morning and drive into town and take her out to lunch. I bet you a tenner to a bob she'll refuse.' He rose. 'Ah! Here we are!'

This was for our housekeeper, waiting, ready to be driven home. She was wearing a small fur hat and a neat, belted tweed coat. From under her hat her dark hair crooked around each cheek. Now that she was wearing high-heeled shoes I noticed how long and elegant her legs were.

'That,' said Mel, surveying her, 'is a darling little hat you have.'

'I had it on this morning,' she said quietly. 'But men never notice anything.'

'Where did you get it?'

'I bought it of course. It's wild mink. I've been saving up for it for years. I got it at Rohu's.'

'Good girl!' he said enthusiastically, and looked at me in approval of his pupil, while I wondered if he knew how much even that little dream of wild mink cost her. She might well have been saving up for it for years. 'I'll bring around the car. I won't be long,' he said to me. 'Play yourself some music while we're away. I've got some good records.'

When he had gone out I said to her, 'Won't you sit down while you are waiting?' and she sat sedately on the arm of his vacated chair and crossed her pretty heron's legs.

'Do you like music, Sheila?'

'I used to like only jazz. Recently I've come to prefer classical music. Mr Meldrum has been introducing me to it. Shall I show you how to work the machine? It's new and he is very particular about it. It has two extensions. They give you the impression that you are surrounded by an orchestra. Oh!' lifting the lid and looking in 'There's a record on it. Yes, here is the jacket – it's *The Siegfried Idyll*. Would you like to play this one. Or would you perhaps prefer something more modern?'

(I thought, 'You may only be a typist in his office but you have the manners of a woman of the world.')

'Yes, I'd like to hear that again. It's years since I heard any Wagner. Do *you* like it?'

'We've played it so often now that I'm just beginning to understand what it's all about.'

'And what is it all about?' I smiled.

She switched on the machine and closed the lid.

'I suppose it's about happiness through love. It takes a little time to warm up. Then it works automatically.'

I glanced at her. Was she a deep one? His horn hooted from the road. For the first time she smiled. She had perfect teeth.

'I must be off. Don't let the fire die down. He sometimes sits up late. There are plenty of logs. And I've fixed the electric blankets at Number Two heat, so they will be nice and cosy before you have finished your last nightcaps. Goodnight.'

When she was gone I walked to the window to look after her and saw that a vast moon had risen over the dark hills surrounding the valley, touching their round breasts as softly as a kiss. He and she stood arm in arm looking at it, he leaning a little over her, pointing up to the moon as if he were showing it to an infant, and saying something that, for once, must have not been off the mark, because she swiftly turned her face up to him and laughed gloriously. Just as he touched her furry cap with his finger the record behind me fell into place and a score of violins began whispering, pulsing and swelling around me as powerfully as the immense moon. In that second I had no more doubts about the pair of them. He released her arm, opened the door of the car for her so that its carriage light fell for a second on her radiant smile. He banged her door, got in on his side and shot away. I returned slowly to my armchair, my brandy and cigar, and stared into the flickering fire.

Gradually the idyll rose in wave after wave to its first crescendo until the bows of the violins were so many lashing whips of passionate sound. The lunatic! Sitting here, of nights, in this silent valley, with her opposite him, listening to music like this Christmas morning music, composed by a lover for his sleeping beloved. If it made me wish to God I was at home in bed with my wife what, in heaven's name, must it do to him? I suddenly remembered some-thing that made me snatch up the jacket of the record. I was right. Wagner wrote that love idyll when he was fifty-seven, having fallen in love with Cosima Liszt when he was in his forties and she in her twenties, and I began to think of other elderly men who had married young women, finding them even in that tight little city a few miles away. Wintering men plucking their budding roses. Old Robert Cottrell, the ship-owner, who married a barmaid out of the Victoria Hotel. Frank Lane, the distiller, who at sixty picked a pretty waitress out of The Golden Tavern. And who was that miller who, after being a widower for twenty-five years, fell in love with one of his mill-girls and had children by her, younger than his grandchildren? It is the sort of thing that can easily happen to men who have lived all their lives by the most rigid conventions, and then suddenly get sick of it all and throw their hats over the moon.

I became more calm as the music slowly died in exhaustion of its own surfeit. He was as open as a book – all that talk of his about men taking the clay of life and making a self-shape of it. Of her I knew nothing except that he had said she lived in a road-side cottage and, as he must know well – and he would be the first to say it – that a rich stockbroker would be a wonderful catch for her. I started to walk restlessly about the house. By error I entered his bedroom. I shut the door quickly, feeling that I was floundering in deep and dangerous tides. The covers of his bed had been neatly turned down at an angle of forty-five degrees and on his pillow there lay a red rosebud. I went to bed and fell into such a sound sleep that I did not hear him return.

When I woke up it was blazing sun outside and the cottage was empty: he had presumably gone to Mass and to collect her. When they came in he was wearing the rosebud in his lapel. After breakfast I took the Jaguar and drove into town to meet my Aunty Anna.

5

The city was full of the sound of church bells but there was hardly a soul out along the quay where she lived. Even the gulls were silent, floating on the river or perched along the quayside walls. I drew up outside her old fabric of a house, its railings crooked, its fanlight cracked, its traditional eight-panelled door clotted with years of paint asking only for a blowlamp and a week's scraping to reveal chiselled mouldings and fine mahogany. I sat for a while in the car thinking of the Aunty Anna I knew and the best way to handle her.

She had always been a soft, slack, complaining creature with, so far as I knew, no keener interests in life than backing horses, telling fortunes on the cups and cards, eating boiled sweets and reading violet-coloured penny novelettes. I should have brought her a box of chocolates. I drove off and managed to find a shop open that sold them. It may have been, it occurred to me, this love of boiled sweets that used to give her so much trouble with her teeth; they used to pain her a great deal and several of them were decayed in the front of her mouth. At that time there was some kind of pulp, paste or maleable wafer that poor country folk used as a dental stopgap to hide these marks of decay on special occasions. Or perhaps it was only white paper chewed-up? She used it constantly and it made her teeth look like putty. The poor woman had also had an operation performed, unskilfully, on her left elbow, which had a moist hollow, like a navel, where the point of the ulna ought to have been; she used to nurse it all the time with her fondling right hand, especially on cold or windy days. Would the poor old thing respond to the idea of going to a good surgeon? Or I could, perhaps, tempt her with some good stout, comfortable dresses: my wife could easily get these for her. Not that I feared, looking up at the crumbling bricks of her tenement, that I would have any difficulty in persuading her to accept an annual gift, and I thought back to those days on the rolling, green Curragh when she had at least had every comfort, the best of food and healthy, country air, and I realised that she should never have left her base, and that the ideal, but now impossible, thing for her to do would be to go back and live in the country where she belonged.

A few minutes later I was holding her weeping in my arms, in her one room where she had cooked, slept and sat day after day, for so many years, and as I smelled the familiar, indefinable musk of urban poverty, suggestive mainly of sour clothes, bad sewage and fried onions, I was overcome with shame that I had not visited her once during the twelve years since I left Cork to be married. I kissed her, and she kissed me, as maternally as if I were still a small boy. Then I stood back, looked at her and got a shock of memory. She had a face like an old turtle, she was humped like a heron and she was rouged. Long ago, my mother had laughed one day and said she did it with geranium petals rubbed lightly in pale-brown boot polish. I noted, too, that all her decayed teeth were replaced by a good denture, and that her hair was tinted and blued. Like a boy I endured the reproaches that she poured over me, and then, eager to be out of that jumbled, stuffy room, I bustled her to get ready and come out to lunch at the Victoria Hotel.

She put on her fur coat, and a small, ancient straw hat, gay with white daisies. Once she was dressed she became rigid with what Cork calls grandeur, as when she said: 'This is quite a nice little car,' and started talking about all the much grander cars she used to drive in at the Curragh Races. At lunch she held her knife and fork at right-angles to her plate, sipped her wine like a bird, drank her coffee with the little finger crooked, hem-hemmed into her napkin like a nun and small-talked as if she were royalty giving me an audience, all of it gossip and chit-chat about the gentry of the Curragh and their fine ladies and great houses. At the end of the lunch she produced a compact, powdered her nose, examined her face intently all over and delicately applied a pink lipstick. She evaded all my efforts to talk of old times until we moved into the empty lounge where I had a stout brandy. She preferred a gin-and-lime. At last I did lure her out of her glorious past to my proposal that I should give her twenty-eight pounds a year (I carefully left Mel out of it) as a little gesture, 'For old times' sake, *Aunty?*' – trying to make her stop being Her Majesty, and become my Aunty Anna again.

She made short work of me.

'No! Thank you very much. Now that I have my divvies I don't need it.'

From there we went back and forth over the whole thing, over more brandy and gin, for two fruitless hours. Gifts she would ('of course') not accept. Her divvies she would ('of course') not renounce. By the end of it I had gained only one point. She said, coldly but with spirit, that if 'that man' denied her her rights she would never darken his door again.

'I will have nothing more to do with this so-called Mister Meldrum. I am finished with all fraudulent stockbrokers for ever.'

It was four o'clock before I surrendered, furious, rejected, humiliated and exhausted. I drove her around the city, slowly at her queenly request, in my white Jaguar (in which, I told her, I had arrived from Dublin that morning), and ended up at her door amid a crowd of lane kids oohing and aahing at what one of them called Snow White's car. I promised faithfully to visit her again next summer, kissed her good-bye, excused my haste by saying that I had to be back in Dublin before nightfall and drove away amid the huzzas of the tiny mob. As soon as I got around a corner I paused to rub off her lipstick. I felt very proud of her, I despised myself, and I hated Mel and all that he and his kind stood for – by which I do not now know what I meant then, unless it had something to do with the corrupting power of money over us all.

I was in no mood to face his guffaws of triumph. I parked the Jaguar on the empty South Mall and went wandering through the silent, Sunday streets of this city of my youth, seeing little of it. I was too angry, and too absorbed in trying to devise some means of helping her, and at every turn bothered by unhappy thoughts about Mel and myself, and about whatever it was that the years had done to us both. Was he right in saying that I knew nothing about poor people like Aunty Anna? His Sheila was a young, pretty Aunty Anna, poor like her, being drawn now, as she had been, close to the world of wealth. What did he really know about her? The question brought me to the point – I was then leaning over the old South Gate Bridge, looking down into the River Lee, far from sweet-smelling at low tide – thinking again not of him alone but of myself and him, as we were when we were here, at college together, years ago. What did I really ever know about him? My Aunty Anna was dead, replaced by what would have been described in one of her violet-covered novelettes as 'Miss Anna Whelan, A Country Lady in reduced circumstances', with nothing left to her from her better days but her memories and her fur coat; defrauded and impoverished of thousands of pounds – her lost fortune would be at least that much within a matter of weeks – by a slick stockbroker. Had my Mel ever existed?

We are not one person. We pass through several lives of faith, ambition, sometimes love, often friendship. We change, die and live again. In that cosy cottage of his I had been the guest of a ghost? Myself a ghost? If he was a new man his Sheila might know him. I did not. For all I knew, she was creating him. All I knew, as I rose from the parapet and walked back to the car, was that I must return to his cottage, as I must leave it, in the most careful silence.

I got back in time to join him and the local curate in another of Sheila's cool five-to-one martinis. Over the dinner, which was just as good as the one the night before, I left the talk to Mel and his guest, all about archaeology, birds, the proposed airport, Cork's current political gossip. I envied the pair of them. Nobody in a capital city can ever be so intimately and intensely absorbed about local matters as provincials always are about the doings and the characters of their city-states. The curate left early. Mel drove Sheila home immediately after. He returned, within twenty minutes.

I was standing with my hand on the high mantelpiece of the fireplace listening to the *verso* of the *Siegfried Idyll*, the end of the last act of *Die Walküre*. As he came in I raised a silencing hand, excited as I was by the heroic loveliness of this music that lays Brünhilde on the mountainside in Valhalla, at the centre of encircling fires through which a young man, who will be Siegfried, will one day break to deliver her with a kiss. Mel threw himself into his armchair, his hands behind his head, and we both listened until the music ended and the silence and the dark of the country began to hum again in our ears. For a while we said nothing. Then I did what I had promised not to do.

'Well?' I asked, looking down at him.

'Well?' he said, looking up at me.

'Do I congratulate you?'

'On what?'

'On your Brünhilde.'

Lazily he rolled his head on the back of his chair.

'Meaning no? Or that you don't know?'

Again he slowly rolled his head.

'Giving nothing away? Mel, you used not to be so damn cautious. What has happened to you? Come on, Mel, take a chance on life. Begin by giving Aunty Anna her divvies.'

'Aha? So she refused our gift?'

'She refused. Also she will trouble you no more. She is now convinced that you are a fraudulent stockbroker who has robbed her of a fortune. Come on, man! Gamble for once in your cautious life. Stop being a fraudulent broker.'

'Are you suggesting that I should let your aunt blackmail me?'

'I'm suggesting that you forget the idol you have made outside in the woodshed. It's not you. It can't be you. The Mel I knew can't be that fancy portrait of an unbreakable, incorruptible, crusty, self-absorbed old man, stiff-necked with principles and pride and priggishness. It is a false god. Kick it out on the rubbish heap. When you have made yourself a real image of yourself you'll find there is nothing so terribly frightening about giving Aunty Anna her divvies – or marrying Sheila.'

I had said 'frightening' because immediately I started suggesting that he was different to whatever he wanted to be I had seen his eyes under his blond eyelashes contract, a blush appear on his cheekbones under their grey outcrops of hair, his mouth begin to melt. With a flick he threw away the sudden fear.

'I haven't changed. I am what I am, always was and intend always to be. And if I am a prig, as you so kindly call me, I'm content to be a prig. It's better than being a cock-eyed dreamer like you and your mad aunt.'

'Then why are you playing with the girl?'

'I am not.'

'In that case you might wipe that lipstick off your cheek.'

'You know nothing about her.' He paused. 'She has a boyfriend He was waiting for her again at her cottage tonight.'

'I shouldn't be surprised if she had a dozen boy-friends. A girl as pretty as that! You have seen him often?'

'I have. He comes around here on his motor-bicycle whenever she stays a bit later than usual. Just to offer her a lift home. Just by way of no harm. Each time, she goes off with him at once. I followed them one night. I saw them kissing and hugging under a tree. If she can deceive him she could deceive me. If I married her I might be unhappy all my life, I'd be jealous and suspicious of her all my life.'

'You make me sick! *You* might not be happy? Why don't you say she might not be happy? What sort of a thing do you think marriage is? One long honeymoon? Happiness is a bonus. You smuggle it. You work for it. It comes and goes. You have to be in the market to snatch it. Where's your realism? He who does not speculate cannot accumulate. Stop being such a coward! Live, man, live!'

'I prefer to be logical.'

'Then you certainly will not give Aunty Anna her imaginary divvies, and you will have to sack your imaginary Sheila, and then you will be very unhappy indeed.'

'It may be. It will wear off. And, anyway, it's none of your damn business.'

For a couple of moments we looked at one another hatefully. Then I turned and without saying goodnight went to my room. Almost immediately I heard the front door slam. Parting the curtains

I saw him stride down the path, out into the moonlit road and around the corner under the deep shadows of the trees towards where we had gone yesterday to watch the kingfishers, the nesting heron and that unlikely, crested, exotic bird. For a second my heart went out to him. Then I shrugged him off in despair. I was awakened – my watch said it was two o'clock – by the sound of the Brünhildeian flames wavering, leaping, pulsing from their mountaintop among the gods. I, in bed, he, by the ashen fire, listened to it together. After it died away I heard his door click.

In the morning I rose to find him already up and in his spotless yellow-and-white kitchen making coffee and toast.

'Morning, Mel!'

'Hello! Sleep well? I'm the cook on Monday mornings. She leaves everything ready, as you see,' nodding to the napery, china and silverware on the table.

She had even left a tiny bouquet of polyanthuses, alyssum and cowslips in a vase.

He was dressed for the city in his black jacket, with black and grey-striped pants, grey Suède waistcoat, stiff white collar and striped shirt, a small pearl tie-pin in his grey tie. Over the coffee he talked about birds, and for that while, as on the Saturday, he was again his old attractive, youthful, zestful self. He talked of the hoopoe, saying, 'It cannot have been one – they pass us by in the spring.' He talked about night-jars. He sounded knowledgeable about owls. When we were ready to go he saw to it that every curtain was drawn ('The sun fades the mahogony') and every window carefully fastened, took down his bowler hat and umbrella, double-locked the door, felt it twice, looked all over the front of the cottage, and we drove off into another sun-bathed morning.

On the way into town we picked up Sheila outside her road-side cottage, and after that we did not speak at all until he dropped her at his office. There I tried to insist on his not seeing me off at the station – he was a busy man, Monday morning and all that, he must have lots to attend to—and he insisted against my insisting, and we almost squabbled again before he gave in so far as to go into his office to ask if there was anything urgent. He brought me in with him, and formally introduced me to his chief accountant and his book-keeper. While he ruffled through his mail, I chatted with them, and noted the Turkish carpet, and all his modern gadgets, and thought that this was the place where Aunty Anna began to change. At the station he insisted on buying me the morning papers, and on waiting by my carriage door until the train should carry me away. I thanked him for our enjoyable weekend, assured him I meant it, praised his cottage, remembered the food and the wine, promised that we would meet again, to which he nodded, and exchanged a few polite, parting words. As the porters started to slam the last doors, and pull up the windows against the rank smells of the tunnel at the platform's end, he said, his pointed face lifted below my window, his eyes sullen above the two little tufts of greying hair on his cheekbones:

'You will be pleased to hear, by the way, that I have decided to give your aunt her dividends, as usual. Naturally, we go halves in that.'

I leaned down and grasped his shoulder.

'And marry Sheila?'

'I know when I'm licked. I'm going to give her the sack this morning. I'll have to get a new housekeeper. I am going to ask your Aunty Anna.'

'But she's seventy! And a lady in reduced circumstances. She will refuse.'

'Not when she sees my cottage,' he said arrogantly. 'I'm only there on weekends. She can imagine she is a real lady for five days in the week. Not bad! And she has been a cook. And she won't tempt my flesh. Hail! And Farewell!'

The train started to puff and chug and he and the platform slid slowly away.

Seconds later I was in the tunnel. My window went opaque. I got the rancid smell of the underworld. 'And Farewell?' Evidently I was not, it was a last judgement on my presumption, to meet him ever again. I had probed, I had interfered, I had uncovered his most secret dream and destroyed it by forcing him to bring it to the test of reality. I had been tiresome in every way. I had counted on finding the Mel I had thought I had always known, felt affronted at finding him rather different, tried to make him more different, and yet at the same time have my old Mel, and was furious when he insisted on remaining whatever he thought he always had been. In such irreducibly plenary moments of total mess, shame and embarrassment the truth can only be trite, though none the less the truth for that. Youth only knows embryos. Life is equivocal. Life is a gamble. Friendship is frail. Love is a risk. All any man can do when fate sends some shining dream his way is to embrace it and fight for it without rest or reason because we do all the important things of life for reasons (It *has* been said!) of which reason knows nothing – until about twenty years after.

For that mile of tunnel I had them all there together with me in that dark carriage, with the cold smell of steam, and an occasional splash of water on the roof from the ventilation shafts to the upper air. Abruptly, the tunnel shot away and I felt like a skin-diver soaring from the sea to the light of day. Green country exploded around me on all sides in universal sunlight. Small, pink cars went ambling below me along dusty side-roads to the creamery. Black-and-white cows munched. Everywhere in the fields men were at their morning work. I opened the window to let in the fresh air. Then, with only occasional glances out at the fields floating away behind me, and at certain images and thoughts that became fainter and fewer with the passing miles, I settled down to my newspapers and the gathering thoughts of my home and my work.

I have never seen him since, although we are both now ageing men, but, perhaps three times, it could be four, as if a little switch went click in my memory he has revisited me – a dubious shadow, with two grey tufts on his cheeks and a long nose like Sherlock Holmes . . . No more. He did write to me once, after – not, I observed, *when* – Aunty Anna died, in his service, aged eighty-one. Piously, he had attended to everything. He enclosed some snapshots that he had found in her bag: herself as a young woman, horses on the Curragh, myself as a young boy. In her will, he mentioned, she had bequeathed her dividends to him.

The Talking Trees

There were four of them in the same class at the Red Abbey, all under fifteen. They met every night in Mrs Coffey's sweetshop at the top of Victoria Road to play the fruit machine, smoke fags and talk about girls. Not that they really talked about them – they just winked, leered, nudged one another, laughed, grunted and groaned about them, or said things like 'See her legs?' 'Yaroosh!' 'Wham!' 'Ouch!' 'Ooof!' or 'If only, if only!' But if anybody had said, 'Only what?' they would not have known precisely what. They knew nothing precisely about girls, they wanted to know everything precisely about girls, there was nobody to tell them all the things they wanted to know about girls and that they thought they wanted to do with them. Aching and wanting, not knowing, half guessing, they dreamed of clouds upon clouds of fat, pink, soft, ardent girls billowing towards them across the horizon of their future. They might just as well have been dreaming of pink porpoises moaning at their feet for love.

In the sweetshop the tall glass jars of coloured sweets shone in the bright lights. The one-armed fruit-machine went zing. Now and again girls from Saint Monica's came in to buy sweets, giggle roguishly and over-pointedly ignore them. Mrs Coffey was young, buxom, fairhaired, blue-eyed and very good-looking. They admired her so much that one night when Georgie Watchman whispered to them that she had fine bubs Dick Franks told him curtly not to be so coarse, and Jimmy Sullivan said in his most toploftical voice, 'Georgie Watchman, you should be jolly well ashamed of yourself, you are no gentleman,' and Tommy Gong Gong said nothing but nodded his head as insistently as a ventriloquist's dummy.

Tommy's real name was Tommy Flynn, but he was younger than any of them so that neither he nor they were ever quite sure that he ought to belong to the gang at all. To show it they called him all sorts of nicknames, like Inch because he was so small; Fatty because he was so puppy-fat; Pigeon because he had a chest like a woman; Gong Gong because after long bouts of silence he had a way of suddenly spraying them with wild bursts of talk like a fire alarm attached to a garden sprinkler.

That night all Georgie Watchman did was to make a rude blubber-lip noise at Dick Franks. But he never again said anything about Mrs Coffey. They looked up to Dick. He was the oldest of them. He had long eyelashes like a girl, perfect manners, the sweetest smile and the softest voice. He had been to two English boarding schools, Ampleforth and Downside, and in Ireland to three, Clongowes, Castelknock and Rockwell, and had been expelled from all five of them. After that his mother had made his father retire from the Indian Civil, come back to the old family house in Cork and, as a last hope, send her darling Dicky to the Red Abbey day-school. He smoked a corncob pipe and dressed in droopy plus fours with chequered stockings and red flares, as if he was always just coming from or going to the golf course. He played cricket and tennis, games that no other boy at the Red Abbey could afford to play. They saw him as the typical school captain they read about in English boys' papers like *The Gem* and *The Magnet*, *The Boy's Own Paper*, *The Captain* and *Chums*, which was where they got all those swanky words like Wham, Ouch, Yaroosh, Ooof and Jolly Well. He was their Tom Brown, their Bob Cherry, their Tom Merry, those heroes who were always leading Greyfriars School or Blackfriars School to victory on the cricket field amid the cap-tossing huzzas of the juniors and the admiring smiles of visiting parents. It never occurred to them that *The Magnet* or *The Gem* would have seen all four of them as perfect models for some such story as *The Cads of Greyfriars*, or *The Bounders of Blackfriars*, low types given to secret smoking in the spinneys, drinking in The Dead Woman's Inn, or cheating at examinations, or, worst crime of all, betting on horses with redfaced bookies' touts down from London, while the rest of the school was practising at the nets – a quartet of rotters fated to be caned ceremoniously in the last chapter before the entire awe-struck school, and then whistled off at dead of night back to their heartbroken fathers and mothers.

It could not have occurred to them because these crimes did not exist at the Red Abbey. Smoking? At the Red Abbey any boy who wanted to was free to smoke himself into a galloping consumption so long as he did it off the premises, in the jakes or up the chimney. Betting? Brother Julius was always passing fellows sixpence or even a bob to put on an uncle's or a cousin's horse at Leopardstown or the Curragh. In the memory of man no boy had ever been caned ceremoniously for anything. Fellows were just leathered all day long for not doing their homework, or playing hooky from school, or giving lip, or fighting in class – and they were leathered hard. Two years ago Jimmy Sullivan had been given six swingers on each hand with the sharp edge of a metre-long ruler for pouring the contents of an inkwell over Georgie Watchman's head in the middle of a history lesson about the Trojan Wars, in spite of his wailing explanation that he had only done it because he thought Georgie Watchman was a scut and all Trojans were blacks. Drink? They did not drink only because they were too poor. While, as for what *The Magnet* and *The Gem* really meant by 'betting' – which, they dimly understood, was some sort of depravity that no decent English boy would like to see mentioned in print – hardly a week passed that some brother did not say that a hard problem in algebra, or a leaky pen, or a window that would not open or shut was 'a blooming bugger'.

There was the day when little Brother Angelo gathered half a dozen boys about him at playtime to help him with a crossword puzzle.

'Do any of ye,' he asked, 'know what Notorious Conduct could be in seven letters?'

'Buggery?' Georgie suggested mock-innocently.

'Please be serious!' Angelo said. 'This is about Conduct.'

When the solution turned out to be *Jezebel*, little Angelo threw up his hands, said it must be some queer kind of foreign woman and declared that the whole thing was a blooming bugger. Or there was that other day when old Brother Expeditus started to tell them about the strict lives and simple food of Dominican priests and Trappist monks. When Georgie said, 'No tarts, Brother?' Expeditus had laughed loud and long.

'No, Georgie!' he chuckled. 'No pastries of any kind.'

They might as well have been in school in Arcadia. And every other school about them seemed to be just as hopeless. In fact they might have gone on dreaming of pink porpoises for years if it was not for a small thing that Gong Gong told them one October night in the sweetshop. He sprayed them with the news that his sister Jenny had been thrown out of class that morning in Saint Monica's for turning up with a red ribbon in her hair, a mother-of-pearl brooch at her neck and smelling of scent.

'Ould Sister Eustasia,' he fizzled, 'made her go out in the yard and wash herself under the tap, she said they didn't want any girls in their school who had notions.'

The three gazed at one another, and began at once to discuss all the possible sexy meanings of notions. Georgie had a pocket dictionary. 'An ingenious contrivance'? 'An imperfect conception (*US*)'? 'Small wares'? It did not make sense. Finally they turned to Mrs Coffey. She laughed, nodded towards two giggling girls in the shop who were eating that gummy kind of block toffee that can gag you for half an hour, and said, 'Why don't you ask *them*?' Georgie approached them most politely.

'Pardon me, ladies, but do you by any chance happen to have notions?'

The two girls stared at one another with cow's eyes, blushed scarlet and fled from the shop shrieking with laughter. Clearly a notion was very sexy.

'Georgie!' Dick pleaded. 'You're the only one who knows anything. What in heaven's name is it?'

When Georgie had to confess himself stumped they knew at last that their situation was desperate. Up to now Georgie had always been able to produce some sort of answer, right or wrong, to all their questions. He was the one who, to their disgust, told them what he called conraception meant. He was the one who had explained to them that all babies are delivered from the navel of the mother. He was the one who had warned them that if a fellow kissed a bad woman he would get covered by leprosy from head to foot. The son of a Head Constable, living in the police barracks, he had collected his facts simply by listening as quietly as a mouse to the other four policemen lolling in the dayroom of the barracks with their collars open, reading the sporting pages of *The Freeman's Journal*, slowly creasing their polls and talking about colts, fillies, cows, calves, bulls and bullocks and 'the mysteerious nachure of all faymale wimmen'. He had also gathered a lot of useful stuff by dutiful attendance since the age of eleven at the meetings and marchings of the Protestant Boys' Brigade, and from a devoted study of the Bible. And here he was, stumped by a nun!

Dick lifted his beautiful eyelashes at the three of them, jerked his head and led them out on the pavement.

'I have a plan,' he said quietly. 'I've been thinking of it for some time. Chaps! Why don't we see everything with our own eyes?' And he threw them into excited discussion by mentioning a name. 'Daisy Bolster?'

Always near every school, there is a Daisy Bolster – the fast girl whom everybody has heard about and nobody knows. They had all seen her at a distance. Tall, a bit skinny, long legs, dark eyes, lids heavy as the dimmers of a car lamp, prominent white teeth, and her lower lip always gleaming wet. She could be as old as seventeen. Maybe even eighteen. She wore her hair up. Dick told them that he had met her once at the tennis club with four or five other fellows around her and that she had laughed and winked very boldly all the time. Georgie said that he once heard a fellow in school say, 'She goes with boys.' Gong Gong bubbled that that was true because his sister Jenny told him that a girl named Daisy Bolster had been thrown out of school three years ago for talking to a boy outside the convent gate. At this Georgie flew into a terrible rage.

'You stupid slob!' he roared. 'Don't you know yet that when anybody says a boy and girl are talking to one another it means they're doing you-know-what?'

'I don't know you-know-what,' Gong Gong wailed. 'What what?'

'I heard a fellow say,' Jimmy Sullivan revealed solemnly, 'that she has no father and that her mother is no better than she should be.'

Dick said in approving tones that he had once met another fellow who had heard her telling some very daring stories.

'Do you think she would show us for a quid?'

Before they parted on the pavement that night they were talking not about a girl but about a fable. Once a girl like that gets her name up she always ends up as a myth, and for a generation afterwards, maybe more, it is the myth that persists. 'Do you remember,' some old chap will wheeze, 'that girl Daisy Bolster? She used to live up the Mardyke. We used to say she was fast.' The other old boy will nod knowingly, the two of them will look at one another inquisitively, neither will admit anything, remembering only the long, dark avenue, it's dim gaslamps, the stars hooked in its trees.'

Within a month Dick had fixed it. Their only trouble after that was to collect the money and to decide whether Gong Gong should be allowed to come with them.

Dick fixed that, too, at a final special meeting in the sweet-shop. Taking his pipe from between his lips, he looked speculatively at Gong Gong, who looked up at him with eyes big as plums, trembling between the terror of being told he could not come with them and the greater terror of being told that he could.

'Tell me, Gong Gong,' Dick said politely, 'what exactly does your father do?'

'He's a tailor,' Tommy said, blushing a bit at having to confess it, knowing that Jimmy's dad was a bank clerk, that Georgie's was a Head Constable, and that Dick's had been a Commissioner in the Punjab.

'Very fine profession,' Dick said kindly. 'Gentleman's Tailor and Outfitter. I see. Flynn and Company? Or is it Flynn and Sons? Have I seen his emporium?'

'Ah, no!' Tommy said, by now as red as a radish. 'He's not that sort of tailor at all, he doesn't build suits, ye know, that's a different trade altogether, he works with me mother at home in Tuckey Street, he tucks things in and he lets things out, he's what they call a mender and turner, me brother Turlough had this suit I have on me now before I got it, you can see he's very good at his job, he's a real dab...'

Dick let him run on, nodding sympathetically – meaning to convey to the others that they really could not expect a fellow to know much about girls if his father spent his life mending and turning old clothes in some side alley called Tuckey Street.

'Do you fully realise, Gong Gong, that we are proposing to behold the ultimate in female beauty?'

'You mean,' Gong Gong smiled fearfully, 'that she'll only be wearing her nightie?'

Georgie Watchman turned from him in disgust to the fruit-machine. Dick smiled on.

'The thought had not occurred to me,' he said. 'I wonder, Gong Gong, where do you get all those absolutely filthy ideas. If we subscribe seventeen and sixpence, do you think you can contribute half-a-crown?'

'I could feck it, I suppose.'

Dick raised his eyelashes.

'Feck?'

Gong Gong looked shamedly at the tiles.

'I mean steal,' he whispered.

'Don't they give you any pocket money?'

'They give me threepence a week.'

'Well, we have only a week to go. If you can, what was your word, feck half-a-crown, you may come.'

The night chosen was a Saturday – her mother always went to town on Saturdays; the time of meeting, five o'clock exactly; the place, the entrance to the Mardyke Walk.

On any other occasion it would have been a gloomy spot for a rendezvous. For adventure, perfect. A long tree-lined avenue, with, on one side, a few scattered houses and high enclosing walls; on the other side the small canal whose deep dyke had given it its name. Secluded, no traffic allowed inside the gates, complete silence. A place where men came every night to stand with their girls behind the elm trees kissing and whispering for hours. Dick and Georgie were there on the dot of five. Then Jimmy Sullivan came swiftly loping. From where they stood, under a tree just beyond the porter's lodge, trembling with anticipation, they could see clearly for only about a hundred yards up the long tunnel of elms lit by the first stars above the boughs, one tawny window streaming across a dank garden, and beyond that a feeble perspective of pendant lamps fading dimly away into the blue November dusk. Within another half-hour the avenue would be pitch black between those meagre pools of light.

Her instructions had been precise. In separate pairs, at exactly half past five, away up there beyond the last lamp, where they would be as invisible as cockroaches, they must gather outside her house.

'You won't be able even to see one another,' she had said glee-fully to Dick, who had stared coldly at her, wondering how often she had stood behind a tree with some fellow who would not have been able even to see her face.

Every light in the house would be out except for the fanlight over the door.

'Ooo!' she had giggled. 'It will be terribly oohey. You won't hear a sound but the branches squeaking. You must come along to my door. You must leave the other fellows to watch from behind the trees. You must give two short rings. Once, twice. And then give a long ring, and wait.' She had started to whisper the rest, her hands by her sides clawing her dress in her excitement. 'The fanlight will go out if my mother isn't at home. The door will open slowly. You must step into the dark hall. A hand will take your hand. You won't know whose hand it is. It will be like something out of Sherlock Holmes. You will be simply terrified. You won't know what I'm wearing. For all you'll know I might be wearing nothing at all!'

He must leave the door ajar. The others must follow him one by one. After that...

It was eleven minutes past five and Gong Gong had not yet come. Already three women had passed up the Mardyke carrying parcels, hurrying home to their warm fires, forerunners of the home-for-tea crowd. When they had passed out of sight Georgie growled, 'When that slob comes I'm going to put my boot up his backside.' Dick, calmly puffing his corncob, gazing wearily up at the stars, laughed tolerantly and said, 'Now Georgie, don't be impatient. We shall see all! We shall at last know all!'

Georgie sighed and decided to be weary too.

'I hope,' he drawled, 'this poor frail isn't going to let us down!'

For three more minutes they waited in silence and then Jimmy Sullivan let out a cry of relief. There was the small figure hastening towards them along the Dyke Parade from one lamp-post to another.

'Puffing and panting as usual, I suppose,' Dick chuckled. 'And exactly fourteen minutes late.'

'I hope to God,' Jimmy said, 'he has our pound note. I don't know in hell why you made that slob our treasurer.'

'Because he is poor,' Dick said quietly. 'We would have spent it.'

He came panting up to them, planted a black violin case against the tree and began rummaging in his pockets for the money.

'I'm supposed to be at a music lesson, that's me alibi, me father always wanted to be a musician but he got married instead, he plays the cello, me brother Turlough plays the clarinet, me sister Jenny plays the viola, we have quartets, I sold a Haydn quartet for one and six, I had to borrow sixpence from Jenny, and I fecked the last sixpence from me mother's purse, that's what kept me so late...'

They were not listening, staring into the soiled and puckered handkerchief he was unravelling to point out one by one, a crumpled half-note, two half-crowns, two shillings and a sixpenny bit.

'That's all yeers, and here's mine. Six threepenny bits for the quartet. That's one and six. Here's Jenny's five pennies and two ha'pence. That makes two bob. And here's the tanner I just fecked from me mother's purse. That makes my two and sixpence.'

Eagerly he poured the mess into Dick's hands. At the sight of the jumble Dick roared at him.

'I told you, you bloody little fool to bring a pound note!'

'You told me to bring a pound.'

'I said a pound note. I can't give this dog's breakfast to a girl like Daisy Bolster.'

'You said a pound.'

They all began to squabble. Jimmy Sullivan shoved Gong Gong. Georgie punched him. Dick shoved Georgie. Jimmy defended Georgie with 'We should never have let that slob come with us.' Gong Gong shouted, 'Who's a slob?' and swiped at him. Jimmy shoved him again so that he fell over his violin case, and a man passing home to his tea shouted at them, 'Stop beating that little boy at once!'

Tactfully they cowered. Dick helped Gong Gong to his feet. Georgie dusted him lovingly. Jimmy retrieved his cap, put it back crookedly on his head and patted him kindly. Dick explained in his best Ampleforth accent that they had merely been having 'a trifling discussion', and 'our young friend here tripped over his suitcase'. The man surveyed them dubiously, growled something and went on his way. When he was gone Georgie pulled out his pocketbook, handed a brand-new pound note to Dick, and grabbed the dirty jumble of cash. Dick at once said, 'Quick march! Two by two!' and strode off ahead of the others, side by side with Tommy in his crooked cap, lugging his dusty violin case, into the deepening dark.

They passed nobody. They heard nothing. They saw only the few lights in the sparse houses along the left of the Mardyke. On the other side was the silent, railed-in stream. When they came in silence to the wide expanse of the cricket field the sky dropped a blazing veil of stars behind the outfield nets. When they passed the gates of the railed-in public park, locked for the night, darkness returned between the walls to their left and the overgrown laurels glistening behind the tall railings on their right. Here Tommy stopped dead, hooped fearfully towards the laurels.

'What's up with you?' Dick snapped at him.

'I hear a noise, me father told me once how a man murdered a woman in there for her gold watch, he said men do terrible things like that because of bad women, he said that that man was hanged by the neck in Cork Jail, he said that was the last time the black flag flew on top of the jail. Dick! I don't want to go on!'

Dick peered at the phosphorescent dial of his watch, and strode ahead, staring at the next feeble lamp hanging crookedly from its black iron arch. Tommy had to trot to catch up with him.

'We know,' Dick said, 'that she has long legs. Her breasts will be white and small.'

'I won't look!' Tommy moaned.

'Then don't look!'

Panting, otherwise silently, they hurried past the old corrugated iron building that had once been a roller-skating rink and was now empty and abandoned. After the last lamp the night became impenetrable, then her house rose slowly to their left against the starlight. It was square, tall, solid, brick-fronted, three-storeyed, and jet-black against the stars except for its half-moon fanlight. They walked a few yards past it and halted, panting, behind a tree. The only sound was the squeaking of a branch over their heads. Looking backwards, they saw Georgie and Jimmy approaching under the last lamp. Looking forwards, they saw a brightly lit tram, on its way outward from the city, pass the far end of the tunnel, briefly light its maw and black it out again. Beyond that lay wide fields and the silent river. Dick said, 'Tell them to follow me if the fanlight goes out,' and disappeared.

Alone under the tree, backed still by the park, Tommy looked across to the far heights of Sunday's Well dotted with the lights of a thousand suburban houses. He clasped his fiddle case before him like a shield. He had to force himself not to run away towards where another bright tram would rattle him back to the city. Suddenly he saw the fanlight go out. Strings in the air throbbed and faded. Was somebody playing a cello? His father bowed over his cello, jacket off, shirt-sleeves rolled up, entered the Haydn; beside him Jenny waited, chin sidewards over the viola, bosom lifted, bow poised, the tendons of her frail wrist hollowed by the lamplight, Turlough facing them lipped a thinner reed. His mother sat shawled by the fire, tapping the beat with her toe. Georgie and Jimmy joined him.

'Where's Dick?' Georgie whispered urgently.

'Did I hear music?' he gasped.

Georgie vanished, and again the strings came and faded. Jimmy whispered, 'Has she a gramophone?' Then they could hear nothing but the faint rattle of the vanished tram. When Jimmy slid away from him, he raced madly up into the darkness, and then stopped dead halfway to the tunnel's end. He did not have the penny to pay for the tram. He turned and raced as madly back the way he had come, down past her house, down to where the gleam of the laurels hid the murdered woman, and stopped again. He heard a rustling noise. A rat? He looked back, thought of her long legs and her small white breasts, and found himself walking heavily back to her garden gate, his heart pounding. He entered the path, fumbled for the dark door, pressed against it, felt it slew open under his hand, stepped cautiously into the dark hallway, closed the door, saw nothing, heard nothing, stepped onward, and fell clattering on the tiles over his violin case.

A door opened. He saw firelight on shining shinbones and bare knees. Fearfully, his eyes moved upwards. She was wearing nothing but gym knickers. He saw two small birds, white, soft, rosy-tipped. Transfixed by joy he stared and stared at them. Her black hair hung over her narrow shoulders. She laughed down at him with white teeth and wordlessly gestured him to get up and come in. He faltered after her white back and stood inside the door. The only light was from the fire.

Nobody heeded him. Dick stood by the corner of the mantel-piece, one palm flat on it, his other hand holding his trembling corncob. He was peering coldly at her. His eyelashes almost met. Georgie lay sprawled in a chintzy armchair on the other side of the fire wearily flicking the ash from a black cigarette into the fender. Opposite him Jimmy Sullivan sat on the edge of a chair, his elbows on his knees, his eyeballs sticking out as if he just swallowed something hot, hard and raw. Nobody said a word.

She stood in the centre of the carpet, looking guardedly from one to the other of them out of her hooded eyes, her thumbs inside the elastic of her gym knickers. Slowly she began to press her knickers down over her hips. When Georgie suddenly whispered 'The Seventh veil!' he at once wanted to batter him over the head with his fiddle case, to shout at her to stop, to shout at them that they had seen everything, to shout that they must look no more. Instead, he lowered his head so that he saw nothing but her bare toes. Her last covering slid to the carpet. He heard three long gasps, became aware that Dick's pipe had fallen to the floor, that Georgie had started straight up, one fist lifted as if he was going to strike her, and that Jimmy had covered his face with his two hands.

A coal tinkled from the fire to the fender. With averted eyes he went to it, knelt before it, wet his fingers with his spittle as he had often seen his mother do, deftly laid the coal back on the fire and remained so for a moment watching it light up again. Then he sidled back to his violin case, walked out into the hall, flung open the door on the sky of stars, and straightway started to race the whole length of the Mardyke from pool to pool of light in three gasping spurts.

After the first spurt he stood gasping until his heart had stopped hammering. He heard a girl laughing softly behind a tree. Just before his second halt he saw ahead of him a man and a woman approaching him arm in arm, but when he came up to where they should have been they too had become invisible. Halted, breathing, listening, he heard their murmuring somewhere in the dark. At his third panting rest he heard an invisible girl say, 'Oh, no, oh no!' and a man's urgent voice say, 'But yes, but yes!' He felt that behind every tree there were kissing lovers, and without stopping he ran the gauntlet between them until he emerged from the Mardyke among the bright lights of the city. Then, at last, the sweat cooling on his forehead, he was standing outside the shuttered plumber's shop above which they lived. Slowly he climbed the bare stairs to their floor and their door. He paused for a moment to look up through the windows at the stars, opened the door and went in.

Four heads around the supper table turned to look up inquiringly at him. At one end of the table his mother sat wearing her blue apron. At the other end his father sat, in his rolled-up shirt-sleeves as if he had only just laid down the pressing iron. Turlough gulped his food. Jenny was smiling mockingly at him. She had the red ribbon in her hair and the mother-of-pearl brooch at her neck.

'You're bloody late,' his father said crossly. 'What the hell kept you? I hope you came straight home from your lesson. What way did you come? Did you meet anybody or talk to anybody? You know I don't want any loitering at night. I hope you weren't cadeying with any blackguards? Sit down, sir, and eat your supper. Or did your lordship expect us to wait for you? What did you play tonight? What did Professor Hartmann give you to practise for your next lesson?'

He sat in his place. His mother filled his plate and they all ate in silence.

Always the questions! Always talking talking at him! They never let him alone for a minute. His hands sank. She was so lovely. So white. So soft. So pink. His mother said gently, 'You're not eating, Tommy. Are you all right?'

He said, 'Yes, yes, I'm fine, Mother.'

Like birds. Like stars. Like music.

His mother said, 'You are very silent tonight, Tommy. You

usually have a lot of talk after you've been to Professor Hartmann. What were you thinking of?'

'They were so beautiful!' he blurted.

'What was so bloody beautiful?' his father rasped. 'What are you blathering about?'

'The stars,' he said hastily.

Jenny laughed. His father frowned. Silence returned.

He knew that he would never again go back to the sweetshop. They would only want to talk and talk about her. They would want to bring everything out into the light, boasting and smirking about her, taunting him for having run away. He would be happy forever if only he could walk every night of his life up the dark Mardyke, hearing nothing but a girl's laugh from behind a tree, a branch squeaking, and the far-off rattle of a lost tram; walk on and on, deeper and deeper into the darkness until he could see nothing but one tall house whose fanlight she would never put out again. The doorbell might ring, but she would not hear it. The door might be answered, but not by her. She would be gone. He had known it ever since he heard her laughing softly by his side as they ran away together, for ever and ever, between those talking trees.

Feed My Lambs

It is about eleven o'clock of a sunny September morning in late September. The unfrequented road that crosses the level bogland from skyline to skyline passes on its way a few beech trees, a white cottage fronted by a small garden still bright with roses and snapdragons, a cobbled path and a small wooden gate bearing, in white celluloid letters, the name *Pic du Jer*. In the vast emptiness of the bog these unexpected and inexplicable beech trees, the pretty cottage, the tiny garden, the cobbled path suggest only a dream in the mind of somebody who, a long time back, thought better of it, or died, or gave up the struggle with the bog.

A young woman in an apron as blue as the sky is sweeping a few fallen beech leaves along the cobbles. She is bosomy, about thirty, with amber hair, and eyelids as big as the two half-domes of an eggshell. Looking idly towards the west she observes, far away, a flash of sunlight. She gives it one thoughtful glance and resumes her sweeping. Whoever the motorist is, he will come and go as slowly as a dot of light emerging from one mirror and as slowly dwindling into another. The bog is as immense as it is flat. It swallows everything.

Pic du Jer? A mountain peak? Asked why, Rita Lamb always says, in her usual saucy, self-mocking way, one quizzical eyebrow cocked: 'Yerrah, it's an old mountain near Lourdes. You go up to it in the funicular. It's where I climbed to the pic of my career. It's where I met Jer.' If she admitted that she really met Jer at the foot of the peak, in the waiting funicular, it would spoil the joke. It would be no joke at all if she said, 'It's where I met Father Tom.'

Under the final whisk of her broom the leaves rustle out through the garden gate. She looks again. The car is half a mile away. Her hands tighten on the broom handle. The cups of her eyelids soar, she runs indoors, tearing off her blue apron, looks at herself in the mirror, punches the cushions of her minute parlour, looks into the sideboard to be sure there is a bottle or two there, and out at the gate again just in time to greet Father Tom with a delighted grin.

He has never failed her. He drops in at least three or four times a year, either on his way up to Dublin or on his way back to his parish on the far side of the Shannon. She takes his overcoat, indicates the settee, and begins to make his usual drink, Irish coffee.

'Now!' she says pertly as a parrot. 'What's y'r news? Tell me everything.'

'I'll tell you one thing, Rita,' he laughs. 'You haven't changed one iota since the first day I met you.'

That day, waiting for the funicular to start, the four of them had got talking at once: the two priests, herself and Jer. The older priest – rosy, bony and bald, easygoing and poorly dressed, his waistcoat flecked brown from his scented snuff – simply leaned across and took her paperback from her hand: Franz Werfel's *Song of Bernadette*.

'Not bad,' he conceded, 'For a modern novel. Tell me, my child, did you ever read a novel by Canon Sheehan called *My New Curate*?'

At this, the young priest had pulled down his elegant white cuffs, and all in one breath laughed, groaned, sighed and said, 'Here we go again. Poor old Tom Timlin off to the guillotine once more.'

'Indeed and I did read it,' Rita gushed. 'I think I've read every single thing Canon Sheehan wrote.'

Father Jordan patted her knee.

'Good girl! Most of ye read nothing nowadays but dirty books like the one his reverence here gave me the other day by some young trollop named ... What was this her name is, Father Timlin?'

'Miss Edna O'Brien,' the young priest said, his natural courtesy qualified by an over-patient smile.

'A fine Irish name! It was the only decent thing about her rotten book. I nearly shoved it behind the fire it made me so mad! Upon my word, Father, I don't know for the life of me what you want to be reading books like that for.'

Father Tom folded the crease of his trousers over his knee and observed urbanely that it is one's duty to know what young people are thinking nowadays.

'After all, one belongs to one's contemporaries, Father Jordan, as Simone de Beauvoir puts it.'

'I read her, too!' Rita exclaimed, and blushed wildly, suddenly remembering the picture of a completely naked woman on the cover of her contraband copy of *The Second Sex*, and how its first chapter was all about the machinery of the inside of a woman and the outside of a man. 'I forget now what book by her it was that I read. I think it was a travel book about France.'

'You probably read *The Second Sex*,' Father Tom said dryly. 'Quite an interesting study. It's a pity she has no sense of humour. Sex can be funny, too.'

The old man threw him a cold look. 'In this excellent novel by the late Canon Sheehan,' he persisted, 'there is a poor old parish priest like myself who has the life plagued out of him by his new curate.'

'I remember the two of them well,' said Rita, patting his knee as approvingly as he had patted hers, 'and, do you know, I felt very sorry for the pair of them.'

'The part I love,' he said with relish, 'is where this poor old P.P. walks in one day into his curate's room and finds him if you please, playing the piano and singing some sloppy German love song about "Roselein, Roselein, Roselein buck – Roselein auf dem heiden"? Wasn't that how the song went, Father?'

Father Tom coughed and said that, yes, it was, indeed, something on those lines.

'Well! Father Timlin here is *my* new curate and he has me plagued out with Italian. Always playing Italian operas on the gramophone. In Italian if you please! Always throwing around words like *Giovannismo*, and *ecumenismo*, and *aggiornamento*, and what's that other word you have, Father, that sounds like an Italian racing car?'

'*La gioventù!*' Father Timlin cried eagerly, and threw his hands out to the two young people seated opposite them. 'And here we have them! Youth at the helm!'

The old priest winked at them.

'He is ancient, you see. He is twenty-six.'

'Ah!' Father Tom said enthusiastically. 'There's nothing like youth. Married or engaged?' he asked.

Rita and the young man beside her looked at one another. He observed that she had eyes as big as a cow, eyelids as sleepy as a cow, soft hair the colour of a Jersey cow, and that she was very well made around the brisket. She liked his grin, his white teeth and his warm voice as he answered, 'We are not even acquainted yet, Father. We just met this minute.'

Father Jordan roared with delight.

'There you are,' he nudged his curate. 'Crashing in as usual.'

'Only anticipating, maybe,' the young priest said, unabashed, and they all introduced themselves. Father Malachy Jordan, P.P., and Father Tom Timlin, C.C., from the parish of Annabwee in the County Galway; Jerry Lamb, farmer and butcher, from Barron in the County Kildare; and Rita Lyons, schoolmistress, from Doon in the County Westmeath; at which point the funicular gave a jolt and they started to climb.

'Talking of marriages,' said Father Tom, paying no attention at all to the descending landscape, 'I suppose ye know that Lourdes is a great place for matchmaking? The best Catholic families in France come here with their children. We have a count, and a prince, and their wives and children in our hotel. The idea is that the best young people in France meet, and if they like one another . . . well, you never know your luck.'

Jerry Lamb chuckled.

'It would be one of the unrecorded miracles of Lourdes if I met a princess here and took a shine to her – and she to me!'

Father Tom waved his hand with a man-of-the-world air.

'It would be no miracle at all! We get all kinds in Lourdes. All sorts and sizes come here to see the pilgrimages, Buddhists, Jews, Muslims, Communists, atheists, everybody!'

Rita turned sideways to consider Mr Lamb.

'Wouldn't that be a good joke,' she said, 'if your Catholic princess met a Communist who was a roaring atheist and took a shine to him?'

The old priest's palms applauded silently, but the young priest was unquashable.

'It might be an excellent thing for them both. She might convert him and he might broaden her.'

'Ha!' said his PP sourly. 'She might! And so might a mouse! And supposing they did get married? A mixed marriage! And what about the children? If they had any children!'

Father Tom smiled benevolently.

'Ah, now, Father, you must admit that since the *Concilio* the attitude of the church to mixed marriages has greatly relaxed. And as for the question of having children, that will come too. Do you believe in large families, Mr Lamb?' he asked their butcher.

'I wouldn't be averse to two or three. Or at most four.'

'Two or three?' Father Jordan said sadly. 'I was the youngest of twelve. Brought up on a scrawny thirty-five-acre farm west of Ballinasloe. An acre to the cow, they say, and three acres to the child, we cut it fine.'

'I was the youngest of six myself,' from Father Tom.

'Ai, ai, ai!' Father Jordan sighed. 'I suppose this is your *aggiornamento*.' He gazed into a distant valley. 'My mother was one of fifteen. Twelve of us. Six of you. Mr Lamb here would like three. And if you have three I suppose they will want one apiece. We progress!'

'What I'd like,' Rita said, looking pensively out over the distant Pyrenees, 'would be to have a boy and a girl.'

'Two?' Father Tom asked her amiably. 'Four?' he asked Jerry Lamb. 'Why don't ye split the difference and make it three?' – at which Father Jordan asked him if he was getting a percentage on this, and all four of them laughed, and the funicular stopped and all the passengers except Rita looked down.

'Maybe they want us to enjoy the view?' Jer suggested.

'My sister Joanie has seven children,' Rita said to the sky. 'She is married to a clerk. He gets eleven pounds a week. Seven children. And they are only married seven years.'

'Fine!' Father Jordan said to the valley. 'Splendid! A proud and happy mother!'

Rita's mouth tightened. Father Tom was watching her closely. 'Is she happy?' he asked, stressing quietly.

'Tell me, Father,' Rita said to him, 'what's all this about the Pill?'

'It is forbidden,' the old priest said shortly.

'Well, now,' the young priest temporised, 'it is certainly not authorised. But it is still under discussion. I hope,' he added, looking around at the crowded carriage, 'we're not stuck forever?'

'Are we stuck?' Father Jordan asked an old Frenchwoman across the aisle from him, and her husband turned back from where he was looking up the peak to say that the one coming down was stuck too. Jer and the old priest crossed over to look out. Father Tom was left with Rita. She was staring moodily at the sky. He leaned forward, elbows on thighs.

'You are very silent, Rita.'

She said nothing.

'What is on your mind?'

'Nothing.'

'There is something. What is it?

Struck by the kindness in his voice, she slewed her eyes towards him, and for the first time took stock of him. He had sandy hair; his eyelashes were golden fair; his eyes were as bright blue as a Siamese cat's; he reminded her of her brother who was a sailor.

She hesitated. Then she spoke very softly: 'I was remembering why I came to Lourdes.'

'Why did you?'

'Everybody comes to Lourdes to pray for something. I prayed that my sister Joanie won't have any more children. And if I ever get married that I'll only have two.'

He looked at her mischievously. She was to become familiar with that mischievous, mocking way of his – his way of calming her, of calling her to use her commonsense.

'When I was young, Rita, I had a small sister who was mad about a sort of sweet called bull's-eyes. The nuns told her one day to pray to the Blessed Virgin to break her of the habit.'

'And did she?' Rita asked with interest.

'She got a terrible pain in her stomach one day and that cured her. Rita! Which are you? Dying to be married, or afraid to be married?'

'I don't want to have a child every year for the rest of my blooming life.'

He smiled at her. She looked away, annoyed.

'Father, you're like every priest. Ye know all about theology and ye know nothing about feelings. Would you like to have a child every year of your life?'

'Not unless I was a rabbit. Still, nathless, and howbeit, and quid pro quo, and all things being carefully considered, and so on, you would like to get married?'

'I'm human.'

'I should hope so, if that means that you are a normal woman with the normal longings and desires of a woman.'

She faced him crossly, at a disadvantage. If he had been a man she could tell him!

'How do I know what I am?'

'Everybody knows what he is. You've had boy friends, haven't you?'

'Yes.' Then she said coldly, 'Am I going to confession to you?'

'Oh, come off it, girl! This talk about confession that women go on with! Why wouldn't you have boy friends? Anyway, nobody confesses any more to a priest. The priest today is only a kind of spiritual telephone operator. To what part of the otherworld do you want a trunk call today, madam? For all faults, inquiries and difficulties kindly dial Tom Timlin, C.C.'

She laughed.

'But you listen in!' she pointed out.

'And interpret now and again. And add up the charges. Come now, Rita! Face up to yourself.' He chuckled at her. '*Vide, visse, amò*. She saw, she lived, she loved. You embraced. You kissed. And you hated it like poison!'

'I did not!' she said furiously. 'I liked it.'

'As *il buon Dio* intended you to. "So long as things are", Saint Augustine said, and he was a tough man, "they are good". Kissing is like Guinness, Rita. It's good for you. The *osculum* . . .'

'The what?'

'The kiss on the cheek.'

His eyes were mocking her again. She waved an airy hand.

'The *basium*. On the lips.'

Even more jauntily, she waved the other hand.

'The *suavium*?' and he shrugged.

She waved both her hands and was enraged with herself for blushing; and more enraged when he laughed delightedly.

Jer turned back to them and shouted, 'I think it is a life sentence!'

'Anyway,' she protested, 'that's all damn fine,' not quite knowing what was fine, 'but seven kids in seven years? Eight in eight? Nine in nine?'

He glanced across the carriage to where Father Jordan and Jerry Lamb were now trying out their French on the old French lady and her husband.

'You can only do your best, Rita,' he said gently. 'When any man or woman comes to me with your problem all I ever say is, "You can only do your best". If I was speaking as your spiritual telephone operator I'd always say, "He is saying, you can only do your best".'

She glared down at the huddled red roofs of Lourdes until he thought she was going to throw herself out. Then she breathed out a long sigh of exasperation.

'These last three days,' she said, 'I was so happy down there.'

He gave her a melancholy laugh. He looked down at the basketful of roofs.

'Ai! Ai! – as Father Jordan says. Such a mixture! The lovely and the tawdry, sincerity and sentimentality, lies and truth, God and Mammon. It would remind you of life! And here we are now like Mahomet's coffin slung halfway between . . . Where was it slung? I always imagine it was held up between walls of magnetic forces. Impossible?' He paused. 'You mustn't be afraid, Rita.' She kept staring sulkily down at the roofs. 'No woman can do more than her best.' This time he was silent a long while. 'I'd say that to you anytime, anywhere.'

He watched her. She got the point. She smiled at him :

'I have a car. Sometime I might pay you a visit.'

'Do!'

'But you will never know.'

'I will never know. All I will hear will be a voice. It will come and go. Like a bird singing in flight.'

The carriage jolted a little, started to move, and the whole carriage cheered and laughed. Father Jordan and Jer rejoined them.

'*E pur si muove!*' Father Tom cried. 'Galileo. The world does go around the sun. Though I'm not sure Father Jordan entirely believes it. George Bernard Shaw,' he went on, 'once said that in Ireland we still believe that the world, if not exactly flat, is only very slightly removed from the spherical.'

They all chuckled and began to discuss such important things as whether they could get a cool refreshing drink on top of the mountain.

From the peak they gazed far and wide about them, silenced by the gleaming wings of the Hautes Pyrénées, still snow-covered, and the eyes of the lakes in the far valleys, and Father Tom, who knew his Lourdes, pointed out famous peaks like the Pic du Midi de Bigorre that local mountaineers had mastered at the risk of their lives.

'Glory be to God,' said Father Jordan, 'but it's a hard country! Is it good for anything at all?'

'Sheep,' said Jer. 'And I bet you there's fine grazing up there for the cattle in the summertime.'

'I read in the paper this morning,' said Father Tom, 'that the shepherds are complaining that the wolves aren't being shot.'

'Feed my lambs,' said the old priest, and the two of them drifted around, and Rita and Jer went in search of a beer.

Sitting on a rough bench a little apart from the other tourists, she amused him by telling him what it is like to teach in a nun's school, and he entertained her by telling her what it is like to be a farmer-butcher in a small village in the middle of a bog as flat as a slate. When Father Tom and Father Jordan came by, the old man looked as if he were going to join them, but the curate took him firmly by the arm and pointed off into the distance and drew him away around the corner. Presently Mr Lamb was asking Miss

Lyons if she had ever been to Biarritz and when she said no, Mr Lamb said he was going by bus the day after tomorrow, and Miss Lyons said she wondered if she ought not to visit it someday.

'Yerrah, why don't you? You earned it. If you like you could come with me. I'm all on my own.'

'But, Mr Lamb,' she said, floating her eggshell eyelids wide open, 'we are hardly acquainted!' – and when his laugh showed his splendid teeth she laughed too, and he went on laughing because she looked so happy, and had such big droopy eyelids and was well made around the brisket.

Father Tom advanced his empty glass of Irish coffee to Rita sideways along the settee, laughed and clinked it with hers.

'So there you have it! That's all my news. Nothing at all since July. I'm the same old three-and-fourpence I always was and always will be.'

She looked at him affectionately.

'We have no news either! Jer goes on with his butchering. I go on with my sweeping. If you are worth three-and fourpence, then between the three of us we're worth exactly ten bob.'

She took up the empty glasses, the bottle, the cream, and the percolator and started to tidy them on the small dining room table by the window. He looked appreciatively at her straight back and her trim legs.

'Rita!'

She turned, observed him and cocked an alert eye.

'You look as if you are about to give birth to a profound thought?'

'Divil a profound thought! It's just that ever since I came within sight of this little cottage of yours this morning I was thinking how you once said to me, five years ago, "I have a car". And you have never once paid me a visit?'

She came back and sat on the settee.

'You are a low scoundrel, Father Tom. You only thought of that just half an hour ago? And in all those five years you never once thought of it before? The truth isn't in you.'

'Well, I admit I did give it a passing thought now and again. I'm not probing, Rita!'

'You are. And I don't mind. Sure we're always probing one another. When we have no news it's all we ever do.'

'Why didn't you?'

'Do you really want to know? I'll tell you. But I think you will be sorry you asked me. One reason I didn't visit you was because I had no need to. I had nothing to tell you. Or to tell any other priest. Now you know!'

Her left hand lay supine on the settee near his. He laid his right hand on her palm. The palm slowly closed on his fingers.

'Poor Rita! I guessed it must be that way. I'm afraid your family hasn't had much luck with Our Lady?'

'Not with three more babies for my sister, and none for me.'

'And poor Jer, too!'

'Oh, he's accepted it now. At first, he minded an awful lot.'

'What was the other reason?'

She looked down at their two hands. She gave him a long silent look – so long that he peered questioningly at her. She leaned over a little and castled her right hand on his.

'Did it ever occur to you, Father,' she said, 'that from the first day we met you called me Rita? Because you're a priest and that made it all right – for you. But I have never once called you Tom. Because I'm a woman, and that mightn't be quite so safe – for me. I love it when you drop in here, Father, and pop off again after an hour or so. I love the chat. I love the way I can say anything I like to you. I love the way you say anything you like to me. I love all the things we argue about. I look forward to it for weeks. I think about it for weeks after you've gone. And that's not just because it's lonely out here on this empty old bog. Now and again friends of Jerry's drop in, and I like them to call too, but I never think of them when they're gone, and if they never came again I wouldn't miss them. I love you to come because you are you. Still, so far, I've always managed to remember that you are a priest and I am a married woman. The other reason I did not visit you is because if I started meeting you outside of here it would be very different. It would be admitting to myself that I am fond of you as a man.'

His golden eyelashes fell. She removed her hand. He laid his on his knee.

'Well?' she asked tartly. 'What's wrong with you? Am I to be the only one to tell the truth today? Or did none of this ever occur to you?'

'You are a wonderful woman, Rita! You are the most honest being I have ever met.'

'Is that all you can say to me?'

'It is all I dare say to you. What the hell is the good of anybody saying anything if he can do nothing about it? What would you want me to say? That I love you? When neither you nor I can ever prove it!'

She shook her amber head at him.

'Well, there's the cat out of the bag at last! Tom! You should never have been a priest. The first day I met you I knew it.'

'Why didn't you say so then?'

'Would it have made any difference?'

He jumped up, walked away from her, whirled and cried, 'I don't know! I was younger then!'

She rose and went over so close to him that he could hear her breathing.

'And now,' she taunted, 'you are a feeble old man?'

He flung his arms around her and kissed her on the mouth. She held his kiss. Then she drew away from him and laid her finger gently but imperatively on his mouth.

'The *basium*?' she mocked. 'You've come a long way in five years. Tom.'

'Do you realize you are the first girl I ever kissed!'

'I do. And I'm the last. You can never come here again.'

He walked away from her and looked angrily at her.

'Is that what you wanted, talking the way you did on that settee?'

'I merely answered your question. I warned you that you might be sorry. You asked for the truth. And you put an end to our story.'

'You didn't have to answer me!'

'I had to. Because immediately you asked me I knew what I'd never let myself know before. And I knew that we both knew it. And I knew something else too. That if it didn't end one day we would explode, and then we'd be torturing one another for the rest of our lives.'

He stared wildly around him.

'There is no sense nor meaning to this. It doesn't hang together. All I ever wanted was a bit of friendship. A bit of companionship. There's nobody else in the world I can talk to but you. That day I first met you I knew that here was somebody at last that I could talk to. Maybe that I could help. That I'd be a better priest if I could ...'

'Tom! It's long ago that I told you that you knew all about theology and all that stuff, and nothing about feelings. Now you know better! This is what love is like.'

He glared at her in misery and longing. Then, suddenly, he calmed, and then as suddenly broke into a long peal of laughter, at himself, at both of them, at the whole of life.

'Honest to God, Rita! You're worth fifty priests. You're worth a thousand of us. And I that began it all by trying to educate the simple, ignorant schoolteacher! Well, I may have learned slow, but you learned damn fast. Where the hell, Rita, did you learn all you know?'

'Where every woman learns everything. In bed. Am I shocking you? Because if I am, then you really are getting very old.'

He considered her answer bitterly.

'The one classroom no priest ever visits. And I suppose the only one that ever tells anyone anything about the nature of love. So! That's it. I'm never to see you again?'

'Why not? I will go my way. You will go yours. If I live I will become an old woman. If you live you will become an old, old parish priest like poor old Father Malachy Jordan.'

'My God! If Father Jordan was alive today and knew about you and me he'd break his heart laughing at me for a botch of a priest and a fool of a man!'

She flashed out angrily at him. He had never seen her so angry.

'Stop that, Tom! Stop it at once! Never say that again! Never think it! I liked you that day in Lourdes because you were honest with me. I grew fond of you, I fell in love with you if you want the whole bloody truth, because you went on being honest with me. You will always be honest, and you will always be a better priest than old Jordan ever was because you will always remember that, if it was only for one minute of your life, you loved your woman and kissed her. When you run yourself down you are only cheapening yourself and cheapening me. I won't have that! I'm not sorry for anything we've done. I'm proud of it.'

Far away a bell gently, faintly tolled. She listened. 'There's the angelus bell in Barron.' Suddenly she became the bright, capable housewife. 'Jer will be back in an hour. Will you stay and have lunch with us, Tom?'

'No!' he said brusquely, and grabbed his overcoat and dived into it. 'But there's one thing I'll tell you, Rita!' He snatched up his hat and gloves. 'If I met you not five years ago but ten I'd have given up God Himself for you!'

He went out the door and down the cobbled path. She followed slowly after him. At the wicket-gate he paused and looked up and down the long, empty road.

'I'll never pass this road again.' He flipped his gloves against the white celluloid letters on the gate. 'Why did you call it Pic du Jer?'

He watched her great eyelids drooping. He watched the sinking of her amber head. She spoke as softly as if she were whispering to the three foreign words.

'To remind me of you.'

She did not raise her head again until his car started and his wheels spurned the gravel of the road. Then she walked out to the middle of the road to watch him dwindling away from her into infinity, diminishing like a dot of light until he vanished out of sight.

She looked around the level bog. Miles away the blue smoke of a turfcutter's fire rose out of the flat emptiness straight up into the blue sky. She heard nothing. Then she heard a soft wind and raised her eyes to the blue above her. A host of swallows were flying south. She watched them until they, too, became lost to sight. Soon it would be winter. The rains and the fogs. She turned briskly indoors to prepare a meal for her man.

Only once did she pause in her task, the knife in one fist, the apple in the other, to look out of the window and murmur aloud to herself, 'I know what he'll do. It's what I'd do. Drive past me every time he goes to Dublin.' She added, 'Until it wears off,' and went on with her work.

Of Sanctity and Whiskey

As Luke Regan drove down to Saint Killian's for the first sitting he kept shifting around the fading cards of his schoolboy's memories of the place and wishing the press had never got on to this thing. It was a pleasant idea, of course, and he could understand the columnists playing it up – but the stupid things they wrote about it! 'Former pupil returns to his old school to paint his old teacher. . . . This portrait of a distinguished Headmaster by a distinguished Academician is certain to reflect two sensibilities in perfect rapport with one another. . . . This new portrait by Mr Luke Regan, RHA, of Brother Hilary Harty, the retired Head of Saint Killian's College, should record not one journey but two journeys from youth to maturity. . . .' He had already confided to his boozing friends that he found the whole bloody thing extremely embarrassing; not least because he could see that they thought he was just boasting about it. He had only been in that school for three years, between the ages of twelve and fifteen. It was forty years ago. He had not the slightest recollection of this Brother Hilary Harty, and he felt sure that old man could not possibly remember him.

Hilary Harty? He hoped he was not that old snob they used to call Dikey, a fellow with a face like a coffin and eyes like a dead hen. Could he be Flossy, who used to collect jokes in a notebook as fat as a Bible: head and a face like a turnip; purple, orange and green – that would be a nice palette to have to work with! Without affection he remembered Popeyes, always blinking at you like the flicker of a motorcar that the driver had forgotten to turn off. But his name was Hurley. Now, little Regis would be a marvellous subject – a pink-and-white angel face with a fierce furrow between the eyebrows. That would be a challenging puss – if you were lucky enough, and had time enough to get him talking about himself. But Hilary? The name rang no chime, sweet, cracked or otherwise. 'Two sensibilities in perfect rapport with one another . . .' Had none of these fellows ever been to school themselves? Didn't they

know well that no boy ever knows anything human at all about
his teachers? Men dressed in black soutanes and bony collars, with
names like ships, or stars, or horses – Hyperion, Aquarius, Berengarius, Arkel – floating into your classroom every morning, saying,
'Irregular verbs today!' or 'Did we polish off Queen Anne yet?'
and if you didn't know your stuff, giving you three on each hand
with the leather strap stuck in their black belts like a policeman's
truncheon. All any boy ever wants from any teacher is that he
might give you a bit of a chance now and again; understand, or
know, or guess that the real reason you did not know your history,
or your maths, was not because you lost the book, or had a headache, or broke your pen but because you saw Molly Ryan yesterday
with high leather boots halfway up her fat legs and you simply had
to dodge out that night to be gassing with her under the gaslamp
by the back gate, watching her swinging her pigtails and admiring
her toes just to provoke you. Little Regis would have understood;
he was the only one of them who understood anything. He would
give you a good clout on the ear, look at you hard and say, 'I'll
give you this one chance, Master Regan, but if you ever do it
again I'll have the hide off you.' And you loved him for it. But the
rest of them? Human? The shock he got the day he saw Popeyes
laughing with a woman in the Main Street! (Jesus! I must have
been a right little prig in those days!) Not to mention the evening
he saw Monsieur Joffre, their French teacher, coming out of a pub
wiping the froth off his Clemenceau moustache. And by the same
token not a drop must pass his lips while he was doing this portrait.
Not with two hundred quid from the Past Pupils' Union depending
on it. Anyway, he had been off the booze for four months now.
'Drop it, Luke!' – his doctor's last words. 'Or it will drop you into
a nice, deep, oblong hole up in Glasnevin. Ninety per cent of your
bloodstream is pure alcohol, and you know where that finally
lodges?' – and he had tapped his forehead. 'DT's. Epilepsy, Neuritis,
Insanity, God knows what!' The memory of it frightened him so
much that when he was passing through Kilcrea he halted for one
last, one absolutely last quick one before he arrived. And, just for
precaution's sake, he packed a bottle of Paddy Flaherty in his hold-
all in case he got a cold, or needed a little nightcap to send him
to sleep after a day's revving-up at the easel.

The only change he could see, guess, presume or infer in Coonla-
han was the rows of cars parked on each side of the Main Street.
Surely, in his time, there were only a few horse-drawn carts or

donkey-butts? Chromium everywhere now and neon strips. The street's surface, asphalted, recalled mud and cowdung on market days. With relief he saw a neat-looking hotel called The Shamrock, and booked himself in there.

'How long, Mr Regan?' the freshfaced young woman said with a welcoming smile.

'How did you know my name?'

'Ah, sure the whole town knows about the painting.'

He winced.

'Four nights, please.'

'Only four?'

He winced again. In the Academy his colleagues called him Luca Fa Presto, after a certain Neapolitan painter who could finish any picture in twenty-four hours.

'It's a small portrait. Head and shoulders.'

Did she think he was going to live in the monastery? All the same he felt a bit ashamed that he was not. There were painters who would have done it, toiling to reveal the habits of a lifetime in a face. Degas must have done it before he began his *Uncle and Niece*. Manet must have known every damned thing about those three people he imprisoned behind the green railing of *The Balcony*. Courbet had put a whole countryside into those three men in *Bonjour, Monsieur Courbet*. Still, when he had driven out of the town and come to the big iron gateway, with SAINT KILLIAN'S COLLEGE half-mooned across it in gilded lettering, and saw the half-mile of avenue leading straight as a ruler up to the barrack-bare front of the college, grim as a tombstone against the sinking sun, he wondered whether Degas, or Monet, or Courbet, or Rembrandt, or Holbein or any of them would have wanted to soak himself in so dreary a joint as this either in the name of literal truth or ideal beauty. Wishing that he had had another drink in The Shamrock before facing this Brother Hilary Harty, he rang the bell.

A cheerful little lay brother, spry and bright as a monkey, showed him into the front parlour where, with painful clarity he remembered the evening his mother had handed him over there to a matron named Miss Wall and with a face like one. The literal truth of the room leaped to the eye: linoleum on the floor, horse-hair chairs, a round table glistening with a mock walnut veneer, a gas-fire unlit. As for ideal beauty: pictures in monochrome, *The Agony in the Garden*, the ghostly face of Christ on the pious fraud called *The Veil of Veronica*, somebody's *Annunciation*, and was

that Breughel's *Tower of Babel* lifting the clouds? The Past Pupils'
Union was going to make him earn every penny of this two hundred quid. The door was hurled open, a powerful-bodied old brother
strode in, jolly-faced and beaming, and on the spot the setting sun
hit face and everything became joyous, and splendid and okay.

'Luke Regan!' he all but shouted. 'After all these years!'

And the two of them were laughing and shaking one another's
hands as energetically and boisterously as only two men can do who
do not know one another from Adam. But what a head! Ripe for
marble! For marble and porphyry! Nose rubicund, eyes blue as
gentians, and an astonishingly protruding lower lip, the sure sign
of a born talker. Hair white, thin on top but curling like the last of
the harpers around his neck. Manet be blowed! Poor old Rembrandt!
It was going to be the portrait of his life. Green curtain behind,
ochre streaks of sunlight, buckets of carmine, lumps of it laid on
with bold hard brushstrokes – half-inch brushes at that. Energy,
strength, tenderness, humour! No more of that blasted pink tooth-
paste enamel that he had been floating all over the gobs of endless
company directors for the last ten years. Not, to be fair, to flatter
them but to flatter their stupid wives. 'Oh, Mister Regan, I think
Eddie is much younger that you are making him out to be!' Or
'D'ye think, Mister Regan, you could make the tie a bit smoother
like? The way you have it makes him look old and careless like.'
Meaning, 'My God, man, do you want people to think *I'm* that old?'

'Brother Hilary, when do you think we can begin?'

He was so excited that when he got back to The Shamrock he
had to go into the bar for a large one to calm his nerves. In its
gold pool he saw the title on the catalogue of the Academy, where
the portrait would be shown publicly for the first time. *The Old
Dominie.* By Luke Regan, RHA. Not for Sale. Or what about *The
Good Shepherd?* Or maybe, *Ex Cathedra.* Or *Post Multos Annos?*
With a neat gold tab at the bottom of the frame saying, *Gladly
wolde he lerne and gladly teche.* Tactile values? His fingers in-
voluntarily began to mould the face. The man sitting beside him
said, 'Hello, Mister Regan.' He sighed and did not deny it.

'My name is Halligan, Harry Halligan. We all knew you were
coming. All Ireland knows about the painting. You have a great
character there in old Leatherlip.'

'Leatherlip?'

Far away a bell chimed harshly, curtains parted on a small red
light at the end of a mile-long corridor.

'Don't you remember? Or didn't ye call him that in your day?'

'How extraordinary! We did call one fellow that. But, surely, not *this* man?'

'*Tempus fugit*. It's twenty-five years since I was at Saint Killian's. He was slim then, bushy black hair, eyes like a razor blade. You knew him in his thirties. And you really can't remember him?'

'He will come back to me. I'll quarry him out. That's how a painter works, working in and in, burrowing, excavating. It's like archaeology, you don't know what you are looking for until you find it. Sooner or later the face speaks.'

Halligan half-turned to the woman on his left: a bosomy, high-coloured little blonde. Horsy type.

'Let me introduce you to my wife. Valerie, this is Luke Regan the famous painter.'

She gave a cool hand and a cooler 'Howdyedo?' in a loud Anglo-Irish voice. No smile. Regan could feel the antagonism in her, and wondered at it. They had two more quick ones together before Mrs Halligan abruptly hauled her husband off with her. Regan took a last one by himself for the road to sleep.

Because of the light he decided to use the front parlour for a studio. It had three tall windows facing north. He could come and go without bother. By two o'clock, when his man would be free and the light good for two hours or so, he had managed to get a throne fixed up, a green curtain hung for background, his easel and work table ready and the inflatable lay figure that he always travelled with (one of his neatest Fa Presto tricks) draped with a black soutane that he would be working on every morning.

'I can't believe, Brother Hilary,' he laughed, as his charcoal lightly and rapidly sketched in the outline, 'that you are really seventy-five. You look about fifty.'

He always talked while he worked to keep his subject from stiffening or sagging.

'Aha!' the old boy laughed triumphantly. 'Mixing with youth all my life, that's what does it. That,' finger magisterially aloft, 'and the regular life. A dull life I suppose, not like you, out in the world, travelling, meeting interesting people, doing interesting things. But I have had my compensations. No worries, no regrets, no tensions. The rut, Luke. The beaten path. The ascetic discipline. Simple food. Good country air. Constant exercise. No excesses of any kind. You wouldn't grow fat on my kind of life, my boy. But that's what turns every monk into a man.'

When he came to the mouth he stared long and hard at the protruding lower lip. Again that far-off bell. Leatherlip? The eyes were curiously small but they gave out sparks when he talked. He would have given anything for an early photograph of the softer eyes of the boy buried behind those sharp orbs. He saw that the nose was red because it was veined all over. If this were a company director he would have said at once, 'Chronic alcoholic.' He knew rosacea when he saw it. Chiefly in elderly women. The wages of virtue. Chronic tea-drinkers. Gastritis. Monastery food. Probably an ulcer. Teeth browning from age and pipe-smoking. There would be black centres on the tip of every one of them. He frowned again at the big lip. A hard mouth in a jolly face. Now, what in hell did that portend? Silence. A good subject – he held the pose patiently.

'The rut?' he murmured, looking up looking down. 'The beaten path? "The path of the just is as the shining light that shineth more and more unto the perfect day." '

'I'm glad to see that you read your Bible, Luke.'

'Now and again, Brother. A little to the left, Brother. Thank you, Brother.'

The light on the lip threw an interesting shadow. The nose became gory.

'Ah, yes!' concentrating on the jutting lip. 'Now and again . . . "Return, return O Shulamite. Thy belly is like a heap of wheat set about with lilies . . . Thy neck is as a tower of ivory . . . Many waters cannot quench love, neither can the floods drown it." '

He glanced up. The eyes were blazing, the whole expression of the face had changed, the brows gathered down fiercely, the cheeks as scarlet as the nose. His charcoal flew, dragging down the eyebrows. That revealing wet light on the lip, thrust out a whole inch – that, above all, *that* he must keep.

'I think, Mister Regan, I think, Luke, it might have been better if you had concentrated on the New Testament.'

By a forty-year-old reflex he glanced at the black belt around the belly to see if he still carried the strap. No time for that now. Now? Memory was now!

'Now, Brother, I begin painting.'

As he mixed his colours he cooled, a sign that he was in tiptop form. He knew they called him Luca Fa Presto. Bloody fools! You boil at the inspiration. You go cold as ice in the execution.

'You're dead right, Brother,' he said soapily. 'The new Covenant. There is the true wisdom. I learned that here in Saint Killy's.'

(Funny how the old slang name came back to him. It was all creeping back to him.) 'I often think, Brother, of those wonderful words of Saint Matthew. "Behold the birds of the air . . . They sow not, neither do they reap . . . Consider the lilies of the fields . . . Even Solomon in all his glory was not arrayed like one of these" '

To his relief the mollified voice quoted back to him.

' "Behold, a greater than Solomon is here." '

He looked up at the veined nose. The tuning fork for a study in *rouge et noir*. He touched the canvas with carmine.

'Oh, a beautiful saying, Brother! A darlint saying, Brother. And so wise, Brother. So very wise.'

Not too red now, for Christ's sake. No wife, but the Past Pupils' Union would have to be pleased. And, after all, two hundred johnny-ogoblins in this job! A long silence.

'And there's another fine phrase. Muscular Christianity. A Jew invented that. Disraeli. A great man in lots of ways.'

'A Jew?' said the voice coldly.

'By the way, Brother,' he said hurriedly. 'Talking of muscle. When I was here in twenty-six, Brother, the Gaelic Football team was going great guns. How is it doing these happy days?'

The old man beamed and told him. The rest of the sitting went as smooth as milk. The only other little lurch came when he looked out at the sky, threw down his brushes, and said that the light was going.

'Can I see what you have done so far, Luke?'

He handled it with expert joviality.

'We never do, Brother, not until we've polished off the victim.'

They parted in laughter and with warm handshakes. He took the key of the parlour with him; he would be working on the lay figure in the morning.

Halligan was waiting for him in the bar; alone this time. Seeing that his glass was at low tide, Regan invited him to freshen it up.

'I won't say no. How's the masterpiece doing?'

A stocky man. Heavy hands, but they could be a craftsman's. A fawn waistcoat with brass buttons. Ruddy cheeks. A gentleman farmer? A fisherman? Not a doctor – no doctor would dare drink at a public bar in a small town like this. The wife had had the smell of money.

'He's coming back to me slowly. Another sitting and I'll have him smoked out.'

'What,' eagerly, 'are you finding?'

Regan eye-cornered him. This fellow might be a member of the Past Pupils' Union.

'A splendid character. I was just wondering did he ever teach me history?'

'Were you a senior?'

'I was only what we used to call a gyb. A Good Young Boy. I came here when I was twelve. Straight from the nuns. Our Ladies of the Holy Bower. You wouldn't think it now to look at me, but I used to be their little angel. Curly hair. They used to make me sing solo at Benediction. In a lacy surplice, purple soutane, red tie. They spoiled me. It was only by the blessing of God I didn't turn into a queer. I may tell you the change from there to here was pretty tough. I only stayed three years.'

'No, you wouldn't have had him. And,' surveying him humourously, 'you may have been a little angel, Mister Regan, but you've put on a bit of weight since then. Thirteen and a half stone? He only taught the seniors, and after he became Headmaster he had no fixed classes at all. Anyway, his particular obsession was English Grammar. He was dotty about it. He was a bit of a megalomaniac, really. Couldn't give it up. Even after he became Head he used to rove around the school from class to class leathering it into us. Of course he's retired now, but I'm told he still does it. Did he never come into your classroom to wallop *I seen* out of you and *I saw* into you?'

Halligan laughed as if in happy memory of the walloping, and, on the spot, Regan had his man whole and entire. The terror of his very first day at Saint Killy's often repeated, seeing the lean black ghost come floating in. Like a starved wolf. One hand waving the leather strap behind his back like a black tail. The rasping voice. 'What is a relative clause? What is an adverbial clause? Decline the verb *see* in the past tense. No, it is not! Hold out your hand. Take that. And that. And that.' And, always, the one thing all boys loathe in teachers, as sarcastic as acid. Oh, a proper bastard!

'Do I take it, Mister Halligan, that you didn't particularly like it at Saint Killy's?'

'I got on there all right. I was good at games. And Leatherlip was mad on games. "The Irish," he was always telling us,"are famous all over the world as sportsmen. Strong men." It was he started boxing at Saint Killy's. He used to knock the hell out of me in the ring. I got so mad at him one day that I deliberately gave him one right under the belt. And I could hit hard that time. When he got his wind back he nearly murdered me. He was the only fly in the ointment.' He leaned over and whispered: 'I often thought afterwards that he was the only wasp in the ointment.' He glanced quickly around the bar and said in a loud voice, 'Mind you, Brother Hilary is a great organiser. He built up a great school here. We are all very proud of Saint Killian's in this town.'

('Fuck *you*!' Regan thought.)

'And most justifiably so, Mister Halligan. By the way are you a member of the Past Pupils' Union?'

Halligan smiled crookedly. His voice fell.

'I didn't tell you I'm the local vet. I look after the Jersey herd up there.' He beckoned to the barmaid. 'The same again, Miss Noble.'

'Family?' Regan asked.

'Three boys.'

'They at school here?'

Halligan shuffled his glass a bit.

'Not exactly. You see . . . Well, the fact is Valerie is a Protestant. We met at the hunt. Actually, she's a niece of Lord Boyne's.' (A good connection for a vet, Regan thought.) 'Before I married her I knew I'd have to do something to smooth the way for her. For myself, of course, I didn't give a damn. To hell with them, But for poor little Valerie . . . You live up in Dublin, you can do what you like there, you don't understand what it's like in small places like this. But,' he winked, 'there's always ways and means. Two months before I got married, do you know what I did?' He nudged and again winked. 'I joined the local Knights of Columbanus. And, by God, it worked. Though I'll never forget the first time I went to the Club after the wedding. The Grand Knight got up and he says, "Since our last meeting I suppose you all know that one of our brothers got married." Christ Almighty, I thought, here it comes! He's going to give me hell for marrying a Protestant. I'm going to be ruined for life in this place. Far from it! He complimented me most warmly. I drove home that night singing like a bird. I knew I'd done one of the smartest things in my life. After a year I dropped them. But when it came to where we'd send the boys to school, Valerie and myself had one hell of a fight. I said we simply had to send them to Saint Killy's We started with the oldest boy. The very first day he came home from school with his two hands red as pulp from Leatherlip's strap. After that Valerie put her foot down. We came to a sensible compromise. We sent them all to school in England. One of the finest Catholic schools in the world. Nobody could object to that.'

'Very shrewd. Very wise move. And after that, no opposition? Miss Noble, fill 'em up again.'

'Not half! The day I whipped Tommy out of school Leatherlip wrote me a stinker. He went all around town saying I was a snob, and a lah-di-dah, and an Anglicised Irishman, and a toady, and God knows what else. Just to show you – it wasn't until he retired that I got the job of looking after the college herd.'

Regan laughed.

'Elephants never forget.'

'It's no joke,' Halligan whispered solemnly. 'Don't delude yourself. That man never forgets anything. Or anybody.'

'I wonder,' Regan said uncomfortably.

Just then Valerie Halligan came in. He noted that after one quick one she hauled her husband away. From her manner it was plain that she did not approve of his latest drinking companion. This time Regan did not wonder why.

Not that he had ever been much leathered by anybody at Saint Killy's, and never once by Leatherlip. On the contrary, he had often wished he would leather him after the day he called him out of the class and sat him on his knee, and said to the rest of them after he had leathered them all, 'Look at this clever little boy. He knows what a dependent clause is. And he's only twelve, and straight from the nuns, as small and fresh and rosy as a cherry. Why don't you slobs know it as well as he does?' His nickname became Cherry. They called him Leatherlip's Lapdog or Leatherlip's Pet. They used to corner him and say things like, 'Cherry, if *he* comes in today for more frigging grammar your job is to suck up to him. Get him into a good humour or he'll leather us and we'll puck the hell outa you.' He used to try, but it was always the same, 'See this bright little boy!' And, after school, they would shove him, and taunt him and puck him. Once he deliberately tried to get leathered by failing to write out six sentences that night before on *shall* and *will*. The strap swished, the brows came down, a grey spittle appeared at each corner of the big lip. Terror shook his bones.

' "I *will* go there tomorrow." Is that correct?'

'No, Brother. Plain future statements in the first person must always have *shall*.'

' "We would not win a single match with a team like that." Is that correct?'

'No, Brother. Plain conditional statements in the first person must have *should*.'

'Come here to me, boy. Now, listen to that bright little boy, straight from the nuns...'

For three years he had suffered hell from the benign approbation of that accursed old fathead.

'Miss Noble, the same again. No, make it a double this time.'

He went to bed plastered.

'Well, Brother Hilary, I hear nothing all over the town but people singing your praises. You've made a great job of this college. The doyen of Saint Killian's.' The old monk beamed softly.

'Ah, well, Luke, I've done my humble best. But, mind you,' rather less softly. 'I had to fight all the way.' Far from softly: 'Opposition. I had to keep my hand on my dagger every moment of the day.'

'Aha, but you fought well, Brother. You fought the good fight, Brother. "To give and not to count the cost, to fight and not to heed the wounds." '

'Who said that?' – suspiciously.

The lip out again with the lovely wet light on it. Porcine. Sensual. Lickerish. Loose. Deboshed by pride and righteousness. Daringly he slapped on a fleck of viridian, And, by God, it was just right. He kept him waiting for the answer.

'Saint Ignatius Loyola said that. A great body of men, the Jesuits.'

The two eyes cold. Turquoise? No! Pine-needle blue? Hell's bells, snow and ice are the one thing no Irish painter can ever get right. Nor the British. Nor the Italians. You have to live with the stuff like the Dutch and the Scans. The gore of the cheeks would have to bring it out. Cherry? Damn you, I'll give you cherry. No ablation here. Warts and all. Maxillae of an anthropomorph. Ears of a bat. That time he had to sit on his lap in class! The hair stuck out of his ears.

'Have you ever had any Protestants in Saint Killy's, Brother?'

The little finger dug into a hairy ear and wagged there twenty times.

'I don't approve of mixed marriages and I don't approve of mixed schooling. Protestants haven't our morality, Luke. The morality of every Protestant I ever met was written into his cheque-book. They are completely devoid of our mystical sense of the otherworld. Not like you and me. I don't like Protestants. You mentioned some

Jew yesterday. I'll be frank with you, Luke. I don't like Jews either.'

'Oh, you're on to something there, Brother. A cunning bloody race. Very able, though. I was talking about Disraeli.' He seized his palette knife for the coarse, oily skin of the cheeks. 'Do you remember what he said the time Dan O'Connell taunted him with being a Jew. "Yes, I *am* a Jew, and when ancestors of the right honourable gentleman were brutal savages in an unknown island, mine were priests in the temple of Solomon." '

The old warhorse out on grass. Teeth bared. Sepia? Burnt sienna?

'For Heaven's sake, Luke! I do wish you'd stop talking about Solomon!'

'All the same, Jesus was a Jew.'

'One of the mysteries of the world!'

'And he chose the Jews.' Laughing delightedly at the furious face on his canvas he quoted. ' "How odd/That God/Should choose/ The Jews." '

In laughter the ritual answer pealed from the throne.

' "Oh no, not odd./They hoped to God/Some day/He'd pay." '

They both cackled.

'Ah, Brother, you understand it all!'

'We understand one another, Luke. Two comrades in Christ!'

He worked on. From the distant playing fields young voices cheered. A long silence. When he looked up he saw a profile. The old man was gazing at the moony face of Christ looming through the Veil of Veronica.

'Do you know Greek, Luke? A pity! There is a wonderful Greek word. *Archiropito*. It is the perfect word for that image of Christ. Painted by no human hand. Painted by the angels. The day I became Headmaster I bought three dozen copies of that angelic image. I put one in every classroom. I gave one to every brother to hang over his bed.'

He sighed. Regan looked at the fraud. Then he looked at his portrait. Never had he felt such a sense of power, energy, truth to life. The light was fading. 'Tomorrow is Sunday. I might do a little work on the background. Then on Monday we'll have the last sitting.'

'And then,' as eagerly as a boy, 'I can see it?'

A laggard nod. As they parted the old man put his arm around his shoulder.

'My dear friend!' He sighed affectionately. 'Take care of yourself, Luke,' who gave one backward glance at his easel; the face was virtually finished, the body half finished, the soul naked. Areas of bare canvas at the edges surrounded it all like a ragged veil.

That evening the Halligans came together, had one quick one and left, promising to call on Sunday afternoon and go out to the college for a secret look at the unfinished masterpiece. He stayed on alone. The Saturday night crowd was dense. He felt he was drinking with half the town. He was the last to leave the bar, pushed out, blind drunk, by the barman and old Noble. He took a bottle of whiskey to bed with him. He woke late. The angelus was slowly tolling and under his window hollow feet were echoing along the pavement to last mass. He drunk some more and slept some more. He was wakened by the maid knocking at his door to ask him did he want to eat something. He ordered her to bring him a bottle of whiskey. When she returned she stamped the bottle distastefully on his chest of drawers and banged the door after her. Halligan came up at four, refused to drink with him, said that Valerie was waiting outside in the station wagon, helped him to dress and all but carried him downstairs. He was tolerantly amused by his stumblings and fumblings as he tried to get into the car, but Mrs Halligan was not. 'Oh, for Christ's sake!' she growled at her husband. 'He needs to be pumped!'

When they had pushed open the hall door of the college and crept cautiously across the empty hall to the parlour, she had to take the key from his helpless hand to open the door. They entered twilight. Regan dragged back the window curtains, bade Halligan switch on the light, and with one forensic arm presented them to the easel. For one minute's silence he watched Halligan's mouth fall open and his eyelids soar. Her eyelashes peered.

'God almighty!' Halligan whispered. 'You have him to a T.'

'T for Truth,' he cried triumphantly.

Halligan turned to his wife.

'What d'ye think, Valerie?'

She looked at him, she looked at Regan, she looked at the portrait. Then she edged Halligan aside, stood before the portrait, and, one hand on her hip, extended her silence to two minutes.

'Isn't it stu – PEN – dous, Valerie?'

She walked away to the window, did a tiny drum roll with her nails on the glass, turned to them and spoke, quietly, coldly and brassily.

'Don't be a damn fool, Halligan. Mister Regan! I know nothing about painting, but I know one thing, for certain, about that paint-

ing. Nobody will buy it. Not here, anyway. Are you, Halligan, going
to get up in the committee of the Past Pupils' Union and say that
portrait is stupendous? Vote for it? Pay for it? And hang it? And
where? There's only one place in this town where you could hang
that picture – in the bar of the Shamrock Hotel, where everybody
would laugh their heads off at it and then go out and say it is a
public disgrace. And do you think even old Noble would dare hang
it? You can vote for that picture, Halligan, over my dead body –
we've had trouble enough in this town and I don't want any more
of it. And I'll tell you one other little thing about that picture,
Mister Regan. If you show it anywhere in this country you might
just as well go out and hang yourself because it would be the last
portrait you'd be asked to paint as long as you live.'

Regan laughed at her.

'To hell with their money. I'll show it at the Academy. I'll sell
it there for twice the price. It'll be reproduced in every paper in
Dublin! In every art magazine in the world!'

Halligan looked at him with funky eyes.

'Luke!' (And if Regan had been sober he would have known
at once by that use of his first name how grave the issue was.)
'Valerie is right. Listen! Would you do one thing for me, and for
yourself and for God's sake. There must be a second key to this
room. Anyone might come in here at any moment.' He cocked a
frightened ear. 'Any second that door might open. Would you take it
back to the hotel for the night, and tomorrow morning look at
it calmly and coldly and make up your own mind what you're going
to do about it. You know,' he wheedled, 'they might even start
pawing it!'

'Pawing? Wise man! Shrewd man! Monkey, monkey,' he
approved. 'See all, hear all, say nothing. Let's get it out of here.'

They restored the twilight, the hallway was as empty as before;
they drove fast, back to the empty, Sunday afternoon Main Street.
Outside The Shamrock she put her head out through the window
of the wagon to say, 'I'll give you one minute, Halligan, no more.'
They were lucky. They met nobody on the way to the bedroom.
They stood the portrait on the mantelpiece. They sat side by side
on the bed and looked at the scarlet, scowling, wet-lipped face of
their old master staring down at them. Halligan accepted one slug
from the neck of the bottle, slapped his companion on the back,
and ran for it. Regan lay back on his pillow, emptying the bottle
gulp for gulp, rejoicing strabismally at the face on the mantelpiece

that, like a wavering fire, slowly faded into the veils of the gathering dusk.

'*Archiropito!*' he wheezed joyfully as he drained the bottle on its head, let it fall with a crash on the ground and sank into a stupor.

It was dark when he woke. He had no sense of time, of date, of day or night. He thought he heard noises downstairs. He groped for the bell, found it and kept pressing it until the door opened and, against the light, he saw the burly figure of old Noble.

'Mishter Noble, shend me up a bottle of whishkey if you please.'

Silence. Then:

'I will do no such thing, Mister Regan. If I was to do anything I'd send for a doctor. Sleep it off.'

The door closed and he was in darkness again.

'The bitch!' he growled, knowing that she had tipped off the old man. *Must* have a drink! If only . . . Suddenly he remembered. That bottle he had bought on the way down from Dublin. Had he drunk that too? He rolled out of bed, crawled on all fours to the light switch, at last found his hold-all, and there was his golden salvation. The colours of the little map of Ireland on the label swam – purple, and red, and yellow and green. With his teeth he tore off the thin metal covering on the neck, wrested out the cork, twisting its serrated edge, lifted the bottleneck to his mouth, engorged the sweet liquor as if it were water, and sank on the floor in a coma. The maid found him there in the morning, and ran from him down the stairs, screeching.

He recovered his senses only for the few minutes during which he was being put to bed in the monastery. Hilary had him brought there immediately he was informed of his sorry condition by old Noble, then by the community's doctor who had driven him at once to the college door, wrapped in blankets, still in a stupor, his breath coming in gasps, his forehead glistening with cold dots of sweat. It took three brothers to lift him from the car and carry him upstairs to Hilary's bedroom. Harry Halligan and Valerie Halligan, also alerted by Noble, came after them, carrying his few belongings stuffed into his suitcase and his hold-all. As they packed them, her eye roving about the room saw the portrait on the mantelpiece.

'Halligan,' she ordered. 'Take that thing down and burn it.'

He looked at her, looked at the closed door, told her to lock it, took out his clasp knife and cut the canvas from its frame. But when he approached the empty grate his nerve failed him.

'I can't do it, Valerie. It's like murder.'

She snatched it from him, tore some paper linings from the chest of drawers, crumpled the canvas on top of them in the grate, put her cigarette lighter to the paper and they watched everything burn to ashes. They drove to the college, laid his two cases inside the door, and drove rapidly down the drive for home and a couple of stiff ones. In the middle of her drink, and her abuse of him, she looked at him and laughed, remembering from her schooldays.

' "To be thus is nothing, but to be safely thus," ' jumped up to ring old Noble and warn him never to mention their names to anybody in the college about this affair.

'Rely on me,' the old voice replied. 'We're all in it together,' from which she knew that he, too, had seen the portrait.

Hilary sat by his bed during his few, limp moments of consciousness.

'My poor Luke,' fondling his icy palm. 'What on earth happened to you at all, at all?'

'Brother,' he said faintly. 'Can I have one, last little drink?'

The old man shook his head, sadly but not negatively.

'Of course you can, Luke. I'll leave you a glass of the best here beside your bed for the night. Tomorrow we'll cut it down to half a glass. Then, bit by bit, between us, with God's help,' glancing up piously at the veiled face over the bed, 'we'll wean you back to your old self.'

In the morning a young lay brother stole into the room with a nice hot cup of tea for the patient. He found the glass dry and the body an empty cell. Touched, it was like stuffed leather.

The obituaries were invariably kind. They all stressed the burned portrait, the symbol of every artist's indefatigable pursuit of unattainable perfection. They slyly recalled his convivial nature, his great thirst for friendship, the speed with which he could limn a character in a few lines, the unfailing polish of his work. But as always, it was some wag in a pub who spoke his epitaph.

'Well, poor old Lukey Fa Presto is gone from us. He wasn't much of a painter. And he had no luck. But what a beautiful way to die! In the odour.' His glass raised. All their glasses lifted. 'Of sanctity and whiskey.'

With solemn smiles they drank.

The Faithless Wife

He had now been stalking his beautiful Mlle. Morphy, whose real name was Mrs Meehawl O'Sullivan, for some six weeks, and she had appeared to be so amused at every stage of the hunt, so responsive, *entrainante*, even *aguichante*, that he could already forsee the kill over the next horizon. At their first encounter, during the Saint Patrick's Day cocktail party at the Dutch embassy, accompanied by a husband who had not a word to throw to a cat about anything except the scissors and shears that he manufactured somewhere in the West of Ireland, and who was obviously quite ill at ease and drank too much Irish whiskey, what had attracted him to her was not only her splendid Boucher figure (whence his sudden nickname for her, La Morphée), or her copper-coloured hair, her lime-green Irish eyes and her seemingly poreless skin, but her calm, total and subdued elegance: the Balenciaga costume, the peacock-skin gloves, the gleaming crocodile handbag, a glimpse of tiny, lace-edged lawn handkerchief and her dry, delicate scent. He had a grateful eye and nose for such things. It was, after all, part of his job. Their second meeting, two weeks later, at his own embassy, had opened the doors. She came alone.

Now, at last, inside a week, perhaps less, there would be an end to all the probationary encounters that followed – mostly her inventions, at his persistent appeals – those wide-eyed fancy-meeting-you-heres at the zoo, at race-meetings, afternoon cinemas, in art galleries, at more diplomatic parties (once he had said gaily to her, 'The whole diplomacy of Europe seems to circle around our interest in one another'), those long drives over the Dublin mountains in his Renault coupé, those titillating rural lunches, nose to nose, toe to toe (rural because she quickly educated him to see Dublin as a stock exchange for gossip, a casino of scandal), an end, which was rather a pity, to those charming unforeseen-foreseen, that is to say proposed but in the end just snatched, afternoon *promenades*

champêtres under the budding leaves and closing skies of the
Phoenix Park, with the first lights of the city springing up below
them to mark the end of another boring day for him in Ailesbury
Road, Dublin's street of embassies, for her another possibly cosier
but, he selfishly hoped, not much more exciting day in her swank
boutique on Saint Stephen's Green. Little by little those intimate
encounters, those murmured confessions had lifted acquaintance to
friendships, to self-mocking smiles over some tiny incident during
their last meeting, to eager anticipation of the next, an aimless tenderness twanging to appetite like an arrow. Or, at least, that was how
he felt about it all. Any day now, even any hour, the slow count-
down, slower than the slow movement of Mendelssohn's Concerto
in E Minor, or the most swoony sequence from the *Siegfried Idyll*,
or that floating spun-sugar balloon of Mahler's 'Song of the Earth,'
to the music of which on his gramophone he would imagine her
smiling side-long at him as she softly disrobed, and his ingenious
playing with her, his teasing and warming of her moment by
moment for the roaring, blazing takeoff. To the moon!

Only one apprehension remained with him, not a real misgiving,
something nearer to a recurring anxiety. It was that at the last
moments when her mind and her body ought to take leave of one
another she might take to her heels. It was a fear that flooded him
whenever, with smiles too diffident to reassure him, she would once
again mention that she was a Roman Catholic, or a Cat, a Papist or
a Pape, a convent girl, and once she laughed that during her schooldays in the convent she had actually been made an *Enfant de Marie*.
The words never ceased to startle him, dragging him back miserably
to his first sexual frustration with his very pretty but unexpectedly
proper cousin Berthe Ohnet during his lycée years in Nancy; a similar
icy snub a few years later in Quebec; repeated still later by that
smack on the face in Rio that almost became a public scandal;
memories so painful that whenever an attractive woman nowadays
mentioned religion, even in so simple a context as, 'Thank God
I didn't buy that hat, or frock, or stock, or mare,' a red flag at once
began to flutter in his belly.

Obsessed, every time she uttered one of those ominous words he
rushed for the reassurance of what he called The Sherbet Test,
which meant observing the effect on her of some tentatively sexy
joke, like the remark of the young princess on tasting her first
sherbet: – 'Oh, how absolutely delicious! But what a pity it isn't
a sin!' To his relief she not only always laughed merrily at his

stories but always capped them, indeed at times so startling him by her coarseness that it only occurred to him quite late in their day that this might be her way of showing her distaste for his diaphanous indelicacies. He had once or twice observed that priests, peasants and children will roar with laughter at some scavenger joke, and growl at even a veiled reference to a thigh. Was she a child of nature? Still, again and again back would come those disturbing words. He could have understood them from a prude, but what on earth did *she* mean by them? Were they so many herbs to season her desire with pleasure in her naughtiness? Flicks of nasty puritan sensuality to whip her body over some last ditch of indecision? It was only when the final crisis came that he wondered if this might not all along have been her way of warning him that she was neither a light nor a lecherous woman, neither a flirt nor a flibbertigibbet, that in matters of the heart she was *une femme très sérieuse.*

He might have guessed at something like it much earlier. He knew almost from the first day that she was *bien élevée*, her father a judge of the Supreme Court, her uncle a monsignor at the Vatican, a worldly, sport-loving, learned, contriving priest who had persuaded her papa to send her for a finishing year to Rome with the Sisters of the Sacred Heart at the top of the Spanish Steps; chiefly, it later transpired, because the convent was near the *centre hippique* in the Borghese Gardens and it was his right reverend's opinion that no rich girl could possibly be said to have completed her education until she had learned enough about horses to ride hounds. She had told him a lot, and most amusingly, about his uncle. She had duly returned from Rome to Dublin, and whenever he came over for the hunting, he always rode beside her. This attention had mightily flattered her until she discovered that she was being used as a cover for his uncontrollable passion for Lady Kinvara and Loughrea, then the master, some said the mistress, of the Clare-Galway hounds.

'How old were you then?' Ferdy asked, fascinated.

'I was at the university. Four blissful, idling years. But I got my degree. I was quick. And,' she smiled, 'good-looking. It helps, even with professors.'

'But riding to hounds as a student?'

'Why not? In Ireland everybody does. Children do. You could ride to hounds on a plough horse if you had nothing else. So long as you keep out of the way of real hunters. I only stopped after my

marriage, when I had a miscarriage. And I swear that was only because I was thrown.'

A monsignor who was sport-loving, worldly and contriving. He
understood, and approved, and it explained many things about her.

The only other way in which her dash, beauty and gaiety puzzled
and beguiled him were trivial. Timid she was not, she was game for
any risk. But the coolness of her weather eye often surprised him.

'The Leopardstown Races? Oh, what a good idea, Ferdy! Let's
meet there . . . The Phoenix Park Races? No, not there. Too many
doctors showing off their wives and their cars, trying to be noticed.
And taking notice. Remember, a lot of my college friends married
doctors . . . No, not *that* cinema. It has become vogueish . . . In
fact, no cinema on the south side of the river. What we want is
a good old fleabitten picture house on the north side where they
show nothing but westerns and horrors, and where the kids get
in on Saturday mornings for thruppence . . . Oh, and do please only
ring the boutique in an emergency. Girls gossip.'

Could she be calculating? For a second of jealous heat he wondered if she could possibly have another lover. Cooling, he saw that
he had to keep a wary eye in his master's direction she had to
think of her bourgeois clientele. Besides, he was a bachelor, and
would remain one. She had to manage her inexpressibly dull, if
highly successful old scissors and shears manufacturer, well past
fifty and probably as suspicious as he was boring; so intensely, so
exhaustingly boring that the only subject about which she could
herself nearly become boring was in her frequent complaints about
his boringness. Once she *was* frightening – when she spat out that
she had hated her husband ever since the first night of their marriage
when he brought her for their honeymoon – it was odd how long,
and how intensely this memory had rankled – not, as he had
promised, to Paris, but to his bloody scissors and shears factory in
the wet wilds of northern Donegal. ('Just me dear, haha, to let 'em
see, haha, t'other half of me scissors.')

Ferdy had of course never asked her why she had married such
a cretin; not after sizing up her house, her furniture, her pictures,
her clothes, her boutique. Anyway, only another cretin would dis-
courage any pretty woman from grumbling about her husband:
(a) because such grumblings give a man a chance to show what
a deeply sympathetic nature he has, and (b) because the information
incidentally supplied helps one to arrange one's assignations in
places and at times suitable to all concerned.

Adding it all up (he was a persistent adder-upper) only one problem had so far defeated him: that he was a foreigner and did not know what sort of women Irish women are. It was not as if he had not done his systematic best to find out, beginning with a course of reading through the novels of her country. A vain exercise. With the exception of the Molly Bloom of James Joyce the Irish Novel had not only failed to present him with any fascinating woman but it had presented him with, in his sense of the word, no woman at all. Irish fiction was a lot of nineteenth-century *connerie* about half-savage Brueghelesque peasants, or urban *petits fonctionnaires* who invariably solved their frustrations by getting drunk on religion, patriotism or undiluted whiskey, or by taking flight to England. Pastoral melodrama. (Giono at his worst.) Or pastoral humbuggery. (Bazin at his most sentimental.) Or, at its best, pastoral lyricism. (Daudet and rosewater.) As for Molly Bloom! He enjoyed the smell of every kissable pore of her voluptuous body without for one moment believing that she had ever existed. James Joyce in drag.

'But,' he had finally implored his best friend in Ailesbury Road, Hamid Bey, the third secretary of the Turkish embassy, whose amorous secrets he willingly purchased with his own, 'if it is too much to expect Ireland to produce a bevy of Manons, Mitsous, Gigis, Claudines, Kareninas, Oteros, Leahs, San Severinas, what about those great-thighed, vast-bottomed creatures dashing around the country on horseback like Diana followed by all her minions? Are they not interested in love? And if so why aren't there novels about them?'

His friend laughed as toughly as Turkish Delight and replied in English in his laziest Noel Coward drawl, all the vowels frontal as if he were talking through bubble gum, all his r's either left out where they should be, as in *deah* or *cleah*, or inserted where they should not be, as in *India-r* or *Iowa-r*.

'My deah Ferdy, did not your deah fatheh or your deah mamma-r eveh tell you that all Irish hohsewomen are in love with their hohses? And anyway it is well known that the favourite pin-up girl of Ahland is a gelding.'

'Naked?' Ferdinand asked coldly, and refused to believe him, remembering that his beloved had been a hohsewoman, and satisfied that he was not a gelding. Instead, he approached the Italian ambassador at a cocktail party given by the Indonesian embassy to whisper to him about *l'amore irlandese* in his best stage French, and stage French manner, eyebrows lifted above fluttering eyelids, voice as hoarse as, he guessed, His Excellency's mind would be on its creaking way back to memories of Gabin, Jouvet, Brasseur, Fernandel, Yves Montand. It proved to be another futile exercise. His Ex groaned as operatically as every Italian groans over such vital, and lethal, matters as the Mafia, food, taxation and women, threw up his hands, made a face like a more than usually desiccated De Sica and sighed, '*Les femmes d'Irlande? Mon pauvre gars! Elles sont d'une chasteté . . .*' He paused and roared the adjective, '. . . FORMIDABLE!'

Ferdinand had heard this yarn about feminine chastity in other countries and (with those two or three exceptions already mentioned), found it true only until one had established the precise local variation of the meaning of 'chastity.' But how was he to discover the Irish variation? In the end it was Celia herself who, unwittingly, revealed it to him and in doing so dispelled his last doubts about her susceptibility, inflammability and volatility – despite the very proper Sisters of the Spanish Steps.

The revelation occurred one night in early May – her Mee-hawl being away in the West, presumably checking what she contemptuously called his Gaelic-squeaking scissors. Ferdy had driven her back to his flat for a nightcap after witnessing the prolonged death of Mimi in *La Bohème*. She happened to quote to him Oscar Wilde's remark about the death of Little Nell that only a man with a heart of stone could fail to laugh at it, and in this clever vein they had continued for a while over the rolling brandy, seated side by side on his settee, his hand on her bare shoulder leading him to hope more and more fondly that this might be his Horizon Night, until suddenly, she asked him a coldly probing question.

'Ferdy! Tell me exactly why we did not believe in the reality of Mimi's death.'

His palm oscillated gently between her clavicle and her scapula.

'Because, my little cabbage, we were not expected to. Singing away like a lark? With her last breath? And no lungs? I am a Frenchman. I understand the nature of reality and can instruct you about it. Art, my dear Celia, is art because it is not reality. It does not copy or represent nature. It improves upon it. It embellishes it. This is the kernel of the classical French attitude to life. And,' he beamed at her, 'to love. We make of our wildest feelings of passion the gentle art of love.'

He suddenly stopped fondling her shoulder and surveyed her

with feelings of chagrin and admiration. The sight of her belied his words. Apart from dressing with taste, and, he felt certain, undressing with even greater taste, she used no art at all. She was as innocent of makeup as a peasant girl of the Vosges. Had he completely misread her? Was she that miracle, a fully ripe peach brought into the centre of the city some twenty years ago from a walled garden in the heart of the country, still warm from the sun, still glowing, downy, pristine, innocent as the dew? He felt her juice dribbling down the corner of his mouth. Was this the missing piece of her jigsaw? An ensealed innocence. If so he had wasted six whole weeks. This siege could last six years.

'No, Ferdy!' she said crossly. 'You have it all wrong. I'm talking about life, not about art. The first and last thought of any real Italian girl on her deathbed would be to ask for a priest. She was facing her God.'

God at once pointed a finger at him through the chandelier, and within seconds they were discussing love among the English, Irish, French, Indians, Moslems, Italians, naturally the Papacy, Alexander the Sixth and incest, Savonarola and dirty pictures, Joan of Arc and martyrdom, death, sin, hellfire, Cesare Borgia who, she insisted, screamed for a priest to pray for him at the end.

'A lie,' he snarled, 'that some beastly priest told you in a sermon when you were a schoolgirl. Pray! I suppose,' he challenged furiously, 'you pray even against me.'

Abashed, she shook her autumn-brown head at him, threw a kipper-eyed glance up to the chandelier, gave him a ravishingly penitential smile, and sighed like an unmasked sinner.

'Ah, Ferdy! Ferdy! If you only knew the real truth about me! Me pray against you? I don't pray at all. You remember Mimi's song at the end of the first act? "I do not always go to Mass, but I pray quite a bit to the good Lord." Now, I hedge my bets in a very different way. I will not pray because I refuse to go on my knees to anybody. Yet, there I go meekly trotting off to Mass every Sunday and holy day. And why? Because I am afraid not to, because it would be a mortal sin not to.' She gripped his tensed hand, trilling her r's over the threshold of her lower lip and tenderly umlauting her vowels. Dürling. Cöward. Li-er. 'Amn't I the weak cöward, dürling? Amn't I the awful li-er? A crook entirrrely?'

Only a thin glint of streetlight peeping between his curtains witnessed the wild embrace of a man illuminated by an avowal so patently bogus as to be the transparent truth.

'You a liar?' he gasped, choking with laughter. 'You a shivering coward? A double-faced hedger of bets? A deceiving crook? A wicked sinner? For the last five minutes you have been every single one of them by pretending to be them. What you really are is a woman full of cool, hard-headed discretion, which you would like to sell to me as a charming weakness. Full of dreams that you would like to disguise as wicked lies. Of common sense that it suits you to pass off as crookedness. Of worldly wisdom still moist from your mother's nipple that, if you thought you would get away with the deception, you would stoop to call a sin. My dearest Celia, your yashmak reveals by pretending to conceal. Your trick is to be innocence masquerading as villainy. I think it is enchanting.'

For the first time he saw her in a rage.

'But it is *all* true. I *am* a liar. I *do* go to Mass every Sunday. I do *not* pray. I *am* afraid of damnation. I . . .'

He silenced her with three fingers laid momentarily on her lips.

'Of course you go to Mass every Sunday. My father, a master tailor of Nancy, used to go to Mass every Sunday not once but three times, and always as conspicuously as possible. Why? Because he was a tailor, just as you run a boutique. You don't pray? Sensible woman. Why should you bother your *bon Dieu*, if there is a *bon Dieu*, with your pretty prattle about things that He knew all about one billion years before you were a wink in your mother's eye? My dearest and perfect love, you have told me everything about Irishwomen that I need to know. None of you says what you think. Every one of you means what you don't say. None of you thinks about what she is going to do. But every one of you knows it to the last dot. You dream like opium eaters and your eyes are as calm as resting snow. You are all of you realists to your bare backsides. Yes, yes, yes, yes, yes, you will say this is true of all women, but it is not. It is not even true of Frenchwomen. They may be realists in lots of things. In love, they are just as stupid as all the rest of us. But not Irishwomen! Or not, I swear it, if they are all like you. I'll prove it to you with a single question. Would you, like Mimi, live for the sake of love in a Paris garret?'

She gravely considered a proposition that sounded delightfully like a proposal.

'How warm would the garret be? Would I have to die of tuberculosis? You remember how the poor Bohemian dramatist had to burn his play to keep them all from being famished with the cold.'

'Yes!' Ferdy laughed. 'And as the fire died away he said, "I always knew that last act was too damned short." But you are dodging my question.'

'I suppose, dürling, any woman's answer to your question would depend on how much she was in love with whoever he was. Or wouldn't it?'

Between delight and fury he dragged her into his arms.

'You know perfectly well, you sweet slut, that what I am asking you is, "Do you love me a lot or a little? A garretful or a palaceful?" Which is it?'

Chuckling she slid down low in the settee and smiled up at him between sleepycat eyelashes.

'And you, Ferdy, must know perfectly well that it is pointless to ask any woman silly questions like that. If some man I loved very much were to ask me, "Do you love me, Celia?" I would naturally answer, "No!" in order to make him love me more. And if it was some man I did not like at all I would naturally say, "Yes, I love you so much I think we ought to get married," in order to cool him off. Which, Ferdy, do you want me to say to you?'

'Say,' he whispered adoringly, 'that you hate me beyond the tenth circle of Dante's hell.'

She made a grave face.

'I'm afraid, Ferdy, the fact is I don't like you at all. Not at all! Not one least little bit at all, at all.'

At which lying, laughing, enlacing and unlacing moment they kissed pneumatically and he knew that if all Irishwomen were Celias then the rest of mankind were mad ever to have admired women of any other race.

Their lovemaking was not as he had foredreamed it. She hurled her clothes to the four corners of the room, crying out, 'And about time too! Ferdy, what the hell have you been fooling around for during the last six weeks?' Within five minutes she smashed him into bits. In her passion she was more like a lion than a lioness. There was nothing about her either titillating or erotic, indolent or indulgent, as wild, as animal, as unrestrained, as simple as a forest fire. When, panting beside her, he recovered enough breath to speak he expressed his surprise that one so cool, so ladylike in public could be so different in private. She grunted peacefully and said in her muted brogue. 'Ah, shure, dürling, everything changes in the bedda-room.'

He woke at three twenty-five in the morning with that clear bang so familiar to everybody who drinks too much after the chimes of midnight, rose to drink a pint of cold water, lightly opened his curtains to survey the pre-dawn May sky and, turning toward the bed, saw the pallid streetlamp's light fall across her sleeping face, as calm, as soothed, as innocently sated as a baby filled with its mother's milk. He sat on the side of the bed looking down at her for a long time, overcome by the terrifying knowledge that, for the first time in his life, he had fallen in love.

The eastern clouds were growing as pink as petals while they drank the coffee he had quietly prepared. Over it he arranged in unnecessarily gasping whispers for their next meeting the following afternoon – '*This* afternoon!' he said joyously – at three twenty-five, henceforth his Mystic Hour for Love, but only on the strict proviso that he would not count on her unless she had set three red geraniums in a row on the windowsill of her boutique before three o'clock and that she, for her part, must divine a tragedy if the curtains of his flat were not looped high when she approached at three twenty o'clock. He could, she knew, have more easily checked with her by telephone, but also knowing how romantically, voluptuously, erotically minded he was she accepted with an indulgent amusement what he obviously considered ingenious devices for increasing the voltage of passion by the trappings of conspiracy. To herself she thought, 'Poor boy! He's been reading too many dirty books.'

Between two o'clock and three o'clock that afternoon she was entertained to see him pass her boutique three times in dark glasses. She cruelly made him pass a fourth time before, precisely at three o'clock, she gave him the pleasure of seeing two white hands with pink fingernails – not, wickedly, her own: her assistant's – emerge from under the net curtains of her window to arrange three small scarlet geraniums on the sill. He must have hastened perfervidly to the nearest florist to purchase the pink roses whose petals – when she rang his bell five cruel moments after his Mystic Hour – she found (to her tolerant amusement at his boyish folly) tessellating the silk sheets of his bed. His gramophone, muted by a bath towel, was murmuring Wagner. A joss stick in a brass bowl stank cloyingly. He had cast a pink silk headscarf over the bedside lamp. His dressing-table mirror had been tilted so that from where they lay they could see themselves. Within five minutes he neither saw, heard nor smelled anything, tumbling, falling, hurling headlong to consciousness of her mocking laughter at the image of her bottom mottled all over by his clinging rose petals. It cost him a brutal effort to laugh at himself.

All that afternoon he talked only of flight, divorce and remarriage. To cool him she encouraged him. He talked of it again and again everytime they met. Loving him she humoured him. On the Wednesday of their third week as lovers they met briefly and chastely because her Meehawl was throwing a dinner at his house that evening for a few of his business colleagues previous to flying out to Manchester for a two-day convention of cutlers. Ferdy at once promised her to lay in a store of champagne, caviar, *pâté de foie* and brioches so that they need not stir from their bed for the whole of those two days.

'Not even once?' she asked coarsely, and he made a moue of disapproval.

'You do need to be all that realistic, Celia!'

Already by three fifteen that Thursday afternoon he was shuffling nervously from window to window. By three twenty-five he was muttering, 'I hope she's not going to be late.' He kept feeling the champagne to be sure it was not getting too cold. At three thirty-five he moaned, 'She *is* late!' At three forty he cried out in a jealous fury, glaring up and down the street, 'The slut is betraying me!' At a quarter to four his bell rang, he leaped to the door. She faced him as coldly as a newly carved statue of Carrara marble. She repulsed his arms. She would not stir beyond his doormat. Her eyes were dilated by fear.

'It is Meehawl!' she whispered.

'He has found us out?'

'It's the judgement of God on us both!'

The word smacked his face.

'He is dead?' he cried hopefully, brushing aside fear and despair.

'A stroke.'

She made a violent, downward swish with the side of her open palm.

'*Une attaque? De paralysie?*

'He called at the boutique on his way to the plane. He said goodbye to me. He walked out to the taxi. I went into my office to prepare my vanity case and do peepee before I met you. The taxi driver ran in shouting that he had fallen in a fit on the pavement. We drove him to 96. That's Saint Vincent's. The hospital near the corner of the Green. He is conscious. But he cannot speak. One side of him is paralysed. He may not live. He has had a massive coronary.'

She turned and went galloping down the stairs.

His immediate rebound was to roar curses on all the gods that never were. Why couldn't the old fool have his attack next week? His second thought was glorious. 'He will die, we will get married.' His third made him weep, 'Poor little cabbage!' His fourth thought was, 'The brioches I throw out, the rest into the fridge.' His fifth sixth and seventh were three Scotches while he rationally considered all her possible reactions to the brush of the dark angel's wing. Only Time, he decided, would tell.

But when liars become the slaves of Time what can Time do but lie like them? A vat solid-looking enough for old wine, it leaks at every stave. A ship rigged for the wildest seas, it is rust-bound to its bollards on the quay. She said firmly that nothing between them could change. He refuted her. Everything had changed, and for the better. He rejoiced when the doctors said their patient was doomed. After two more weeks she reported that the doctors were impressed by her husband's remarkable tenacity. He spoke of Flight. She now spoke of Time. One night as she lay hot in his arms in his bed he shouted triumphantly to the chandelier that when husbands are imprisoned lovers are free. She demurred. She could never spend a night with him in her own bed; not with a resident housekeeper upstairs. He tossed it aside. What matter where they slept! He would be happy sleeping with her in the Phoenix Park. She pointed out snappishly that it was raining. 'Am I a seal?' He proffered her champagne. She confessed the awful truth. This night was the last night they could be together anywhere.

'While he was dying, a few of his business pals used to call on him at the Nursing Home – the place all Dublin knows as 96. Now that the old devil is refusing to die they refuse to call on him anymore. I am his only faithful visitor. He so bores everybody. And with his paralysed mouth they don't know what the hell he is saying. Do you realise, Ferdy, what this means? He is riding me like a nightmare. Soaking me up like blotting paper. He rang me four times the day before yesterday at the boutique. He rang again while I was here with you having a drink. He said whenever I go out I must leave a number where he can call me. The night before last he rang me at three oclock in the morning. Thank God I was back in my own bed and not here with you. He said he was lonely. Has terrible dreams. That the nights are long. That he is frightened.

That if he gets another stroke he will die. Dürling! I can never spend a whole night with you again!'

Ferdy became Napoleon. He took command of the campaign. He accompanied her on her next visit to 96. This, he discovered, was a luxury (i.e., Victorian) nursing home in Lower Leeson Street, where cardinals died, coal fires were in order, and everybody was presented with a menu from which to choose his lunch and dinner. The carpets were an inch thick. The noisiest internal sound heard was the Mass bell tinkling along the corridors early every morning as the priest went from room to room with the Eucharist for the dying faithful. The Irish, he decided, know how to die. Knowing no better, he bore with him copies of *Le Canard Enchaîné, La Vie Parisienne,* and *Playboy.* Celia deftly impounded them. 'Do you want him to die of blood pressure? Do you want the nuns to think he's an Irish queer? A fellow who prefers women to drink?' Seated at one side of the bed, facing her seated at the other, he watched her, with her delicate lace-edged handkerchief (so disturbingly reminiscent of her lace-edged panties) wiping the unshaven chin of the dribbling half-idiot on the pillow. In an unconsumed rage he lifted his eyebrows into his hair, surveyed the moving mass of clouds above Georgian Dublin, smoothened his already blackboard-smooth hair, gently touched the white carnation in his lapel, forced himself to listen calmly to the all-but-unintelligible sounds creeping from the dribbling corner of the twisted mouth in the unshaven face of the revolting cretin on the pillow beneath his eyes, and agonisingly asked himself by what unimaginably devious machinery, and for what indivinable purpose the universe had been so arranged since the beginning of Time that this bronze-capped, pastel-eyed, rosy-breasted, round-buttocked, exquisite flower of paradise sitting opposite to him should, in the first place, have matched and mated with this slob between them, and then, or rather *and then,* or rather AND THEN make it so happen that he, Ferdinand Louis Jean-Honoré Clichy, of 9 *bis* rue des Dominicains, Nancy, in the Department of Moselle et Meurthe, population 133,532, altitude 212 metres, should happen to discover her in remote Dublin, and fall so utterly into her power that if he were required at that particular second to choose between becoming Ambassador to the Court of Saint James's for life and one night alone in bed with her he would have at once replied, 'Even for one hour!'

He gathered that the object on the pillow was addressing him.

'Oh, Mosheer! Thacks be to the ever cliving and cloving Gog I khav mosht devote clittle wife in all Khlistendom . . . I'd be chlost without her . . . Ah, Mosheer! If you ever dehide to marry, marry an Irikhwoman . . . Mosht fafeful cleatures in all exhishtench . . . Would any Frenchwoman attend shoopid ole man chlike me the way Chelia doesh?'

Ferdy closed his eyes. She was tenderly dabbing the spittled corners of the distorted mouth. What happened next was that a Sister took Celia out to the corridor for a few private words and that Ferdy at once leaned forward and whispered savagely to the apparently immortal O'Sullivan, 'Monsieur O'Sullivan, your wife does not look at all well. I fear she is wilting under the strain of your illness.'

'Chlstrain!' the idiot said in astonishment. 'What chlstrain? I khlsee no khlsignch of kkchlstrain!'

Ferdy whispered with fierceness that when one is gravely ill one may sometimes fail to observe the grave illness of others.

'We have to remember, Monsieur, that if your clittle wife were to collapse under the chlstr . . . under the *strain* of your illness it would be very serious, for *you*!'

After that day the only reason he submitted to accompany his love on these painful and piteous visits to 96 was that they always ended with O'Sullivan begging him to take his poor clittle, loving clittle, devoted clittle pet of a wife to a movie for a relaxation and a rest, or for a drink in the Russell, or to the evening races in the park; whereupon they would both hasten, panting, to Ferdy's flat to make love swiftly, wildly and vindictively – swiftly because their time was limited, wildly because her Irish storms had by now become typhoons of rage, and he no longer needed rose petals, Wagner, Mendelssohn, dim lights or pink champagne, and vindictively to declare and to crush their humiliation at being slaves to that idiot a quarter of a mile away in another bed saying endless rosaries to the Virgin.

Inevitably the afternoon came – it was now July – when Ferdy's pride and nerves cracked. He decided that enough was enough. They must escape to freedom. At once.

'Celia! If we have to fly to the end of the world! It won't really ruin my career. My master is most sympathetic. In fact since I hinted to him that I am in love with a *belle mariée* he does nothing but complain about his wife to me. And he can't leave her, his career depends on her, she is the daughter of a Secretary of State for Foreign Affairs – and rich. He tells me that at worst I would be moved off to someplace like Los Angeles or Reykjavik. Celia! My beloved flower! We could be as happy as two puppies in a basket in Iceland.'

She permitted a meed of Northern silence to create itself and then wondered reflectively if it is ever warm in Iceland, at which he pounced with a loud 'What do you mean? What are you actually asking? What is really in your mind?' She said, 'Nothing, dürling,' for how could she dare to say that whereas he could carry his silly job with him wherever he went she, to be with him, would have to give up her lovely old, friendly old boutique on the Green where her friends came to chat over morning coffee, where she met every rich tourist who visited Dublin, where she made nice money of her own, where she felt independent and free; just as she could never hope to make him understand why she simply could not just up and out and desert a dying husband.

'But there's nothing to hold you here. In his condition you'd be sure to get custody of the children. Apart from the holidays they could remain in school here the year round.'

So he had been thinking it all out. She stroked his hairy chest.

'I know.'

'The man, even at his best, you've acknowledged it yourself, over and over, is a fool. He is a moujik. He is a bore.'

'I know!' she groaned. Who should better know what a crasher he is? He is a child. He hasn't had a new idea in his head for thirty years. There have been times when I've hated the smell of him. He reminds me of an unemptied ashtray. Times when I've wished to God that a thief would break into the house some night and kill him. And,' at which point she began to weep on his tummy, 'I know now that there is only one thief who will come for him and he is so busy elsewhere that it will be years before he catches up with him. And then I think of the poor old bastard wetting his hospital bed, unable to stir, let alone talk, looking up at his ceiling, incontinent, with no scissors, no golf, no friends, no nothing, except me. How *can* I desert him?'

Ferdy clasped his hands behind his head, stared up at heaven's pure ceiling and heard her weeping like the summer rain licking his windowpane. He created a long Irish silence. He heard the city whispering. Far away. Farther away. And then not at all.

'And to think,' he said at last, 'that I once called you a realist!'

She considered this. She too no longer heard the muttering of the city's traffic.

'This is how the world is made,' she decided flatly.

'I presume,' he said briskly, 'that you do realise that all Dublin knows that you are meanwhile betraying your beloved Meehawl with me?'

'I know that there's not one of those bitches who wouldn't give her left breast to be where I am at this moment.'

They got out of bed and began to dress.

'And, also meanwhile, I presume you do *not* know that they have a snotty name for you?'

'What name?' – and she turned her bare back for the knife.

'They call you The Diplomatic Hack.'

For five minutes neither of them spoke.

While he was stuffing his shirt into his trousers and she, dressed fully except for her frock, was patting her penny-brown hair into place before his mirror he said to her. 'Furthermore I suppose you do realise that whether I like it or not I shall one day be shifted to some other city in some other country. What would you do then? For once, just for once in your life tell me the plain truth! Just to bring you to the crunch. What would you really do then?'

She turned, comb in hand, leaned her behind against his dressing table and looked him straight in the fly which he was still buttoning.

'Die,' she said flatly.

'That,' he said coldly, 'is a manner of speech. Even so, would you consider it an adequate conclusion to a love that we have so often said is forever?'

They were now side by side in the mirror, she tending her copper hair, he his black, like any long-married couple. She smiled a little sadly.

'Forever? Dürling, does love know that lovely word? You love me. I know it. I love you. You know it. We will always know it. People die but if you have ever loved them they are never gone. Apples fall from the tree but the tree never forgets its blossoms. Marriage is different. You remember the day he advised you that if you ever marry you should marry an Irishwoman. Don't, Ferdy! If you do she will stick to you forever. And you wouldn't really want that?' She lifted her frock from the back of a chair and stepped into it. 'Zip me up, dürling, will you? Even my awful husband. There must have been a time when I thought him attractive. We used to sail together. Play tennis together. He was very good at it. After all, I gave him two children. What's the date? They'll be home for the holidays soon. All I have left for him now is contempt and compassion. It is our bond.'

Bewildered he went to the window, buttoned his flowered waist-coat. He remembered from his café days as a student a ruffle of aphorisms about love and marriage. Marriage begins only when love ends. Love opens the door to Marriage and quietly steals away. *Il faut toujours s'appuyer sur les principes de l'amour – ils finissent par en ceder.* What would she say to that? Lean heavily on the principles of love – they will always conveniently crumple in the end. Marriage bestows on Love the tenderness due to a parting guest. Every *affaire de coeur* ends as a *mariage de convenance.* He turned to her, arranging his jacket, looking for his keys and his hat. She was peeking into her handbag, checking her purse for her keys and her lace handkerchief, gathering her gloves, giving a last glance at her hat. One of the things he liked about her was that she always wore a hat.

'You are not telling me the truth, Celia,' he said quietly. 'Oh, I don't mean about loving me. I have no doubt about you on that score. But when you persuade yourself that you can't leave him because you feel compassion for him that is just your self-excuse for continuing a marriage that has its evident advantages.'

She smiled lovingly at him.

'Will you ring me tomorrow, dürling?'

'Of course.'

'I love you very much, dürling.'

'And I love you too.'

'Until tomorrow then.'

'Until tomorrow, dürling.'

As usual he let her go first.

That afternoon was some two years ago. Nine months after it he was transferred to Brussels. As often as he could wangle special leave of absence, and she could get a relative to stay for a week with her bedridden husband, now back in his own house, they would fly to Paris or London to be together again. He would always ask solicitously after her husband's health, and she would always sigh and say his doctors had assured her that 'he will live forever.' Once, in Paris, passing a church he, for some reason, asked her if she ever went nowadays to confession. She waved the question away with a laugh, but later that afternoon he returned to it pertinaciously.

'Yes. Once a year.'

'Do you tell your priest about us?'

'I tell him that my husband is bedridden. That I am in love with another man. That we make love. And that I cannot give you up. As I can't, dürling.'

'And what does he say to that?'

'They all say the same. That it is an impasse. Only one dear old Jesuit gave me a grain of hope. He said that if I liked I could pray to God that my husband might die.'

'And have you so prayed?'

'Dürling, why should I?' she asked gaily, as she stroked the curly hair between his two pink buttons. 'As you once pointed out to me yourself all this was foreknown millions of years ago.'

He gazed at the ceiling. In her place, unbeliever though he was, he would, for love's sake, have prayed with passion. Not that she had said directly that she had not. Maybe she had? Two evasions in one sentence! It was all more than flesh and blood could bear. It was the Irish variation all over again: never let your left ass know what your right ass is doing. He decided to give her one more twirl. When she got home he wrote tenderly to her, 'You are the love of my life!' He could foresee her passionate avowal, 'And me too, dürling!' What she actually replied was, 'Don't I know it?' Six months later he had manoeuvred himself into the consular service and out of Europe to Los Angeles. He there consoled his broken heart with a handsome creature named Rosie O'Connor. Quizzed about his partiality for the Irish, he could only flap his hands and say, 'I don't know what they have got. They are awful liars. There isn't a grain of romance in them. And whether as wives or mistresses they are absolutely faithless!'

An Inside Outside Complex

So then, a dusky Sunday afternoon in Bray at a quarter to five o'clock, lighting up time at five fifteen, November 1st, All Souls' Eve, dedicated to the suffering souls in Purgatory, Bertie Bolger, bachelor, aged forty-one or so, tubby, ruddy, greying, well known as a dealer in antiques, less well-known as a conflator thereof, walking briskly along the seafront, head up to the damp breezes, turns smartly into the lounge of the Imperial Hotel for a hot toddy, singing in a soldierly basso 'my breast expanding to the ball'.

The room, lofty, widespread, Victorian, gilded, over-furnished, as empty as the ocean, and not warm. The single fire is small and smouldering. Bertie presses the bell for service, divests himself of his bowler, his vicuna overcoat, his lengthy scarf striped in black, red, green and white, the colours of Trinity College, Dublin (which he has never attended), sits in a chintzy armchair before the fire, pokes it into a blaze, leans back, and is at once invaded by a clear-cut knowledge of what month it is, and an uneasy feeling about its date. He might earlier have adverted to both if he had not, during his perambulation, been preoccupied with the problem of how to transform a twentieth-century Buhl cabinet, now in his possession, into an eighteenth-century ditto that might plausibly be attributed to the original M. Boulle. This preoccupation had permitted him to glance at, but not to observe, either the red gasometer by the harbour inflated to its winter zenith, or the haybarn beside the dairy beyond the gasometer packed with cubes of hay, or the fuel yard, facing the haybarn, beside the dairy beyond the gasometer, heavily stocked with mountainettes of coal, or the many vacancy signs in the lodging houses along the seafront, or the hoardings on the pagoda below the promenade where his mother, God rest her, had once told him he had been wheeled as a coiffed baby in a white pram to hear Mike Nono singing 'I do liuke to be besiude the seasiude, I do liuke to be besiude the sea,' or, most affectingly of all, if he had only heeded them, the exquisite, dying leaves of the hydrangeas in the public gardens, pale green, pale yellow, frost white, spiking the air above once purple petals that now clink greyly in the breeze like tiny seashells.

He suddenly jerks his head upright, sniffing desolation, looks slowly about the lounge, locates in a corner of it some hydrangeas left standing too long in a brass pot of unchanged water, catapults himself from the chair with a 'Jaysus! Five years to the bloody day!', dons his coat, his comforter and his bowler hat, and exits rapidly to make inland towards the R.C. church. For days after she died the house had retained that rank funereal smell. Tomorrow morning a Mass must be said for the repose of his mother's soul, still, maybe – Who knows? Only God knows! – suffering in the flames of Purgatory.

It is the perfect and pitiless testing date, day and hour for any seaside town in these northern island. A week or two earlier and there might still have been a few lingering visitors, a ghost of summer's lukewarmth, a calmer sea, unheard waves, and, the hands of the Summer Time clocks not yet put backward, another hour of daylight. This expiring Sunday the light is dim, the silence heavy, the town turned in on itself. As he walks through the side avenues between the sea and the Main Street, past rows of squat bungalows, every garden drooping, past grenadiers of red brick, lace curtained, past ancient cement-faced cottages with sagging roofs, he is informed by every fan-light, oblong or halfmoon, blank as night or distantly lit from the recesses behind each front door, that there is some kind of life asleep or snoozing behind number 51, *Saint Anthony's, Liljoe's, Fatima*, 59 (odd numbers on this side), *The Billows, Swan Lake*, 67, *Slievemish, Sea View*, names in white paint, numbers in adhesive celluloid. Every one of them gives a chuck to the noose of loneliness about his neck. I live in Dublin. I am a guest in a guest house. I am Mister Bee. I lunch of weekdays at the United Services Club. I dine at the Yacht Club. Good for biz. Bad for Sundays, restaurants shut, homeless. Pray for the soul of Mrs Mary Bolger, of Tureenlahan, County Tipperary, departed this life five years ago. Into thy hands, O Lord.

On these side avenues only an odd front window is lit. Their lights flow searingly across little patches of grass called front gardens, privet-hedged, lonicera-hedged, mass-concrete hedged. Private. Keep Off.

As he passed one such light, in what a real estate agent would have called a picture window, he was so shaken by what he saw inside that after he had passed he halted, looked cautiously about him, turned and walked slowly back to peep in again. What had gripped his attention through the unsuspecting window had been a standing lamp in brass with a large pink shade, and beneath its red glow, seated in an armchair with her knees crossed, a bare-armed woman reading a folded magazine, one hand blindly lifting a teacup from a Moorish side table, holding the cup immobile while she concentrated on something that had detained her interest. By the time he had returned she was sipping from the cup. He watched her lay it down, throw the magazine aside and loop forward on two broad knees to poke the fire. Her arms looked strong. She was full-breasted. She had dark hair. In that instant B.B. became a *voyeur*

The long avenue suddenly sprang its public lights. Startled he looked up and down the empty perspective. It was too cold for evening strollers. He was aware that he was trembling with fear. He did not know what else he was feeling except that there was nothing sexy to it. To calm himself he drew back behind the pillar of her garden gate whose name plate caught his eye. *Lorelei.* He again peeped around the side of the pillar. She was dusting her lap with her two palms. She was very dark, a western type, a Spanish-Galway type, a bit heavy. He could not discern the details of the room beyond the circle of light from the pink lamp, and he was glad of this: it made everything more mysterious, removed, suggestive, as if he was watching a scene on a stage. His loneliness left him, his desolation, his longing. He wanted only to be inside there, safe, secure, and satisfied.

'Ah, good evening, Bertie!' she cried to the handsome man who entered her room with the calm smile of complete sang-froid. 'I am so glad, Bertie, you dropped in on me. Do tell me your news, darling. How is the antique business? Come and warm your poor, dear hands. It is going to be a shivering night. Won't you take off your coat? Tea? No? What about a drink? I know exactly what you want, my pet. I will fix it for you. I have been waiting and waiting for you to come all the livelong day, melting with longing and love.'

As he gently closed the door of the cosy little room she proffered her hand in a queenly manner, whereupon our hero, as was fitting, leaned over it – because you never really do kiss a lady's hand, you merely breathe over it – and watched her eyes asking him to sit opposite her.

The woman rose, took her tea tray, and the room was suddenly empty. Her toe hooked the door all but a few inches short of shut.

He was just as pleased whether she was in the room or out of it. All he wanted was to be inside her room. As he stared, her naked arm came slowly back into the room between the door and the jamb, groping for the light switch. A plain gold bangle hung from her wrist. The jamb dragged back the shoulder of her blouse so that he saw the dark hair of her armpit. The window went black.

He let out a long, whistling breath like a safety valve and resumed his long perambulation until he saw a similar light streaming from the window of an identical bungalow well ahead of him on the opposite side of the roadway. He padded rapidly toward it. As he reached its identical square cement gate-pillars he halted, looked backward and forward and then guardedly advanced a tortoise nose beyond the edge of the pillar to peep into the room. A pale dawnlike radiance, softly tasselled, hinted at comfortable shapes, a sofa, small occasional chairs, a pouffe, a bookcase, heavy gleams of what could be silver, or could be just electroplated nickel. Here, too, a few tongues of fire. In the centre of the room a tall, thin, elderly man in a yellow cardigan. but not wearing a jacket or tie, stood so close beside a young girl with a blonde waterfall of hair as to form with her a single unanalysable shape. He seemed to be speaking. He stroked her smooth poll. They were like a still image out of a silent film. They were presumably doing something simple, natural and intimate. But what? They drew apart abruptly and the girl, while stooping to pick up some shining object from a low table, looked in the same movement straight out through the window. B.B was so taken by surprise that he could not stir, even when she came close to the window, looked up at the sky, right and left, as if to see if it was raining, turned back, laughed inaudibly, waved the small silver scissors in her hand.

In that instant, at that gesture, some time after five fifteen on the afternoon of November 1st, the town darkening, the sky lowering, his life passing, a vast illumination broke like a sunrise upon his soul. At the shut-time of the year all small towns become smaller and smaller, dwindle from out-of-doors to in-of-doors; from long beaches, black roads, green fields, wide sun, to kitchens, living rooms, bedrooms, locked doors, drawn blinds, whispers, prayers, muffling blankets, nose-hollowed pillows; from making to mending; to littler and littler things, like this blonde Rapunzel with a scissors and a needle; all ending in daydreaming, and nightdreaming, and dreamless sleeping. How pleasant life could be in that declension to a white arm creeping between a door and a jamb, bare but for a circle of gold about a wrist and a worn wedding ring on one heavy finger. But I am outside. When the town is asleep in one another's arms I will sleep under the walls. No wife. No child. Mister Bee.

The headlamps of a motor car sent him scurrying down an unlighted lane that may once have led to the mews of tall houses long since levelled to make room for these hundreds of little bungalows. In this abandoned lane the only window-light was one tiny, lofty aperture in the inverted V of a gable rising like a castle out of tall trees. Below it, at eye level the lane was becoming pitch dark. Above it, a sift of tattered light between mourning clouds. Hissing darkness. A sheaving wind. The elms were spiky as if the earth's hair was standing on end. He stiffened. A bird's croak? A sleepless nest, A far-off bark? He stared up at the tiny box of light whose inaccessibility was so much part of its incitement that when it went black like a fallen candle he uttered a 'Ha!' of delight. He would never know who had put a finger on the switch of that floating room. A maidservant about to emerge into the town? To go where? To meet whom? A boy's den? An old woman lumbering down the long stairs

That Monday morning B.B. was laughing happily at himself. Bertie Bolger, the well-known dealer! The Peeping Tom from Tipperary! That was a queer bloody fit I took! And Jaysus, I forgot all about the mother again: well, she will have to wait until next year now though surely to God they'll let her out before then? Anyway, what harm did she ever do bar that snibby way she treated every girl I ever met; if it wasn't for her I might have been married twenty years ago to that Raven girl I met in 1950 in Arklow. And a hot piece she was, too... Mad for it!

The next Sunday evening he was padding softly around the back roads of Bray. He could not locate the old-man-blonde-girl bungalow. He winked up at the little cube of light. But *Lorelei* was dark. The next two Sundays were raining too heavily for prowling. On the fourth Sunday the window of *Lorelei* was brilliantly lighted, and there she was plying a large dress-maker's scissors on some coloured stuff laid across a gate-legged table under the bare electric bulb whose brightness diminished the ideality of the room, increased the attractions of the dress-maker. Broad cheekbones, like a Red Indian; raven hair; the jerky head of a blackbird alert at a drinking pool. He longed to touch one of those fingers, broad at the tip like a little spade. Twice the lights of an oncoming car made him walk swiftly away, bowler hat down on nose, collar up. A third time he fled from light pouring out of the door of the adjacent bungalow and a woman hurrying down its path with her overcoat over her head and shoulders. Loping away fast he turned in fright to the running feet behind him and saw her coat-ends vanish under the suddenly lighted door lamp of *Lorelei*. Damn! A visitor. Spoiling it all. Yet, he came back to his watching post, as mesmerised as a man in a vast portrait gallery who returns again and again to *Portrait of Unknown Woman*, unable to tell why this one unidentified face makes him so happy. The intruder, he found, made no difference to his pleasure.

'Jenny! Isn't that a ring at the door? Who the divil can that be?'

'I bet that will be Mrs Ennis from next door, she promised to give me a hand with these curtains, you don't mind, darling, do you?'

'Mind! I'm glad you have friends, Molly.'

'Hoho! I've lots of friends.'

'Boyfriends, Katey?'

'Go 'long with you, you ruffian, don't you ever think of anything but the one thing?'

'Can you blame me with a lovely creature like you, Peggy, to be there teasin' me all day long, don't stir, I'll let her in.'

In? To what? There might be a husband and a pack of kids, and at once he had to sell his *Portrait of Unknown Woman* for the known model, not being the sort of artist who sees a new face below his window, runs out, drags her in, and without as much as asking her name spends months searching for her inner reality on his canvas.

Every Sunday he kept coming back and back to that appealing, rose-pink window until one afternoon, when he saw her again at her tea, watched her for a while, and then boldly clanged her black gate wide open, boldly strode up her path, leaped up three steps to her door, rang her bell. A soft rain had begun to sink over the town. The day was gone. A far grumble of waves from the shingle. She opened the door. So close, so solid, so near, so real he could barely recognise her. His silence made her lift her head sideways in three slow, interrogatory jerks. She had a slight squint, which he would later consider one of her most enchanting accomplishments – she might have been looking at another man behind his shoulder. He felt the excitement of the hunter at her vulnerable nearness. He suddenly smelled her. Somebody had told him you can always tell a woman's age by her scent. *Chanel* – and Weil's *Antelope* – over sixty. *Tweed* – always a mature woman. *Madame Rochas* – the forties. The thirties smell of after-shave lotion: *Eau Savage*, *Mustache*. Wisps of man scent. The twenties – nothing. She had a heavy smell. Tartly she demanded, 'Yes?' Unable to speak, he produced his business card, handed it to her spade fingers. *Herbert Bolger/Antiques/2 Hume Street, Dublin*. She laughed at him.

'Mister Bolger, if you are trying to buy something from me I have nothing, if you are trying to sell me something I have even less.'

He was on home ground now, they all said that, he expected it, he relied on them to say it. His whole technique of buying depended on knowing that while it is true that the so-called Big Houses of Ireland have been gleaned by the antique dealers, a lot of Big House people have been reduced to small discouraged houses like this one, bringing with them, like wartime refugees, their few remaining heirlooms. Her accent, however, was not a Big House accent. It was the accent of a workaday countrywoman. She would have nothing to sell.

'Come now, Mrs. Eh? Benson? Well, now, Mrs Benson, you say you have nothing to sell but in my experience a lot of people don't know what they have. Only last week I paid a lady thirty pounds for a Georgian saltcellar that she never knew she possessed. You might have much more than you realise.'

He must get her alone, inside. He had had no chance to see her figure. Her hair shone like jet beads. Her skin was not a flat white. It was a lovely, rich, ivory skin, as fine as lawn or silk. He felt the rain on the back of his neck and turned up his coat collar. He felt so keyed up by her that if she touched him his string would break. She possessed one thing that she did not know about. Herself.

'Well, it is true that my late husband used to attend auctions. But.'

'Mrs Benson, may I have just one quick glance at your living room?' She wavered. They always did. He smiled reassuringly. 'Just one quick glance. It will take me two minutes.'

She looked up at the rain sifting down about her door lamp.

'Well? All right then . . . But you are wasting your time. I assure you! And I am very busy.'

Walking behind her in the narrow hallway, he took her in from calves to head. She was two women: heavy above, lighter below.

He liked her long strong legs, the wide shoulders, the action of her lean haunches, and the way her head rose above her broad shoulders. Inside, the room was rain-dim, and hour-dim, until she switched on a central hundred-and-fifty-watt bulb that drowned the soft pink of the standing lamp, showed the furniture in all its nakedness, exposed all the random marks and signs of a room that had been long lived in.

At once he regretted that he had come. He walked to the window and looked out through its small bay up and down the avenue. How appealing it was out there! All those cosy little, dozing little, rosy little bungalows up and down the avenue, those dark trees comforting the gabled house with its one cube of light, and her window being slightly raised above the avenue, he could see the scattered windows of the other cosy little houses coming awake all over the town. An hour earlier he might have been able to see the bruise-blue line of the Irish Sea. I could live in any one of those little houses out there, and he turned to look at her uncertainly – like a painter turning from easel to model, from model to easel, wondering which was the concoction and which was the truth.

'Well?' she asked impatiently.

His eye helicoptered over her cheap furniture. Ten seconds sufficed. He looked at her coldly. If he were outside there now on the pavement, looking in at her rosy lamp lighting . . .

'There is,' she said defensively, 'a mirror.'

She opened the leaves of large folding doors in the rear wall, led him into the room beyond them, flooded it with light. An electric sewing machine, patterns askew on the wall, a long deal table strewn with scattered bits of material, a tailoress's wire dummy and, incongruously, over the empty fireplace, a lavish baroque mirror, deeply bevelled, sunk in a swarm of golden fruit and flowers, carved wood and moulded gesso. Spanish? Italian? It could be English. It might, rarest of all, be Irish. Not a year less than two hundred years old. He flung his arms up to it.

'And you said you had nothing! She's a beauty! I'd be delighted to buy this pretty bauble from you.'

She sighed at herself in her mirror.

'I did not say I have nothing, Mr Bolger. I said I have nothing for you. My mirror is not for sale. It was my husband's engagement present to me. He bought it at an auction in an old house in Wexford. It was the only object of any interest in the house, so there were no dealers present. He got it for five pounds.'

He darted to it through an envious groan. He talked at her through it.

'Structurally? Fine. A leaf missing here. A rose gone there. Some scoundrel has dotted it here and there with commercial gold paint. And somebody has done worse. Somebody's been cleaning it. Look here and here and here at the white gesso coming through the gold leaf. It could cost a hundred pounds of gold leaf to do it all over again. Have you,' he said sharply to her in the mirror, 'been cleaning it?'

'I confess I tried. But I stopped when I saw that chalky stuff coming through. I did, honestly.'

He considered her avidly in the frame. So appealing in her contrition, a fallen Eve. He turned to her behind him. How strongly built and bold she was! Bold as brass. Soft as silk. No question – *two* women!

'Mrs Benson, have you any idea what this mirror is worth?'

She hooted at him derisively.

'Three times what you would offer as a buyer, and three times that again for what you would ask as a seller.'

He concealed his delight in her toughness. He made a sad face. He sighed heavily.

'Lady! Nobody trusts poor old B.B. But you don't know how the game goes. I look at that mirror and I say to myself, "How long will I wait to get how much for it?" I say, "Price, one hundred pounds," and I sell it inside a month. I say, "Price two hundred pounds," and I have to wait six months. Think of my overheads for six months! If I were living in London and I said, "Price, three hundred pounds," I'd sell it inside a week. If I lived in New York, I could say, "Price fifteen hundred dollars," and I'd sell it in a day. If I lived on a coral island it wouldn't be worth two coconuts. That mirror has no absolute value. To you it's priceless because it has memories. I respect you for that, Mrs Benson. What's life without memories? I'll give you ninety pounds for it.'

They were side by side, in her mirror, in her room, in her life. He could see her still smiling at him. Pretending she was sorry she had cleaned it! Putting it on! They do, yeh know, they do! And they change, oho, they change. Catch her being sorry for anything. Smiling now like a girl caught in fragrant delight. Listen to this: –

'It is not for sale, Mr Bolger. My memories are not on the market. That is not a mirror. It is a picture. The day my husband bought it we stood side by side and he said,' she laughed at him in the mirror, ' "We're not a bad looking pair." '

He stepped sideward out of her memories, keeping her framed.

'I'll give you a hundred quid for it. I couldn't possibly sell it for more than a hundred and fifty pounds. There aren't that many people in Dublin who know the value of a mirror like yours. The most I can make is twenty-five percent. You are a dressmaker. Don't you count on making twenty-five percent? Where are you from?' he asked, pointing eagerly.

'I'm a Ryan from Tipperary,' she laughed, taken by his eagerness, laughing the louder when he cried (untruthfully) that he was a Tipp man himself.

'Then you are no true Tipperary woman if you don't make fifty percent! What about it? Tipp to Tipp. A hundred guineas? A hundred and ten guineas? Going, going ... ?'

'It is not for sale,' she said with a clipped finality. 'It is my husband's mirror. It is our mirror. It will always be our mirror,' and he surrendered to the memory she was staring at.

As she closed the door on his departure there passed between them the smiles of equal strangers who, in other circumstances, might have been equal friends. He walked away, exhilarated, completely satisfied. He had got rid of his fancy. She had not come up to his dream. He was cured.

The next Sunday afternoon, bowler hat on nose, collar up, scarfed, standing askew behind her pillar, the red lamp glowing, will now always glow above the dark head of Mrs Benson, widow, hard-pressed dressmaker, born in Tipperary, sipping Indian tea, munching an English biscuit, reading a paperback, her civil respite from tedious labour. How appealing! She has beaten a cosy path of habit that he lusts to have, own, at least to share with her. 'I can make antiques but I can't make age, I could buy the most worn bloody old house in Ireland and I wouldn't own one minute of its walls, trees, stones, moss, slates, gravel, rust, lichen, ageing.' And he remembered the old lady in a stinking dry-rotted house in Westmeath, filled with eighteenth-century stuff honeycombed by wood-worm, who would not sell him as much as a snuff-box because, 'Mister Bulgey, there is not a pebble in my garden but has its story.'

Bray. For sale. Small modern bungalow. Fully furnished. View of sea. Complete with ample widow attached to the front doorknob. Fingerprints alive all over the house.

He pushed the gate open, smartly leaped her steps, rang.

A fleck of biscuit clung childishly to her lower lip. Her grey eye, delicately defective, floated beyond his face as disconcertingly as a thought across surprise.

'Not you again!' she laughed lavishly.

'Mrs Bee! I have a proposition.'

'Mister Bee! I do not intend to sell you my mirror. Ever!'

'Missus Bee! I do not want your mirror. What I have to propose will take exactly two tics. I swear it. And then I fly.'

She sighed, looked far, far away. Out over the night sea?

'For two minutes? Very well. But not *one* second more!'

She showed him into the living room and, weakening – in the name of hospitality? of Tipperary? of old country ways? – she goes into the recesses of her home for an extra cup. In sole possession of her interior he looks out under the vast umbrella of the dusk, out over the punctured encampment of roofs. Could I live here? Why does this bloody room never look the same inside and outside? Live *here*? Always? It would be remote. Morning train to Dublin. In the evenings, this, when I had tarted it up a bit, made it as cosy, lit inside, as it looks from the outside.

'My husband,' she said, pouring, 'always liked China tea. You don't mind?'

'I am very partial to it. It appeals to my aesthetic sense. Jasmine flowers. May I ask what your husband used to do?'

'Ken was an assessor for an English insurance company. He was English.'

He approved mightily, fingers widespread, chin enthusiastically nodding.

'A fine profession! A very fine profession!'

'So fine,' she said wryly, 'that he took out a policy on his own life for a bare one thousand pounds. And I am now a dressmaker.'

'Family?' he asked tenderly.

She smiled softly.

'My daughter, Leslie. She is at a boarding school. I am hoping to send her to the university. What is your proposition?'

Her profile, soft as a seaflower, changed to the obtuseness of a deathmask, until, frontally, its lower lip caught the light, the eyes became alert, the face hard with character.

'It is a simple little proposition. Your mirror, we agree, is a splendid object, but for your business quite unsuitable. Any woman looking into it can only half see herself. What you need is a great, wide, large, gilt-framed mirror, pinned flat against the wall, clear as crystal, a real professional job, where a lady can see herself from top to toe twirling and turning like a ballet dancer.' He smiled mockingly. 'Give your clients status.' He proceeded earnestly. 'Worth another two hundred pounds a year to you. You would be employing two assistants in no time. I happen to have a mirror just like that in my showrooms. I've had it for six years and nobody has wanted it.' He paused smiling from jawbone to jawbone. 'I would like you to take it as a gift.'

Shrewdly he watched her returning her teacup between her palms as if she were warming a brandy glass, while she observed him sideward just as shrewdly out of an eye as fully circled as a bird's. At last she smiled, laid down her cup, leaned back and said, 'Go on, Mr B.'

'How do you mean, "go on"?'

'You have only told me half your proposition. You want something in return?'

He laughed with his throat, teeth, tongue and gullet, enjoying her hugely.

'Not really!'

She laughed, enjoying him as hugely.

'Meaning?'

He rose walked to the window, now one of those black mirrors that painters use to eliminate colour in order to reveal design. The night had blotted out everything except an impression of two or three pale hydrangea leaves wavering outside in the December wind and, inside, himself and a lampshade. He began to feel that he had already taken up residence here. He turned to the woman looking at him coldly under eyebrows as heavy as two dark moustaches and flew into a rage at her resistance.

'Dammit! Can't you give me credit for wanting to give you something for your own sake?' As quickly he calmed. The proud animal was staring timidly, humbly, contritely. Or was she having him on again? She could hide anything behind that lovely squint of hers. He demanded abruptly, 'Do you ever go into Dublin?'

She glanced at the doors of her workroom.

'I must go there tomorrow morning to buy some linings. Why?'

'Tomorrow I have to deliver a small Regency chest to a lady in Greystones. On my way back I could call for you here at ten o'clock, drive you into Dublin and show you that big mirror of mine, and you can take it or leave it, as you like.' He got up to go. 'Okay?'

She gave an unwilling assent but as she opened the front door to let him out added, 'Though I am not at all sure that I entirely understand you, Mister B.'

'Aren't you?' he asked with an impish animation.

'No, I am not!' she said crossly. 'Not at all sure.'

Halfway across her ten feet of garden he turned and laughed derisively, 'Have a look at the surface of your mirror,' and twanged out and was lost in a dusk of sea-fog.

She returned slowly to her workroom. She approached her mirror and peered over its surface. Flawless. Not a breath of dust. With one spittled finger she removed a flyspeck. What did the silly little man mean? Without being aware of what she was doing she looked at herself, patted her hair in place, smoothed her fringe, arranged the shoulder peaks of her blouse, then, her dark eyebrows floating, her bistre eyelids sinking, her back straight her bosom lifted, she drawled, 'I really am afraid, Mister B., that I still do *not* at all understand you,' and chuckled at the effect. Her jaw shot out, she glared furiously at her double, she silently mouthed the word 'Fathead!' seized her scissors and returned energetically to work. She would fix him! Tomorrow morning she would let the ten o'clock train take her to Dublin.

He took her to Dublin, and to lunch, and to her amused satisfaction admitted that there was a second part to his proposition. He sometimes persuaded the owners of better class country hotels to allow him to leave one or two of his antiques, with his card attached, on view in their public rooms. It could be a Dutch landscape, or a tidy piece of Sheraton or Hepplewhite. Free advertisement for him, free decor for them. Would she like to co-operate? 'Where on earth,' some well-off client would say, 'did you get that lovely thing?' — and she would say, 'Bolger's Antiques.' She was so pleased to have foreseen that there would be some such *quid pro quo* that she swallowed the bait. So, the next Sunday, though he did not bring his big mirror, he brought a charming Boucher fire screen. The following Sunday his van was out of order, but he did bring a handsome pair of twisted Georgian candlesticks for her mantelpiece. Every Sunday, except during the Christmas holidays when he did not care to face her daughter, Leslie, he brought something: a carved, bronze chariot, Empire style, containing a clock, a neat Nelson sideboard, a copper warming pan, so that they always had something to discuss over their afternoon tea. It amused and pleased her until the day came when he produced a pair of (he swore) genuine Tudor curtains for her front window and she could no longer conceal from herself that she was being formally courted, and that her living room had meanwhile been transformed from what it had been four months ago.

The climax came at Easter when, for Leslie's sake, she weakly allowed him to present her with two plane tickets for a Paris holiday. In addition he promised to visit her bungalow every day and sleep there every night while she was away. On her return she found that he had left a comic 'Welcome Home' card on her hall table; that her living room was sweet with mimosa; that he had covered her old-fashioned wallpaper with (he explained) a hand-painted French paper in (she would observe) a pattern of Notre Dame, the Eiffel Tower, the Arc de Triomphe and the Opéra; replaced her old threadworn carpet – she and Ken had bought it nearly twenty years ago in Clery's in O'Connell Street – by (he alleged) a *quali* Persian carpet three hundred years old; and exchanged her central plastic electric shade for (he mentioned) a Waterford cluster. In fact he had got rid of every scrap of her life except her mirror, which now hung over her fireplace, her pink lamp and, she said it to herself, 'Me?'

The next Sunday she let him in, sat opposite him, and was just about to say her rehearsed bit of gallows humour – 'I am sorry to have to tell you, Bertie, that I don't particularly like your life, may I have mine back again please?' – when she saw him looking radiantly at her, realised that by accepting so many disguised gifts she had put herself in a false position, and burst into tears of shame and rage. Bertie, whose many years of servitude with his mother had made all female tears seem as ludicrous as a baby's squealing face, laughed boomingly at her, enchanted to see this powerful woman so completely in his power. The experience filled him with such joy that he sank on his knees beside her, flung his arms about her, and said, 'Maisie, will you marry me?' She drew back her fist, gave him such a clout on the jaw that he fell on his poll, shouted at him, 'Get up, you worm! And get out!'

With hauteur he went.

She held out against him for six months, though still permitting him to visit her every Sunday for afternoon tea and a chat. In November, without warning, her resistance gave out. Worn down by his persistence? Or her own calculations? By her ambitions for Leslie? Perhaps by weariness of the flesh at the prospect of a life of dressmaking? Certainly by none of the hopes, dreams, illusions, fears and needs that might have pressed other hardpressed women into holy wedlock; above all not by the desires of the flesh – these she had never felt for Bertie Bolger.

He made it a lavish wedding, which she did not dislike; he also made it showy, which she did not like; but she was soon to find that he did everything to excess, including eating, always defending himself by the plea that if a man or a woman is any good you cannot have too much of them; a principle that ought to have led him to marry the Fat Lady in the circus, or led her to marry Paddy O'Brien, the Irish giant, who was nine feet high and whose skeleton she had once seen preserved in the College of Surgeons. 'Is he all swank and bluff?' she wondered. Even on their honeymoon she discovered that after a day of boasting about his prowess compared with all his competitors, it was ten to one that he would either be crying on her shoulder long past midnight, or yelping like a puppy in one of his nightmares; both of which performances (her word) she bore with patience until the morning he dared to give her dogs' abuse for being the sole cause of all of them, whereat she ripped him with a kick like a cassowary. She read an article about exhibitionism. That was him! She read a thriller about a manic-depressive strangler, and peeping cautiously across the pillows, felt that she should never go to bed with him without a pair of antique duelling pistols under her side of the mattress.

Within six months they both knew that their error was so plenary, so total, so irreducible that it should have been beyond speech – as it was not. He said that he felt a prisoner in this bloody bungalow of hers. He said that whenever he stood inside her window (and his Tudor curtains) and looked out at those hundreds of lovely, loving, kindly, warm, glowing little peaked bungalows outside there he knew that he had picked the only goddam one of the whole frigging lot that was totally uninhabitable. She said she had been as free as the wind until he took forcible possession of her property and filled it with his fake junk. He said she was a bully. She told him he was a bluffer. He said, 'I thought you had brains but I've eaten better.' She said, 'You're a dreamer!' He said, 'You're a dressmaker!' She said, 'You don't know from one minute to the next whether you want to be Jesus Christ or Napoleon.' He shouted, 'Outside the four walls of this bungalow you're an ignoramus, apart from what little I've been able to teach you.' She said, 'Outside your business, Bertie Bolger, and that doesn't bear close examination, if I gave you three minutes to tell me all *you* know, it would be six minutes too much.' All of it as meaningless and unjust as every marital quarrel since Adam and Eve began to brawl with one voice, 'But *you* said . . . ,' and 'I know what *I* said, but you said . . .' 'Yes but then *you* said . . .'

His older, her more recent club acquaintances chewed a clearer cud. At the common table I once heard three or four of them mentioning him over lunch. They said next to nothing but their tone was enough. Another of those waxwork effigies that manage somehow or other to get past the little black ball into the most select clubs. Mimes, mimics, fair imitations, plausible impersonations of The Real Thing, a procession of puppets, a march of masks, a covey of cozens, a levee of liars: chaps for whom conversation means anecdotes, altruism alms, discipline suppression, justice calling in the police, pleasure puking in the washroom, pride swank, love lust, honesty guilt, religion fear, patriotism greed and success cash. But if you asked any of those old members to say any of this about Bertie? They would look you straight in the top button of your weskit and say, without humour, 'A white man.' And Maisie? 'A very nice little wife.'

Dear Jesus! Is life in all clubs reduced like this to white men and nice little wives? Sometimes to worse. As well as clubbites there are clubesses to whom the truth is told between the sheets and by whom enlarged, exaggerated, falsified, and spread wide. After all, the men had merely kicked the testicles of his reputation; the wives castrated him. They took Maisie's part. A fine, natural countrywoman, they said; honest as the daylight; warm as toast if you did not cross her, and then she could handle her tongue like the tail end of a whip; a woman who carried her liquor like a man; as agile at Contract as a trout; could have mothered ten and would never give one to Bertie, whom she had let marry her only because she saw he was the sort of weakling who always wants somebody to lean on, and did not find out until too late that he was miles away from what every woman really wants, which is somebody she can rely on. Their judgement made him seem much less than he was, her much more. The result of it was that he was soon feeling the cold wind of Dublin's whispering gallery on his neck and had to do something to assert himself unless he was to fall dead under the sting of mockery.

Accordingly, one Sunday afternoon in November, a year after his marriage, he packed two suitcases, called a cab, and drove off down the lighted avenue to resume his not unimportant role in life as the Mister Bee of some lonely guest house. It had not, at the end, been her wish. If she had not grown a little fond of him she had begun to feel a little sorry for him. Besides, next autumn Leslie would be down on her fingers and up on her toes at the starting line for the university, waiting eagerly for the revolver's flat 'Go!'

'This is silly, Bertie!' she had shrugged as they heard and saw the taxi pulling up outside their window. 'Husbands and wives always quarrel.' He picked up his two suitcases and looked around the room at his lost illusions, a Prospero leaving for the mainland. 'It's nothing unusual,' she had said, to comfort him. 'It happens in every house,' she had pleaded, 'but they carry on.'

'You bitch!' he had snarled, making for the door. 'You broke my heart. I thought you were perfect.'

She need not have winced, knowing well that they had both married for reasons the heart knows nothing of. Nevertheless she had gone gloomily into her dining room, which must again become her workroom. The sixty pounds that he had agreed to pay her henceforth every morrth, though much more than she had had before they met, would not support two people. Looking about it she noted, with annoyance, that she had never got that big mirror out of him.

So then, a dusky Sunday afternoon in Bray, at a quarter to five o'clock, lighting up time five fifteen, All Souls' Eve, dedicated to the souls of the dead suffering in the fires of Purgatory, Bertie Bolger, half Benedict half bachelor, aged forty-four, tubby, ruddy, greying, walking sedately along the seafront, sees ahead of him the Imperial Hotel and stops dead, remembering.

'I wonder!' he wonders, and leaning over the promenade's railings, sky-blue with orange knobs, rusting to death since the nineteenth century, looks down at the damp pebbles of the beach. 'How is she doing these days?' and turns smartly inland toward the town.

At this ambiguous hour few houses in Bray show lighted windows. The season is over, the Sunday silent, landladies once more reckoning their takings, snoozing, thinking of minute repairs, or praying, in *Liljoe's, Fatima, The Billows, Swan Lake, Sea View*. Peering ahead of him Mr B. sees, away down the avenue, a calm glow from a window and feels thereat the first, delicate, subcutaneous tingle that he has so often felt in the presence of some desirable object whose value the owner does not know. Nor does he know why those rare lighted windows are so troubling, suggestive, inviting, rejecting, familiar, foreign, like any childhood's nonesuch, griffin, mermaid, unicorn, hippogriff, dragon, centaur, crested castle in the mountains where there grows the golden rose of the world's end. Not knowing, he ignores that first far-off glow, turns from it as from a temptation to sin, turns right, turns left, walks faster and faster as from pursuing danger, until his head begins to swim and his heart to drumroll at the sight, along the perspective of another avenue, of a lighted roseate window that he knows he knows.

As he comes near to *Lorelei* he looks carefully around him to be sure that he is not observed by some filthy Paul Pry who might remember him from that year of his so-called marriage. He slows his pace. He slowly stalks the pillar of his wife's house. He peeps inside and straightway has to lean against the pillar to steady himself, feeling his old dream begin to swell and swell, his old disturbance mount, fear and joy invade his blood at the sight of her seated before the fire, placid, self-absorbed, her teacup in her hand, her eyes on her book, the pink glow on her threequarter face, more than ever appealing, inciting, sealed, bonded, unattainable.

I *have* neglected her. I owe her restitution. He enters the garden, twangs the gate, mounts the steps, rings the bell, turns to see the dark enfold the town. A scatter of lights. The breathing of the waves. The glow of a bus zooming up Kilruddery Hill a mile away, lighting the low clouds, bare trees, passing the Earl of Meath's broken walls, his gateway's squat Egyptian pillars bearing, in raised lettering, the outdated motto of his line, LABOR VITA MEA.

'Bertie!'

'Maisie!'

'I'm so glad you dropped in, Bertie. Come in. Take your coat off and draw up to the fire. It's going to be a shivering night. Let me fix you a drink. The usual, I suppose?' Her back to him: – 'As a matter of fact I've been expecting you every Sunday. I've been waiting and waiting for you.' She laughed. 'Or do you expect me to say I've been longing and longing for you since you abandoned me last November?'

He looks out, shading his eyes, sees the window opposite light up. They, too, have a pink lampshade.

'That,' he said, 'is the Naughtons' bungalow, isn't it? It looks very cosy. Very nice. I sometimes used to think I'd be happy living there, looking across at you.'

She glances at it, handing him the whiskey, sits facing him, pokes the fire ablaze.

'We're all alike, in our bungalows. Why did you come today, Bertie?'

'It's our marriage anniversary. I didn't know what gift to send you, so I thought I would just ask. Hello! Your mirror is gone!'

'I had to put it back in my workroom. If you want to give me a present give me your mirror.'

'Jesus, I never did give it to you, did I? Next Sunday, I swear! Cross my heart! I'll bring it out without fail. If the van is free.'

In this way they chatted of this and that, and he went on his way, and he came back the next Sunday, though not with his mirror, and he came every Sunday month after month for tea or a drink. On his fourth visit she produced, for his greater comfort, an old pair of felt slippers he had left behind him, and on the fifth Sunday a pipe of his that she had discovered at the bottom of a drawer. He did not come around Christmas, feeling that Leslie would prefer to be alone with her mother. Instead he spent it at the Imperial Hotel. In a blue paper hat? She refused to let him send them both to Paris for Easter but she did let him send Leslie. For her own Easter present she asked, 'Could I possibly have that mirror, Bertie?' – and he promised it, and did not keep his promise, saying that someday she would be sure to give up dressmaking and not need it, and anyway he was somehow getting attached to the old thing, it would leave a big pale blank on his wall if he gave it away, and after all she had a mirror of her own, but he promised, nevertheless, that he would sometime give it to her.

The music of the steam carousel played on the front, the town became gay, English tourists strolled up and down the lapis lazuli and orange promenade, voices carried, and now and again he went for a swim before calling on her, until imperceptibly it was autumn again, with the rainy light fading at half past four and her rosy window appealing to him to come inside, and in her mirror he would tidy his windblown hair and his tie, and look in puzzlement around the room, and speculatively back at her behind him pouring his drink, just as if he were her husband and this was really his home, so that it was a full year again, and November, and All Saints' Eve before she saw him drive up outside her gate, accompanied by his man Scofield, in his pale blue-and-pink van, marked along its side in Gothic silver lettering, BOLGER'S ANTIQUES, and, protruding from it his big mirror, wrapped in felt and burlap. She greeted it from her steps with a mock cheer that died when Scofield's eye flitted from the mirror to her door, and from door back to mirror, and Bertie's did the same, and hers did the same, and they all there knew at once that his mirror was too big for her. Still, they tried, until the three of them were standing in a row in her garden looking at themselves in it where it leaned against the tall privet hedge lining the avenue, a cold wind cooling the sweat on their foreheads.

'I suppose,' Bertie said, 'we could cut the bloody thing up! Or down!' – and remembering one of those many elegant, useless, disconnected things he had learned at school from the Benedictines, he quoted from the Psalms the words of Christ about the soldiers on Calvary dicing for his garments: – *'Diviserunt sibi vestimenta mea et super vestem meam miserunt sortem.'*

'Go on!' he interpreted. 'Cut me frigging shirt in bits and play cards for me jacket and me pants,' which was the sign for her to lead him gently indoors and make three boiling hot toddies for their shivering bones.

He was silent as he drank his first dram, and his second. After the third dram he said, okay, this was it, he would never come here again, moving with her and Scofield to the window to look at his bright defeat leaning against the rampant hedge of privet.

And, behold, it was glowing with the rosiness of the window and the three of them out there looking in at themselves from under the falling darkness and the wilderness of stars over town and sea, a vision so unlikely, disturbing, appealing, inviting, promising, demanding, enlisting that he swept her to him and held her so long, so close, so tight that the next he heard was the pink-and-blue van driving away down the avenue. He turned for reassurance to the gleaming testimony in the garden and cried, 'We'll leave it there always! It makes everything more real!' At which, as well she might, she burst into laughter at the sight of him staring out at himself staring in.

'You bloody loon!' she began, and stopped.

She had heard country tales about people who have seen on the still surface of a well, not their own hungry eyes but the staring eyes of love.

'If that *is* what you really want,' she said quietly, and kissed him, and looked out at them both looking in.

Something, Everything, Anything, Nothing

I

Somebody once said that a good prime minister is a man who knows something about everything and nothing about anything. I wince – an American foreign correspondent, stationed in Rome, covering Italy, Greece, Turkey, Corsica, Sardinia, Malta, Libya, Egypt and the entire Middle East.

Last year I was sent off to report on pollution around Capri, steel in Taranto, which (as journalists say) 'nestles' under the heel of the peninsula, the Italo-American project for uncovering the buried city of the Sybarites, which is halfway down the coast from Taranto, the political unrest then beginning to simmer in Reggio di Calabria, around the toe of the continent, and, of course, if something else should turn up – some 'extra dimension', as my foreign editor in Chicago likes to call such unforeseens . . .

Summer was dying in Rome, noisily and malodorously. Down south, sun, silence and sea. It was such a welcome commission that it sounded like a pat on the head for past services. I was very pleased.

I polished off Capri in two hours and Taranto in three days – a well-documented subject. After lunching at Metaponto, now one of Taranto's more scruffy seaside resorts, I was salubriously driving along the highway beside the Ionian when, after about an hour, 'something else' did crop up. It happened in a place too minute to be called a village, or even a hamlet: an Italian would call it a *loguccio* (a rough little place), named Bussano. I doubt if many travellers, not natives of these parts of Calabria – barring Karl Baedeker some sixty years or so ago, or the modern Italian Touring Club guide, or a weary Arab pedlar – had ever voluntarily halted in Bussano. The Touring Club guide is eloquent about it. He says, and it is all he says: – 'At this point the road begins to traverse a series of monotonous sand dunes.' Any guide as reticent as that knows what he is not talking about.

Bussano consists of two lots of hovels facing one another across the highway, one backing on that wild stretch of the Calabrian Apennines called La Sila, the other on an always empty ocean; 'always' because there is no harbour south of Taranto for about a hundred and fifty miles, nothing but sand, reeds, a few rocks, the vast Ionian. I presume that during the winter months the Ionian Sea is often shaken by southwesterly gales. In the summer nothing happens behind those monotonous sand dunes except the wavelets moving a foot inward and a foot outward throughout the livelong day, so softly that you don't even hear their seesaw and you have to watch carefully to see their wet marks on sand so hot that it pales again as soon as it is touched. The *loguccio* looked empty.

The only reason I halted there was that I happened to notice among the few hovels on the sea side of the road one two-storied house with a line of brown and yellow sunflowers lining its faded grey-pink walls on which, high up, I could barely decipher the words *Albergo degli Sibariti*. The Sybarites' Hotel. It must have been built originally for travellers by stagecoach, first horse then motor, or by hired coach and horses, or by private carriage, or in the later years by the little railroad along the coast that presently starts to worm its slow way up through those fierce mountains that climb seven thousand feet to the Serra Dolcedorme where, I have been told, snow may still be seen in May. It was the same friend who told me about a diminutive railroad in this deep south – could it be this one? – grandiosely calling itself *La Società Italiana per le Strade Ferrate del Mediterraneo–Roma*, five hundred miles from the smell of Rome and barred by the Apennines from the Mediterranean. The *Albergo degli Sibariti* would have flourished in the youth of Garibaldi.

I was about to move on when I glanced between the hotel and its nearest hovel at a segment of sea and horizon, teasingly evoking the wealth of centuries below that level line – Greece, Crete, Byzantium, Alexandria. Once again I was about to drive off, thinking how cruel and how clever of Mussolini, and also how economical, to have silenced his intellectual critics (men like, for instance, Carlo Levi) simply by exiling them to remote spots like this, when an odd-looking young man came through the wide passageway, halted and looked up and down the highway with the air of a man with nowhere to go and nothing to do.

He was dark, bearded and long-haired, handsome if you like mushy Italian eyes, dark as prunes, eyelashes soft and long, cheeks tenderly browned, under his chin hung a great, scarlet blob of tie like a nineteenth-century Romantic poet, his shirt gleaming (washed and ironed by whom?), his shoes brilliantly polished (by whom?), pants knife-pressed (by whom?), on his head a cracked and tawny straw hat that just might have come many years ago from Panama, and he carried a smooth cane with a brass knob. His unshaven jaws were blackberry blue. His jacket was black velvet. His trousers were purple. All in all more than overdressed for a region where the men may or may not wear a cotton singlet, but a shirt never except on Sundays apart from the doctor if there is one, or the teacher if there is one, or the local landowner, and there is always one of them.

What on earth could he be? Not a visitor, at this time of the year, and in this non-place. An adolescent poet? More likely an absconding bank clerk in disguise. (Joke. In empty places like this the sand-hoppers for fifty miles around are known by their first names.) The local screwball? I alighted. He saw me. We met in the middle of the road – the roads down here are wide and fine. I asked him if he might be so kind as to tell me where I might, if it were not too much to ask, find the lost city of the Sybarites. At once he straightened his sagging back, replied eagerly, rapidly and excitedly, 'Three kilometres ahead fork left after the gas station then first right along a dirt track can I have a cigarette where are you from may I show you my pictures?'

Well, I thought, this is odd, I am on Forty-second Street, Division, Pigalle, the Cascine, the Veneto, Soho, Pompeii, show me his dirty pictures, what next? His sister? A pretty boy? Cannabis? American cigarettes? I told him I was an insurance salesman from Chicago and bade him lead on. He led me rapidly through the passage to a wooden shack in the untidy yard behind the house, where, as he fumbled with the lock, he explained himself.

'I am a Roman I am a great painter I came down here two years ago to devote my life to my art I have been saving up for years for this a professor of fine arts from New York bought four of my paintings last week for fifty-thousand lire apiece.'

I knew this last to be not so immediately he flung open the door on lines of paintings stacked around the earthen floor – there were three or four canvases but he had mostly used chipboard or ply-wood. His daubs all indicated the same subject, mustard yellow sunflowers against a blue sea, each of them a very long way after van Gogh, each the same greasy blob of brown and yellow, each executed (appropriate word!) in the same three primary colours straight from the tube, chrome yellow, burnt umber, cerulean blue, with, here and there as the fancy had taken him, a mix of the three in a hoarse green like a consumptive's spittle. They were the most supremely splendid, perfect, godawful examples of bad art I had ever seen. As I gazed at them in a Cortes silence I knew that I simply must possess one of them immediately.

Snobbery? A kinky metropolitan taste? I know the feeling too well not to know its source in compassion and terror. To me bad art is one of the most touching and frightening examples of self-delusion in the world. Bad actors, bad musicians, bad writers, bad painters, bad anything, and not just the inbetweeners or the border-liners but the total, desperate, irredeemable failures. Wherever I have come on an utterly bad picture I have wanted to run away from it or possess it as a work of horror. Those 'original' gilt-framed pictures in paper elbow guards displayed for sale in the foyers of big commercial hotels, or in big railroad terminals. A quarter of a a mile of even worse 'originals' hanging from the railings of public parks in the summer. Those reproductions that form part of the regular stock of novelty stores that sell china cuckoo clocks, nut-crackers shaped like a woman's thighs, pepper pots shaped like ducks' bottoms. The poor, sad, pathetic little boy with the one, single, perfect teardrop glistening on his cheek. Six camels forever stalking across the desert into a red ink sunset. Three stretched-neck geese flying over a reedy lake into the dawn. That jolly medieval friar holding up his glass of supermarket port to an Elizabethan diamond-paned window as bright as a five-hundred-watt electric bulb.

We know the venal type who markets these *kitsch* objects and we know that they are bought by uneducated people of no taste. But if one accepts that these things are sometimes not utterly devoid of skill, and are on the edge of taste, who paints them? Look-ing into the earnest, globular eyes of this young man in Bussano (who insofar as he had no least skill and no least taste was the extreme example of the type) I felt once again the surge of com-passion and of fear that is always the prelude to the only plausible answer I know: that he was yet another dreaming innocent who believed that he had heard the call to higher things. His type must be legion: young boys and girls who at some unlucky moment of their lives have heard, and alas have heeded that far-off whir of wings and that solitary midnight song once heard, so they have been told, in ancient days by emperor and clown, the same voice that flung magic casements open on the foam of perilous seas and faery lands forlorn. The frightening part of it is that there can be very few human beings who have not heard it in some form or another. If we are wise we either do nothing about it or do the least possible. We send a subscription, join something, vote, are modest.

As I offered him a cigarette I felt like the man in charge of a firing squad; not that I, or anybody else can kill such lethal innocence. As he virtually ate the cigarette I saw that his eye sockets were hollowed not by imagination but starvation. He was a living cartoon of the would-be artist as a young man who has begun to fear that he possibly may not be the one and will certainly never again be the other. To comfort him I irresponsibly said, 'You might one day become the van Gogh of Calabria,' to which he said quickly, 'I sell you any one you like cheap.' Should I have said they were all awful? I said I liked the one that, in characteristic burlesque of the real by the fake, he had labelled *Occhio d'oro, Mar' azzurro.* 'Golden Eye, Azure Sea.' Whereupon he said, 'Fifty dollars,' and I beat him down to two. As he pouched the two bills I asked him what he was proposing to do with all that lovely money. He laughed gaily – the Italian poor really are the most gutsy people in the world, as well as the most dream-deluded – 'Tonight I will bring my wife to the hotel for two brandies to celebrate my first sale in two years. It is an omen from heaven for our future.'

All this, and a wife too? I invited him into the hotel for a beer, served by a drowsy slut whom he had imperiously waked from her siesta. I asked him about his wife.

'Roman,' he said proudly, 'And *borghese.* Her father works in a bank. She believes absolutely in my future. When we married she said, "Sesto" – I was a sixth child, my name is Sesto Caro – "I will follow you to the end of the world." ' He crossed two fingers. 'We are like that.' He crossed three. 'With our child, like that. The first, alas, was stillborn.'

(The harm innocence can do!)

He said that he, also, was a Roman. And he was! He knew the city as well as I do, and I have spent twenty years living there as a nosy reporter. I found him in every way, his self-delusion apart, an honest young man. He agreed that he had done all sorts of things. Run away from home at fourteen. Done a year in the galleys for stealing scrap. Returned home, spent two years in a seminary trying to be a monk, a year and a half in a *trattoria* in the Borgo Pio. Was arrested again and held for two years without trial for allegedly selling cannabis. Released, he spent three years in Germany and

Switzerland to make money for his present project. Returned home, was apprenticed as an electrician's assistant...

He was now twenty-nine. She was now twenty-one. When she was turned off by her father they had come down here to beg the help of her godfather-uncle Emilio Ratti, an engineer living in what I heard him lightly call 'the Cosenza of Pliny and Varro.' I looked out and upward toward the Sila.

'Cosenza? A godfather so far from Rome?'

'He was exiled there by Mussolini and never went back.'

Unfortunately, or by the whim of the pagan gods of Calabria – he contemptuously called it *Il Far Ouest* – his wife, then nineteen, and big with child, got diarrhoea so badly in Naples ('Pollution around Capri?') that they finally tumbled off the train at a mountainy place called Cassano in the hope of quickly finding a doctor there; only to be told as the train pulled away into the twilit valleys that the station of Cassano was hours away from the village of Cassano, whereas their informant, a carter from Bussano, offered to drive them in one hour to his beautiful village by the sea near which (equally untrue) there was a very good doctor. So, with their parcels, their cardboard suitcases, their paper bundles and bulging pillow-cases they had come to this *casale* and stayed. Uncle Emilio had visited them once. Still, like her father, he occasionally disbursed small sums of money on condition that they stayed where they were.

2

We shook hands cordially, I gathered my bad painting and drove off fast. I had walked into the middle of a frightening story and I had no idea what its end would be. Murder? Suicide? If I could wait for either that could be a good something else for Chicago. Not now. No lift. No human interest. I looked eagerly ahead of me along the straight highway to my meeting with the skilled Italo–American technicians and archaeologists at Sybaris. About this, at least, van Gogh was accurate. After exactly three kilometres I saw the yellow and black sign of a gas station, whose attendant directed me, without interest, towards a dirt track leading into a marshland of reeds and scrub.

As I bumped along this dusty track I could see no life whatever, nothing but widespread swamp, until I came around a bend in the track and saw ahead of me a solitary figure leaning against a jeep, arms folded, pipe-smoking, well built, idly watching me approach.

High boots to his knees, riding breeches, open-necked khaki shirt, peaked cap, sunglasses, grizzled hair. In his sixties? I pulled up beside him, told him who and what I was and asked him where I could see the buried city of Sybaris. Immobile he listened to me, smiled tolerantly, or it might be boredly, then without speaking beckoned me with his pipe to follow his jeep. I did so until he halted near a large pool of clear water surrounded by reeds and mud. Some ten feet underwater I perceived a couple of broken pillars and a wide half-moon of networked brick.

'Behold Sybaris,' he said and with amusement watched me stare at him, around the level swamp at the immensity of the all-seeing mountains and back to him again.

'You mean that's *all* there is to see of it?'

'All, since, if you believe the common legend, its enemies deflected its great river, the Crathis,' he in turn glanced westward and upward, 'to drown it under water as Pompeii was smothered in volcanic ash. Crathis is now brown with yellow mud. "Crathis the lovely stream that stains dark hair bright gold." '

He smiled apologetically at the quotation

'But the archaeologists? I was hoping to find them all hard at work.'

He smiled unapologetically. He relit his pipe.

'Where is the hurry? Sybaris has been asleep a long time. They have finished for this year. They have had to work slowly. They have been experimenting with sonic soundings since 1964. They have had to map the entire extent of the city with their magnetometers. It was six miles in circumference. But I am only an engineer. Consultant engineer. Of Cosenza.'

I stared unhappily at the solitary eye of the once largest and most elegant city of the whole empire of Magna Graecia. I recalled and mentioned an odd detail that had stuck in my mind's tooth, out of, I think, Lenormant, supposedly typical of the luxury of the city in its heyday – its bylaw that forbade morning cocks to crow earlier than a stated number of hours after sunrise. He shrugged dubiously. I did not know that it was Lenormant who a hundred years ago looked from the foothills of the Sila down at this plain and saw nothing but strayed bulls, long since gone wild, splashing whitely in its marshes. He said he had been much struck by this legendary picture.

'Legendary? You *are* a sceptical man.'

'In this country legend is always posturing as history. We are a wilderness of myths growing out of myths. Along the coast there, at Crotone, my wife, as a girl, walked to the temple of Juno, the Mother of the Gods, in a procession of barefooted girls singing hymns to Mary, the Mother of God. Here Venus can overnight become Saint Venus. *Santa Venera.* A hill once sacred to Cybele becomes sanctified all over again as Monte Vergine. I do not deride any of this. Some myths point to a truth. Some not. I cannot always distinguish. And I have lived in Calabria for thirty years.'

'Not a born Calabrese, then?'

'I am a Roman. I was exiled here by the Fascisti in 1939. Not in this spot! Back up there in a small village called San Giovanni in Fiore. A pretty name, situated beautifully, poor and filthy when you got there. The night they arrested me in Rome they allowed me five minutes and one suitcase. I grabbed the biggest book I could find. It was *Don Quixote.* That winter I reread it by daylight and by candlelight three times. I had nothing else to read, nobody to talk to, nothing to do. Every fine day I tramped over those mountains, sometimes twenty and more miles a day.' He laughed cheerfully. 'Wearing out the Fascist spies detailed to follow me. Today the same men, as old as I am now, joke with me over it. They were bastards every one of them. And would be again if it suited them. They say, "Ah, the good old days, Emilio! You were so good for our bellies. If only we could lead one another that dance all over again!" I came everywhere on old stories written on old stones – myths, charms, omens, hopes, ambitions. The cerecloths of Greece. The marks of Rome. Those bits in that pool are probably Roman. You can tell it by the *opus reticulatum* of the bricks. That was only uncovered in '32. They call this place the *Parco del Cavallo.* What horse? Whose horse? I came on remnants of Byzantium, the Goths, the Saracens, the Normans. Our past. When my spies saw what I was after they stopped following me – I had become a harmless fool – doors opened to me, a land-owner's, then a doctor's, even a schoolmaster's, a learned priest's in Rossano. I met and fell in love with a doctor's daughter from Crotone. It was a charming little port in those days. Good wine of Ciro. Good cigars. Very appealing. One day in September 1943 the British Fifth Army entered Crotone and we were married. Well before then,' he laughed, 'every Fascist of San Giovanni in Fiore had burned his black shirt and started shouting *Viva il Re.* The old woman with whom I had lodged sold me for ten thousand lire to the doctor, who sold me for twenty thousand to the police marshal, who sold me for

fifty thousand to a landowner who drove me into Crotone to show
the British commanding officer the victim of Fascism whom he had
protected for the last four years. I did not give him away. I had
fallen in love so much with Calabria that I even liked its ruffians.
I settled in Cosenza.'

Why was he unburdening himself like this to a stranger? I said
that in September 1943 I was with the American Eighth Army across
these mountains.

'My God!' I wailed, throwing a bit of silver wrap from my chew-
ing gum into the pool of the horse. 'Do you realise that all that is
over a quarter of a century ago?'

He smiled his tender, stoic's smile.

'I realise it very well. My youngest son is a lieutenant in the Air
Force. His brother is studying medicine in Palermo. My eldest child
is due to have her first baby at any hour.'

'Why did you not return to Rome?'

He again glanced towards Cosenza. The sun, I observed, sinks
early behind those Apennines. For no reason there flashed across
my eyes the image of this plain covered by sheets of water made of
melting snow.

'I have told you why I never went back to Rome. Because I had
fallen in love with a woman and a place, with a woman who was
a place. I saw my Claudia as a symbol of the ancientness, the
ancestry, the dignity, the unforgettable beauty of Calabria, of its
pedigree, its pride, its arrogance, its closeness to the beginning of the
beginnings of man and the end of the ends of life. I believed then
and believe still that outside Calabria it would be impossible to find
such a woman as my Claudia.'

I did not suggest that fifty million Italians might not agree. If
a young man in love, and an old man remembering his young love
is not entitled to his dreams, who is? I merely suggested that there
is also some 'ancientness' in Rome.

'In museums? In Rome the bridge is down. It has no living past.
It is just as venal, vulgar, cowardly, cynical and commercial a city
as any other in the world.' He jerked his body to a soldierly attention.
'I must get back to Cosenza. We have been warned by the doctor
that the birth may be difficult. There may have to be a caesarean.
My wife will be praying for an easy birth. When I get back she may
have more news.'

No relatives? Ageing both. Alone. I did not say that my own
daughter has married far away from me into another continent.

All dreams have an ending somewhat different from their beginnings.

'Your daughter is in Cosenza?' I asked hopefully, but he waved his right hand towards the south.

'No. She married a splendid young man in Reggio, an *avvocato*. Bartolomeo Vivarini. It is not very far but it is far too far for my wife and me at a time like this.'

We shook hands warmly. We had in some way lit in those few minutes a small flame to friendship. He waved and went his way. I continued along the coast, deeper into his South, his beloved Past.

I slept in Crotone, badly, woke wondering if I had been as unwise about my food as one so easily can be anywhere south of Rome, or dreamed oppressively, or failed to do something along the road that I ought to have done. It was not until I had dived into the sparkles of the sea and had been driving fast for a good hour that the reason for my dejection struck me. I had caught the *mal du pays*. Four days out of Rome and I was already homesick for it. And why not? I am not married to Old Calabria. I am a political animal, a man of reason, interested in the world as it really is. My job is to do with today, occasionally with tomorrow, never with yesterday. I had been seeing far too many memorials to that incorporeal, extra-mundane, immaterial, miasmic element that is food and drink to men like Emilio Ratti and that Carl Sandburg called a bucket of ashes.

One ancient temple had been exciting, like those fifteen Doric columns at Metaponto deep in weeds and wild flowers. The next, less than a mile away, had been too much. A cartload of stones. Decline, decay, even death is Beauty's due. Never defeat. The South is littered with decay and defeat. Farther on a bare few megaliths recorded another defeated city. A duck pond to call up great Sybaris! Not even a stone had marked another lost city. Juno's great church had been worn by time, weather and robbery to a naked column on the edge of a bleak moor and a bare cliff outside Crotone. All as empty now as the sea, except for ageing women remembering the garlanded girls who once walked there in a line singing hymns in May. At Locri I had paused for gas and found the local museum ill-kept and dusty. *Aranciata Pitagora*. One of Greece's great philosophers advertising orange juice over a wayside stall.

I covered my final forty miles in half an hour. I swept into a Reggio bristling with carabinieri, local police, armed troops, riot squad trucks crackling out constant radio reports. The hotel was like a Field HQ with pressmen and photographers, cinema crews and TV crews. All because it was widely and furiously feared that Rome intended to pass Reggio over in favour of either Cosenza or Catanzaro as the new provincial capital. Posters all over the walls announced that at four o'clock there would be a Monster Meeting in the Piazza del Popolo. This would leave me just enough time to interview the chief citizens of Reggio: mayor, archbishop, city councillors, parliamentary deputies, labour bosses, leading industrialists if any. For some five hours, lunchless, I patiently gathered from them thousands of flat-footed words, to which at the afternoon meeting a sequence of bellowing orators added their many more.

Weary, hungry and bored I remembered with a click of my fingers the name Vivarini.

3

Twenty minutes later, in a quarter of the city far removed from the noisy piazza, I was admitted by an elderly woman in black – wife? housekeeper? secretary? – to the presence of a very old man in a dusky room cluttered with antiquated furniture, bibelots, statuettes in marble, alabaster and bronze, old paintings, vases, boxes of papers, books, bowls, crystal paper-weights, signed photographs in silver frames. It was the kind of room that made me wonder how he ever found anything he might require there. A Balzac would have been delighted to list all its telltale signs, markers or milestones of the fortunes of a business and a family, especially those signed photographs – King Vittorio Emmanuele III, Dr Axel Munthe, one Peter Rothschild, Prime Minister Giolitti (the one who held out against Mussolini until 1921), Facta (who fell to Fascism in 1922), Mussolini's son-in-law Galeazzo Ciano, Marshal Badoglio. As for me, one look and I knew what I was in for. And I was!

'Ah, *signore*, this was once a city of the rarest elegance. My son whom you must meet – he is at the hospital – does not realise this, he is too young. But I myself heard d'Annunzio say that our *lungomare* is one of the most gracious seaside promenades in Europe. What do you think of that?' (I refused to say that if the so-called Prince of Montevenoso ever said so he must have said it before 1908 when this city was flattened by its terrible earthquake, and at that date Signor Vivarini would have been a very small boy indeed.) 'But, now, alas, *signore*, we have been taken over by the vulgar herd, the *popolazzo*. Corruption. Vendettas. Squabbles for gain.

Maladministration. And all because our natural leaders, our aristocracy, the landed gentry of Calabria, started to abandon Reggio immediately after the earthquake of 1908 . . .'

In the distance an irritable rattle of rifle fire. He did not seem to hear it. He went on and on. And I should be back there at the rioting.

'Nothing can save us now but a miracle . . . When I was a youth . . .'

I rose at the sound of a distant, dull explosion, ready to run from him without ceremony, when from the doorway I found myself transfixed by the stare of a man whom I took to be his son – a tall, thin, challenging, cadaverous man of about thirty-five, eyes Atlantic grey, peering through eyelashes that hid nothing of his patent awareness of his own merits, his inquisitorial mistrust, his cold arrogance of a pasha. I would have been utterly repelled by him if his clothes were not so much at odds with his manner. His lean body was gloved in a light, metallic, bluish material suggestive of shimmering night and stars, his skintight shirt was salmon pink, his lemon tie disappeared into the V of a flowered waistcoat, the silk handkerchief in his breast pocket lolled as softly as a kitten's tail, or as its eyes, his shoes were sea-suede, and his smoke of hair was blued like a woman's. After all those big mouths in the piazza he looked so promisingly ambiguous that I introduced myself at once, name, profession, nationality. In a courteous and attractively purring voice, and in the unmistakable English of Cambridge (Mass.), i.e., of Harvard, he replied that he had also spent some time in America. In return I told him that I had begun my career as a journalist on *The Crimson*. His laugh was loud, frank, open and delighted. We shook hands amiably. I was on the point of deciding that he was really a most engaging fellow when I recalled his first ice-cold air, his arrogance and his suspicion. I glanced at his clothes and I looked at his face, where now it was the mouth that impressed me : a blend of the soft, the mobile, the vulpine, the voracious, the smiling that made me suddenly think that the essence of his first effect on me had been the predatory and the self-protective nature of a born sensualist. Obviously a man capable of being very attractive to women, but also, I feared, capable in his egoism of being cruel.

'You enjoyed America,' I stated cheerfully.

For a second or two his peering mask returned and he smiled, not unhappily, yet not warmly either, the way I fancied an inquisitor might when watching a heretic slowly gyrating over the flames that would soon deliver his soul to paradise. He said that he had endured the arid rigidities of Harvard University for three years. He laughed gaily at another rattle of gunfire, saying, 'That nonsense will be over in an hour.' He did not so much invite me to dine with him, as insist that I should give him the pleasure.

'And the consolation. I am going through a difficult time.'

The next second he was blazing with fury at his father's tremulous question, 'How is Angelica?' This – I had observed in some embarrassment – had already been iterated four times.

'She has been in labour now for eight hours!' he ground out savagely. 'If she has not given birth within three more hours I insist upon a caesarean.' The old man waved protesting hands. 'My dear father,' he raged at him in a near whisper. 'I have told you twenty times that there is nothing scientifically wrong with a caesarean.'

He turned suavely to me. 'I do wish my dear father would realise that even after three caesareans my wife could still bear him a long line of grandchildren.' He laughed lightly. 'Of course there is no truth in the legend that Julius Caesar was so delivered. I will call for you at your hotel – The Excelsior I presume? – at half past seven. We will dine at the Conti. It is not very much but it is our best.'

I would have preferred to catch the plane for Rome. But I remembered, and shared, some of Emilio Ratti's quiet troublement over his daughter. My own daughter had not had an easy time with her first. There bounced off my mind the thought that a nameless young woman in Bussano had lost her first. Actually it was none of these things decided me but the sound of more shots. I ran from the pair of them.

The rioting was well worth it, water cannon, baton charges, rubber bullets, the lot, women howling Jesu Marias, hair streaming, children bawling, fat men behaving like heroes, the finest fullest crop of De Sica clichés, vintage 1950, and not a cat killed. And all for what? For, at least, more than Hecuba, if for less than Hector. For pride, honour, family, home, ancient tradition, *Rhegium antiquum* so often raped by Messinaians, Syracusans, Romans, Goths, Normans, Saracens, Pisans, Turks, Aragonese, Fascisti, Nazis, and the liberating armies of Great Britain and the U.S.A. Also, no doubt, for something to do with real estate, tourism, air travel, emigration, IRI, Bernie Cornfield's *fonditalia*, Swiss hooks in Chiasso, the Mafia, the

Cassa per il Mezzogiorno, the Demochristians' majority in parliament . . . But the journalist's classical symptom is cynicism, the
boil of his inward frustration, the knowledge that he will never
get at that total truth reserved for historians, novelists and poets
who will reduce his tormented futilities to a few drops of wisdom.

By the time Vivarini called for me I was calmed, and if apart from
Crotone's morning moonshine coffee still unfed, I was by now not
unslaked, braced by two martinis which I insisted that he and I,
at the bar, make four; as, in Conti's he at once ordered not one
but two litres of *vino di Ciro* – reminding me of that drunken night,
it was in Peking (Oh! Jesus!) years and years ago, that I first became
a father.

'No!' he groaned aloud to the totally empty restaurant. (Its usual
clients afraid to emerge at night?) 'No baby yet!'

His father ('Don't touch the *scampi*! Even here we have possible
pollution!') was a Polonius, a foolish, fond old man whom nobody
would mistake for his better, three generations out of date. A sweet,
kind man. With fine sensibilities. But, like all Italians, a besotted
sentimentalist.

'By comparison I, Bartolomeo . . .'

'Hi, Bart! Call me Tom!'

'Hi, Tom . . . am a cold Cartesian. My wife,' he informed me
secretively, evidently making some point, 'is a mortal angel. I have
selected her with the greatest care. For I have also had my sorrows.
My betrayals. But she is an angel with a Gallic mind. She also loathes
all this traditional nonsense of her father's and of my father, all
this ridiculous adoration of the Past. Down with Tradition! All
it is is confusion! Mythology! Obfuscation!' He hammered the
table, a waiter came running and was dismissed. 'I insist on a
caesarean! Those two old men with their folksy minds think it
bad, wrong, a threat to the long line of children they dream of
as their – *their!* – descendants. Excuse me,' he said quietly. 'May
I telephone?'

He returned, swaying only a very little, shook his head, looked
at his watch, while I thought of my engineer and his wife waiting
by the telephone in Cosenza, and that agonised girl hauling on a
towel tied to the end of a bedpost, and the old lawyer somewhere
up the street moaning to himself among his portraits and his trophies
of the dead and I said, 'Look't, for Chrissake, forget me! I know
you want to be back in that hospital, or nursing home, or whatever
it is. Do please go there!' – to which, intent on behaving as calmly

as a Harvard man, that is to say as a Yank, that is to say as an English gentleman (period 1850) would have behaved, he replied that if his papa was irrational his father-in-law Emilio was far more so.

'I can guess how my father explained those riots to you. The decay of the aristocracy? All that shit? But did he once mention the Mafia? With whom, of course, he worked hand in glove all his life? Whereas, on the other hand, Emilio would know all about the Mafia, but he would also tell you that the rioting would have been far worse if it had not been for,' here one could almost hear his liver gurgling bile, 'the "wisely restraining hand of Mother Church." Two complementary types of total unreason.'

At this he bowed his face into his palms and moaned into them.

'If only my love and I could get out of this antiquated, priest-ridden, Mafia-ridden, time-ridden, phony, provincial hole!'

He quickly recovered control of himself sufficiently to beg me, concernedly, to give him the latest news from the States. I did so, keeping it up as long and lightly as I could since the narration seemed to soothe him. But it was only a seeming, because he suddenly cried out, having obviously not heeded one word I had been saying: –

'The Church here is, of course, a master plotter and conspirator. Have you seen their latest miracle?' – as if he were asking me whether I had seen the latest Stock Exchange reports. 'You must. It is a masterpiece. It is only five hundred metres away. A weeping Madonna. Weeping, of course, for Reggio. Like Niobe, from whom the idea most certainly derives. What a gullible people we are! Madonnas who weep, bleed, speak, go pale, blush, sway, for all I know dance. Did you know that before the war Naples possessed two bottles of milk supposed to have been drawn off the breasts of the Virgin which curdled twice a year? Excuse me. May I telephone?'

He disappeared. This made the restaurant twice as empty. The patron asked me solicitously if all was well. Signor Vivarini seemed upset? I said his wife was expecting a baby.

'A baby!'

Within a minute the restaurant came alive. A fat female cook bustled from the kitchen. After her came a serving woman. The *padrone*'s wife appeared. Two small children peeped. An old man shuffled out in slippers. In a group they babbled about babies. It was nine o'clock. I had lost my plane. I had not yet written my report on Reggio. But he did not come back and he did not come back, and I was cross, bothered, bored and bewildered. The restaurant again emptied – the whole company of family and servitors had gone off in a gabble to regather outside the telephone booth. I had decided to pay the bill and leave when a mini-riot burst into the place, all of them returning, cheering and laughing, to me as if I was the fertile father, and in their midst Bartolomeo Vivarini, swollen as the sun at noon, beaming, triumphant, bestowing benedictions all around, proclaiming victory as smugly as if he was the fertile mother.

'*Un miracolo gradito!*' he laughed and wept, 'a son! I am the father of a son! I have telephoned my father and my mother, my father-in-law and my mother-in-law. They are all such good people. Are they not?'

The company laughed, clapped, declared that it was indeed a miracle, a splendid miracle, a *miracolo gradito.*

'There will be more children!' the cook assured him.

'And more sons,' the *padrone*'s father assured him.

He sat, sobbed, hiccuped, called for champagne, but this I firmly forbade.

'You haven't yet seen your wife!' I pointed out. 'She must have suffered terrible pain,' at which his sobs spouted like champagne.

'I had forgotten all about her!' he wailed and punished his bony breast. 'I must light a candle for my wife to the Madonna. To the weeping Madonna! Let us go, my dear friend. To the Madonna! She, perhaps, may make them give me one peep at my son. You will drive me? I dare not! It is not far away.'

So, we left, led noisily by all to the door. And nobody asked us to pay the bill.

His car was a Lancia. I drove it furiously to somewhere up the hill, this way, that way, until, above the nightness and lightness of the city, of the straits, of all Calabria and all Sicily, we halted on the edge of a tiny *piazza* crowded with worshippers or sightseers where there stood an altar, and on the altar a pink and blue commercial statue of the allegedly lachrymose Virgin Mary. A hundred breathless candles adored her, and four steady electric spotlights. Bartolomeo crushed me through the crowds to the altar, bought two candles, one for himself, one for me, refusing to take any change from his thousand-lire bill, lit his candle, fixed it in position and knelt on the bare ground to pray, his hands held wide in total wonder and belief.

As far as I was concerned the miracle was, of course, like every popular Italian miracle preposterous – a word, I had learned at high school, that means in Ciceronian Latin arse-to-front. The object was to me simply an object, brought from some statue vendor in Reggio, with, if even that ever happened, a drop or two of glycerine deposited on its painted cheek by some pious or impious hand. But why should anybody want a miracle so badly? And gradually, as I looked about me and felt the intensity of the human feeling circling the altar like a whirlpool of air, or bees in a swarm, or butterflies over a wave, or fallen leaves whispering in a dry wind, I began to feel awed and even a little frightened. As I moved through the murmuring or silent crowds, conscious of the eloquent adoration of the old, the unexpected fervour of the young, the sudden hysteria of a woman carried away screaming, the quiet insistent stare of two Franciscans fixed on the painted face, I became so affected that at one point I thought that I, too, could, might, perhaps – or did I? – see one single, perfect teardrop gleaming in the spotlights on the face of the mother of their God. I blinked. 'It' vanished.

But had it ever been there? Who had the proof that it had not been an illusion for us all? The night was inflammable, the country explosive, I had too much respect for my skin to ask why even one teardrop had not been looked at through a microscope capable of distinguishing between glycerine, that is to say $C_3 H_5 (OH)_3$ and the secretions of the lachrymal gland. I might as well have committed instant suicide as suggest that a similar test could be applied to the wine said to change during their Mass into the blood of their God. I found myself beside the two motionless friars. I cautiously asked one of them if he had seen, or knew anybody who had seen, a tear form in the Madonna's eye. He answered skilfully that this was not wholly relevant since if one saw the tear it was so, and if one did not see a tear it was not so, which he took pleasure in explaining to me courteously, but at some length, marks the difference in Kantian philosophy between the *phenomenon* and the *noumenon*. My mind swam.

Bartolomeo had vanished. I stayed on in that haunted *piazzetta* until well after one in the morning. I collected some opinions, two asserted experiences, stories of miraculous cures. The crowds thinned, but at no time was the statue unattended by at least one worshipping believer. Only when a palsied dumb woman asked me the time by tapping my watch with her finger did I remember that by now the huntsmen might be asleep in Calabria but the foreign editors of America would be wide awake, for who could be drowsy at that hour whose first edition frees us all from everlasting sleep? A few steps away I found a lighted café whose owner must have nourished the same views as Sir Thomas Browne. There, over a couple of Stregas, I disposed in twenty minutes of Reggio's political troubles. Inside another half an hour I evoked the miracle of the Madonna in one of the most brilliant pieces I have written during my whole life. The best part of it was the coda, which I doubted I would ever send – they would only kill it at once. In it I asked Chicago, still daylit, still dining or well dined, rumbling like old thunder, smelling as rank as a blown-out candle, how it is that the Mediterranean never ceases to offer us new lamps for old. I opined that it is because it is in the nature of that restless Mediterranean mind to be divinely discontent with this jail of a world into which we are born. It is always trying to break out, to blow down the walls of its eyes, to extend time to eternity so as to see this world as nobody except the gods has ever seen it before.

No! Not for Chicago. Not that I cared. What is every journalist anyway but an artist *manqué* spancelled to another who is tethered to a third, and a fourth and a fifth up to the fiftieth and final *manqué* at the top?

I passed slowly back through the little *piazza*. The candles were guttering, the spotlights still shone, it was empty except for one man kneeling in the centre of it before the sleepless statue. I bade her a silent farewell, Juno, Hera, Niobe, Venus, or the Virgin, and went on walking through the sleeping streets downhill to the shore. It was a still night. The sky gleamed with stars like Vivarini's blue coat. I thought of my dauber of Bussano, my van Gogh *manqué*, and I decided that the distinction between Emperor and Clown is irrelevant. Every virtue is woven into its opposite, failure built into ambition, despair into desire, cold reason into hot dreams, delusion into the imagination, death into life, and if a youth does not take the risks of every one of them he will not live long enough to deserve peace.

I paused. In the straits was that a purring motorboat? Not a sound. Here, at about five twenty o'clock one equally silent morning sixty-one years ago – it was in fact December 28th – people like the father and mother of old Mr Vivarini the lawyer felt their houses sway and shiver for thirty-two seconds, and for twelve miles north and south every house swayed and shook in the same way for two months. At widening intervals the earthquake went on for a year